MW00790989

CUTTER

A novel

By

FORD SIMPSON, M.D.

Copyright © 2013 by Ford Simpson, M.D.

ISBN 978-0-7414-9840-3 Paperback
ISBN 978-0-7414-9841-0 Hardcover
ISBN 978-0-7414-9842-7 eBook
Library of Congress Control Number: 2013915305

Printed in the United States of America

Published October 2013

INFINITY PUBLISHING
1094 New DeHaven Street, Suite 100
West Conshohocken, PA 19428-2713
Toll-free (877) BUY BOOK
Local Phone (610) 941-9999
Fax (610) 941-9959
Info@buybooksontheweb.com
www.buybooksontheweb.com

For all of my Tuscaloosa friends and family in and out of the hospital who encourage me and inspire me daily!

α

Its rider was named Faithful and True, for he judges fairly and wages a righteous war.
Rev. 19:11

Ω

CHAPTER 1

The overhead lights, blinding like the dentist's, hovered like UFOs then descended in formation. The room was all action, ants too busy to follow. The scene was blurred from the premedication that had dripped into his intravenous line minutes ago. He knew what he was seeing would simply vanish from his memory after the operation—the green uniforms of nurses and anesthesiologists; the hum of circulators; and the high intensity, cool, bright lighting he saw every day—any recall extinguished because of the fast-acting medicines.

He knew the slightly acidic yet sweet smell of background gases well, the pleasing aroma of the disinfectant on the floor that made the wintry air seem fresh and clean, the beeps and buzzing of monitors, the whispers. He recognized them all. The extra breeze of oxygen on his face and the warmth under toasty blankets in this arctic room of blue tile and icy air, the vents active with a deep chill, gave him a feeling of peace and let him nestle in for a sleep.

His right lower quadrant abdominal pain that had led him to the Emergency Room only an hour ago wasn't even present now. The narcotic floating through his veins and numbing his brain had replaced his constant ache and kidney-punch nausea with euphoria. He knew he had appendicitis when he woke up that morning. He had all of the classic signs he learned as a resident in surgery: dull aching around his navel last night, more localized pain to the right of his navel when he climbed out of bed, queasiness deep inside his stomach. When he pressed his hand into the area of his appendix and buckled to his knees, he was absolutely certain. Still, he confirmed it in the emergency room with a CT scan.

"Are you doing okay, Dr. Miller?" The voice drifted through his consciousness.

His facemask, balanced over his mouth and nose and held in place only by the plastic tubing attached to the anesthesia machine, was delivering a slow flow of oxygen. He nodded.

"It won't be long now!"

He recognized Jenny's voice. She was his nurse anesthetist for the morning and had worked with him for years. When he first came to Tuscaloosa as a cardiac surgeon, she was working in an intensive care unit. However, as an excellent nurse on the floor, she was able to go to Nurse Anesthesia School to become an anesthetist. It seemed that all nurse anesthetists were attentive, competent and attractive, and Jenny was no exception. Her green eyes peered over her mask, checking everything. The breathing tube was ready when the anesthesia kicked in completely, and the drugs to achieve total anesthesia were in syringes, marked and ready for the anesthesiologist. The intravenous lines were all running, and the machine had been checked and all monitors were working.

"Alright, Grant!" said a not-so-gentle voice. It belonged to Quan, his anesthesiologist, who was second-generation Chinese-American, brilliant, and a body builder. "What you doing on your back?" Moving like a ghost, he was above Dr. Miller at the head of the table before Grant could open his eyes. "You supposed to have two hearts to do today! You play hooky?" His laugh was as strong as his hand.

"Ha, ha, ha." He picked up the syringes that Jenny had prepared and fired them into the intravenous setup.

"You have good sleep, Grant!" His hands were magical, the fingers working with serpentine precision, almost as if without joints. Everything was rapid. Everything was precise. Everything was dependable. Quan didn't waste time. His life and work had always been tactical. Nothing was different here, not even with a fellow physician.

Grant Miller, M.D., was out. He was scheduled to perform two coronary bypass operations today, both cancelled now. Like every day of his professional career, the unexpected was expected. He had survived training at Texas Heart working 25 hours a day, 8 days a week. He had lived in the surgical ICU for six months, never emerging for fresh air or to see daylight. He had endured six years of general surgery residency and three years of cardiac surgical training, never asking for relief and never complaining about the hours. Now was his chance to rest.

He was always responsible for his patients, always at the hospital, always the captain of the ship, the one to blame or the one to praise. But today, he rested, confident that his surgical team was able to perform a routine appendectomy without incident.

The nurses worked in concert now, two shaving his abdomen and another placing a urinary catheter and then painting his abdomen and right groin with antiseptic. Finally, as though the rest of his body had no importance, they placed drapes in a square, isolating his abdomen and excluding every body part that was not necessary for the procedure.

"Scalpel!" Jack Wade, Grant's buddy, had entered the room as the last drape was placed. He was in residency training at Houston with Grant and had returned to Tuscaloosa as a general surgeon instead of spending extra years in training.

"For a sissy, this ol' boy sure has tough skin!" He used a number 10 blade, pressing firmly on Grant's umbilicus. The carbon-infused steel popped through Grant's skin, leaving a blush of red behind. Next he pushed a rounded tube with a metal point into the hole. More pressure and he felt the resistance end as the trocar slipped into Grant's abdomen.

"Fifteen millimeters of pressure," Jack said as he sprayed carbon dioxide through the tube and into Grant's abdomen, expanding the insides for better visibility and to avoid sticking additional trocars into the intestines. Two more stabs and he inserted other tubes in a triangular pattern to the left of midline.

"Hey, Jack!" Quan looked over the drapes separating the anesthesia domain from the surgeon's sterile field. "How many surgeon it take to change a light bulb?"

Jack kept working, never looking at Quan but only staring at the camera before him. He was now manipulating the intestines with instruments to find the appendix.

"No one know!" Quan laughed at himself, hoping to get a rise out of Jack. "Surgeon so busy, after take out socket and wires, only their assistant know how to put everything back!" Quan's laughter bounced off the walls.

Jack never blinked. "Two people enjoying themselves at a hotel bar decided to go up to a room." His hands and instruments danced through the abdomen, dissecting blood vessels from the appendix and dividing fat.

"After a few hours of frolic, the man grins at the woman and says, 'You must be a surgeon!' She says, 'Yes, but how did you know?' He says, 'Because you were so good with your hands!' She responds, 'And you must be an anesthesiologist!' He was amazed, 'Yes, and how did you know?'" Jack paused for effect. "'Because I hardly felt a thing!'"

The room erupted, all except Quan. His grasp of English and cultural differences left him slow to pick up on the humor, but after the laughter slowed, Quan's eyes lit. "Ahhhhh, you got me!"

Jenny, knowing Jack's hands were the best, lifted her head above the drapes to watch him operate. She knew he noticed her. He never missed anything. She also knew he was on call and would be in his call room all night.

"Your muscle relaxant must be wearing off!" Jack was struggling with the instruments. "The abdomen is really tight!" The muscles on Grant's stomach were rigid, fighting Jack as he tried to angle them and curve them toward his targets.

Jenny pulled a vial from her cart and pushed a few milliliters of liquid into the intravenous line. "That ought to take care of it!"

One of the monitors had been beeping, but Jack's joke had been distracting.

"We're still tight!" Jack pulled the instruments out of the abdomen and looked at the anesthesia monitors. "Is that right?"

"What?"

"The heart rate is 120 and..."

Jenny followed his eyes to the temperature reading.

"Forty degrees Celsius!!" Jack's hands went down on Grant's abdomen as though they were working clay. "That's 104 degrees, isn't it?" His hands were pressing and molding. "He's hot as fire and his belly's as tight as a board!"

"Shit!" Quan knew that word of English and shouted it like a command.

Everyone's head turned to the anesthetic gas canister. The soda lime granules were turning blue, indicating rapid carbon dioxide absorption. The beeping monitor was the carbon dioxide alarm in Grant's breathing tube. Jenny suddenly identified it. "Oh no, the CO_2!"

"Malignant hyperthermia!" Jack's voice was calm but firm. "Dantrolene! Do you have it in the cart?"

He'd only seen one case of malignant hyperthermia, which can be caused by inhalation gases or muscle relaxants and results in uncontrolled rapid metabolism in skeletal muscle that overwhelms the body's ability to regulate temperature, depletes the oxygen stores in the body, and causes progressive accumulation of CO_2 in the body. It happened during a congenital heart operation at Texas Heart. He was the only resident in the ICU an hour after the operation had been completed when the baby went rigid, temperature shooting up like a geyser and urine turning to brown syrup. The baby went into rigor mortis before his eyes. At the time, he knew the diagnosis and the treatment and dantrolene was given immediately, just as the baby's heart went into ventricular tachycardia, reaching a heart rate of 200. The baby died within minutes, despite all the right treatment.

"No, sir!" Jenny reached the telephone beside her to call the pharmacy. "John, we need dantrolene! Now! Malignant hyperthermia!" Her body was shaking from adrenalin.

"I'm sorry, Dr. Wade," Jenny choked. "The recent federal regulations make us get all of our medicines from the pharmacy. We can't even keep Lidocaine on the cart."

Quan was already out the door. He ran to the pharmacy, reaching it just as John had pulled the drug from the shelf. The door to the operating room crashed behind him as he blew back to Jack's side.

Cold fluid poured into Grant's intravenous line and cold water circulated through a plastic blanket placed under the drapes. The dantrolene was in and Jack was back at work, his hand dancing with syncopations, using surgical clips to divide tissue. Then he revealed the appendix, which stuck out like a baby's little finger, swollen and red and pulsing like it had been slammed with a hammer. He applied a final clip to the appendix.

Luckily Grant's appendix was in the normal position, attached to the right side of his colon and poking out where the small intestines and large intestines converged. Yesterday Jack had to fish one out that sank backward, stuck to the muddy debris it had formed after it ruptured.

"For a tiny pouch of intestines that doesn't do anything good for the body, this son-of-a-bitch sure causes its share of problems." Jack slipped a final trocar tube into the abdomen and placed a bag through it, dropped the appendix into the bag, and with gentle tugs, slipped it out of the abdomen. Other than a few sutures to close the holes, the operation was over.

Grant's temperature was still 104. His body was slightly less stiff after the dantrolene, but his six-pack still bulged with the strain of muscles that wouldn't release their energy. Marcia, one of the nurses, pulled off the drapes as Jack emptied his rubber gloves and gown in the garbage. She washed the blood from Grant's abdomen and then patted it dry with a towel, taking more strokes than necessary in order to look intently at his condition. The muscle relaxant should have done its work by now, but every fiber was violin-string tight, his body sculpted with perspiration that glistened like oil. He had attended the Air Force Academy on a wrestling scholarship prior to medical school, but his medical training had taken time away from any physical exercise and replaced lean muscle with fat. However, after he began his practice, he took up wrestling again, sparring with local enthusiasts, and worked with his personal trainer to maintain agility, balance, and strength. He had regained most of his tone. He was 45 years old, but he was in better shape than most his age.

"Call the ICU and the pulmonologist. Tell them we need to start the Arctic Sun protocol." Jack was helping Marcia now, pulling the remaining drapes and sheets away. He spread Band-Aids over the surgical sites on Grant's flesh and pulled the cooling blankets over him, draping him with anything that would cool him down.

The temperature probe was still in his throat, measuring his core warmth. It went through his mouth into his esophagus, allowing the central body heat to be registered.

"Is that right, Jenny?" Jack's voice broke. "Forty-five degrees Celsius? What is that in Fahrenheit?"

"I think it's 113, sir! What happened."

Quan had taken over up top. He had turned the oxygen delivery to 100% and was adjusting the ventilation rate to maximum, trying to allow Grant's carbon dioxide to be blown off through his breathing tube.

Jack replied, "Grant's reaction to one of the anesthetic agents triggered his muscles to release calcium, leading to a type of nuclear meltdown. The muscle spasm and accelerated metabolism leads to carbon dioxide production that causes acid buildup in the body, which is turn releases potassium that can stop the heart or make it develop a lethal rhythm. The release of calcium compounds the chemical disturbances and heart irritability. While all of these reactions are taking place, the muscle activity causes overheating. This, also, causes cardiac rhythm disturbances. But at baking temperature, the brain can "melt down" as well!"

"Beta Blocker is in!" Quan had just squirted Esmolol into the IV. "That should slow down heart rate!"

Grant's heart rate was 160, and the ventilator was kicking in a respiratory rate of 30. His body was still board-like, his facial muscles contracted with pit bull force. The room was electric—telephones ringing, monitors beeping, people racing about—but for Grant there was peace.

CHAPTER 2

Governor Sands knew that body language was as important as verbal skills in dealing with Chinese businessmen. Power and confidence had to be blended with equal parts humility and certainty. He had been waiting for 10 minutes, just as he had for each of the past five days. Punctuality was a prerequisite with the Chinese. His interpreter was in another room with his negotiators, aware that the governor would call them in when the "little people" were needed.

"Governor Sands!" Wang Chien entered but stood barely inside the threshold.

"Mr. Wang!" The governor stood quickly and walked with purpose in his gait toward the steel-haired owner of Beijing Automotive.

Sands was the first to bow, aware from their first meeting that age was as important as title. He also knew not to touch Wang. Often, the Chinese will acquiesce to Western customs like handshakes, but not Wang. They exchanged courtesy bows, and then the governor motioned with an open hand for Wang to join him, indicating the place opposite his own at the table. He knew that this was proper etiquette for Wang's importance.

The governor tapped a button and his staff entered through one door as Wang's staff stepped through another, the same door their boss had entered. Everyone had already been introduced, 40 hours of negotiations earlier.

The governor, then Wang, followed by the others all sat in order of importance. Behind Wang, always within arm's distance, stood his personal bodyguard with sovereign vigilance, his arms folded, ready to crush anyone who threatened his boss.

Wang's clothes hid a well-fed belly, and his teeth were stained orange from tobacco. However, his guard, who looked like the henchman Oddjob from Goldfinger with a massive forehead and broad chest, demanded all the respect his boss's appearance did not. His eyes never stopped and did not miss a movement in the room.

"Mr. Wang, after our meeting yesterday I discussed the issues with our attorneys and contractors." The governor's eyes locked with Wang's, which never seemed satisfied and were always suspicious, or maybe they simply radiated greed.

Governor Sands suspected that Wang understood every word, but he waited for the Chinese interpreter to repeat in Pekingese, the Mandarin dialect spoken in urban Beijing.

"As you know, our state has already proven our willingness to develop partnerships with the automotive industry of any country." He waited between sentences for the interpreter to repeat. "We are the home of Mercedes-Benz, Honda, and Hyundai manufacturing."

Before the interpreter could speak, the governor marked a twitch in Wang's eye when he mentioned Hyundai. He was aware that the South Korean car manufacturer seemed to have gotten under Wang's skin. Beijing-Hyundai seemed to have a growing empire in China, the Elantra taking over Wang's market. That was one reason he was looking for more international visibility.

"We have almost a hundred automotive suppliers in the state, and plants like Siemens, Michelin, and Eaton Corporation. Organized labor has a minimal presence in our state, and so our workers don't pose a problem—and they are hard workers and loyal!"

Again, Wang gave the simplest of gestures, his brow wrinkling ever so slightly. But the governor was good. Skirmishes in politics had taught him how to look another in the eye while studying any nuances in demeanor for a hint of deceit or emotion. So far, he hadn't identified the least clue of honesty in Wang. The governor had made it clear in previous meetings that he would oppose any attempts of organized labor to gain control in Alabama, including any attempts to organize foreign-owned factories in his state, but he had also heard of such attempts recently and so too had Wang.

"If you plan to build in Tuscaloosa County, Mercedes-Benz has already expanded production. Its plant exceeds 3 million square feet and has almost 40 suppliers in the state. It has invested 2 billion dollars in a fifth model joining the assembly line that makes their entire investment 4 billion."

Governor Richard Sands was no novice. He had founded and was still CEO of Sands Electronics. Against the advice of businessmen and his professors to join the Silicon Valley technology corporations after he graduated from MIT with a Masters in electrical engineering and computer science, he saw promise in Alabama and acted accordingly. He started with production of his own semiconductor, and through a billionaire venture capitalist, was able to develop a billion-dollar plant in Mobile, just inland from Mobile Bay with silver sand, and hence a play on words in the name of his company that he found appealing, and turquoise water as backdrop. Math and science were second nature to him, but he loved people and could sit at a campfire and listen to or tell jokes and stories all night long. Thus meetings were no problem. His intuition and communication skill usually allowed discussions to be streamlined and to the point. Many urged him to take up poker because the governor could identify deceit with the sensitivity of a bloodhound on a man's trail, and with his intellect and instinct, he would have excelled. But gambling on cards was of no interest to him. His energy came from accomplishment, which was not purely monetary for him.

Wang sighed and then scratched his face, a sign of irritation and a shame-on-you response. His voice rattled the glasses of water on the table.

"I don't want to know what you already have in Alabama." The translator toned down the volume. "I want to know what you can do for me! If I have to pay American wages for American labor, I want to know how you can make a plant profitable for me."

"By building in America, you avoid the export tax. Some in America would tax incoming goods from China at 25%! Your own economy is lagging while America's is rebounding. Alabama has not only proven itself in the automotive industry but we are willing to make tax exemptions and allow additional land rights. You can be the pioneer Chinese automaker in America. It can only be profitable for you."

The governor knew how to use pride as a weapon and a tool, and he felt it was worth a try with Wang. "Besides, the Chinese are smart enough to let Americans work for you already." He smiled. "And we are making good on our debt to your country, paying off trillions of dollars. You can all probably quit working soon and let us work forever, American workers your piggy bank." Governor Sands was prepared. He did his best to pronounce *puman*, knowing that the Chinese had historical and cultural ties to piggy banks.

Richard's assumption that Wang understood every word was verified when Wang couldn't restrain a smirk at this last remark. He also knew from Wang's history, as much as from his tone, that there wouldn't be an agreement today. This was the last day of their meeting, and the governor had already offered specifics. He wasn't going to be pressured into more than he could honestly guarantee.

"As long as the automobile is a quality product, it will sell and be popular in America. I have seen the Astor and it is perfect for the American market. Sleek, gas efficient, and sturdy. It is what SUV lovers need and what sedan seekers want. Alabama is just your launching pad."

"I will have to think about it!" The translator spoke quickly as the entire Chinese team rose.

Sands knew that Wang wanted more. He knew that the Chinese considered politicians in America corrupt and wanted money under the table. A gesture with his hand to his face already suggested that he looked down on his potential American partner. The other Chinese recognized it, but so did Governor Sands.

The Americans rose, waiting for the exiting party to stop and turn. Then, in unison, they bowed and the Chinese headed back to Beijing by way of Detroit.

CHAPTER 3

Induced hypothermia, or mechanically created low body temperature, has been shown to reduce brain damage in patients suffering cardiac arrest with a comatose state. Jack knew that Arctic Sun was available at DCH and had been used with success. He'd never used it, but he had seen patients wrapped in a blue cooling jacket to maintain a temperature of 89^0 F to minimize their metabolism and preserve brain tissue at threat from swelling and damage.

"You can't do that!" Rashad Bemini arrived in the intensive care unit just as Jack, Quan, and almost the entire OR crew came crashing into room 112.

"Why not?" Jack demanded!

"We don't know if he's in a coma, and the only indication for using Arctic Sun is cardiac arrest with coma." Rashad was the on-call pulmonologist.

"Screw your protocol indicators. Grant's temperature is 114 degrees! If it stays that high much longer his temporal lobe will be dripping out of his ears!" Jack usually played by the rules and was aware he didn't know if Grant met the criteria for this treatment, but he had never played by the rules when it was a life or death situation. He was especially not prone to following protocol just for the sake of following it when it was a friend in danger, especially if said friend was Grant.

"We can cool him, but with a standard protocol." Rashad stood his ground. He had dealt with surgeons before. "If we have a bad outcome, we won't have a legal foot to stand on."

"I don't give a shit about a legal foot or a fucking attorney." Jack was shaking. "I don't give a shit about anything right now except saving this man and sending him home to his wife and children with a fucking brain that hasn't been poached."

Rashad bowed his head gracefully. "That's my goal, also, sir."

Jack frowned, then yelled, "Go get ice, as much as you can find, and bring it back in a fucking sleigh if you have to! But get back here before I finish beating the shit out of this bastard!" Jack looked at anyone who wasn't running out of the room. He turned to Rashad. "If you're worried about getting sued more than you're worried about using your brain, then you need to..." Jack was still shaking.

"Just stop there, Jack! We've worked together for years and we can work together here. Let's just get to work!" Rashad nodded with confidence.

Jack was too close to Grant and too revved up. He rarely peaked, but when he did the eruption was violent. He knew this about himself and usually held his tongue until he got control. He realized he had crossed the line and Rashad was right.

Nurses and attendants returned with bags, carts, and gurneys of ice. An avalanche began, everyone pouring their cache on Grant.

"Have you started the Diprovan drip to keep him knocked out and the Pavulon to keep him paralyzed?" Rashad was in control now.

In the operating room surgeons rule. Nurses, attendants, and even M.D. anesthesiologists realize that the surgeons bring in the patients and are ultimately responsible for outcomes, and so they allow surgeons considerable leeway. But on the floor and in intensive care units, too much has changed in critical care medicine over the last 10 years for surgeons to be fully informed and competent in ventilator management, antibiotic therapy, federally mandated quality indicators, and hospital generated improvement trackers. Jack acknowledged Rashad's competence and control.

"Is Pavulon safe? It may have been a paralyzing agent in the OR that caused the problem." Jack was calm now.

"It was succinylcholine we used," Quan piped in.

"Pavulon is a nondepolarizing agent and so doesn't cause malignant hyperthermia. It has to be given so Grant doesn't shiver, which could increase his metabolism." Rashad was checking the ventilator. He made adjustments to maximize Grant's breathing rate, still trying to get rid of his carbon dioxide.

In the midst of ice packs, melting ice, ventilator adjustments, laboratory values, beeping monitors, scurrying nurses, and window watchers, Jack sat beside Grant and prayed. It wasn't unusual. He and Grant had prayed together and for each other. When he had lost his wife, Grant was there. When Grant had asked for help with his family, Jack was more than eager to return the favor.

Things were quiet now, except for the EKG monitor and occasional IV signal that another bag of fluid needed to be hung. The thermal monitor was gradually creeping down. Jack sat with his eyes closed, but he wasn't asleep. Grant lay in ice, but he wasn't asleep anymore either.

The Pavulon kept him paralyzed and he was unable to breathe on his own or even to blink, unable to give anyone the signal that he was home, awake and freezing.

He knew what was happening. His Diprovan drip had stopped. He had used Pavulon frequently if he was concerned that a patient would be too active, possibly pulling out vital tubes or lines. And if a patient was extremely sick and needed all their energy preserved, the

Pavulon would keep their muscles from expending energy. Grant knew that Pavulon couldn't be given alone, that there must be something added to the Pavulon to erase pain and allow the patient to sleep. Otherwise, they would have the pain of needle pricks, the discomfort of a breathing tube stuffed down their throat, the agony of a recent operation but be paralyzed and unable to ask for relief.

In Grant's case, the Diprovan was the medicine that kept him down, that hypnotized him into a deep sleep without pain. But the pump wasn't working and the alarm wasn't beeping.

He had the mixed discomfort of burning up inside, his muscles crushing with exhaustion and his skin numbed yet biting from the ice. His body was in revolt, punishing him with every pain sensation available. The breathing tube was lodged in his throat, making him feel the need to gag, but his paralysis prevented even this. His eyes had been taped shut to prevent injury to his corneas since he had no control over his eyelids. So he lay in darkness. The urinary catheter pulled at him from below, dangling beside the bed unrestrained, tearing inside and out and his pelvis knifed with its pull. He tasted medicines in his blood stream, but he couldn't smell because the ventilator prevented any air movement through his nose. But most of all he simply hurt, every muscle fiber in his body stretched and worked to its limit.

He had no idea what had happened. He had gone in for an elective appendectomy. Now this. Then it registered. Through the pain he figured out what was happening. He knew there was nothing to do but wait.

He tried to take his mind off of his body by thinking of home. He had told Carol, his wife of 20 years and the mother of his two beautiful daughters, that he would have someone call after the operation to come pick him up.

"God, how lucky I've been," he thought, the silence inside him deafening.

Carol was the thin blonde that usually develops hips at 35, but at 120 pounds and with perfect blonde hair, no hint of gray and no evidence of three pregnancies, she, like Grant, seemed to be winning the battle against time. She would do anything for Grant. Her goal was to protect him, from the strain of work, from himself.

When he got home before bedtime, they would often take a walk. Whether it was evening in the Alabama summer heat or winter's dreariness, they could still share their day, their dreams, their fears, and their plans. It didn't happen every day, and maybe not for weeks, but it happened and that was enough for him.

Carol had grown up in Houston and worked at Texas Heart as a statistician. She knew her numbers and she knew what she wanted. When she and Grant met, their fate was sealed. She understood that Grant was driven by his work, that his patients, his operations, and his reputation were the fuel that powered his day. She also recognized that his devotion to work wasn't limited to his time at the hospital. He was always at work. When he was with her or his children, he was always looking for more. Something to do. Something to fix. Somewhere to go.

Carol knew from the beginning who he was. She also knew that his concern, dedication to and love for her and the children were uncompromised. He knew how lucky he was to find a wife who encouraged him in his work and who made the most of her time with him when they were together.

They'd had their struggles. When they lost their first child, times were tough. Luckily, he had his work, but things were different for her. She had struggled for years, feeling responsible even though it had been a crib death situation. She had only released the guilt and sorrow recently.

She had more monitors and cameras in their children's rooms than lights as they passed through the stages of childhood. Now that they were in their teens, she pulled the electronics, but she knew where they were and who they were with every moment of every day. But now that Beth had her driver's license, he knew it would be hard for both of them.

Surely Carol was out there somewhere. Someone must have called her. Jack would have been the first to think of it. When she was close, Grant could sense her presence. He knew her aroma, with or without perfume. But now he couldn't smell, couldn't see, couldn't feel anything but pain. He wanted her close but didn't want her to worry. He knew he'd be okay if something happened, but she wouldn't!

"V-tach!"

Grant heard the scream. He knew it was a deadly heart rhythm and that it was his. Then he drifted away. The cold was gone, the pain lifted, and only light remained shining even through his taped eyelids.

19

CHAPTER 4

"Governor, if you're thinking about bringing more industry into our county, we need to start planning."

The word was out. There are no secrets in politics or industry. Billy Fields, the mayor of Tuscaloosa for the last five years, was all over it. He knew the city and the county. He knew who could make things happen. He knew where land could be purchased and that more jobs meant a stronger city, county, and mayor.

Tuscaloosa, the home of the Crimson Tide, was Billy's home. In western Alabama and 60 miles from Birmingham, the city had grown to over 100,000. Originally named after Chief Tuskaloosa, the chieftain of the Muskogean-speaking tribe who defeated Hernando de Soto in 1540 in the Battle of Mabilia, it received a nickname during the Civil War because of the abundant old oaks and hardwoods that lent an air of mystery and eeriness to the city. The Druid City was a reference to the ancient Celtic sect whose name was associated with the occult, its members labeled as demonic by Julius Caesar who accused them of animal and human sacrifice. Billy was glad, therefore, that the Druid City Hospital revised its name to DCH Regional Medical Center just before he was born. The association of a pagan name with a hospital in the Deep South simply didn't make good sense.

The governor had planned to fill Billy in on details after his meeting with Wang, but he got sidetracked with other issues. It had only been a couple of days, though.

"Sorry, Billy. I was planning to come to Tuscaloosa in the near future. Maybe we can get together to discuss things."

"So it's true that the Astor is gonna be manufactured in our neighborhood?"

"I didn't say that, Billy. As a matter of fact, I've learned not to say anything of significance over the telephone. But if you heard that negotiations are underway, I can't deny that!"

"So when are you coming to T-Town?" Billy knew Richard was a man of his word, but he also knew the governor could be slippery.

"Hopefully, soon. But I'd like to have an agenda when I come. It may take some time to get that together."

"Come on, Governor! Does that mean a few weeks, months?"

"Can't say, Billy. I'm not being evasive. I really don't know for sure where we're headed with this. But I promise that, when I know for sure if the Chinese will sign on, then you'll be the first to know!"

"That's good enough for me, Governor. I'll wait for a call."

....

Billy believed in preparation and action. He was young but had already proven himself in local politics, blistering his incumbent-rival years ago with promises of jobs, growth, and honesty. So far he had lived up to his word. He had organized property owners along the Black Warrior River, also named after Chief Tuscaloosa and underutilized for years, to develop a novel multi-operational complex that would include a vacation haven along the river. Lake Tuscaloosa, a dammed reservoir, empties into the river; and between the two are hills, waterfalls, streams, and wildlife that had been untapped for centuries. The mayor encouraged businessmen and builders to create a wildlife refuge and a rustic-appearing, but with state of the art conveniences, cabin retreat. Part of the development included marathon training facilities, restaurants, and shopping along the river, with a convention center and international trade shows. Most of the power was hydroelectric from the river, and any part of the project that could be "green" was. Tourism and money flowed into the city throughout the year, added to by extra spending on Saturdays during football season.

The mayor established yearly reviews and open forums for the public to ask questions and give suggestions or critiques, and to hear an accounting for the money being spent. He respected the governor and liked him personally, but Billy saw no reason he couldn't be the governor one day.

CHAPTER 5

Jack was exhausted. He had spent the entire last day at Grant's bedside. There was little to do except babysit, but he knew Grant would do the same for him. It was two in the morning and he had cases in only a few hours, but late night, or in this case early morning, sleep in the hospital was Jack's favorite. He didn't have to waste time on the road and the rooms were sound proof. Within minutes, the darkness and silence would pull him into emptiness.

"You did a great job." He had just turned the key, opening the door to his call room, when the voice teased through the empty hallway.

Jack knew the voice. He had heard it many times before. Jenny was usually silent in the operating room but had no problem with volume when she was alone with Jack.

"Thanks. So did you." He turned to watch her glide toward him. She wore scrubs like a Cosabella chemise. Her green eyes were fixed on his, catlike, and he knew she'd been waiting for him like so many times before.

"Are you exhausted?" she asked, hoping for his usual response.

"Never too tired for the bed." He looked to his right and left, knowing the halls were empty already.

Jenny never used perfume. Her skin had a natural fragrance, sweet and slightly musty, that drifted through the air like Spanish saffron. Jack let her pass in front of him, entering the room as though it was hers, and right now it was. He hadn't been in the room all day, but when he turned on the fluorescent overhead, he smiled as he saw fresh sheets tucked in the sleeper.

Jack's heart always gave him away. Whether it was the call bringing him out of a dead sleep a car wreck in the emergency room or the scent and touch of femininity, his neck pounded with surges of blood. The tugs of weariness loosened their grip as he watched Jenny step toward the bed. Every inch of her 5'4 frame was designed for motion. Her tightly fitted green scrubs fit her hips with the snugness necessary to outline the string panties underneath. Each sway of her cheeks beckoned and teased him until she turned to face him. He didn't look at her face. Her body was the only thing he wanted, the only thing that reminded him of Kate.

Jenny's face was already flushed with expectation. She stood at the bed, waiting for his approach. They always started the same way, but endings wrote new novels every time. Jack knew it had been a long day, but time seemed eternal when his motor was running. He popped a peppermint as he planned his advance. He thought of things like that, continuously. Every moment, at work or play, needed to be perfect. But he knew it didn't matter to Jenny. She wanted wild, whether it was performance or an appeal to the senses or the imagination. Nevertheless, he always had a mint in his mouth, so distractions wouldn't be a problem for him. Jenny liked to stand for a while, him exploring her, and so she waited for the safari to begin.

She stood, eyes partly open but not really watching. With Jack, most of the experience was in the hunt. He searched her body like a Hemmingway hunter, tracking for signs of delight. Though she could watch him work, desire and fantasy made the encounters more exciting, allowing her to follow his lead, always open to new ideas. She waited for the first touch, smelling the mint that was

24

still strong on his lips. His hands started on her hips, first moving up. His long powerful fingers studied her ribs, enjoying her tightness. They stopped below her breasts, his thumbs pressed beneath them, waiting for the gentle touch to do their work. Lingering, playing, taunting...

Jack lifted her scrub shirt, feeling the heat of her skin as he lowered his lips to her neck. He remembered how Kate used to react to his kisses, how she never wanted him to stop, how kisses were enough at times and told the whole story. But not for Jenny. His whiskers made her shiver as he softened their bristle with the moisture of his tongue. Her skin was dessert, delicious but never enough. His tongue traveled to her right breast, now fully engaged. Her pant brought complete fullness to his scrubs.

"You are the best," she whispered, more to herself than to Jack.

He stooped to his knees, enjoying the scent as he moved south, and stopped at her navel, taking a quick pull with his teeth at the tiny ring that was mounted on its bottom rim. The tug was just enough. Playfulness with a hint of pain made her captive. She placed her palms on his cheeks and closed her eyes. She didn't direct him with her touch but let her hands enjoy the journey.

The tip of his tongue traveled further, staying midline as he loosened the tie of her pants and let them fall. Warmth steamed outward as he squeezed her buttocks and pulled the strap downward. The cleft between her legs widened as she spread her legs slightly and pressed her pelvis forward. He continued, enjoying the pursuit as much as she did.

She felt the sudden warmth that never took long. Her body convulsed with satisfaction as she felt her lower body become his. His hands never lost their strength, massaging her buttocks and drawing every ounce of energy from them.

"Now. Now." She pulled his head back to her lips, their tongues sporting with each other.

They collapsed to the bed, acting as though they were fighting for position but both knew Jack would win. He always did.

....

Jack's eyes popped open at 5:00 in the morning, like they did every day whether his alarm rang or whether he had closed them an hour ago. His left arm reached to an empty space. The sheets were tossed, her scent still fresh. He reviewed his performance with a smile, then drifted into a lonely fog. It was like this every time, with Jenny or the countless others. He wanted to be more, wanted to be true to his faith, to be true to Kate.

Jack's wife had died shortly after their marriage. Cancer knows no age, and in spite of all available treatments, Leukemia won. He knew everything that could be done had been done, and yet he blamed himself for missing her early signs.

Absorbed in his training, trying to be the best surgery intern in history, he told Kate not to worry when she kept getting sinus infections, then bronchitis, then pneumonia. Having only limited funds and time, he treated her himself. The antibiotics worked for a while, but then she became dotted with red blotches. He didn't worry about them when she mentioned them and did not see them because he was stuck in the hospital for a week. If he had been given a test, he would have nailed the signs of acute lymphoblastic leukemia. Of course, the malformed white blood cells can't fight infection and the lack of platelets lead to easy bruising. He could have placed her lack of appetite, headaches, and vomiting in a multiple choice line up. She was less likely than a child to get it, but a third of those with the diagnosis are adults.

When he finally asked her to see another doctor, his first reaction was disbelief when her biopsy and spinal fluid showed advanced cancer of the bone marrow. When reality sunk in, he was as devoted as a husband could be. He wept with her when her hair fell out, and they laughed together when he shaved his own head. When she had surgery to place a pump in her head for direct brain chemotherapy, he wore a party hat like a cone-head.

For months, he balanced his duties at hospital with his devotion to her, asking to work an extra year to be able to be with her. He was still paying off debt for the bone marrow transplant, living, and travel expenses for her parents, who lived in Connecticut. Her mom worked as a bank teller, her father a carpenter. They thought nothing of it when Jack offered to pay their expenses to fly out and stay in a hotel in Houston during her last weeks because he was a doctor. They had no idea he was already living in debt. But money really meant nothing to him when he had nothing.

Now, when he paid bills each month, reminders of his time with Kate—debts both monetary and emotional—nearly overwhelmed him and he tried to forget the Jennies, the Julies, and the Bonnies. All he could think of when he wrote the checks was his failures: to diagnose Kate earlier, to be faithful to her memory in other relationships, and to the faith that they once shared.

He still remembered, as Kate started her treatments, their first real conversation. Sure, they had discussed marriage, work, the past, the future, even children. But everything was fun, all youth and excitement. They had never talked about why they did what they did, what they were doing it for.

"I'm so glad you're here today!" Kate smiled, as he came into her isolation room the first day that her blood counts were worrisomely low. "Do you know why you're here?"

"Because I love you." He remembered his response, but knew now that he had no idea what he meant. It was the flippant word he tossed out in conversation or in privacy but without taking ownership.

He remembered today, and every month he signed checks, her look and her response.

"I wish I could give you my disease." Her smile had a glow. In spite of her anemia and the poisons eating away at her body, there was peace, tranquility and release in her words. Her skin seemed phosphorescent, radiant with life.

They often played word games and made light of major issues. He remembered his response and still struggled with it.

"I wish I could take it from you." It was the honest truth. If he could he would exchange places for her in a moment, then and now. But that wasn't what she was asking him to do.

"Do you realize that we haven't gone to church since we got married." Again, her lines of thought and reason seemed zigzagged, which he thought was perhaps due to the chemotherapy. He let her go on.

"I'm going to die. I know I am!" She pulled his hand to her chest. "Thank God I have had this chance to live these last months."

He had wanted to say something profound, something powerful.

"I've never been so happy in all my life as right now, Jack." She held his hand with all her might, unwilling to turn loose until he was as free as she felt. "Do you know how much Jesus loves us?"

He'd never been there with her before. Sure, they were both Christians and had both been raised in the church. She was a Baptist and he was Methodist. They were married in the Methodist church. They went through marriage counseling, saying the right things to please the minister such as promising to raise children in a godly manner. But surgery residency had to be his god right then. Furthermore, if God was really God, if God wanted them to do what they had promised, then He needed to heal her. As a matter of fact, if He didn't heal her, Jack would probably never forgive Him.

The last thing he remembered before she closed her eyes were words that still haunted him.

"Jack. I think we all have to die before we can really live." Her eyes closed and she whispered, "I can't wait for you to find out."

Those were her last words.

God didn't heal her. Kate was gone and he did die a little bit. Now, his only way to embrace her was through the touch of other women. Yes, God had taken his only love, but he found his own way to show God that he could still enjoy life, his own way to remember Kate.

CHAPTER 6

Gossip in the hospital was faster than Twitter. Dr. Miller was going to live and Dr. Jack Wade was a hero. Everyone knew where Dr. Wade had been for the last 72 hours. In addition to his time at Dr. Miller's bedside, Jack had operated the last three nights on three gunshot victims, one multiple trauma, two hot appendixes, and the ruptured gallbladder of the wife of a local minister. Jack was the buzz.

Jack wore fatigue like a leather jacket. Going for days without sleep was becoming harder as he trickled into his forties, but sleepless nights were a badge of honor. His heavy whiskers and early wrinkles simply added mystery to his pitch eyes and muscular jaw. He was naturally slim, but the no carb diet of the last 24 had left him with a teen's look from behind. His scrubs were worn but fit tightly.

"You don't want that!" He said with certainty.

The tiny Asian recoiled, pulling her arm back. He had been watching her as he stood behind her in the cafeteria line. Her T-shirt was over bleached, the yellow now tan. It clung to her with the tenacity of overuse, tight but not improper. It was neatly tucked into her jeans that proved hips could have curves without fat.

"What?" She looked back anxiously.

"Never eat soup on a Friday. You can be sure it's only leftovers." He winked at her as their eyes met.

"But I love leftovers." Her English was good but not native. Her soft consonants and nasal tenor matched her Asian hair. "That's what I eat every day."

"But do you know where leftovers come from in a hospital?" He cocked his head.

"No! Where?" Her eyes were even darker than Jack's, dancing with energy and youth but also uncertainty now.

"I saw the chef visiting the operating room the other day." He paused. "He said they needed some bones for the stew."

"Ah. That's disgusting." She looked at the cup of soup she had put back. "You have to be joking."

"Yes, I'm joking." He saw that the girl was still studying the soup, horrified. "I'm going to have the soup, also."

Fatigue seemed to be a catalyst for Jack, making him more talkative and bold. He loved people and enjoyed flirting, and he never considered himself more than 20-something. He didn't usually eat in the doctor's dining room. The cafeteria was where the rest of the staff and the families of the sick ate. These were the people he enjoyed most. He was tired of the constant whining about government intrusion, red tape, low pay, and constant work even though everyone in the doctor's lounge had a job and a house. Jack enjoyed surgery and people, in that order. If he wasn't operating, he wanted to talk, but not politics and not doom and gloom.

The woman ahead of him in line was petite and had perfect posture. Her Lucy Liu eyes were narrowed, held tightly by cheekbones that lifted her silky skin. Her movements were graceful, he noted, direct yet nimble. She placed her tray in front of the server who wasn't paying attention. He partially dropped the plate of noodles and beef on the corner of her tray. The entire plate crashed to the ground.

"Oh, no!" Her words were filled with surprise and distress but almost lost in the clamor of broken dishes.

The server was taken by surprise as well. He stepped back, ready to apologize, but when he saw the young Asian standing in shock, his vision narrowed and his mouth recoiled.

"What are you doing? You need to pay attention. When somebody puts a plate on your tray, you need to be holding it with both hands." He glanced at his supervisor, raising his hands in disgust as if another fool had just embarrassed him.

"Excuse me, but did you mean to say you are sorry?" Jack moved between the girl and her server, his voice predatory, his jaw tucked. He lowered his forehead slightly to get a better look at the server.

"I..." He gave a quick look at the supervisor and at Jack's scrub clothes. "I guess no one is to blame here, but..." He stopped, aware that he'd said enough.

"I'll tell you what. Why don't you just put two bowls of that on my tray. I can assure you I won't drop it."

Jack had seen the same server cause accidents before. Most likely he was already under the scrutiny of his supervisor, and Jack didn't want to humiliate him but he wasn't going to allow him to transfer blame to the girl.

"And we'll both have a strawberry parfait."

The woman had caught her breath but stood motionless, her pale skin empty of blood. Her hands shook with embarrassment. "I am so sorry."

"You have no reason to apologize. Please, will you join me for lunch?" Jack's voice was soft, fatherly.

"I... I..." She seemed unsure of the situation, or perhaps of what proper etiquette might consist of in this situation.

"Were you going to dine alone?"

"Yes, well okay... I mean..." She examined Jack quickly, obviously completely unnerved. Another look at Jack's eyes and face and she collected herself, however. She saw something that she hadn't seen in years, compassion and honor. "Sure. I'd like that very much!"

Jack carried the tray, now topped with food and beverage, ushering her to a four-seat table. Carrying a loaded tray was no problem for a guy who benches 300 pounds and still was in the shape he had been in at Vanderbilt where he played linebacker. He avoided a two-seat table next to it, aware of the girl's uneasiness. "Is this okay?" It was in the middle of the room.

"Sure!" She followed obediently.

They sat across from each other, Jack placing her servings on the table first.

"Do you always start food fights in hospitals?" Jack smirked.

"I don't know what happened, honestly."

"I do. I saw the whole thing. Relax." He reached out his hand, a peace gesture. "I'm Jack Wade! I'm one of the surgeons in this hospital."

She shook hands, her grasp brief but sincere. "Hi. I'm Suzy Yuan."

"Do you have someone you're visiting here?" Jack didn't want to pry, but he was truly interested.

"No." She smiled sheepishly. "I'm a student at the University of Alabama. I am working on my PhD."

"So why are you in the hospital, if you don't mind my asking?"

Again, a self-conscious hesitation. "I'm working on a dissertation in neuropsychology. My field of research is connectionism and artificial neural networks."

Jack's eyes rounded. "Huh?"

She giggled. "It has to do with neural pathway damage and how it affects people clinically. I am working with people who have brain injury in the hospital as part of my research."

Suddenly Jack remembered that he had seen her before in the Neuro Intensive Care Unit talking with patients. He was always in a rush during rounds, but he had been peripherally aware of her presence.

"You have operated on some of the patients I work with, trauma patients with head injuries. I know you are a great surgeon." Her tone held more than admiration, he noted, almost reverence.

"Where are you from?" Jack asked.

"I was born in Shanghai, China. My parents died in an automobile accident when I was young. I was sent to live with my aunt and uncle, who live in Atlanta, Georgia, by the government. I've been at the university for the last four years. So..." She grinned. "I'm not really sure where I'm from. But I guess when I finish my degree, I'll be going back to China."

"So that's why your English is so good and you even have a hint of a Southern accent."

Another grin.

"You wouldn't want to stay in the States?"

"I'd love to. I love it here. But I'm here on a student visa. I will have to go back home when I'm no longer a student."

Jack's cell phone buzzed. It was the emergency room. A stab wound to the belly.

"I'm sorry. I have to run to the E.D. It's been very nice talking with you, Suzy. Good luck on your work. I hope to see you around the hospital."

CHAPTER 7

It had been a couple of weeks since his surgery and Grant was home, his body slowly recovering. Creatine kinase is an enzyme released from muscle as a result of injury. Normally it is in single figures, but Grant's maxed out at 14,000. Once all of the medicines had left his system, his body was essentially depleted of all energy stores. That didn't mean that the pain was gone. Even when he was perfectly still, the flu-like throb never left; but any movement brought toothache-severe pounding that hammered him back to bed. Even his eyes hurt. The simple action of looking around caused pounding in his brain, a migraine on steroids. At least he wasn't frozen, paralyzed and in rigor mortis, he told himself, but alive, home, and recovering.

"Dad, are you doing okay?" Ree, his oldest, came to check on him before heading to school.

She'd just had her 16th birthday. Twenty-four hours before Grant was admitted to the hospital, she woke up to a new life. Finally, she had wheels. She'd never imagined that anything would make her happier than the freedom of being alone in her car. Driving wasn't every-thing, however. She and her sister, Beth, had practically camped at their father's bedside in the hospital. Having their father alive was the gift they prayed for, but having him home instead of at work was like candy.

"Yeah, sweetie. I'm really fine. You go on to school, and be careful driving."

"Honey, I'll take you to school today." Carol jumped into the exchange.

"Mom! We've been through this!" Ree's voice frowned as much as her face.

"Sweetheart, your dad just got home and you don't have plans after school. It would be easier for me to take you," Carol pleaded more than insisted.

"Mom." Ree planted her feet. "I'm going to be careful. I'm not going to wreck or run over anyone. I've been driving for a year now, and you've been with me every time I even looked at a car for the last year. It's time." She pulled her keys out defiantly.

"Hey, Dad!" Beth pranced in, taking her place beside Ree.

"You two are the most beautiful sights my poor tired eyes could see!" His eyes really were pounding, but his heart danced when he saw his daughters. "Perfect timing!" he thought. He didn't want to be in the middle of a tug-of-war between Carol and Ree.

Ree was wearing a new dress she had gotten for her birthday. Muted pastels in silk allowed her cheeks, which she had just learned how to dust into a rosy blush with her new makeup, to take center stage.

Beth, 13 and spirited, couldn't wait to give him a hug.

"I love you, Dad. I'll see you after school." She wrapped his head in her arms, then released him. Clenching her hand, she gave two fist pumps. "This is awesome, my sister driving me to school."

Carol remained quiet, apparently deciding it wasn't worth it. Her daughters didn't understand how terrified she was, but arguing now would unravel into another verbal brawl. Grant had never experienced one of their meltdowns, and it wasn't the time for him to see one.

"Okay. You win. But be careful," Carol surrendered to Ree. "Drive slowly and carefully." She made sure Ree made eye contact with her. "Don't forget how to merge onto McFarland Boulevard."

"Mom!" Ree snapped. "My car has heard you tell me so many times, it knows how."

"Kisses and hugs! Love you, Dad!" the girls said in unison. They rushed out of the bedroom, a quick confirmatory glance back before rushing downstairs.

"Good job." Ree high-fived Beth as they hit the stairs. She knew Beth had played her part well. It took teamwork to beat Mom!

The front door slammed and the new Jeep Compass whirred away. Carol crawled back in bed and nudged in close. She knew the pain of the unexpected and the vacuum of loss. Her mother had passed only a year ago with a cerebral bleed. She and her mother were like sisters, her loss ripping the fibers of her stomach for months. Grant had been her crutch.

She was an only child, her father and mother divorced at an early age. She hardly knew her father and wasn't sure about men in general. Grant had met her during his residency, a time that his hours were spoken for and his ability to give energy outside of the hospital limited. However, when he met Carol, his priorities, focus, and sense of being suddenly reversed.

They found time to meet before rounds, between cases in the OR, or in the cafeteria. If there was a chance to catch their breath away from work, it was shared. Carol saw his exhaustion but understood his drive for she had the same inner fire. No matter how high the mountain, if she had a goal, there was no stopping her. They both understood well the term "delayed gratification," but life in Tuscaloosa was going to be great.

But it wasn't. Grant seemed to spend more and more time away from home, more and more time away from her. But she understood as well as he did that hard work upfront would pay off down the road, and so she was willing to give him up to the hospital, hoping that events in their lives would shape them, that time together would return.

Then her first child died. The most precious things in her life—her father, her daughter, her mother—were simply vapor waiting to blow away. She couldn't hold on to them. The harder she tried, the faster they escaped. She had almost lost her husband, now her other girls were off...

"Do you remember how we met?" Carol gently stroked his arm, escaping into a memory.

"Are you kidding? I remember what you were wearing, what you were gonna do that night, and what time it was!" Grant sometimes bluffed his way through these little quizzes, but not today.

"Refresh my memory."

"You were wearing a pink polo shirt with a popped collar, tight jeans, a Rachel haircut, and the cutest cowboy boots I'd ever seen. You looked like Dale Evans and Olivia Newton John rolled into one. I had just been raked over the coals by Dr. Elders for forgetting to check a potassium on a patient, Elder's personal friend and a big oil guy."

Grant enjoyed telling the story, no matter how many times he delivered it. "I had traded call with John Ballard so I could go to a Madonna concert that night. Dr. Elders was so mad that he told me to stay outside the guy's room all night so I wouldn't forget what needed to be done with him. As soon as the air was completely out of my balloon, you tripped on a trash can outside Dr. Elder's office. He walked past you like you didn't exist. You'd been working stats for him on his carotid endarterectomy stroke rates. I ran to help you up, knowing you were working with him and hoping you could put in a good word for me. Instead, we talked for a while and I gave you my ticket to Madonna."

"Is that all?" She loved his memory. He seemed to photograph every event in his life.

"Not at all. I looked at you on the floor and felt like an angel had fallen to Earth."

He turned to Carol, the motion painful but worth it. "My last thoughts, before they beat on my chest and apparently thought I was dead, were about you!"

"What were you thinking?"

"I knew you had to be there, but I couldn't see you and I couldn't smell you. I had no sense of you being there." His voice faded, entering the emptiness he had experienced. "It was the most frightening thing I've ever known."

Her eyes stung with gratefulness, then filled with tears.

"I'm glad." She held him as tightly as she could, afraid she might hurt him.

CHAPTER 8

Wang Chien didn't bow to many people. He had been visited by Yao Ming several times. The first visits were cordial. Yao came to Wang's office at Beijing Automotive to examine Wang's business plan and financials. Later meetings went from information gathering to strategy.

Today Wang walked up the front steps of *Guojia Anquan Bu*, which had a Greek Revival appearance similar to the Alabama State Capitol. The building stood as a source of honor and fear among the Chinese. Wang knew its history and took each step with reverence. The building was the home of the Ministry of State Security (MSS), the most powerful agency of state and international intelligence in the China and perhaps the world. Little was known about the agency by the Chinese, except for its central role in their protection and world dominance. Political dissidents feared the MSS, and Washington knew it for its general disregard for international law. The MSS had hacked into American intelligence systems, infiltrated American businesses to steal technology secrets, and used espionage to discover military plans and weapons. And the Chinese made no apology when such actions exposed.

Wang now quickened his pace, taking two steps at a time up toward the entrance. His chin stuck out strongly but a chill traveled down his spine. He assumed that he was being watched from Yao's window. He wasn't used to walking alone. Usually his ape was at his side.

An officer waited for him as he entered and took him to a nearby room where he was undressed, x-rayed, and redressed in traditional Chinese tangzhuang attire. The simple dress made Wang feel like a peasant, which he knew was the intent. It was the uniform Mao wore to symbolize the simplicity of a commoner.

Upon entering Yao's office, Wang was first to bow. "*Nin hao!*" Wang used the honorific address of hello. It wasn't like their earlier meetings when he considered Yao an equal and greeted him with *ni hao*. Not only did he lack the confidence he once had, there was no longer any familiarity between them.

Wang raised his head, making quick eye contact with Yao, then shifted his forehead downward. Yao kept his eyes on Wang.

"Have you completed the initial negotiations?" Yao's voice seemed to bellow out of a well.

"*Shi de!*" Wang's eyes were on the table. He thought he had done everything expected of him, but he was prepared for a reprimand.

"*Lianghao,*" Yao grunted. He already knew that Wang had contacted the governor. He knew where the deal stood and knew that Wang had done everything he had been told to do. "Good" came like a verdict of "Innocent."

"Now, you will do this. We will need to use American workers, Tuscaloosa and Birmingham workers. They will not keep production high for they are weak and slow, but they will be our strength."

Yao continued, his mouth a snarl. "The *gwailo* foreign devil has opened its gates to us. We will enter! We will work! We will grow!"

Wang didn't know exactly what Yao's plans were. He was mainly interested in building his automotive empire. As long as Yao was happy, he could enjoy his mistresses, tobacco, and opium.

"You will demand that any company doing business with you must be subject to investigation. The *gwailo* know the Chinese do not trust them. They will do anything to appease us. If another company supplies Beijing Automotive or if you provide services to them, you must be able to review their business plans and financials. I want to know as much about the American companies as I do about yours." He paused, waiting for Wang to look up. "And I know everything about yours!"

Wang knew not to be arrogant but also to be confident. "Beijing Automotive is strong and successful because of our commitment to hard work and Chinese tradition. We will continue to do what is best for the company and the mainland."

"*An jing!*" Yao snapped. "Beijing Automotive is successful because WE allow you to be successful. If the People's Republic wants you to be successful, you will be! If not..." Yao slammed his fist on the table.

Yao knew that Wang was a shrewd businessman. He had dealt with others. Some were still in his circle but others had fallen out. Yao knew that Wang understood it was safer to be in the circle.

CHAPTER 9

Everything happened faster than the governor had expected or than the mayor could anticipate. Mr. Wang had called two weeks after his departure from Detroit. The Astor would be built in Tuscaloosa County. Billy was electrified with the prospects of planning and organizing. The anticipation of incoming jobs and growth—and of his increased popularity—was overwhelming.

Local and national news vans choked the streets. Video cameras bounced to the courthouse like camels to water as microphones emerged, stalks newly sprouted, waiting for the broadcast. The sun pounded into the concrete, shaded only by the recently built 48 million-dollar federal building and courthouse. The massive Doric columns, made of Indiana limestone, seemed to adorn the house of Zeus himself.

Tuscaloosa, once the capitol of Alabama, was making a comeback, and Billy could not be more pleased that it was on his watch. The Alabama Crimson Tide was reigning in glory athletically, the University of Alabama had recently been named in the top 10 public universities nationally, DCH Regional Hospital had achieved national recognition by the newly formed Bureau of Hospital Performance as a leader among non-profit hospitals in overall outcomes, and the Chamber of Commerce of Tuscaloosa had been recognized by the *European and Asian Market Magazine* as number one in recruiting foreign businesses to America.

Billy approached the microphone, all of his 6'6 stature necessary to have a presence in front of the massive Pantheonic columns. His voice echoed outward as though blown by the Gods of old as he looked out over the hundreds of reporters, thousands of locals, and six or seven helicopters that were circling for aerial views.

"Thank you all for your support of Tuscaloosa and our state." He paused, giving an eye to the governor.

"As you all know, we in Tuscaloosa have encouraged businesses to come to our city and county. We are all about hospitality and we are all about growth."

He pulled forward a poster outlining all of the businesses in Tuscaloosa, the real estate projects that had been completed and that were underway, and the economic success of the last few years.

"I don't want to waste time reviewing our successes and looking at the past, however. I come before you today to announce our new partnership with China and to peer into the future with you."

The cheers and applause continued for almost a minute. "Today, I can proudly announce that Beijing Automotive will open a plant in our southern city limits that will bring the first Chinese automobile into production in America." Again the air before courthouse shook with whistles, clapping, and the firing of cameras.

"Tuscaloosa has been chosen for several reasons. We are the heart of the South. We believe in hospitality, and we believe in ourselves and our neighbors."

Again, he paused, waving to the state troopers behind him. They parted, allowing Wang to step forward.

"I want to introduce you to Mr. Wang Chien, President and owner of Beijing Automotive."

Wang walked quickly to join the mayor at his podium. With a humble bow, he looked out over the masses, opening his arms as if to absorb every cheer. His ape stood at Wang's command nearby. He didn't like crowds, but he knew this was necessary. He watched his boss walk forward, but then his gaze was everywhere: looking at hands, looking at movements, aware of everyone around him and anyone close to his master.

"Mr. Wang has been in negotiations with the governor and business leaders for months. He has looked elsewhere for locations to build, but because he trusts us and values our commitment to honesty and hard work, the plant to build the first Chinese car in America will be located in our hometown. The Astor will be one more product that will bring us pride."

Wang grinned and swayed, waving like Stevie Wonder into the air, as though he had no idea what Billy had said. He opened his arms toward the crowd, again waving in the applause and absorbing every cheer.

"Now, I'd like to introduce the man who, with Mr. Wang, has put this partnership together. Please join us, Governor Richard Sands." Billy looked back once again to the troopers, waiting for the governor to step forward.

Richard had been standing next to Wang, the excitement of the moment and the Alabama sun doing their work on his heart rate and perspiration. Wang's ape was behind him, too close for his tastes. Everyone was too close to him. He was hot and needed space. He'd never panicked before, but he was sensing discomfort that was totally foreign. There had been a sting in his back, then his chest heaved for breaths that were void of oxygen. A tightness across his chest seemed to grip him like a vice. Crushing pain ached his heart with every beat as it raced, each beat trying to outrun the next. As though a knife was ripping his shoulder to his left hand, all he could do was stand still.

The troopers parted, waiting for him to step forward. But he simply stood, perspiration dripping from his face and all blood drained from his head. Then he felt his knees buckle and the ground crash against his face.

CHAPTER 10

Suzy Yuan, due to a constant inflow of trauma patients, was well known to the ICU nurses; but she also knew the nurses on most units as trauma and head injury patients were sent to any available room once they were stable. The electronic sensing devices she carried in her backpack, which was almost as big as she was, as she walked the halls were sophisticated and diverse. The smallest gadget fit in her pocket, which was where she kept it at all times. She came to the hospital every day and one way or another she was able to pass by every room in the hospital once a week. If the apparatus in her pocket made a beep, she would punch a button, recording a message. Several beeps had registered today.

Arriving at room 707, she tapped lightly at the door. "Hello!" Her voice sang with hopefulness. "May I come in?"

A tired bleat came from inside. "Come in!"

She gently entered the room, aware of the grief and pain in front of her. "My name is Suzy Yuan. I am working with patients who have suffered spinal cord and brain injury, trying to help families understand the injuries and to provide data that will contribute to a cure."

Lizzie White was 10 years old. She lived in a trailer park next to a busy street. Her brother was teaching her how to ride the bike that he had just bought from a friend. He just couldn't run fast enough to stop her when she started rolling down the hill toward the street. When the car hit her, he saw her head snap back like it was not attached to her body. Unbelievably, there was almost no visible major injury. He was even able to speak to her when he reached her on the pavement, but from that moment on, she was completely paralyzed from her neck down.

"I am studying these injuries and doing research at the University. I have a grant to do this through the university and approval through the hospital. If it is okay with you, I will need you to sign this HIPPA form saying that I can have access to Lizzie's records and that I can share her records and my findings with others." Suzy was addressing the girl's mother.

"Now what?" Lizzie's mother was in her mid-twenties. She had been stroking Lizzie's forehead when Suzy came in.

Suzy placed her backpack on the ground and walked to the bedside. Lizzie's hair was braided, and her dark skin made Asian complexion seem ghost-like. But her gentleness in speech gave a peace to the room.

"I want to try to help you all understand Lizzie's injury and to maybe help Lizzie. But there are rules that the government makes us follow to protect Lizzie's privacy. I would never do anything to violate her privacy, but you have to give me permission to be involved in her care by law."

Suzy hadn't noticed the middle-aged woman sitting quietly in the corner reading her Bible. "Sweetheart, anything you can do to help my grand, you go on ahead."

Lizzie's grandmother sat with the peace of ages. Her eyes showed that she had seen pain and suffered grief, but they had the sparkle of hope that Suzy had seen only in America, especially in those who read that book. She was familiar with Christianity, which had grown in popularity throughout the People's Republic recently. Beginning in 1949, under communist rule, Christianity had been discouraged and even banned, and during the

Cultural Revolution from 1966 to 1976 Christians were tortured and killed. When Suzy left for the United States, she had witnessed the imprisonment of several of her friends who had been identified as Christians for meeting without authorization. She was intrigued by this faith that seemed strong enough to overcome grief and powerful enough to risk punishment, a religion making a comeback in her country against such great odds.

"May I examine little Lizzie?" Suzy's hands cradled Lizzie's face. The little girl's eyes immediately softened from fear to trust as if her touch carried special powers.

Methodically, Suzy touched and memorized every inch from head to toe. Then, she went to her bag, pulling out a series of needles and wires and a miniature console. For the next two hours she made recordings, charted results, and developed a map of Lizzie's responses to stimuli. She left the room to review her chart and returned.

"Lizzie has a complete spinal injury in her neck." She knelt down speaking softly so Lizzie wouldn't hear. Lizzie's mother and grandmother held hands, sitting next to each other.

"That means that her spinal cord is completely severed, or cut in two."

"We been told that!" Lizzie's mother had hoped after all this time that there would be something new to report.

"Yes, but have you been told that research has shown that these injuries can be completely healed?" Suzy pulled out her laptop.

She showed the two ladies pictures of rats, then pigs and finally monkeys. The before and after pictures were too incredible to believe. Lifeless animals appeared to have been restored.

"Them's just pictures. Are you saying our Lizzie can be cured?" Grandma held tightly to her book. A tear tried to form in her eye but she wiped it away.

Suzy clicked on her laptop again. This time she showed a video. Suzy herself was in a lab on the video operating on a monkey. She cut the neck of a spider monkey, leaving it lifeless except for mouth and eye motions. The video showed weeks of time lapse action with the monkey lying limp in a cage. Then Suzy injected a syringe of fluid at the exact site she had cut the monkey's neck. Again, time lapse filming showed the monkey gradually regaining all arm, leg, bowel, and urinary function. Finally the monkey was shown jumping from tree to tree in a zoo.

There was silence in the room as Lizzie's mother and grandmother wept.

"You must be patient." Suzy cautioned. "I have also shown that, in injuries like Lizzie's, you have to wait several months before injecting stem cells and the injury to the backbone has to be fixed." She looked back at Lizzie. "But Lizzie will walk again." Her encouragement was more than wishful. "I will be back tomorrow."

Suzy left as quietly as she had entered. Her backpack bounced behind her with new information and new hope as she glided down the hall to the elevator trying to decide whether to go back to the lab or do computer work at her residence. As the elevator door opened, Jack Wade stepped off.

"Well, Suzy!" Jack's face brightened.

"Hello, Dr. Wade!" She looked down automatically, a sign of honoring another in her culture.

"Are you making any discoveries today?"

The elevator closed behind him, leaving them alone in the hall. Jack could see that Suzy was uncomfortable. Her eyes darted through the empty halls, hoping not to be seen alone with a man.

"Suzy." He waited for her to look back up. "This isn't China and I'm not an emperor." Another pause.

"Yes, sir!" She maintained eye contact, grinning uneasily.

Jack hoped to say more but the words wouldn't come. He was rarely lacking when it came to conversation, but Suzy left him vacant. Her frail stature, cultural mystique, and graceful beauty mesmerized him. He simply stood watching her.

Suzy was the first to notice the activity. Her eyes left Jack, spotting two Pinkerton guards rushing toward them. She froze, staring in disbelief. The guards shoes clicked on the linoleum floor and their nightsticks danced on their belts. Jack and Suzy stood motionless.

The two guards ran past them and threw open the adjoining stairwell door. One of the guards recognized Jack and yelled back as they rumbled down the stairs. "The governor's in the Emergency Room!"

CHAPTER 11

In fact the governor had already passed through the Emergency Room. His EKG on the way to the hospital showed severe ST changes, indication of a huge heart attack. He was awake but the elephant remained on his chest, and there was no time to waste in the ER. He was rushed back to the catheterization lab where the team was already assembled and waiting.

"Here he comes." Janet watched the EMS team wheel Governor Sands around the last corner before the cath lab.

A face mask delivering oxygen was strapped to his face and orange safety straps were buckled on top of him to prevent him from falling off the gurney. State troopers multiplied behind him.

"You'll have to stay out here," Janet said to the contingent of troopers as she held her hand out like a school teacher. "This is a sterile area. No one can come in without scrubs and a mask."

The nurses and techs waiting for him at the entrance to the lab took over. The governor was rolled into the lab, unstrapped, and on the table before the troopers outside had taken a breath.

There is no dignity in the hospital. The governor's clothes were taken off and his groin shaved, then painted with disinfectant. A large blue drape was placed over him, with only a tiny opening that exposed the position of his femoral artery.

"Needle!" Dr. Wu had performed thousands of cardiac catheterizations and angioplasties. He placed the needle into the skin between Richard's pubis and hipbone. A narrow jet of blood sprayed into the air.

"Wire!" He threaded a long silver wire through the needle and stepped on a pedal. The room dimmed as the screen in front of Dr. Wu came to life. He navigated the wire up, around, and into the shadow of Richard's heart. Then he delivered a catheter over the wire, removing the wire and positioning the catheter at the origin of the main artery feeding the heart.

"Call Dr. Miller!"

A single blush of dye showed that Richard had a complex blockage in his left main coronary artery that extended into the big branches feeding 70% of his heart. This was no situation for angioplasty or stents, and no situation to be a hero.

"Right catheter!" Another injection showed blockage on the right side of the heart.

"Governor!" Dr. Wu spoke loudly, waking him from light anesthesia. "You're going to need emergency surgery for blockage in your heart."

"I thought that's what was going on here." Sands looked around, puzzled.

"No, this is not surgery. We cannot fix your blockages with balloons and stents. Your blockage is too complex and you will die without open-heart surgery."

"You mean cracking my chest?" He flinched.

"That's right."

"Dr. Wu," Phil called from the observation annex, "Dr. Miller is on the phone."

Within moments Grant was in the lab. He had been back at work for a week and had already finished his second operation of the day. He had heard that the governor was in the cath lab and a sixth sense told him that he would get this call. He clicked through the images stored in the review area and approached the governor's side.

"Governor, I'm Grant Miller, a heart surgeon."

Richard looked him over. He looked a bit younger than he had hoped. "Okay." He shifted uncomfortably on the table. "So, tell me. Am I about to die or do I have a choice of going to another hospital like..."

"Governor, you can do anything you want. All options are open. But you have a 99% blockage in the main artery going to your heart and additional blockages that are critical. If the main artery closes, you will die." He'd had this conversation hundreds of times before. Even speaking to the governor, it seemed rote.

"My advice is that we get you fixed before that happens. You've had a big heart attack already. Anything more and it's over." There was compassion in his voice but also conviction and confidence, which seemed to reach Richard first.

"Okay, let's get it on!" He looked around. "Where's Frank? I need him to let Molly and my son know what's happening." He stopped. "Better yet, can I call right now on my cell phone?"

Grant left the room briefly, giving the governor his privacy and a second chance to request transfer to another hospital. He knew that DCH Regional didn't have the glamour of some other places, but the best thing for this man was to have a an operation without delay.

When he reentered, Dr. Wu had already placed an intra-aortic balloon where the catheter had been, in the aorta above the kidney arteries and below to collar bone, beating every time the heart relaxes to provide extra blood flow to. and to take stress off, the heart.

"Governor, we are ready to go to the operating room. The procedure will take about three hours. Anything can happen: stroke, kidney failure, wound infections, problems in the OR during the operation, or afterward pneumonia or death..."

CHAPTER 12

Lee was also aware of the governor's arrival in the hospital. Born Li Zhang in China, he found it easier to succeed in the business world of America with a Western common name. He had been able to make a regional success of the popular Yida Tech instruments and surgical disposables. Yida Industries, which had broken into a multi-billion dollar market by offering an excellent product but also by underbidding, was known for producing ergonomically designed instruments that conformed to the human hand. The company had also developed an inventory of stapling devices that required minimal effort from the surgeon.

Typically, there is a "pop" or a "firing" motion with surgical staplers. This moment of commotion can be disruptive on highly sensitive or fragile tissue, and veins, arteries, intestines, or nerves can easily be damaged by the instability. Yida Tech had overcome this obstacle with an automated mechanism that required only slight pressure on the trigger, an innovation surgeons had needed for years. Recent advances in robotic surgery and video-assisted techniques demanded a new concept in suturing and stapling tissue that was distant from the surgeon's hand.

Lee was meeting with Butch Robbins, the Chief Financial Officer, and Jennifer Owens, the Central Purchasing officer for the hospital. The meeting had been scheduled for weeks and he was excited to offer a new product.

"Thank you for meeting with me again." Lee surrendered his customary nod. "This is an exciting day for Tuscaloosa, the state of Alabama, America, and China." He hesitated, then a bit more than a whisper. "I understand that Governor Sands has had a heart attack. Yida Technology and all of China wish him well."

"Thank you, Lee. He's in good hands here!" Butch said confidently.

"I will get straight to business. I know you will both be busy today." Lee opened his briefcase, pulling out a piece of plastic folded like a handkerchief. Unfolding it, he inserted a wire attached to his cell phone. The display came to life like a 24-inch 3D television.

"This is our new line of orthopedic implants. You will be able to purchase total hips, total knees, screws, rods..." He watched the animation with pride.

Again, Yida had developed a totally new design. Instead of the traditional ball and socket joint, the new design was based on five individual universal joints with side hinge joints for stability. Lee waited for the animation to demonstrate its surgical implantation and design features, and then before and after video of patients. Butch and Jennifer marveled at videos of men, women, and children, even some athletes, who were barely able to walk in the before videos running and playing sports in the post-operation videos.

"Your doctors at DCH have asked me about this product. I haven't been soliciting them," he continued. "But I know you are very interested in whether you can afford it. The recent healthcare laws are causing hospitals to close, and part of the reason is the expense of implantable devices like hips, knees, and shoulders. Here's the breakdown."

Lee tapped on his cell phone and new graphics appeared on the plastic screen. "Hospitals now receive $15,000 for a hip replacement. That's down from $17,500 in 2012. Of that, $5,000 goes to buy a hip prosthesis. It doesn't affect you, but the surgeon makes $2,000, down from $2500 in 2012, and the anesthesiologist makes $800, down from $1,000. Each day a patient stays in the hospital costs you $1600, and so the cheaper the prosthesis and the quicker a patient is discharged, the more savings to the hospital."

Butch and Jennifer knew all of this; they were simply waiting for the bottom line. DCH was feeling the squeeze of mandated cuts and private insurance failure. High cost items were a huge problem. Consideration had been given to discontinuing services that were a drain on the hospital's resources.

"For a total hip replacement, the Yida-Hip will cost the hospital only $3,000." Lee watched Butch and Jennifer brighten. "And the typical hospital stay is only three days due to the simplicity of implantation. The hospital makes money again and the doctors are happy, and the patients have quicker recovery and a better joint. Everybody wins."

Lee then showed the breakdown for knees, shoulders, and even new hand prostheses. "We have FDA approval as of this year. We follow all guidelines regarding implants, just as we follow the appropriate guidelines for every stapler you use and implantable we offer. Every name is recorded, and the implant is recorded and submitted to the FDA for tracking. So far, we haven't had any failures. Blood-clot complications have decreased by 25% and surgery date to return to work has decreased by 20%.

"Since Tuscaloosa has opened its doors to China, and since you already are using our products, we are willing to even give an additional 10% cost reduction if you use our products exclusively."

"Thanks, Lee," Butch spoke up. "You have been fair with us before and your product has been embraced here at DCH with excitement. DCH has always placed patient care above the bottom line, but it looks like we win on both ends with Yida products. Jennifer and I will present this to our CEO and get back with you."

Lee wanted to make sure that Yida was well established and had branded a reputation before Beijing Automotive came to town. He had heard stories of Wang Chien, known in Beijing as Jiang Shi, or hopping vampire, because he would suck the life spirit out of anyone who crossed him—or anyone he wished to conquer. Lee had a good job and good reputation he didn't want tarnished.

He left the meeting and went directly to the Operating Room. He was diligent in checking inventory. If any supplies were low, he would restock the shelves. He had learned the benefits of devotion to duty and the focused pursuit of his ambitions.

CHAPTER 13

The governor was in OR Room 5, which had recently been upgraded to a hybrid operating room with state of the art radiographic imaging for delivery of stents to repair aneurysms in the chest and heart valves that could be replaced through a single incision in the groin.

"Governor, you'll be going to sleep in a moment. Happy dreams. We take good care of you." Quan was at the helm.

Grant was assisting the nurses, shaving Richard's legs. Quan's voice and words made him hesitate. He'd heard them before. A shiver ran down his back. Memories of his hyperthermia and near death were too close.

This would be a standard coronary artery bypass. Erica was checking the lines on her bypass machine. She had been a perfusionist since she was 25, and now at 65 she had seen it all. In order for the surgeon to operate on the heart, techniques had evolved to stop it from beating without interrupting blood circulation to rest of the body. Earlier methods involved blood draining into a large well where oxygen bubbled into the blood before being returned to the body with roller pumps. Now a centrifugal pump whirled blood through plastic tubing, pushing it through hollow fiber membranes that exchanged oxygen almost like capillaries in the body. Erica knew that any misconnection could be disaster. Any air in the bypass circuit would impede the hydraulic flow of blood. She checked all circuits and alarms. Any problem wouldn't be her fault.

"Lines." Grant took the sterile tubes from the surgical tech and passed them to Erica.

Richard was somewhere below the antiseptic plastic barrier, blue drapes, and loops of hosepipes. Clear fluid circulated through them, allowing air or particles to be captured by a filter. Any debris in the line or air could circulate to the brain once bypass was initiated, leaving Richard with a stroke, which could be worse than death.

"Scalpel." The overhead lights were directed toward his chest and legs, but a beam of white light lasered its way from Grant's headlight. The intense beam pinpointed his view. He wore binocular glasses that increased his magnification by 3.5 times so that the only field of view was the two-inch circle in front of him.

The scalpel slid downward into Richard's chest and met the underlying bone. Blood trickled into the field, leaking out of vessels in the underlying fat. Each bleeding spot was quickly cauterized with electrocautery. A simple touch of a button on the device allowed electric current to vaporize the site of bleeding.

"Saw!" Grant reached for the battery-powered bone cutter that looked like a carpentry saw. Within two seconds the breastbone separated, leaving a whiff of smoldering mineral behind.

As Grant spread a silver retractor, exposing the underlying activity, an assistant busily extracted a long vein from Richard's leg. "Good vein, sir!"

Again the electrocautery Bovie crackled over the severed bone, turning bleeding tissue into char. Beneath, Richard's heart struggled under a sac of wax paper confinement. It bounced slowly, exhausted with blood starvation.

"Dr. Miller, the blood pressure is low. Can we start some dopamine?" Vickie, a nurse anesthetist, peeped over the drapes.

"That's fine." He kept working, using the electrocautery to dissect the internal mammary artery from the undersurface of Richard's chest wall. The two-millimeter artery under the chest wall was the perfect size for one of the bypasses but took extra time to dissect and use.

"Clip." Grant reached for the Yida-Clip. With a gentle touch, Lee's stapler did the rest. A four-millimeter clip slid along a rail, contacted a thready branch of the artery, and squeezed down imperceptibly. He repeated the maneuver, placing two clips on each side of the branch and cutting between them.

The Bovie buzzed and the clips fired until the internal mammary artery fell from its perch on the chest and thumped with each heartbeat, eager to restore blood flow to the heart.

"We're fibrillating!" Quan shouted.

Grant didn't need to look at the monitors. He had heard the rhythmic beep of the heart stop. He knew Quan could look at the monitors. It wasn't time for looking.

"Scalpel." He slit the membrane confining the heart, and watery fluid sloshed out and the heart bulged like a balloon underneath, no longer beating but wiggling toward death.

"Metzembaums." Grant snatched the scissors and completed the opening, slicing the sac from top to bottom.

His right hand slipped around the heart and he started squeezing. The first efforts were careful not to puncture the thin muscle that could easily rupture and lead to immediate exsanguination.

"Paddles! Charge to 10 joules!"

Quan hit the defibrillator button. A whirring and beep signaled that the paddles were fully charged.

"Clear!" With a paddle on the right and left side of the heart, Grant waited to make sure no one was in contact with the patient.

Pop! Richard's entire body jerked with electricity, but the heart still quivered. No spontaneous beats.

"Charge to 20!" The governor's body bounced and then went limp. His heart still quivered.

"Okay, we're crashing on. Give heparin."

The assistant knew what that meant. He left the vein and leg below, jumping into position across from Grant.

"Scalpel." With a snake like strike, the scalpel popped into the aorta. The two inch wide vessel exiting the heart squirted blood, but no sooner had the blood found freedom than a plastic cannula closed the opening. Grant connected the tubing from Erica's bypass machine to the plastic pipe in the aorta.

"Almost there."

The room was silent. There was nothing anyone could do until the governor was on bypass. Each second seemed like minutes. Everyone in the room knew the drill. They'd seen it before and knew the consequences of failure. After the first minute without blood flow, the brain cells begin to die, and after three minutes brain injury is likely. After 10 minutes, the patient is unlikely to recover.

Grant's hands moved quicker than his thoughts. They had been here before. The scrub tech had as well, and without a word, the knife was in Grant's hands again. Another strike into the heart, and this time the right atrium poured black blood into the chest. It was under such backpressure from the dying heart that it filled the entire chest cavity with blood.

The assistant held the aortic cannula in place, aware that if it became dislodged, they would never be able to find the hole in the aorta and replace the cannula with so much blood everywhere.

"Pump sucker on." With a free hand the assistant placed a metal tip into the rising well of blood.

"On bypass!" Grant watched blood drain into his assistant's suction tubing, travel through Erica's machine, and back into the tubing that his assistant had been holding.

"Venous cannula." With the blood level lower, Grant could identify the hole in the atrium. He slipped another tube into the atrium and connected it to another of Erica's pipes. The heart collapsed. It had been bigger than a softball and almost as firm, but now the blood no longer circulated through it but around it, bypassing the heart and lungs to give oxygen and nutrients to a suffocating brain.

"Two minutes." Quan panted.

"What?"

"Only two minutes from the time he fibrillated until we were on bypass!" He checked the clock again. "Good job. His brain should be okay."

Grant was placing sutures around all the cannulas. Now that the heart could rest and blood flow was restored to everything else, he could secure the tubing so it wouldn't fall out of the entry sites.

"Cool to 32."

Erica turned the cooler on, chilling the blood as it swirled through her machine. The lower the temperature the more protection to the heart. She knew the normal body temperature was 37. At 32 there would be less metabolic work of a damaged heart and the brain.

Grant noted that Richard's heart was thickened from the heart attack. The front was barely moving. He examined the blood vessels that needed to be bypassed, picking target sites for new vessels to be sewn into place.

"Cross clamp!" He placed a long clamp across the aorta, just below the cannula, then popped a needle into the aorta between the heart and the clamp.

"Plegia, on!" Erica turned on a pump that injected potassium into the needle, delivering the same concentration to the heart that prisoners receive on their last day on death row.

The cardioplegia solution did its work and Richard's heart lay flaccid. It was time to sew new blood vessels past the blockages to bypass the obstructions.

"Beaver blade." Grant slid a blade the length of a pencil lead and sharper than a razor into a vessel on the back of Richard's heart. The opening was visible only to Grant with his magnified glasses.

"Yidas!" He completed the opening with the fine nickel and chromium alloy scissors that Lee had promised would be precise and never fail. The cut was precise, even through a plaque of calcium.

Within moments Grant was suturing a vein from the leg to the opened artery. The wall of the artery was as thin and fragile as a lemon pulp divider. As a matter of fact, during his residency, he had spent hours practicing his skills on the thin membranes inside lemons or limes. The vessel was only a millimeter and a half in diameter, and so each bite with the suture had to be perfect. If a suture was misplaced, the operation could turn out poorly.

A final twist of his hand and the suturing was complete. Now his fingers danced, whipping seven knots into the silk-thin suture. Then he moved on to the artery on the right side of Richard's heart, and finally he attached the internal mammary artery to the vessel on the front of the heart.

"Clamps off!" He released the clamp on the aorta, allowing blood to return to the heart. The blockages remained but the internal mammary was now flowing to the front of the heart.

"Twenty-eight minutes." Erica marked the time that the clamp was removed. Grant knew that his grafts were well placed and that 30 minutes without blood flow to the heart was not a problem.

"What you think?" Quan grunted.

"About what?"

"You think he come off bypass?"

Grant was sewing the veins to the aorta now, the last connection to restore flow to Richard's blocked vessels.

"Your guess is as good as mine. The gov has had a big one. I'm afraid we're looking at a VAD."

It had been years since a VAD was necessary. With angioplasty and stenting and excellent cardiologists, the victims of big heart attacks could usually avoid emergency surgery. Cardiologists were able to restore flow in the cath lab more quickly than going to the operating room. But sometimes, even with surgical bypasses, the heart is so badly damaged that it isn't strong enough to beat on its own. The only option for survival is a Ventricular Assist Device that continues to function as a bypass, allowing the heart to rest and recover.

"You remember what happened with our last VAD?" Grant kept working, placing temporary pacing wires on the heart.

"No. What?"

"We put it in and the patient's heart was never strong enough to take it out. We sent him to Birmingham for a heart transplant and he died in transport. The machine clotted in the air and he died in the helicopter."

"Oh, crap!" Grant backed away from the table. "The stapler misfired. A clip squirted out of the Yida and hit my glasses."

"Do you know where the clip went?" The circulating nurse's alarm was immediate.

"Not really! It hit my loupes and who knows where it went."

"If it went back in the governor's chest, it could be contaminated and cause a bad infection."

No one knew that better than Dr. Miller. He hadn't had a case of mediastinitis recently, but he knew how bad a chest infection after heart surgery could be. Usually the entire breastbone has to be removed and replaced with muscle from the chest wall in order to clear the infection and allow healing. A complication like that in the governor would be disastrous.

CHAPTER 14

Suzy Yuan hurried to the 7th floor. All of her work was done. Now, all she wanted was to hear more from Lizzie's grandmother.

"Well, hello, Miss Suzy!" Hattie almost sang the greeting.

Suzy bowed politely. "Hello, Miss Hattie."

Suzy had been by daily to track Lizzie's progress but also to listen to her grandmother. She had never talked to anyone with so much optimism, so much certainty that everything was, and would be, all right. Suzy had seen pain in her life, had disappointments, even regrets. She accepted her past, striving to be everything her parents had taught her. Every day was an opportunity to be humane and righteous. Knowledge was her quest, and she vowed to use it with integrity and etiquette, to be virtuous. But after her parents died, her life turned upside down and she had failed in so many ways. She woke up every day ashamed of her failures and afraid of what lay ahead. Miss Hattie had brought something new into her life, a path to leave her failures and regrets behind, a chance to look into the future without fear.

Lizzie had recently been sedated, and a peaceful smile lingered on her lips as she slept. Suzy kissed her gently on her forehead and proceeded with her electrical tracings and stimulations. Nothing had really changed since her initial exam, but she charted her findings meticulously.

"Miss Hattie? Do you really believe that Lizzie will recover?" She looked back to make sure Lizzie was sleeping.

"Child." Hattie never stopped rocking as she laid her Bible across her lap. It was never out of her grasp. "Do you really want to know?" She tapped the Good Book and looked cautiously at Suzy.

"I do." Suzy watched Hattie's wrinkled finger. The tapping became louder until it sounded like knocking. "I want you to believe me. I really think I can make her walk," she told the old woman.

The tapping stopped. "Child." Her voice wasn't singing anymore. It was stern. "I trust you to try to help my Lizzie, but my faith isn't in you." Her tone was sharp. Not mean but direct.

"Do you remember what we talked about the last few days, about Jesus, about His miracles?" Hattie started rocking again.

"Yes." Suzy remembered but it was still too spooky, like ghosts. There were no facts, no data, no proof.

"Do you remember that Jesus healed the man who was paralyzed, not because He felt sorry for the paralyzed man but because of the faith of the men who brought him to Jesus!" Hattie was singing again, not like the choir sings just joyful cadence and rhythmic tones.

"Yes," Suzy acknowledged.

"Well, I have the faith that those men had," Hattie continued. "Maybe more!" Hattie closed her eyes. "Child, you might be Lizzie's angel. You might be the one Jesus has sent to help heal my baby." She opened her eyes and looked directly at Suzy. "But you aren't the one who will do it."

Suzy bowed. "I didn't mean any disrespect."

"None taken, child." Hattie smiled. "If little Lizzie walks again, it will be Jesus who did it." She tapped the book again. "She is here because it was God's will, and you are here because it is God's will. Whatever happens, it isn't by chance and it isn't because of you or me!"

Suzy fidgeted. "You mean everything, whether bad or good, is because of God?"

Hattie laughed with confidence. She'd had this discussion many times with other people. She had it with her daughter earlier in the week. "You tell me what 'good' is and I'll answer you."

Suzy puzzled. "How about if I tell you what 'bad' is?"

"Fine!"

"It's bad that you're grandchild has been injured," Suzy whispered, looking back at the little child. "It's bad that she is paralyzed."

"Is it, now?" Hattie rubbed her chin. "Is it bad that you are here?"

"No. It's good, good for me," Suzy returned defensively. "And I hope it's good for your granddaughter."

"Well, you wouldn't be here if it weren't for Lizzie, her injury and her paralysis."

"Okay!" Suzy squirmed. "But it will be bad if Lizzie doesn't recover."

"Why?" Hattie rocked.

Suzy became anxious, wondering if she understood the grandmother. "Because no little girl deserves to be confined to bed, stuck in a hospital forever."

"What does she deserve?" Hattie smiled. "What do you deserve? What do I deserve?"

Suzy shifted from side to side, wishing she'd never started the discussion.

"Child." Hattie saw that Suzy was lost. "Every moment is precious." She closed her eyes, drifting into the past. "I never knew my parents. My Auntie, who never had a baby, raised me. I was her Lizzie, and I was a bad girl!" She shook her head. Her eyes, already closed, tightened, screening out memories. "But my Auntie never gave up on me and was always there for me, always took up for me.

"We never missed church, Sunday or Wednesday, until she was raped and killed. We was going home from church Wednesday night when the man came from behind. He grabbed me but Auntie beat him down and told me to run." Her voice still sang but in a higher register. "I ran and I ran!" She was silent for a moment.

"Auntie saved me, but left me alone." She paused again. "I thought I was alone anyway, but I wasn't!" She opened her eyes again and looked toward heaven. "Oh, no! I wasn't left alone!"

She looked at Lizzie. "I pray every minute of every day that little Lizzie will walk again." A tear danced in her eye but wouldn't fall. "But I have faith that whether Lizzie recovers, whether your drugs work, whether I die tonight, that it is GOOD!" She smiled. "No sweetie, you don't know good and bad, and neither do I."

For Suzy it was all too confusing. Life itself seemed cruel. She simply watched Hattie's eyes close again, watched her start rocking again, slowly, drifting into another world. One Suzy had never seen.

CHAPTER 15

"They're in the OR, Molly. As far as I know, everything is okay!" Frank Arnold had been Richard's right-hand man since he assumed office. At this moment, he couldn't be with the governor. His duty now was to make sure Molly arrived safely at DCH.

He had grown up with Richard in Mobile. They went to junior high and high school together, played basketball, and enjoyed the bay together. Frank would never forget the events of their teens, especially when he, Frank, almost died.

He and Richard had been snorkeling off of Dauphin Island, a barrier island separating the Gulf of Mexico from Mobile Bay. They had seen some Redfish and Triple Tails, but they were out of range of their spear guns. Even if they hit food for dinner, they were wary because of the recent shark sightings. But the water was clear and the sun was bright, the day perfect to be a teenager in the bay.

Richard was ahead of Frank, bobbing and occasionally submerging toward the white sand below. They were aware of each other, trying to stay close enough in case one had a problem. They were about 50 yards off shore when Frank went down. First, he felt the piercing bite in his leg, then the tug and weight of the ocean swept him into the underwater current. The pull was somehow different than he would have expected from a shark. He never had a chance to take a breath before going down. All he knew was that he couldn't see what was holding him even as he knew that it wasn't going to let go. The jerk made him lose his snorkel and his first reflex was to take a breath. Salt water entered his lungs, making him cough, which led to additional flooding of his lungs.

He found out later that Richard had spotted him drifting with the current. A large fishing hook had snagged him in the leg, the fishing line tangled in a web of seaweed and netting. Richard was able to cut him free and pull him to shore. Richard had remained at his bedside, never leaving for the two weeks Frank spent in the Intensive Care Unit.

Frank was the first at Richard's side when he collapsed at the courthouse and would be the last at his bedside if he remained in the hospital.

"What happened, Frank?" Molly was driving back from a church retreat in north Alabama. Her cell phone didn't have reception initially.

"It looks like he had a heart attack, Molly. He was about to talk to the crowd at the courthouse here and he just went down. The doctor said he had blockages and they rushed him to the operating room."

"I thought they usually fixed blockages with stents these days." Her voice was cracking.

"I don't know, Molly. They said surgery was the only option in Richard's case. They rushed him right up, and as far as I know, they're already underway."

"He's never had chest pain, and he eats right and exercises." She was trying to put things together in her own mind. "He even went for his yearly exam and EKG a few months ago. Everything was perfect."

"I don't know, Molly. The doctor said that happens a lot. Apparently an EKG doesn't always show blockages. He said people come in like Richard every week."

"Are you in the OR with him?"

"No. They don't allow anyone in there who isn't a hospital employee or a physician. I'm in a waiting room."

"Frank..." Her voice quivered. "He's gonna be okay, isn't he?"

"If I have anything to do with it, he will. You know that, Molly. But they said he had a big heart attack." He didn't want to say that, but he knew she deserved the truth.

"Where are you now?"

"Highway 43. I'm about an hour and a half away."

"Well, you drive carefully, Molly. I'll let you know if I hear anything."

CHAPTER 16

Lee was waiting outside the operating room when Grant walked out. He had been checking inventory when a nurse told him of the problem with the stapler. Immediately, he was on the phone long distance discussing the problem and possible consequences.

"Dr. Miller, I am so sorry." He could see that Grant didn't have time to discuss the stapler, but Lee needed to apologize for his own sake.

"Thanks, Lee. We'll talk about the stapler later. I need to go talk to the family."

"Yes, sir." He squirmed. "I will get the faulty stapler and our company will do a full investigation. I've already talked to my boss."

"Dr. Miller, did you find the missing clip?" Lee was still trailing.

"No."

"I'll stick around and see if I can help."

Grant was already on his way.

. . . .

Dr. Miller walked up the stairwell to the waiting room. He had learned to choose his words carefully with family members after an operation. Generally, they only hear one of several things: he/she is alive or dead; he/she had complications or not; he/she will be okay or not. He had never told a family if a patient would be okay or not, but that was what they heard.

The corridor was packed with overflow from the waiting room. State troopers were positioned around exits. Suits and dresses were everywhere. As he opened the door to the 4th floor, chatter escaped, pouring into the stair well. He stepped into the hall, searching the crowd for anyone who looked like family. The noise turned to silence. Every face was on him. He was either the hero or the goat.

"Is any family here?" Grant knew the rules, and HIP-PA rules and regulations had stung him before. He would make sure he talked to the right person. He wasn't about to break the rules, especially regarding the governor.

Frank stepped forward. "Mrs. Sands is back here."

There must have been a hundred people packed into the room, which was designed for 20. Faces shifted and bodies parted as he moved through.

"Mrs. Sands, I'm Grant Miller, your husband's surgeon."

A moment of relief brightened her eyes. He hadn't said "I WAS his surgeon." Grant marked her attention to his words.

"I have to ask you before I say anything else if I can speak freely about your husband in front of all these people." He glanced quickly side to side and behind him, catching everyone with the sweep.

"Everyone in this room is family. We have no secrets among us, so feel free to tell me...us...everything we need to know!" She reached out her hand, anxious for his words. "Thank you for everything you have done."

"Your husband is alive." Grant paused, feeling her grasp tighten with hope. "He had a massive heart attack, and we actually almost lost him when we were underway in the operating room."

She held back a breath, holding it until Grant continued.

"He would not have survived if he had gone to another hospital. He needed this operation as quickly as he got it." Grant tried to separate emotion from facts, but now he allowed optimism in his tone. "Your husband is a strong man. Most people with a heart attack like his wouldn't have survived, and those few who survived would have been looking at a possible heart transplant. But your husband came off of the bypass machine without difficulty."

He waited once more to allow his words to be fully grasped.

"But let me be clear," he continued. "Before surgery, the cardiologist placed a balloon pump that remains in him. It helps relieve some of the work of his heart. We also had to start epinephrine and milrinone, two medicines that support the blood pressure and heart strength."

"So when..." She held her words. She knew it was a time simply to listen.

"Governor Sands will be coming upstairs in half an hour or so. He will still be on the breathing machine, which probably won't be removed for at least a day or two."

"But you're saying that you think he will just be in the Intensive Care Unit for two days or so?" Her tone was hopeful, almost pleading.

"Listen to me, Mrs. Sands." Grant had learned that starting a statement like this was about the only way to redirect focus. "Your husband almost died. He is critically ill and may not survive. The next six hours are very important, but the next several days will really give a better picture of his prognosis. He is a strong man, and we are going to care for him in every way that modern medicine can. But right now, it's up to the machines, the medicines, and your husband's body."

Molly shrugged, tightening her jaw. "Thank you, Dr. Miller. I understand. You can count on me to be here for you and for Richard. I can't begin to thank you for your care and skill. I know..." She looked upward. "I know that, no matter what happens, you and your staff will do everything to save Richard." Moisture glistened in her eyes."

"I just have one other thing to report. During the operation a surgical clip flipped off of the delivery device. It flew up and hit my face, but we don't know where it landed. It is possible that it is in the governor's chest and could potentially cause problems with infection." He expected the look of concern that iced over Molly's face. "But we couldn't find it and we just have to cover him with antibiotics. I don't expect it to be a factor in his recovery, but I plan to be honest with you about every concern I have."

Molly paused, then seemed to reconsider her words. "Doctor, the fact that you told me this gives me even more confidence in you. Thank you for your honesty!"

The room was silent until the clang of an elevator door rang in the hallway. Within moments, buzzers were blasting, Richard's bed rolled out and six people in scrubs pushed him toward the ICU. His face, camouflaged with tape and tubes and blood, was swollen. One assistant squeezed a bag every few seconds, providing oxygen to the governor. His pale color signaled his low blood count. Monitors beeped with each heartbeat and squealed if breaths didn't come fast enough. A plastic bucket collected blood that was still draining from tubes in his chest while urine collected in a neighboring plastic bag. The governor was somewhere inside the blur as the team rushed him back to a room.

Everyone in the hall stood silent, reverence coated with shock. This morning the governor was a political star and now he was courting death. Grant had witnessed the scene countless times before. He had said all that was necessary. It was best to leave now.

By the time he arrived in the ICU, the receiving nurses were already untangling spaghetti loops of intravenous lines. Five nurses worked with precision: one recording vital signs, medications, chest tube drainage; another checking the swan ganz catheter, a line in the governor's heart measuring his fluid volume and heart function; another was assessing every intravenous site, tube, wound, and pulse; one was taking the report from the operating room team, making sure of every event that had occurred and every medicine that the governor should be receiving; the final nurse was available for assistance, scrambling to help where needed.

Grant stood in the corner, out of the way. He watched the action like so many times before. In the midst of constant activity, simple omissions can be the difference between life and death and so he knew better than to interfere with the nurses. They knew their jobs and didn't need suggestions. His only role was to identify problems and address them.

As he glanced from monitor to drainage tubes to the activities of the nurses, his eyes drifted to his shoe coverings. Everyone in the OR must wear paper coverings for their shoes, but they are to be removed before leaving the OR Part of the reason for removing them is to prevent tracking germs and blood out of the operating room, but partly, also, to keep families from seeing the spillage. Grant looked at his booties splattered with blood, now dried and cracking off of the surface. "Great!" he thought. "Hopefully the governor's wife won't have that as her last memory of her husband."

Then he spotted the shimmer of metal.

CHAPTER 17

The United Auto Workers had gradually worked its way back into meaningful existence, and the Big Three US automakers had brokered individual deals with the union. But union organizing in foreign automobile companies on US soil had been a failure from the time those companies started arriving in America. The UAW had made inroads in health care, universities, aerospace. and agricultural industries; and gaining a foothold in transplant automobile companies was the Hammer's target now.

Wang had visited with Bob DeLaney before returning to the mainland. Never before had the president of the UAW actually met with a foreign automaker before production began, but Bob had a way of negotiating that appealed to Wang. The Hammer knew people. He knew corporations. He knew money.

Wang had flown back to Detroit immediately after the ceremony in Tuscaloosa. This was a private meeting. No more ceremonial posturing and cultural sensitivies like Wang had endured at the governor's office. He brought his own translator and they met at the Waterfront Diner. Ape man never left his side.

"I hope the governor is down for a while." The Hammer knew Wang understood him but waited for the interpreter to speak.

Wang grinned, his tobacco-stained teeth peeping between his lips. "He has served his purpose to this point. Beijing Automotive will get tax benefits and land purchase agreements that will make it possible to be competitive, even with American labor."

The Hammer didn't flinch. Wang had tried to needle him before. "Look, we might have different ways to get what we want, but we both want the same thing. You want to make money in America, and I want workers in my union, which means money. What separates us is the cost of labor."

Wang listened. He knew where this was going.

"Workers in America have come to realize that they can't expect the benefits that they once had. They realize that the Mideast oil crunch has shocked the automobile industry. They know that pensions are a thing of the past. But they understand when a company cares about them. Giving workers benefits with discounts on your automobiles, guaranteeing that workers don't have to work more than eight hour shifts, and allowing them to invest in your company are things they understand."

Wang scratched his face with his finger. They both knew Bob wasn't getting to the point.

"I will give you workers with different tiers. Those with experience in high-level jobs will get a certain hourly wage, and those down the scale, to entry-level line workers, will get a different wage. Your average hourly expense per worker will be $25 an hour."

"How about the governor? He doesn't want your unions in the state at all. He has talked to the insurance companies and kept you out of the universities. He will be a problem!" Wang was still scratching his face.

"The governor won't be a problem," the Hammer said firmly.

"So, if I agree to union representation of the workforce, you will make sure your workers report any concerns to you?" Now Wang's scratching stopped. "If we place things in the cars that the workers don't understand, you will make sure there is no problem?" Bob nodded.

"Why do they call you the Hammer?" Wang already knew but wanted to see what this man would say.

Bob hesitated, then lowered his voice. "I don't give up. I will hammer away until a job is finished."

"I heard there was more to it than that!" Wang persisted.

"Okay. When I was working the line at one of the plants, only 20-something, one of my supervisors tried to make our crew work extra hours. I wouldn't do it; we wouldn't do it. I knew that I had an obligation to my team and myself to hold the company to its word. The supervisor was found with a hammer in his head." He made sure Wang was looking at him. "I guess they thought I did it."

Wang smiled. He let the Hammer's words drift into silence. "I like that," he finally replied, his voice guttural. "If someone backs away from their word with me, I would use a hammer!"

"I think we have an understanding, then." Bob's eyes burned into Wang's. "You will let the union in and I will make sure that unspecified additions to the cars are not questioned."

CHAPTER 18

"Have you gotten any sleep, big guy?" Jack Wade popped his head into the ICU room.

Grant was standing at the governor's bedside adjusting the rate of a drip. "Hey, Jack!"

"The last time anyone was this sick in the hospital, it was you." Jack smiled.

"I'm just hoping this guy has the same result I did." Grant knew Jack had never left his bedside when he was in critical condition. Grant hadn't left the governor's.

"I'm not sure your patient's doctor is as good as the one you had." Jack walked in and looked around. He was fully capable of managing critically ill patients, but open-heart surgery patients were a different class.

Five micro drip machines were stacked on a single pole by the bedside. Each drip was precisely titrated to deliver the exact micrograms per kilogram per minute that would maintain Governor Sand's blood pressure and cardiac output at acceptable levels. The monitor above his head had several colored lines constantly painting out valleys and ridges. One represented the blood pressure in the superior vena cava, and another the blood pressure in the pulmonary artery. A number on the right of the screen provided a constant read-out of the oxygen level in the blood returning to the heart and another showed the oxygen level in the artery circulation. All of these numbers had significance, and each microdrip affected the numbers, the aggregate of numbers representing the governor's chance of survival.

At the foot of the bed was the intra-aortic balloon pump for the balloon implanted before his operation. The balloon kept perfect time with the EKG, its power leaving a muffled thump after each beep representing Richard's heartbeat.

The ventilator to his left pumped a breath through white corrugated tubing 20times a minute, lifting his chest briefly, the only movement of the governor's body. Each time the ventilator triggered, a small amount of watery blood trickled down the drainage tube at the base of his chest.

"How's he doing?" Jack really couldn't tell. He simply saw a pasty face that could have been made of clay.

"Surprisingly well. Thanks. We've already taken him off the epinephrine and we are now weaning him off the milrinone. I've got him on a diprovan drip. His kidneys are working well and his heart seems to be rallying."

"I knew, if anyone could pull him through, you could." Jack patted Grant on the back.

"I'll check back with you, buddy. You get some rest." Jack pointed at one of the nurses. "You make sure he gets some sleep."

Barely 21, the bright eyed girl responded. "Yes, sir, Dr. Wade. I'll make sure he gets as much sleep as you do!"

She winked at him, the kind of wink that says, "I know how busy you are. Who are you to tell him to get some rest." It was also the kind of wink that Jack had seen each day and said, "God, you look hot. Why don't you ask me my name."

Jack did look hot, and he knew it but resisted thoughts about himself. He didn't like wearing white coats. They made him feel confined and labeled. Though proud of being a surgeon, he didn't need to advertise it with scrubs and a white coat. All of the nurses and most of the staff wore scrubs and so Jack fit in like everyone else. Except his scrubs fit differently than most.

Jack was 6'5, and his scrubs were loose enough to allow his arms to move freely. His arms showed the scars and gristle of having grown up on a farm but had the polish of daily workouts. His shirt, tucked neatly into his pants, fit with firmness, showing he wore briefs instead of boxers. Everyone who wore scrubs had their personal designs and colors, except the surgeons who wore the navy blues provided by the OR. But Jack bought his own, every one black and accenting his bristly ebony hair and shadowy five o'clock. He proudly ironed his own scrubs, aware that tidiness outwardly was a reflection of his work in the operating room.

He ignored the nurse's wink and walked out with an innocent smile. As soon as he turned to continue rounds, his throat tightened. He flushed, aware that he felt like a teenager again.

"Hey, Suzy." The words sounded smooth, but he felt like his throat was in a vice-tight grip.

"Dr. Wade!" Startled, Suzy instinctively bowed. Her voice, soft but musical, floated toward Jack and seemed to linger.

"What are you doing here?" His question stumbled out. He'd just had the conversation yesterday with her. Somehow she stymied him, pinning him with her simplicity and natural beauty. He wasn't used to it.

She bowed again, almost as if to hide. Then, lifting her head but not making eye contact, her voice returned. "I have duties throughout the hospital. Today I was given this unit to observe."

Jack carefully placed his finger under her chin, lifting her jaw upward until their eyes met. "In America, if people avoid eye contact, it usually means they have something to hide."

Her eyes widened apologetically. "Oh, no, Dr. Wade. Please forgive me. I have not learned all of your customs. I am not trying to hide anything. I am so sorry."

"The only way I'll forgive you is if you meet me in the cafeteria at noon. If I can buy lunch for you again, then all is forgiven." His eyes told stories. They had a hardness that came from crushing pain and fear: pain from the loss of Kate and fear of relationships that might require devotion and emotional commitment.

"I have to run to the operating room." He looked at his watch. "I'm already late. You don't have long to decide."

Suzy seemed unwilling to let her words out. "It would honor me, Dr. Wade." Again she bowed but quickly returned her gaze to his face.

"Perfect. I'll see you at noon." Jack hurried away, his heart racing.

As Suzy took a step forward, the device in her front pocket beeped. The tone was almost inaudible but she had learned to recognize it instinctively. She quickly pressed the button. She was directly outside the governor's room.

CHAPTER 19

Lee and the Operating Room staff had searched all night long. There was no evidence of the clip in there. It must have flipped into the governor. Hopefully the antibiotics would prevent any infection from developing.

The president of Yida Technology was the son of the Party Secretary of Chongqing. The central Communist Party had imprisoned his father after playing carelessly with organized crime in that region. It was common practice for local leaders to harass and extort criminal and legitimate businesses, but the problem always came when local leaders developed so much power that they represented a threat to the Party. That's where his father made his mistake. He ran Chongqing like his own country. He required payoffs for companies to operate and allowed the black market to thrive, skimming 20% off the top of their revenue.

His father had taken over several businesses, sending the owners who didn't play ball with him to prison or feeding them to the catfish in the Guangdong reservoir. He had taken over Yida's precursor company, imprisoning the owner and accusing him of unfaithfulness to the state and failure to pay taxes. After Yida Technology became prosperous, he turned the company over to his son, Hu Xilai. Mr. Hu was smarter than his father. He made sure that the Party got its money and that he avoided conflicts with the Ministry of State at all costs. He hated Yao Ming for imprisoning his father, but he was also terrified of him. He'd had his own visit to the Guojai

Anquan Bu, at which time Yao told him he might be able to get his father out of prison if he did what he was told. So far, he had done everything right.

"What do you want, Lee?" Mr. Hu had already been told that there were problems. He also knew that Li Zhang had been a reliable and faithful employee.

"Sir, we have identified the faulty clip applier and have sent it back to the company for examination." Lee knew to be very careful when he called the mainland because all telephone traffic was carefully monitored. He knew someone else was listening to every word he spoke.

"As far as we can tell, the clip has not been found. It must have ricocheted into Governor Sands' chest cavity during the operation."

"Have you used all possible means to locate the missing clip?" Hu knew to be precise with his words also.

"I have recorded the serial number of the Yida clip and confirmed that we have all of the information on the patient."

"Has the patient been informed that there was a problem." Hu had been through this before and didn't want to miss anything.

"*Shi de*," Lee confirmed.

Hu sensed that there was something Li wasn't saying. "Is there still a chance that the clip is not in the governor?"

"As far as we can determine, it's in the governor."

"If you find out otherwise, inform me and take the necessary action." Lee knew exactly what Hu meant.

One reason Lee was such a good employee of Yida Technology was that his family remained in Beijing. Lee made a good income with the company and sent his money home, allowing them to live comfortably. But he knew that Hu demanded results and loyalty. The catfish weren't particular in what they ate and Hu wasn't reluctant to feed them.

CHAPTER 20

It was finally visiting hour. Molly had never left the waiting room and hadn't slept once. People from all over the state had kept her cell phone busy while others kept the coffee hot and conversation upbeat. She had been back to the ICU a few times, but only for a few moments to see him, kiss him, and confirm that he was alive. Though her dress had wrinkles, she showed no signs of fatigue. Her lips were naturally pink, highlighting her cheeks that revealed her age. At 65, there were lines but only if one studied her closely. Whether her hair was natural or not, the simplicity of its soft blond texture gave her dignity and natural beauty. Her blue eyes wouldn't allow any streaks of redness to suggest that they were fatigued.

Her son walked by her side. Like his father, he had graduated with honors from MIT. He was the Chief Science and Research Officer at Sands Electronics. Next to his wife and two daughters, his mother carried his heart. Breast cancer had almost taken her when he was a teenager, and since then, he was with her as often as his life would allow, whether by phone or in person or just in his thoughts. When he heard of his dad's situation, his immediate thought was that his father would be okay. His father was a survivor, a fighter. His mother was too but he couldn't bear the thought of her suffering in spirit without his being at her side.

They walked back to the Cardiac Surgical Unit. Molly had been back several times through the night, but this was the first time for her son. She had told him what to expect, but nothing could prepare him.

"Dr. Miller, this is our son, Dick!" Molly whispered.

She wasn't sure how much her husband could hear, and she didn't know what might be good or bad for him to hear if he was able.

"Nice to meet you, Dick." He offered a firm hand-shake. "Please, would you both just call me Grant?"

Dick thought that this would be easy, simply sup-porting his mother through his father's recovery. What he hadn't expected was the helplessness and visceral anguish he felt at seeing his father—his hero — vulnerable under the armor of machines.

Dick could break bones with a handshake, but his grip was that of one distracted. "Yes, sir. That' s fine. Thank you so much for everything you've done for my father." His voice was stronger than he had expected.

"How's he doing?" Molly was still holding Dick's hand. It tightened slightly.

"Actually, he's doing very well, better than I ever ex-pected at this point. He's a strong man. I'm thinking about removing his balloon pump at some point. But first I want him to start waking up and coming off of the breathing machine."

Dick was studying the room and machines. He didn't know biology, but he knew biotech. The computers and machines were simply mathematics and logic packaged in circuits, busses, and wires with logic gates and a central processing unit. The cardiac output was simply oxygen consumption divided by 10 times the arteriove-nous oxygen difference. His time in the labs hadn't been for nothing.

Molly placed her hand on his forehead. There was more warmth than earlier. "Can I talk to him?"

"Of course. At this point, I want him to start waking up. Any voice that he recognizes might help him come out of hibernation."

"Richard." She stroked his forehead and then kissed him. "I love you!"

Richard's eyelids were swollen shut, but there was a sudden movement. They didn't have the power to separate, but the effort was unmistakable.

"Dad, it's Dick. We're here. I love you. You're looking good." His words came out forcefully though his stare indicated dubious hope at best.

They stayed at Richard's side for some time, Grant returning to the chair where he'd spent the last thirteen hours.

Molly tried to bring more movement to his eyes but was satisfied that her husband was still inside and would emerge eventually.

"Tell me more about that clip, now." Dick joined his mother beside Grant.

"Well, as I was telling your mom earlier, I found the clip that I was concerned about. I can tell you with certainty that it didn't go into your dad's chest, and so infection is not a concern at this time."

Grant reached into his pocket and pulled out his billfold. A small piece of metal was taped to one of his credit cards.

"This is the clip." He handed the credit card to Dick.

"I was initially so relieved to find it that I taped it to the card. As the night went on and your dad stabilized, I got bored!" Grant nodded an honest apology.

"I had my loupes with me, magnifying glasses I use to perform heart surgery. They magnify objects about three and a half times."

"Three point five power!" Dick echoed Grant, confirming that he understood optics.

"Yes. Anyway. As I looked at the clip and noticed that there was a black dot on the tip of the clip." He gave his loupes to Dick and pointed at the clip.

Dick placed the glasses on his eyes and adjusted one of the lenses. He looked carefully, angling it and adjusting the glasses occasionally. He recognized the design but had never seen one under magnification. The clip had a black square on its tip with prongs and fencing. He'd worked with radiofrequency biometric devices like it before, but this one looked different not just smaller. Was the clip a surveillance device? Were they being observed now?

Eventually, his eyes widened as he brought his finger to his lips. Then he whispered to his mother and Grant. "Give me your cell phones."

He took the cell phones out of the room, placed them in a drawer, and returned, leaving the clip with the phones.

"This is all crazy." His voice was still low but audible.

"Dad was telling me the other day that the FBI had contacted him. Apparently there was some concern that a mob boss was targeting him." He wiped his brow. "Possibly even to hurt him."

Molly's hand went to her mouth, catching a gasp. "What?"

"Mom he gets warnings all the time. He tells me most of them, just in case." He looked back at the drawer.

"But just in case this one was really a threat, be careful what you say and to whom." He continued. "Back in 2004, the FBI started using a "roving bug" to track criminals by turning their cell phones into listening devices. They simply turned on the phones, remotely activating them, and listened to conversations." Looking through the window, he saw two men dressed as construction workers staring at them.

Dick continued to stare outside, appearing to be enjoying the sunlight. The two men turned, puffed on cigarettes, and shuffled out of sight.

He placed his hand over his mouth as if to scratch his bristly face. "Now anyone can use the same technology to listen in on conversations. That's why Dad uses the case he does to carry his phone. It's made with woven steel to block signals and all his conversations are encrypted."

One of the construction workers stepped back into view. He leaned down to pick up a pen on the ground, stood, and shot a quick glance back through the window. Dick faked a yawn.

Turning back toward Grant, he said, "You are right to be concerned. That looks like more than simply a defect in the clip. It could be a number of things."

Dick borrowed one of Grant's pens and scribbled a note.

CHAPTER 21

Suzy had been waiting for 10 minutes. She looked at her watch every 30 seconds hoping to speed up the cadence. She knew not to miss her checkpoints. She couldn't risk that! She had already confirmed 15 new patients, but Dr. Wade would be here any moment and then she could get her work done.

"Hey, Suzy!" The voice came from her left, high pitched and squeaky.

She felt her throat tighten. Frozen for a moment, she took shallow short breaths trying to remain calm. Then, her eyes focused on her feet and head down, she quickly turned in reverence. "Yes, Master Li!" She knew too well that he was Master Li, not the simple salesman, Lee.

"What are you doing down here!" His Pekingese dialect of Mandarin was familiar to Suzy.

"I am meeting someone for lunch," she responded immediately without thinking. Her response was in her native Wu Chinese of Shanghai, a dialect Lee disdained.

"Lunch?" Lee spat flatly. "You have work to do. What are you thinking?"

"I was asked..." She quickly stopped using her Wu in favor of Lee's Pekingese.

"Follow me!" Lee's order was military in tone.

Suzy stepped into position behind him, never looking back. All she could do was respond by reflex and surrender again. She was such a failure, to her family, her country, and herself.

As a child, she was more than capable in all her studies and excelled in school. Her parents were proud of their Shanghai culture and persisted in speaking the native Wu dialect. Unfortunately, the government was trying to unify language in China, making Mandarin the national tongue. Suzy continued to use her parent's dialect, learning Mandarin but speaking Wu outside class. Her parents discouraged her from using their dialect, realizing that Mandarin would be the language of the future. But Suzy knew that her parents were too old to learn a new dialect and wanted to honor them. She spoke Wu with pride.

Her parents were important people. Her father was a deputy party chief in Shanghai and in line to move to a higher position in the National Party when he and his wife were killed in a car accident. Fortunately, Yao Ming had taken her under his wing. He explained to Suzy that her resistance to following the National Party had upset her parents so much that it caused their car accident and their death. He explained that she was a disgrace to their country.

Suzy was brought to Beijing, where Yao Ming had developed an orphan center for children with similar family tragedies, and she finished school. The orphans lived together, attended school, and to Suzy's knowledge, had all been sent to the United States for further education and training.

The only responsibility of the children was to do what they had failed to do in the past. Honor the Party. That meant working at Mr. Yao's house, cleaning the rooms, yard, pool, and cars. It meant making perfect grades on all exams in school. It meant telling on their classmates if they said or did anything that dishonored the Party, and that included dishonoring Yao. The other children had their jobs and responsibilities, and none could share with the others what their job was. But for

Suzy, she was to soothe Yao and relieve his stress by letting him have her body whenever he wished.

For her faithfulness, trustworthiness, and scholastic aptitude, she was given another chance. Yao had sent her to America. Her job was to study in an American university, learn everything possible about artificial neural pathways, and to do everything that Li Zhang told her to do.

Yao had already proven himself to the Central Committee of the Communist Party. Through his efforts, the Chinese had been able to steal American technology and nuclear secrets from many labs in America. Without the expense of research and development, China was able to develop smaller warheads and catch up to America's generation of weapons for a pittance. Now one of Yao's goals was to accumulate so much data on American business practices, technology secrets, military weaponry and tactics, and international trade that China would know more about the United States than the country knew about itself. Suzy didn't know what Yao's title was, only that he was a member of the Ministry of State Security and had an office in the Guojia Anquan Bu.

When Suzy moved to Atlanta, her aunt and uncle were very gracious. They welcomed her and allowed her to live with them. She studied neuropsychology at Emory, working with a team of experts on stem cell rejuvenation of spinal injuries. It was exciting work, until she met Li Zhang.

When Li came to the house one day, her aunt and uncle seemed to know him. He shared dinner with them, then walked Suzy outside. Mr. Li explained that he was her American Yao. She would do as he commanded or she be sent back to China, directly to Yao, for having dishonored the Party and country again. He explained that his name was Lee in America, but that he would always be Chinese and would always be her master.

Suzy asked her aunt and uncle, after Lee left, if they thought it was right to take pictures of her research and the folders in her lab or to give him her access code to the computer system at the university.

Her aunt and uncle were terrified when she simply asked these questions and demanded that she leave their home. Mr. Lee was Suzy's only other contact, and so she had no choice but to go to him. After he provided her a place to live, she finished her work and took orders from him. He had a key to her place and would come and go as he had the desire. This gave him access to her and to her research and information. It was Lee who arranged for her to complete her doctorate at the University of Alabama. It was Lee who provided her living expenses.

"Who are you meeting?" Lee scolded.

Suzy had followed him to an empty conference room. A dim LED provided enough background red to paint a ghostly shadow in front of her. "A doctor. Dr. Wade."

The light was too dim to see it coming, but she quickly felt the fingernail of his little finger under her jaw. The pointed nail knifed its way upward, bringing her lips to his. She smelled the staleness of unbrushed teeth and the lingering odor of last night's sushi and cigarettes. His purchase on her jaw was too powerful to move and her jaw was too high to breathe through her mouth, so his breath went straight into her nose.

Lee bit her lower lip, not enough to draw blood but enough for him to taste her and for her to feel his power.

She knew not to resist. She must be loyal to the Party. She had no one else. Lee's tongue followed the bite. He had never kissed her. Anything physical had always been impersonal, never requiring her return of affection. He lowered his nail enough for her to open her mouth.

She took a quick breath through her mouth, allowing an escape from his odor, but his tongue pushed deeply into her mouth, exploring. His left hand lifted her from behind, pulling her pelvis to his.

"You want to dine with Dr. Wade?" He softened his finger even more.

"I didn't know how to refuse." The taste he had left in her mouth made her want to gag. She held her throat from anything more than a quick gulp, but it made her swallow his saliva.

"So if you have time to dine with the *gwailo* you must be through with your data collection." His left hand was still pulling her buttocks to him.

"Yes. Master Lee! I have been to all checkpoints to-day." She pulled the device out of her pocket, hoping to prove her success and to allow her release. Her eyes were adjusting to the darkness. The redness seemed to encase him, but the glow covered them both.

"Well, you know your job and your duty." His right hand joined his left, pulling her even tighter to his groin.

His hands separated her buttocks, then pulled them up and down, working them like he had done so many times before. He even liked it more with her clothes on, like a challenge. The red light and shadows reminded him of some videos he had watched recently. He licked her, chin to nose.

She felt the familiar bulge but hoped to escape. "You can come tonight and see what I have if you like."

"Yes, that sounds like a good idea." He pushed from the front, enough for her to know he could perform anywhere, anytime, then released his grip completely. "I would like to see everything you have tonight!"

………

Jack was between cases. He had waited at the entrance to the cafeteria, at first with eagerness and then confusion. As he strolled back to the OR, he wondered if he had missed Suzy. Maybe she had been confused about the time. Maybe she got tied up with her work. Maybe she forgot. Maybe...

He had finally defeated the teenage jitters and had decided on some lines that might work. Maybe they would have dinner together, not just lunch in the cafeteria.

Maybe...

CHAPTER 22

Grant decided things were stable enough. The governor was off his drips, waking up and responding. It was his chance to zip home and take a shower.

He lived in the Highlands, one of the historic neighborhoods in the city. It was only walking distance from the hospital. Several years earlier, a tornado had swept through the city, almost destroying the hospital, and the Highlands was almost destroyed as well, leaving shells of houses and splintered trees. But after rebuilding, the neighborhood was reshaped and the replanted trees were already gaining height.

Grant enjoyed the short walk. It was his chance to breathe fresh air, to watch the seasons change, and to let the sun strengthen him or the moon relax him. Usually residents of the neighborhood were out for a walk, but now the street was empty. He had regained most of his strength after being drained by the hyperthermia, and his long strides felt good. Dusk was his favorite time to walk. The sun was still leaving its presence in grays and shadows, giving a lone lark something still to celebrate. The early evening air still had warmth and the drumbeat of high school Friday-night football was still distant.

Perhaps the evening mystique distracted him or the hybrid van was too quiet. His steps were deliberate, but his thoughts were scattered as a white service van drifted toward Grant on his left, the shaded windows reflecting the last of the evening light. As it paralleled him, the right window lowered and a thin tube eased out of the window, aiming at Grant's neck.

With the power of a single breath, the small dart flew through the air at 400 feet per second, twice the speed of an arrow. It hit Grant in the middle of the neck. The sting was sudden and biting. Instinctively, he swatted what surely was a late evening wasp only to push the remaining nicotine and curare into his neck.

He took one more step, then went down, his entire body losing all tone. Before his head hit the ground, two people jumped from the van to protect his fall. As quickly as the van had arrived, they lifted him into the back of the vehicle. "*Hen kuai!*" said the largest of the two as he pulled an oxygen tank beside Grant and began squeezing breaths into the face mask he pressed against Grant's cheeks.

"Not again!" Grant thought. He was fully conscious, his body simply flaccid. He knew the powerless dependence on others to breathe for him when his body wouldn't respond to his mind. His lungs filled with oxygen as they worked.

The one who had attached the face mask shut Grant's eyelids, but before his vision was extinguished, he captured images of all of them. The driver had pulled to the side, joining the other two. Big Guy was round-faced and his eyebrows merged above a flat nose. The driver was thin and moved like a monkey, his teeth billowing out below a contracted upper face. The other was pale, almost albino, but his eyes were pitch black and sunken like a ghost's. Grant knew he could remember any of them if he ever saw them again. What he didn't know was that the dart contained an amnestic stronger than Versed that would wipe away any memory of the next few minutes.

Grant felt one of them pulling at his back pocket, then felt his billfold escape.

"*Zai nali?*"

As Big Guy pumped air into his lungs, he also was looking at the work in front of him, allowing one of Grant's eyelids to lift ever so slightly. But it was enough for a dimmed view.

Monkey man was flipping through his billfold, examining each credit card with frustration. "*Zai bu zai!*" Every card was swiped by his eyes at least four times.

The Ghost, seeing no results from the credit cards, excavated his pockets. They were all empty. Panicked, he looked at Big Guy. "*Meiyou yunqi!*"

"*Yiqie!*" Big guy barked.

Monkey and Ghost pulled all of Grant's clothes off, straining the fibers as they jerked them off of him, examining everything with microscopic focus.

Big Guy spat orders and waved his hand like a sword.

Now, Monkey and Ghost gave up on the clothes and inspected him from his toes upward. No spot was missed. Big Guy was screaming now.

They dissected his billfold, tearing it apart, frantically unsuccessful in their search. Big Guy grunted some more and they threw the remains of his billfold into a plastic bag. They wiped every credit card carefully to remove their finger prints and then returned them to the top pocket of his scrubs. They struggled, but redressed him.

Big Guy was still growling. He looked into Grant's face, unaware that the one eye still had a view. "*Goupi!*"

Grant felt another prick next to the spot on his neck where it all began.

CHAPTER 23

Dick had instincts like his dad. He knew something wasn't right. He asked Frank and his mother to leave their cell phones in another room, just to be cautious.

"Frank, I know my father trusts you more than anyone outside our family." He closed the door to a separate waiting room behind them.

"You're right!" he agreed proudly. "He saved my life and I'd give mine for him. He's given me jobs, taken me on trips, and supported me through my divorce..." His eyes reddened. "He's more like family to me than anyone I know."

Molly reached for his hand. Her grip said it all, but she added, "And you're family to us, Frank."

"Okay, here's the deal." Dick pulled out the clip that Grant had given him. "I have an idea what this is, but I want to go back to our lab and run some tests."

"What are you talking about?" Frank held back a laugh. "It's a piece of metal." He looked closer. "It's a clip or something. It looks like a miniature staple."

"Look closer, Frank, at the tip." Dick pointed at the dot.

"Looks like a piece of dirt to me." Again, he was more amused than concerned.

"Yes, well dirt isn't glued onto surgical products." He let Frank take another look. Indeed, the dot was clearly manufactured to be on it. "It is a surgical clip, one that was almost used in Dad. But it misfired and Dr. Miller found it on his clothes. The dot is what bothers me."

"What do you think it is?" Frank studied Dick, seeing his concern.

"I'd rather not say yet."

"Honey, what are you so worried about?" Molly had learned that, when her son was evasive, there was usually a reason for apprehension.

"Mom, I'm not worried, just interested." He kissed her on the cheek. "Dr. Miller said he felt really good about Dad's prognosis. He said if anything changed, he would personally contact me. I'm going to our lab to check something out. It won't take long. I should be back by tomorrow evening." He smiled. "Dr. Miller assured me that Dad was doing well, that it would be okay for me to leave town for a day or so."

Molly knew that Dick was on his way. When he made his mind up about something, it was pointless to argue.

"Drive carefully, then!"

Dick opened the door to leave, swinging it somewhat carelessly. He heard it make a thump and then ricocheted back toward him.

"Oh my gosh!" He reached to catch the young girl he had swung the door into.

"I'm so sorry." He saw that the door had knocked her backward. "I had no idea anyone was there."

The girl recovered immediately and bowed. "I'm so sorry. I should have been more careful."

Frank rushed to assist them both. "Are y'all okay?" Frank saw that they were both simply surprised, not damaged. He saw a gadget at the girl's foot and bent over to pick it up. "Is this yours?"

She had already seen it when she bent down but had hoped no one would notice. When she saw Frank bend down, her hand rushed to retrieve it first. "Yes, thank you."

She stood up, a quiver in her lip. Staring back at the floor, she backed away. "I am so sorry. I must go."

Suzy hurried away. She knew that, if they suspected her or her device, her life was in peril.

Frank and Dick watched her walk away, then looked at each other. Molly had just joined them. Neither said a word. The Asian girl seemed spooked but unharmed.

....

Dick thought it might be faster to travel at night on the back roads than going through Montgomery and Greenville or through Meridian. Nighttime had always been his favorite. It was when he read as a child, studied while in school, and worked in the lab. No one was around to interrupt him. It was his private time.

He loved his two girls and never missed a softball game, ballet recital, or helping with homework. He adored his wife, Crista, and together they enjoyed the opera, museums, and travel. They had both grown up in Mobile but didn't meet until their return. She was an architect, specializing in Creole cottages, and had partnered with several developers producing communities along the Bay. Dick and Crista also enjoyed quiet strolls along Mobile Bay. Their house on Point Clear allowed them to amble on the shore, breathing the sea mist that had filled the hearts and souls of generations of those with a taste for Southern antiquity.

Dick's new BMW whirred down the road, his audio tuned to Gov.query.speak. He had read about the new microchips that the FBI was developing and so he wanted more information before deciding which authorities to approach. Why would the FBI be risking its reputation by monitoring his father? What could his father possibly be doing that any federal agency would need to monitor him?

His scanner obeyed his commands, but thus far he hadn't heard what he was hoping to find.

"No, I want to know what the FBI or CIA has developed in microchip technology."

"Do you have an FBI password?" He had programmed Hal, the voice simulator, as his wife's voice. It was like traveling with her.

"No. But I want any information you can give me that isn't confidential."

"Fine." It was the response his wife usually used when processing her thoughts. "The Federal Bureau of Investigation is reportedly developing fine microchips for crime investigation. Do you want to know what has been reported, or what is known by fact?"

"Reported."

"Fine." A brief pause.

"*The Daily Observer,* Washington, reported last month: 'Although restricted by law for personal use, there are reports that the FBI has used microchips in criminal investigations recently. Similar devices were manufactured by Verichip in 2004, but production was discontinued due to evidence that the chip, in laboratory animals, was associated with increased risk of cancer. Positive ID Corporation discontinued marketing its implantable human microchip in 2010.

'Under federal law, these devices cannot be implanted without the consent of the individual who will have it implanted. Shillings, a biotech giant, has reportedly been working with the FBI to implant similar devices in criminals who agree to implantation. The newer generation of microchip can be tracked by GPS, can carry the criminal's history of offenses, can provide biologic and physiologic feedback, and can initiate alarms if the criminal passes outside boundaries set by the terms of their release.'"

Dick hadn't heard anything new. Most of the reports Hal had given were common knowledge to those who read the newspaper and popular magazines. He understood that, if New York and Washington reporters were aware of FBI activities, microchip technology was in reality generations ahead of what these reporters had discovered.

The sound of his wife's voice, the serenity of the night air, the cushion of the BMW seats, and his mind buzzing faster than the 500 horsepower engine under him distracted him from the three headlights approaching at rocket speed.

Three Ducati 2000s ripped through the night air. One whirred past Dick almost the moment he was aware of them. The other two took purchase in the left lane, pinning him to the right. The first rider was just past the reach of Dick's headlights when he dropped his package to the ground, making sure it was in the middle of the right lane. Then he shot forward about 300 yards.

Dick, unfamiliar with this road, didn't think it was safe to slow down, and he knew that he couldn't out run two sport bikes. He tapped his steering wheel to engage his telephone just as he saw and hit the bag in the middle of the road. His car bounced, then rattled, coming almost to a stop. The bag had an anchored cable, one used recently by law enforcement to stop vehicles on the road. A toggle hung on his chassis dragging the metal anchor under him.

His vehicle clunked down the road, all three motorcycles behind, tracking him.

"Shit! Dad asked me over and over to get a gun permit and carry a weapon with me on the road." His telephone wouldn't pick up a signal. He reached for his cell phone, which had no signal either.

Dick's heart was pounding. He had never been prey before. The three riders were simply waiting for the right moment to finish whatever job they were given.

There was only darkness ahead and headlights behind him. He decided to attack the motorcyclists and turned the car completely around, but the anchor wedged into a rear tire left the BMW limp in the road.

His headlights blinded the three bikers long enough for him to jump from the car and run for the tree line. But the Ducati's weren't silent for long. He heard their engines roar into action and suddenly their beams were on him again. A laser show of lights bounced around him as the street bikes vaulted forward over mounds of grass freshly mowed.

Dick's thighs burned with the strain of keeping his balance over roots and anthills, and his lungs sucked in air faster than he could exhale. He knew he couldn't make it before the first cyclist was upon him. He turned, crouched, and aimed his empty hands at the lead headlight as if he had a handgun. It worked. The headlight made a sudden turn to the right and he heard the bike topple and skid. Dick took off for the tree line again.

The other motorcycles were right behind him, but he stumbled past the forest's edge and the trees were too much a barrier for machines. The headlights glittered through the leaves, vines, and hardwoods, catching a reflection of Dick's escape.

Dick knew Southern woods. He had been quail hunting in thickets, and duck hunting in flooded timber was second nature to him. Luckily, he had even enjoyed coon hunting at night as a teen. Forests were like museums to him, all similar but all different.

The moon was full above the canopy, but on the floor Dick settled into the base of a tree where only needles of light poked through. He had the advantage now. He could hear if anyone was approaching and should have the benefit of seeing flashlights if they were close. He felt safe for the moment.

Five minutes passed, then ten. He never heard the bikes crank back up, only the crickets and frogs singing and the buzz of mosquitoes. The mosquitoes were all over him, buzzing in his face, crawling on his ears, swarming around his nose. Occasionally, he swatted or struck wildly into the air, clearing them for a moment.

Then crickets and frogs went silent and Dick held his breath, certain that something or someone was out there. He heard branches cracking and twigs shuffling. The noise was coming from different directions. No lights. No voices. Just the forest holding its breath for the action to come.

Dick assumed they had night vision technology. Maybe they were watching him now. His throat tightened.

His eyes had adjusted a bit to the dark as he pulled out his wallet. Grant had given him the clip, which was now wrapped in tissue paper. He pulled a packet of chewing gum from his pocket. Carefully, he took the clip from the tissue, discarded a piece of gum, and wrapped the clip in the aluminum film. He folded the aluminum in different directions, creating a mesh. Then, with the other pieces of gum, he created a lattice of layers of thin metal.

The rustle of leaves and undergrowth had stopped. Now he heard whispers. He couldn't tell how far away they were, but he knew his pursuers weren't moving. His body was shaking uncontrollably. The mosquitoes had no mercy, they buzzed and bit and swarmed him from every direction.

Penlights were now all around him. The beams crisscrossed the trees and branches, methodically studying each tree from the roots to upper branches. The whispers continued.

Dick bunched up as much as he could, minimizing his profile. He studied the penlights, navigating a course that he might take to escape again. In front of him was a swampy bog, and so that direction was not an option. He would be easy pickings for them if he got stuck in the mud, or the water moccasins might get him. To the right was more thicket, but it seemed that two of his pursuers were over there.

Then the forest was all silence again. The penlights were extinguished. The forest waited.

To his left Dick heard a snap. Someone was travelling quickly. It seemed to be coming from a different direction than the whispers and headed directly toward him. It was now or never. Time to run.

Dick pulled up to a squat, ready to spring forward, as the whispers to his right started again. Then two penlights found their target.

"It's Frank!" Dick thought. Frank squinted as the penlights burned his retina. Startled, then defensively, he turned a pistol toward the light. "Who's there?" He barked as a dart hit his neck.

Frank swatted his neck but it was too late. He went down.

The three were upon him in a moment. They crunched through the underbrush, thrashing through branches and crashing over stumps.

Dick backed carefully away, finding a different spot from which to view the activity. The three pursuers, all wearing black facemasks, quickly emptied Frank's pockets and then removed his clothes and scanned him with a device of some kind. The biggest of the three scanned the perimeter one last time with his penlight. He whispered as the others worked as though he was talking to the air around him.

Dick remembered that he had left his chewing gum on the ground. If the man with the penlight spotted it, these men would surely continue their search. He felt his stomach twist with anger and helplessness. Frank would never leave his father on the ground and possibly dying. But Dick knew any attempt to distract or challenge Frank's captors would be futile.

CHAPTER 24

"Dad!" Ree screamed, dropping her fork on the table.

"What happened to you?" Carol was already standing.

Dried blood painted the scrape on the left side of his forehead and his eyes were glassy as he staggered into the kitchen. His scrubs were streaked with dirt and grass stains and he had a bruise on his left neck. He wobbled forward, then collapsed.

"911!" Carol screamed. "Call 911!" She looked at Beth and then Ree.

Grant was awake but simply absent. "I don't know what happened." His voice was as distant as his eyes.

"I don't think I've had a stroke, but..." Carol had placed her finger over his lips.

"They're on the way!" Beth knelt beside him.

Ree was already beside him, her face streaked with tears. "Dad, what's wrong? What happened to you?"

"I don't know, sweetheart." He tried to focus on Ree, but his eyes were too heavy. She was a blur.

Ree ran to get a pillow from the living room and placed it under his head, terrified at his weakness.

"I hear them!" Beth shouted. "It's the ambulance."

Beth rushed to the door, reaching it as the ambulance pulled to a stop. Two paramedics ran toward her.

"What's the matter?" The first one to reach Beth had a full beard. He was already looking through the entrance for an answer.

"It's my dad. We don't know what's wrong with him." She broke down in sobs. "He may have had a stroke."

Beth was still weeping, following them to the kitchen. The other paramedic ran back to the ambulance to retrieve a gurney while the bearded one examined Grant.

"Hey, doc. What happened?" He knew Dr. Miller from the Emergency Room. He took his blood pressure and felt his pulse. "Blood pressure looks okay. 120 over 80. Pulse 90."

He hooked up a heart monitor, pasting leads to his chest. The monitor came to life, beeping rhythmically. "EKG looks fine, doc."

"Are you hurting anywhere?" The younger was back.

"No." Grant's thoughts and strength were returning slowly. "I really feel fine, just weak and drunk."

Beth's face paled. "Dad, you don't drink!"

"No, honey." He smiled. "I just feel like I would if I'd been at a bar."

The two men hoisted Grant onto the gurney and rolled him toward the door. "Y'all can meet us in the E.D. We'll be there in a second. Luckily, y'all live right around the corner."

....

"Grant, you're toxicology screen came back positive for benzodiazepines and nicotine." Clint was the emergency room doctor taking care of him.

"Benzos?" He scratched his jaw. "That might explain why I have no memory of the last few hours." He grinned to himself. "Hell, maybe I WAS at a bar. I sure as hell don't smoke."

"The head C.T. scan was normal. No evidence of a stroke or subdural." Clint continued. "Your lab work was all normal. No evidence of hyperglycemia, electrolyte disturbance, or hypoxia."

"What is the last thing you remember, sir?" A policeman stood at the foot of his bed.

Carol, Beth, and Ree were standing nearby, white powder on their cheeks indicating the paths of their tears an hour ago. They hadn't left their positions beside him.

"I had left the governor and was going home to shower, planning on returning for a final check. I was walking down the road toward home. I had just passed the Darling's house." He paused, then touched his neck. "I remember getting bitten by a wasp and falling to the ground." He searched his memory. "I almost remember someone catching me, breaking my fall."

The policeman wrote everything he said word for word. "What next?"

"The next thing I remember is being in here, in the emergency room."

Carol stroked his forehead. "You don't remember coming home? Being in the kitchen?"

"All I remember is being stung, falling, and being in here." He scratched his five o'clock again. "I wonder if I had an anaphylactic reaction to a bee sting."

"That would explain your passing out and being confused, possibly everything." Clint, said, thinking out loud.

"Well it doesn't explain your missing billfold or the credit cards in your top pocket," the policeman said as he continued writing.

"And it doesn't explain the benzodiazepines or the nicotine." Clint, all too familiar with the consequences of breaking HIPPA rules by sharing medical information, even with family members, almost caught himself but his words were already out. If Grant was secretly using Valium, Librium or Klonopin, if he was smoking or had a drug addiction, he could be in big trouble.

Grant recognized the sudden concern on Clint's face. He'd too had wished he could suck back words in the past. "Don't worry, Clint. I can assure you that I don't smoke and don't use any medications, including prescription drugs. Not even Tylenol. You are free to discuss or share any medical information with any of my family."

Clint smiled. "Thanks, Grant." His relief then molted, replaced by a snarl. "The damn bureaucrats and government agencies are gonna kill us. If they don't break us with law suits, they'll prevent useful medical information transfer and replace it with useless Electronic Medical Records."

"Back to what happened..." the policeman said, urging Grant onward. "Did you have anything else in your billfold that might have been stolen?"

Grant thought for a second, and then the lights went on. "Yes, maybe some money, but..." He caught his breath. "The clip."

The policeman looked up from his notes. "What clip?"

Grant knew how Clint felt moments ago, wishing he had filtered his thoughts. Dick had mentioned the FBI almost suspiciously, and if there was something going on with law enforcement, something that might endanger the governor, he had better be careful.

"I keep a clip on my bills, a gift from my wife, a keepsake. I've had it for years. I doubt she could find another like it." He squeezed Carol's hand harder than a possible emotional loss might indicate.

She took the hint, smiling affectionately back at him. She'd never given him a bill clip. The policeman studied their exchange and appeared satisfied.

"So nothing else appears stolen or lost?"

"No."

"How much cash would you estimate you lost?"

"Maybe a hundred," Grant answered dismissively.

"So you don't have any other injuries and no other losses?" He flipped his notepad closed and returned it to his pocket.

"I really don't." He looked at his family. "I just want to go home and sleep this off."

"Alright, sir." The policeman studied Grant and his wife carefully. "I guess I'll wrap this up. Call me if anything else comes up or if you have any other concerns."

He turned to walk out, then twirled back. "By the way. I'd advise that you contact your credit card companies to have the current ones deactivated and new ones sent to you. And are all your identification cards and driver's license in your pocket?"

"Yes, all of them."

"Well, you should probably go to the courthouse and have the driver's license number changed just in case."

"Okay, thanks." Once again, Grant answered more indifferently than the officer expected. He turned and was gone.

Carol asked, puzzled, "Are you really okay?" She looked at Beth and Ree, then held any other questions.

"Yeah. It's been a long day, a long few days, a long month or so." He sighed. "Let's just go home and get some rest."

Grant was trying to put everything—the FBI, the clip, the microdot, the benzodiazepines and nicotine—together, but the wires weren't connecting.

CHAPTER 25

Wang Chien snored despite the ringing above his head. His two Boerboels sat at attention, motionless at the foot of his bed. Two others stood watch outside. He had tried several breeds of watch dog, but the muscular mastiff breed was his favorite because of their strength and loyalty. Two of his servants had snuck into his compound one night when he was away. Apparently they thought the dogs would recognize them and let them pass. In fact, the dogs did recognize them, otherwise they would have torn the servants apart. When Wang returned home the next day, the two servants lay on the ground, one with a leg severed, one of the dogs standing guard.

As the ringing grew louder, his eyes squinted toward the clock. His head was spinning from the bottle of Chateau Lafite he had polished off before turning out the light. The speakers over his ivory headboard rarely were active at this hour.

"*Nin*," he grunted.

"This is Yao Ming!" The speakers blasted.

Wang sat straight up, throwing the sheets off the bed. Touching another switch, the overheads dimmed, then gradually brightened. Two girls tossed restlessly. He spanked them to attention, pointing for them to leave the room. They jumped up holding their teen breasts and raced out of the room. The Boerboels growled hungrily.

Wang flipped the bedside switch, silencing the overhead speaker, and picked up his bedside telephone.

"Yes. How can I help you?" The wine still glued his tongue.

"We have trouble in America, in Tuscaloosa." Yao watched Wang. The video surveillance hadn't been easy to install in Wang's bedroom, especially with the dogs, but it was worth the effort. There wasn't much that Yao couldn't do.

Wang wiped the thickness from his eyes. "What do you mean?" He was sitting straight up.

"The governor." Yao toyed with him, seeing how he reacted to different prompts.

"Did he... What about the governor?" Wang gave himself away but didn't know it yet.

"The governor is getting better. He will survive." Yao watched.

"So what is the matter? What are you worried about?" Wang scratched his groin.

Yao's jaw tightened, angered at Wang's last action. Even though Yao wasn't there, he still expected respect. "Is there anything about the governor I need to know?"

Wang's eyes narrowed, looking around. "What do you mean?" He swept the room, disturbed, feeling eyes upon him.

"Did you have anything to do with the governor's heart attack? That's what I mean?" Yao screamed.

Wang stood straight up. The empty bottle next to his bed rattled. "No, sir. I mean no... What do you mean?" Wang wobbled helplessly.

Yao sent visual daggers, watching each hit their mark. "If the governor dies, or if you had anything to do with his heart attack..." Yao paused.

Wang was a naked fat blob who didn't deserve to live in such luxury. Yao peered at him with disgust. Yao was pure muscle, pure work, pure energy, pure Party. Wang's lips were purple with the stain of wine. His pot belly was still digesting the kung pao squid, marinated bean curd sheet, and duck soup.

"No. I had nothing to do with his heart attack." Wang captured his composure, straightening up and reaching for his robe. "The Americans are always sick, always having heart attacks." He looked out the window, searching the grounds. "I am sure the governor will be okay."

Wang was steady now. "But why do you care about the governor? He is just an obstacle now? If you want me to do my job, it would be better without the governor." Wang was back on his game.

"You don't need to worry about that. You just better be sure that you can't be linked to his illness," Yao returned. He already had the answers he was seeking.

"Don't worry about me! I know my job." Wang scratched his groin again, turning from side to side.

Yao hung up the phone, then made another call.

CHAPTER 26

Frank, lying on the ground as Dick peeped through the branches, had been shot with the same kind of poison dart that hit Grant. One motorcyclist continued to scan their position with a penlight while another pulled a body bag from his backpack and quickly stuffed Frank into it with the help of the third man. The governor's longtime friend was all but dead, his muscles paralyzed by the poison and his mind numbed by it. The only activity was his heart, which continued to pump blood through darkness. Without Frank being able to breath, without oxygen, each heartbeat gradually slowed and weakened and occasionally fluttered, threatening to surrender to fibrillation, the wormlike movements of a heart muscle before complete rest.

The one with the penlight whispered in garbled speech. He was too distant and his words too indistinct for Dick to understand. He was obviously talking to someone but no one close to him. The other two were too busy to listen. He reached toward Frank, pulled out a pocketknife, cut off the tip of his thumb, then zipped the bag closed.

Once Frank was cocooned, they quickly retreated toward the highway. Dick stayed still briefly watching three penlights depart, confident that no one was lingering. He could see a glimmer of moonlight where Frank lay and quickly but quietly rushed to the bag.

Unzipping the bag, Dick found Frank's head and neck mainly by feel. The splinters of light weren't enough to see his face. Feeling his neck, a thready pulse tapped slowly underneath. He placed his head above Frank's face, listening for an audible breath, which came after too long a wait and with too little strength.

Dick started pushing on Frank's chest. He was aware of first aid recommendations to begin chest compressions before mouth to mouth breathing. He pushed for a minute or so but realized that Frank wasn't taking any breaths. So he found Frank's mouth with his and took deep breaths, blowing with all of his strength into Frank's lungs. He felt Frank's chest expand with each effort. After 20 breaths and continued chest compressions, he felt for a pulse again. There was a strong pulse now, much faster and rhythmic.

Dick continued to exchange breaths, about 20 per minute, until his head felt like it would explode from the force of blowing and his own hyperventilation. His hands, feet, and lips became numb. Lightheaded, nauseous, and exhausted, Dick continued breathing for his father's friend. Every once in a while, he checked Frank's pulse. It remained strong and steady.

"Maybe he is brain dead," Dick thought. He knew people could be kept on a breathing machine indefinitely, their heart working and their other body parts functional but with no brain function. But he wasn't going to leave Frank. If his father could save him, Dick could too.

The breathing continued for an hour. Then, suddenly, Frank began to hiccup. He had been flaccid to this point, but now there were twitches in his arms and hands. His own breaths were still too shallow and faint, and Dick continued the breaths until Frank was breathing on his own, which took another half hour. He was moving now but not enough.

"What the shit happened?" Frank managed to say.

"I wish I knew. All I know for certain is that you saved my life." Dick was finally able to relax. He fell on his side beside Frank.

"That was some crazy shit."

"Do you have any idea who that was?"

"None."

"How did you find me? What were you doing here?"

Frank was massaging his mouth, trying to make the muscles work. "I told your mom that I had a bad feeling about this whole thing. I was concerned that your whole family might be in danger. She told me what you said about the threats to your dad, about the microdot, the clip. When things sound suspicious, they usually are. I told your mom I was going to have your back at the lab." He was sounding stronger. "I just didn't expect to see your car being rolled off the road by those three men."

"They rolled my car off the road?"

"At first I thought their car had just quit on them, but then I realized it was yours. I had already passed, and so I had to back up to where your car was and the men were gone by then." He was sitting up now. His voice was normal. "I saw lights in the woods, and so I backed farther past them and started searching."

"Did you see them or hear them?"

"The only thing I remember is being blinded by those damn lights, then getting smacked in my neck, and then nothing." He tried to stand, stumbling slightly. "Where the hell are my clothes? MY SHOES?? Shit, what the hell is going on?" He hadn't noticed his thumb until now. Touching his hands together, he groaned, "My thumb. My fucking thumb is gone."

Dick was pulling his thoughts together as Frank checked his other body parts. "I think you got shot with something. I was watching you come toward me but I could hear the bikers closing in on me and had to stay hiding. You got hit with something in your neck that put you down. They must have thought you were me. I think they were tracking me with this clip." He pulled the clip out of his pocket. "It must have GPS capacity in it."

Frank was testing his feet now. A shard of a broken branch bit into the soft of his arch and he cursed. "So they thought I was you, shot me with something that paralyzed me, and then bagged me, leaving me for dead?" Anger lathered in his thoughts. "I guess they took my clothes, hoping to find that clip."

"Either that or to ID you. That's probably why they took your thumb, DNA and prints."

"Shit!" Frank's thumb was a raw nerve now, pulsating with hammer-pounding intensity. "They must have my cell phone too. It won't take long to figure out I'm not you. It wasn't locked."

"You're right. We better get out of here."

The occasional car on the highway helped stay oriented as they crept through the underbrush. Frank tested each step, careful not to injure himself any more, and they paused occasionally to listen, aware that an ambush was possible.

Frank's right hand, buried in his armpit for protection, continued to pulse with dull bursts of pain as he followed Dick's steps, but his strength was returning rapidly. He felt that, if necessary, he could probably run.

The lines of light were becoming more visible as they cleared the last yards before the highway. The moonlight was bright on the highway ahead.

"We'd better travel in the woods back to my truck," Frank whispered. "They might be watching your vehicle."

"I don't even see my car, Frank." Dick could see the highway clearly now. "Over there is where I went into the woods." He saw the sheared bank where one of the cycles had skidded. "My car should be right up there."

"They must have taken it to search for the clip," Frank said, thinking out loud. "My truck should be back there about 50 yards. I didn't want to park too close. Thought I would be less conspicuous." He cupped his thumb. "Guess that didn't work."

They paralleled the highway, staying deep enough in the woods to be invisible. The branches and stumps were merciless, striking Frank's naked body from every angle and he felt the warmth of blood trickling from head to toe.

The moon was still bright, making both sides of the road clear to see. They saw no motorcycles, no evidence of people except an occasional car traveling down the road. They continued to trudge through the thicket but were certain that Frank's truck should be visible by now.

"Shit!" Frank sat on a fallen tree. "We don't have any transportation and no communication. I'm naked as a fish, and somebody tried to kill me thinking I was you. My neck feels like a grenade exploded on it, and..." He stood up again. "I'd hitch for a ride if I had a thumb!"

Dick was at the edge of the forest, watching headlights approach, wondering whether to take the risk and run out for assistance. It wouldn't have made any difference. Just as the thoughts surfaced, there was a screech of brakes as the car darted off the road, shining its lights into the woods and directly at them.

CHAPTER 27

Grant had been up all night. The left side of his neck was bruised and firm, too much damage to have been caused by an insect. He searched the Net. Answers had to be out there.

Benzodiazepines had been found in his blood. That would explain his lack of recall for the events of the evening. Versed had been used in most operations for years. Recently, Dormez had become the agent of choice because it had fewer side effects and had immediate onset of activity. It could be given orally or intravenously. If someone drugged him with it, he would have no memory of the events over an hour or so.

That left the nicotine. He'd never smoked and hadn't been around smokers. He searched periodicals and toxicology reports. Then, finally, he found recent data that nicotine taken intravenously protects a body that has low oxygen content. Nicotine keeps the heart beating even when oxygen depletion would stop the heart. In fact, the combination of curare and nicotine had been used by South American hunters and gatherers for centuries. They shot animals in the tops of trees with a blow gun, the dart tipped in curare and nicotine, so the animal fell to the ground still alive.

That was the answer. Curare is a muscle relaxant that paralyses the body temporarily. Even the diaphragm is paralyzed, causing people or animals to die of suffocation. Either artificial breathing through a machine or from another person would be necessary to stay alive.

Grant pulled information on poison darts. Surely that's what hit him. Poison projectiles have been used throughout the world for hunting and warfare. Now someone had used it on him.

"Molly, this is Grant." It was crazy to call at this hour. He knew that. But he also knew that something crazy was going on, something that couldn't wait.

"Yes, Dr. Miller." Her voice cracked, sharing her exhaustion.

"I need to talk to you, but not over the phone."

"I'm here in Richard's room. Do you want to come here?"

"Sure. I'll be there in a second."

Grant climbed into his jeans, running shoes, and T-shirt. It didn't take long to make the car ride to the hospital and the elevator up to the unit. Molly was in Richard's room, five state troopers at her side.

"Is everything okay?" The troopers were in protection formation.

Grant saw Richard behind one of the troopers. He was wide awake. The breathing tube had already been removed and he looked great. The gathering wasn't for the governor.

"It's our son, and maybe Frank. We've lost contact with them. They were going to our company in Mobile to do some studies on that clip." Tears welled in her eyes. "What does all this mean?" She looked at Grant, searching for an answer.

"Can we talk privately?" He ignored the troopers.

"Surely." She nodded them away.

Grant shut the sliding doors, separating them from the troopers. "Do you have your cell phone in here?"

"Yes." She handed it to him.

"Dick was concerned about these." He took his and Molly's phones outside, closed the doors again, and looked at the governor. "I don't think I've introduced myself." He offered his hand.

Richard looked unbelievably good. His color had returned, and the monitors confirmed that his blood pressure was perfect, his rhythm normal, and his oxygenation good. "I think I owe you a debt of gratitude." His voice was still raspy from the breathing tube that had irritated his vocal cords.

They shook hands, both with strength.

Molly joined her husband, standing by his side. "Grant, we don't have any idea where they are. The state troopers have been searching for hours and there's an APB out for them. Dick always calls on his way to different places, and I kept waiting for his call, but it never came and so I called him. He never answered, and so I got the troopers involved." She tried her best to be strong. "It's like he vanished. There is no sign of him, his phone, or his car."

Grant wasn't surprised. That's why he wanted to talk to her. "I was afraid of that. I am guessing the same thing happened with your friend, Frank?"

"Yes." The governor tried to sound strong, but his voice betrayed him.

"Were they together?" Grant turned to Molly, hoping Richard would save his strength.

"No. Frank was following him, kind of being a guardian angel. He has always felt like our family's personal protector and he was making sure Dick got to the lab without problems."

"What kind of car does Dick have?" Grant asked.

"BMW, a new 8 series."

"Well they have the new Field Sweep technology, don't they?" Grant asked hopefully. "You should be able to track where the car is and where it's been." He looked at Molly. "Do you have Dick's driver's license and car tag number by any chance?"

"Yes, as a matter of fact. All of that information is in my cell phone." Molly went out with Dick to retrieve the phone. She tapped in the request and showed it to Grant.

Grant went to a nearby computer and logged in. Pulling up BMW Field Sweep, he typed in Dick's information with a request for the last eight hours. Immediately the screen plotted out the time and location of Dick's car.

"There it is." Grant pointed at the screen. "He's not far from here."

"What is that?" Molly read the location markers. "It looks like his car is in that creek." She held back a scream.

"Yes." Grant pulled her next to him. "But look. The car came to a stop here and then moved slightly." He zoomed in. "It looks like it moved to the side of the road, stayed there for 45 minutes..." He zoomed back out slightly. "Then it moved at a slow pace and stopped on the bridge." He zoomed back in. "It looks like it is in the creek but not like it was an accident. I'll bet anything he's back here." He pointed to the original stopping point.

Grant took a picture of the screen with his cell. "Come on, let's go back inside." He ushered Molly back to Richard, leaving their phones outside and shutting the doors again.

"I think I know where Dick is," Grant told Richard.

"Well, let's get the troopers on it." Richard's eyes danced.

"Just a minute." Grant wasn't ready to move. "Well, I was hit this evening." He showed the bruise on his neck. "I think someone shot me with a dart that paralyzed me."

"What?" Molly recoiled.

"I was walking home when I got hit in my neck with something that put me to sleep. I woke up at home with my billfold was gone and my credit cards in my front pocket. I think someone put me down and searched me and couldn't find the clip that Dick took."

Molly's tears made it to her cheeks. "What is so important about that clip?" She tried to hold back her sobs, but her body was shaking with fear. "Dicky seemed to think the FBI or CIA might be involved."

Both Molly and Grant looked at Richard. "Is there any reason that the FBI or CIA would be investigating you?" Grant found the courage to ask.

"I don't think so." He searched his thoughts. "Let me say this. They both have reason to investigate all governors and politicians, but I have nothing to hide." His voice strengthened as he looked directly at Molly. "Nothing!"

Both Molly and Grant relaxed. They knew, with their son at risk, that Richard would be honest.

"Governor." Grant looked at the monitors and then at Richard. "I'm not sure at all what's going on here. Your son seemed to suspect the FBI or CIA. He said you had received warnings about threats to your person."

Richard squirmed, more out of discomfort than apprehension. "Politics is a dangerous business. You make friends that turn out to be enemies, and you make enemies that can be dangerous." He sat up in bed. "This deal with Beijing Motors has been difficult from many angles. The Chinese don't trust us and we don't trust them. We want their business; they want our business. Getting them to open shop in Alabama comes with its own set of snags." Richard sighed.

"Labor unions have been the fly in the ointment with this deal." Richard continued.

"Labor unions?"

"Yes. They want in. They want to expand their reach in the automobile business to foreign automakers with plants here. They also want into the universities, the government... I've made enemies with them and maybe even with the Chinese."

"You mean because of the Astor deal?"

"Yes." He sat up in bed. "Beijing Automotive wants cheap labor. They don't really want labor unions to set workers' salaries. Alabama, a right-to-work state, doesn't really want the unions here either. Once they get their foot in the door in a big way, they tend to follow with a stampede."

"So why are they a problem?" Grant asked. "It sounds like no one wants them, which would make them a non-issue."

"You'd think so, but apparently the owner of Beijing Motors was in Detroit recently talking to a boss."

"How did you find out about that?" Molly asked.

"That's where things get muddy," Richard continued. "I didn't hear from the CIA or FBI, but they're the ones who probably saw the meeting and should have passed the information on to me. I found out from a friend of mine who works in Washington."

"So how is this a threat to you?"

"Well, as you know, three governors have died, presumably of natural causes, in the last year." He glanced at Molly, deciding not to guard her from his thoughts. "All of the governors were actively soliciting foreign manufacturing to come to their states." He paused, again making sure Molly was alright. "I knew one of the governors, Paul Jenkins. We had talked about foreign companies and agreed that they were good for our states and good for the economy. As a matter of fact, we talked about a month before he died of his heart attack."

Grant's lips pursed. "I remember reading about him." He was thinking more about the evening, about himself and who it was that could have killed him.

"Well," the governor continued, "he told me that he wasn't so much concerned about local politics or unions or being reelected. He was more concerned about Big Brother. He told me that every move he tried to make was blocked and every plan he had was failing. He also felt like someone was listening to every word he said. He was convinced that the FBI, or someone with its power and scope, was interfering with his attempts to bring business to his state."

"Why would the FBI be doing anything like that?" Grant asked, puzzled.

"He didn't have an answer, but he was always a thinker and maybe a bit of a conspiracy theorist. He told me that, ever since Homeland Security was formed but the FBI and CIA were kept as independent organizations, he worried that the FBI or CIA might have lost some of their capacity to take care of matters involving business and national security. He felt like he was being sabotaged and speculated that it might be American businesses that kept losing market share because of foreigners." Again, he paused. Grant had a faraway look, like he was listening to the babbling of madman.

"I'm with you, Governor. I'm just trying to figure a lot out here."

"Well, the FBI or some rogue entity could be giving information away that could be used to kill foreign competition or maybe to damage the reputation of Homeland Security. The FBI and the CIA have both been under pretty hard criticism recently by the Department of Homeland Security for their failures." Another pause. "Anyway, I simply shared these concerns with Dick, told him exactly what I've shared with you."

Grant's chest was pounding. He remembered the feeling he had before wrestling tournaments, the explosion waiting to ignite inside him. Someone was on to them all. Someone knew everything they were saying. Dick had placed the cell phones out of range and so must have suspected that it was the cell phones that allowed for surveillance. Grant had seen enough movies that he was aware of the possibility of coordinating all communications, even those in the ICU, for investigations. But there was no audio system in the ICU. There were visual monitors, however, and perhaps someone could read their lips, but he thought it would take an entire agency to coordinate an effort like this.

The clip. Only the FBI or CIA could have technology so sophisticated that something so small could be used for surveillance.

CHAPTER 28

Dick was certain of the point he had entered the woods. Frank knew that they had walked far enough back that his truck should have been seen by now. Both vehicles were gone. Frank's feet were bruised and bloodied from the trek through the woods. His thumb was a crust of dried blood and stringy fibers. He lay on the dried fallen tree to catch his breath and gather his strength. At some point they were going to have to hitch a ride.

Dick stood at the edge of the woods. He'd never picked up a hitchhiker and had never needed to beg for a ride. He figured anyone who would stop on a lonely road in the dark was suspect to begin with, but how in the world was he going to convince any driver to give two strangers a ride, one of them naked.

An automobile was approaching from the north. It slowed seconds before the headlights filled the night, the lights shining near where Dick and Frank crouched. The closer it came to them, the slower it moved.

"What do you think?" Frank crept next to Dick.

"I don't like it!"

The xenon blue headlights turned the highway into daylight. Dick could see the motorcycle tracks in the buffalo grass and dirt mounds, the bikes' paths leading to the woods and traveling away. Ahead, down the road, was a bridge. It looked like a creek crossing. If necessary, he and Frank might have to swim the creek to escape.

It was a Lexus Hybrid, black with tinted glass, that inched by them. When it got to the point that the motorcycle trails began, it pulled off the road, shining its beams into the woods. Then, back on the road, it crept to the bridge.

"Do you think someone is looking for us?" Dick asked.

"I'm sure they are, but to help us or to finish the job those other guys started?"

The car stopped again at the bridge and pulled off the road. The driver stepped out of the car and looked down into the creek. There were two men, but Frank and Dick couldn't identify them from here.

The men climbed back in the car and the Lexus backed to the place it had stopped before. The two men stepped out of the car again.

"Holy shit!" Frank was almost crying. "It's Harper Deal, a trooper."

"And that's Dr. Miller!" Dick was racing out of the woods.

Both of them were screaming as they ran toward the car.

Grant heard them before he saw them. They were on the highway within seconds. He and Harper jumped back in the SUV, backing to pick them up.

"What in the hell is going on?" Dick gasped as they jumped in the vehicle.

"Somebody wants that clip you're carrying. I don't know what's so important about it, but it must have tracking and communication capability." Grant was already on the road gunning his engine.

"I figured that out myself," Dick returned. "Three guys on motorcycles were tracking me. I figured they must be doing it through the clip. I wrapped it with aluminum foil, blocking any signal. I felt like I was in

Professor Odin's class, blocking communications with abstract techniques."

"So, I'm assuming you still have the clip," Grant queried.

"You bet your ass."

"Well, we're all going to that lab to figure this out." Grant hit the accelerator on a straightaway and hit 90 miles per hour.

"Harper's packing. I made sure someone was around for protection."

"What the hell happened to you?" Harper looked over his shoulder at the two men in the back seat.

Frank was a mess, torn from head to toe. "I was following Dick, trying to watch out for him. I saw his car on the side of the road and bikers who looked like they were up to no good." His voice betrayed his exhaustion. "I guess I got the raw end of a case of mistaken identity." A weak laugh followed. "I think I got shot in the neck with a tranquilizing dart as I was trying to find Dick."

Grant hit the brakes. "What?" He pulled the Lexus to the side, gravel spraying off the asphalt.

"I was searching for Dick in the woods when I got hit with something in my neck. It put me down. I don't remember shit until I woke up with Dick doing mouth to mouth on me. The fuckers stripped me and left me in a body bag." His voice broke, emotion collapsing on him. "They cut off my fucking thumb and left me to die in that bag. I've seen those bags before. They're airtight. Not even hound dogs can sniff out bodies in them."

Grant examined the mark on Frank's neck, then shared his bruise with them. "It looks like the same group hit me. I'm sure they were trying to find the clip. They must have heard me say that it was on a credit card. Maybe they were tuned in to my cell phone. My billfold was taken and the credit cards were stuffed in my pocket. Whatever was in the dart that hit us must include a benzodiazepine to block our memory. I don't know how I survived. I should have suffocated."

"Are you sure that clip can't transmit communications at this point?" Frank asked.

"I'm assuming it can't or they would have found me," Dick replied. "Speaking of which, are your cell phones active?"

"We turned them off when we left. We have no idea who is doing all this, But whoever it is, they must have access to high-end technology," Harper said. "I know you want to give a message to your mom and dad. I told them if we found you and you were okay, we'd text them the word 'red.' Why don't you do that now?"

Dick took Harper's cell phone, activated it, and sent the text. He started to write more but realized it could be dangerous. He turned the cell back off.

"Do you really think a government agency would be doing this?" Grant was driving again. "That just seems crazy that the FBI or CIA, or even a rogue outfit representing God-knows-who, would be doing this."

"Not so crazy, Dr. Miller!" Dick spoke up. "Don't forget the power the FBI and the National Security Agency have been granted, to track emails, Facebook entries, Twitter messages, texts. They can do this to any citizen down to three or four or more contacts removed to come up with so-called communities of interest. Dragnet surveillance allows members of the FBI, CIA, NSA and probably others to pull all kinds of information together. Any rogue agent could then work alone or with others outside these agencies for their own purposes."

"I understand that you're saying that data gathering is already being done and the techniques for spying on us are increasing, and this clip or microchip, or whatever it is, could simply be one more surveillance option. But can a clip like that be powerful enough to transmit conversations as well as locations?"

"That's what we're gonna have to figure out in our lab," Dick replied.

"Well, if the clip was being monitored, they already know you were on the way to Sand's Electronics." He was playing mental chess. "We can't contact the FBI because it might be them or one of their agents gone rogue, and we can't contact our own people because we might be monitored... We definitely know that at least three people are willing to kill for the clip." He paused. "What about the troopers or police? At least we could get some protection?"

Harper said confidently, "I thought of that, and I have some troopers following us. They should be within a mile or so of us. They are tracking this car with GPS. If I need them, all I have to do is turn on my cell and call."

"So we're on communication lockdown until we interrogate that clip at your plant?" Grant asked Dick.

CHAPTER 29

Yao squirmed in his office as the automated English to China interpreter relayed their conversation. He listened to every word they spoke. The clear night sky made reception flawless.

"Everything is in jeopardy now." He pounded his desk.

Hu, the Tiger, stood by his side, stone-faced and waiting for orders. He had been Yao's faithful servant for years. Ice ran through his veins as he recruited his *qi*, the life force, which strengthened him and prepared him for missions.

"There are now four and maybe more who suspect the clip has communication capability. All four *lǎowài* must die before they know more and before they talk!" Yao's face was crimson.

Hu was well trained in Hung Gar, a Shaolin Tiger style of kung fu. He had trained in the traditional way, spending his first three years in stance training, squatting in horse stance for hours at a time. He then learned the leaping action and ferocity of a tiger for five years. His fingers were thickened from death blows to many victims, the sinews of his hands and forearms taut elastic cords groomed for a whipping power with each strike. He had seen many victims fall, his strikes merciless and his soul fortified with each fatality.

"Our three men are on their way and know what they must do, but you must make sure the mission is completed," Yao grunted to the Tiger. "The good news is that they are afraid of their own people. They suspect the FBI of being after them. That will work in our favor until they discover that the Chinese have infected them. Once they discover that we are responsible, that we have the capability to destroy them with our technology, we will have lost the element of surprise."

They watched the satellite feed on Yao's monitor. An infrared picture captured Grant's Lexus as it sped toward Mobile. A mile behind it, they watched another vehicle mimic the Lexus.

As Yao watched the screen he waved at Wong. "Go. You must hurry. We don't have time to waste."

Hu's hands tightened into claws as he thought of the thrill he would feel again. It had been too long since his last chance to release his energy, his last chance to feel the snap of a bone or a chest being crushed, to watch the last breath of a *gwailo*. He was gone like a ghost.

Yao continued to watch the monitor. His mouth twisted into a grin as he watched three smaller images flash into the screen. They were beside the rear vehicle in a moment. His bikers were good at what they did, and they did whatever Yao demanded.

"They better make it fast, before the troopers have a chance to send out a call," Yao thought.

Yao watched the lead motorcyclist pull in front of the car and throw his payload, oil too thick to wash off the windshield with the wipers. In the dark, the troopers would be blind. The driver of the troopers' car hit the brakes, but it was too late. The second cyclist had already fired his shots. The car veered to the left, then flew into the woods.

Yao was amazed at the thickness of the Alabama forest. The vehicle was almost invisible under the canopy. He smiled slightly but remembered that it was the thickness of the woods that blocked the images of Dick Sands earlier in the evening. He blamed himself for zooming in on the hunt earlier, missing the approach of the other *gwailo*, the one they mistook for Dick Sands.

He watched one of the cyclists follow the car into the woods to make sure the job was done as the other two zoomed ahead. They wouldn't fail this time. The Lexus wouldn't escape.

"They have no idea I am listening to everything they say." He smirked.

Watching and listening to people had become an addiction. Yao rarely went home, instead tuning into various frequencies and alternating from cameras to satellites and coordinating visual and audio feeds at his office at all hours. The automated language interpreter allowed him to move from country to country with ease. Since he had planned and facilitated the surveillance program, he had full access to its use. But he knew that, if the program blew up in his face, Wang's loyalty to his own interests and to the Party were greater than his loyalty to him. He had no desire to feel the bite of the tiger.

One of the motorcycles charged past the Lexus and zipped forward.

"Shit!" Yao heard Dick scream.

Yao expected Dick's reaction to the Ducati as it ripped through the night.

"That's how everything started. Stop the car," Dick yelled. "A motorcycle like that flew past me and dumped something on the ground that wrecked my car."

Grant slowed but didn't stop. He watched the Ducati disappear ahead of them and he didn't see the third cyclist join his buddy a quarter of a mile behind them. The sun was breaking through the darkness to the east, muting the headlights on the motorcycles.

"I don't see it anymore." Yao heard Grant say.

"Well let's make time. The sooner we figure this out, the better," Harper said.

CHAPTER 30

The Mobile River empties into the northern end of the Mobile Bay, forming a delta with extensive marshland. Sand's Electronics was somewhat hidden in the estuary by the towering tupelo gums and bald cypress trees. Richard Sands picked the location for his plant due to the natural beauty and because of his passion for maintaining the environment. After the recent oil spills, he teamed with several groups to build an eco-friendly state-of-the-art facility. Spanish moss draped from the surrounding trees, carrying the staff and visitors to an earlier time when life was breezy and simple.

Flooding in the area was common, and the underlying alluvium made construction of the plant a challenge. However, the sand bar at the foot of the plant was deemed a workable site and, two stories high and just below the horizon of the gums with a lower level for parking, its foundation had taken three years to sink. But built to withstand hurricane velocity storms and the natural erosion of floodplains, the building was more natural in appearance than Richard had ever anticipated. Glassed siding made the majority of the building transparent, while the remainder was granite, the exact color of the surrounding cypress trees. Since hurricanes and tornadoes were common in the area, Richard made sure the windows were impact resistant.

Richard had demanded a wireless plant and had developed a water hydrolysis system to produce hydrogen, the energy source for the plant. Sand's Electronics was essentially free standing, with no need for wires or pipes. The sewage was self-contained, processed in a septic system that turned waste water to fresh water. He allowed tours of the plant and assisted other companies in developing their own self-sufficient facilities.

By the time Grant drove into the parking deck, the morning sun was in full action. Green fly orchids looked like honeysuckle, shaded from the direct light by the swamp tupelo on which it grew. Two red bellied turtles, an endangered species for decades, enjoyed a sun bath on a nearby fallen tree. The world around them was enjoying the day, but none of the passengers in the Lexus took notice.

"How long do you think it will take to figure out what's going on with that clip?" Harper asked as Dick stepped out of the car.

"Who knows? I hope it won't take more than a day, though."

"A day!" Frank almost shouted. "I was hoping this would lead to a quick answer so we'd know who was responsible, who we can trust."

"That's what I'm hoping for too, but I just don't know how sophisticated the technology is." Dick placed his finger on the biometric door lock.

"Welcome, Mr. Sands," a gentle voice said.

"Who is that?" Harper asked. "I thought you said no one would be here on a weekend!"

"It's just a robotic voice generator." Dick grinned. "You don't see anyone else parked in here do you?"

....

Yao was watching their arrival until they slid into the parking area. He could still hear every word, and now he knew they were alone. Soon they would be more alone than they thought.

CHAPTER 31

Jack had just stepped off the elevator on the 7th floor to continue his rounds when he heard sniffles and cries coming from behind the chairs. It was Suzy.

"I should be the one crying," Jack said. "You're the one who stood me up!" He realized that his silly comment was untimely when he saw her eyes.

Suzy looked up, her eyes redder than her face. She heaved uncontrollably, trying to push out words. "Dr. Wade, I am so sorry." She buried her head in her hands, unable to control herself.

"It's okay." Jack sat beside her, careful not to pull too close. "Can you talk?" His voice was paternal, soothing but strong.

She was alone, sitting on the floor in a corner next to the south window. Jack waited for her to speak. It took a while.

"Liz... Lizzie!" she stammered, her syllables staccato. "She died!"

Jack waited. He had learned that patience brings more information than questions.

Suzy lifted her eyes again, almost hopeful. She searched his eyes, desperate almost for someone to care. "I had visited her several times recently." Her words were more understandable now. "She was paralyzed and I had given her and her mother and grandmother information on treatments, treatments that might cure her."

Again she sobbed. All she could think about was last night. All she could see in her mind was Li Zhang. Master

141

Li had come to her apartment unannounced, which wasn't uncommon. He often showed up for his pleasure. Maybe it started that way last night. He had his own key and let himself in while she was showering. When she stepped out of the shower, he was sitting, perched like a leopard. He wore a rage she had never seen before.

He must have had time to look at her computer and probably at a lot of her work. He must have seen that Suzy had made connections in China with spinal specialists who were helping her over the Internet with her work, specialists who were restoring paralyzed patients back home. He must have seen that Suzy had implanted a physiologic monitor under Lizzie's skin. She had developed the monitor but it required one of Lee's clips to transmit information to China.

She didn't care about the belt. He had hit her before. She could forget about him tightening the belt around her throat, relaxing it, tightening it, waiting for her to pass out and then slapping her back into consciousness. The whips of the belt and the strangulation were simply temporary. Though she hoped the belt would stay in place that she would never wake up, the night went on.

Suzy understood pain. Pain was an escape. It was a friend. She deserved so much worse. Lizzie's mother and grandmother both knew pain, too. Lizzie's mother and grandmother had shared their lives with Suzy for they saw the same emptiness in her that they had once known. Lizzie's mother left town when she was 14, ran out on her mother. She had rebelled against Hattie and her strict rules and her Jesus. She wanted to have fun, to run her own life. She found her "fun" as a crack whore. She never understood love until her first daughter was stolen by a child trafficker. Then she understood love and shattered love and how pain can feel good when it is deserved. She tried to kill herself, first with drugs and then with a knife. The first was painless and the second was painful but not painful enough. Pain was her friend calling upon her to pay her debt for her past. She hoped for it, sought it out and relished in it. Then she had Lizzie. Then she understood that pain wasn't the answer for the past and that love was the answer for the future, that the only hope for love and for the future was through forgiveness. That's when she returned to Tuscaloosa, to her mother, to even more.

Lizzie's mother and grandmother studied the Bible, read stories to Lizzie, and laughed with a child who could only smile. They became family to Suzy. Suzy had learned about someone she had never known, someone who was concealed in China and hidden from her until Lizzie in Room 707. Suzy had found that pain didn't have to be a crutch.

Suzy learned about a man who was beaten more than she had ever dreamed. She learned about a man who didn't deserve the beatings but wanted to be beaten and killed to take away her pain and the pain of everyone who has ever been born.

Suzy did her work every day. She did her studies. She did her research. She performed her duties at the hospital. But her life came from Room 707, from Lizzie and her mother and Hattie...

Suzy wept. She didn't weep because of the pain that Lee Zhang dealt her. She didn't weep because he raped her through the night as he had done so many times before. She didn't weep because Lee threatened to cut her into pieces with surgical scissors that he paraded in front of her eyes. She didn't even weep when he spread her legs apart, proud of the blood he had caused. She didn't weep when he snipped her clitoris off and then put it in his mouth, chewing it like a stale piece of gum.

She didn't weep for fear that Lee would do what he promised. She could care less if she was shipped back to China, back to Yao. Suzy wept because the surgical scissors she had seen last night, the surgical scissors she had felt last night, had been laid at the foot of Lizzie's bed. The ventilator tubing was sliced cleanly. Lizzie was perfectly still when Suzy walked into the room. The ventilator was pushing air into the room but not into Lizzie. Lizzie's last thought probably wasn't that she couldn't move, that she couldn't breathe, that she was going to die. She must have wondered why her mother simply watched with a blank stare.

Lizzie didn't know that a dart had hit her mother as she rested. Her mother woke but couldn't move. All her mother could do was watch Lee cut the tubing to her baby's lungs, watch her baby take her last breath even as she took her own last breath. What would Hattie think when she returned to find her two loves were gone. If only Hattie had been there to die as well.

Suzy kept looking at Jack. Gradually, the visions of Lee faded and she saw familiar eyes, Lizzie's mother's eyes and Hattie's eyes, eyes that care and soothe like balm. "I have done terrible things." Her tears were gone.

Jack started to say, "Like standing me up for dinner?" But he could tell that this was a time to listen. He carefully drew close to her, wrapping his arm around her. She buckled in his grasp, drawing into a ball and letting him give warmth to her, letting him touch her as she had never been touched before, with concern rather than desire.

Jack thought he had forgotten the touch of his wife. He remembered how she bathed in his arms in her last days when the leukemia had drained her of all energy and sucked away her color and her strength. But when Jack held her and she felt his strength and his spirit, it was nourishment for them both. He spent years trying to remember her touch, her smell, her surrender. Even her last breath was precious. Her last sigh was not one of death but of gratitude.

As Jack held Suzy, he felt her fear. Shivers traveled through her and into him. He pulled at them, tugging for them, hoping with all of his might to absorb her distress. Slowly the sobs and the shaking slowed, then stopped.

"Code Blue. Room 707!" the overhead speaker blasted.

Nurses and aides rushed down the hall toward 707. Two pushed a crash cart. Others were on their cells.

"Don't move," Jack whispered to Suzy. "I have to give a hand down the hall." He wiped her brow, then her forehead. "Don't leave. I'll be back."

Jack ran down the hall, following the crowd. Stepping in the room, he took quick assessment. The crew had placed a plastic sled under Lizzie, a frail black girl with a tracheostomy. Obviously, the girl was unable to breathe on her own, requiring a tube through her neck to provide artificial breathing. One nurse was providing breaths to her. Another male nurse was pushing on her chest, trying to squeeze blood through her body. Jack felt her groin, searching for a pulse in the femoral artery. She was cold. An EKG was hooked up. Her rhythm was totally flat.

Lizzie's mother was on the floor, which was firm enough that she didn't need anything under her. Someone pounded her chest while another placed a mouthpiece on her, providing breaths connected to an oxygen tank. Jack felt for a pulse. Nothing.

Medicines and intravenous lines were flying into their veins while the chest compressions and artificial breathing proceeded. Neither the girl nor her mother developed any cardiac activity. No shocking was necessary. They were dead and had been for some time.

After 10 minutes of pounding and pushing, Jack pronounced. "That's it...they're gone."

He noticed an unusual cut on the girl's neck below the tracheostomy, the blood already dry. Since they were on the neurosurgery floor and the girl had a tracheostomy, he surmised that the level of the cut was probably where her spinal injury had occurred, but it wasn't the mark of an injury. It was the wound of something that had been removed from her neck.

He looked at the woman on the ground. Except for a bruise on her neck, there were no other external signs of injury.

The room had already emptied as Jack left. He started to chart the events of the code when he saw the product representative for the Yida clip run from the waiting room where he had left Suzy. He knew Lee but had never seen him on the floor. There were hospital rules against reps roaming the halls without authorization.

He walked quickly to the entry.

"Shit!" He screamed back at the nursing station he had left, "I need help, right now."

Suzy was slumped over, blood squirting in bursts out of her neck. Trauma surgery and stab wounds to the neck were second nature to Jack. He had managed these wounds on a weekly basis, but he stopped, blank and horrified for a moment, thoughtless. Then he pushed his right hand on Suzy's neck, threw her over his shoulder, and ran toward the stairwell.

"Call the Operating Room and tell them I'm on my way. They need to prepare for a carotid artery injury."

Jack took the steps two at a time, Suzy limp on his shoulder. His right hand never moved, maintaining pressure on her injury. He could still feel a weak pulse under his grasp.

Breaking through the second floor door, he bolted for the OR.

"What room?" Jack yelled as he exploded into the operating arena.

"Room 9," the nurse at the front desk said, following him to the room.

A crew was waiting as Jack crashed through the swinging doors. He flipped Suzy onto the operating table, his right hand sturdy in its position.

"What happened?" the anesthesiologist asked.

"I'm not exactly sure, but it looks like a stab wound to her carotid."

"We'll do a rapid sequence induction for intubation," she said. "Hopefully her blood pressure can take it and she won't aspirate."

Quan was next in the room. He didn't have to ask questions. Pulling a kit from the head of the table, he slid IV's into Suzy's arms. As the medicines followed and Quan pushed the breathing tube into Suzy's throat, Jack poured antiseptic over and around his hand.

"Give me a gown and gloves!"

"Aren't you going to go scrub?" one of the techs asked.

"Yeah. I'll go scrub for five minutes and then figure out if there's an ounce of blood left in this girl." He waved at the scrub nurse. "Just give me a gown."

Exchanging one hand for the other, the nurse helped Jack maneuver the gown, his pressure never leaving Suzy's neck. Then one hand at a time his hands flew into sterile gloves.

"Give me some more paint." He doused her neck once more with antiseptic and draped Suzy with a prefabricated apron, a small hole cut out for an isolated injury.

Another scrub tech positioned himself opposite Jack at the table, adjusting the lights to shine on the surgical site.

Jack's left hand held its position as his scalpel parted Suzy's skin. He used the electrocautery to burn bleeding vessels, preventing blood from welling in the wound and obscuring his vision. He knew that a moment of delay in cases like this could work for good or for bad.

He continued with his cautery pencil, burning through the tissue layer by layer. Suzy's fat under her skin was white instead of the typical hay yellow, indicating her blood count was low.

"Have you called for blood? Just get O negative and start with two units. Stay two ahead at all times." He assumed the anesthesia team would have already done this, but in emergencies the simplest of actions are often forgotten.

"Do you have a blood pressure?" Jack could feel a thready pulse under his hand, Suzy's heart racing to compensate for the blood loss. He knew that she had a chance as long as her body was reacting to the blood loss with a rapid heart rate. If he felt the heart slow and weaken, Suzy might not survive.

His Bovie, the electrocautery unit, flashed as it continued its descent. The platysma was the next level, a thin muscle that made her neck jerk as he burned through it. Jack took a retractor from the nearby tray of instruments and spread the thin layer of muscle widely.

Continuing with his Bovie, he separated the flimsy film between the sternocleidomastoid muscle, the oblique muscle traveling from the center-base of the neck to the back of the ear, and Suzy's trachea. The tissue was stained with blood from her injury, making the passage difficult.

As he placed a second retractor, the carotid artery came into view. The surrounding tissue was thickened with clay-like redness from the bleeding into the tissue, but the artery itself was glistening white, the appearance of a nonsmoker and healthy young person.

"Vascular clamp." Jack reached for the metal clamp, a gentle device that squeezes down on blood vessels without injuring them. He placed one below and one above the injury.

"Five-O!" The scrub nurse popped a needle carrier load with thin blue nylon into his hand. He knew that the repair had to be fast. Without delivering blood thinner, the blood inside of Suzy's carotid artery could clot, leading to a certain stroke. But he didn't want to risk additional blood loss by delivering the blood thinner.

The needle carrier whipped stitches into the vessel mechanically as Jack's hands coordinated the maneuvers. In less than a minute, he removed the clamp closest to Suzy's brain, making sure there was back-bleeding and no clot. Then he opened the other clamp, allowing forward flow of blood and washing out any other source of clot. Then, tightening the suture, the repair was completed.

Jack relaxed a bit, his job mostly completed. Now it was up to the anesthesiologist to replenish lost blood and support her blood pressure with saline fluid and medicines. He knew that Suzy would survive at this point, but would her brain function? Had the injury slowed blood flow to her brain long enough to cause permanent damage?

"Dr. Wade, are you sure you've got the bleeding under control?" the anesthetist asked.

"Why?"

"The blood pressure isn't responding. Her blood pressure keeps falling. We keep giving blood and fluid, but every time we stop, the pressure drops. Could there be another injury somewhere?"

The drape on Suzy hid everything except her neck. Removing it at this point would lead to infection. But if she was still bleeding, he had to identify the source.

"Two-O Spider." It only took a moment to zip Suzy's neck wound closed. The inner layer he closed with absorbable Spider suture, and then he snapped staples into her skin.

Suzy's blood-soaked clothes were still on, limiting Jack's exam. "Shears!" He took heavy scissors from the scrub tech, slashing her shirt and pulling it from her chest. The circulating nurse pulled her jeans off.

Suzy lay on the table fully exposed, a spectacle of bruises, scars, and blood. Her panties were crusted with blood from the night before, her recent belt injuries only streaks of red on blue.

"My God," the circulator gasped. "She could be bleeding from anywhere with all of those wounds."

"Stethoscope!" Jack reached for the rubber tubing hanging from the anesthetist's neck. He listened to both sides of her chest, then her abdomen. There were no breath sounds on the left side, the side of Suzy's neck wound.

"Whoever did this knew what they were doing," he thought. The knife wound in the carotid artery was a distracter, appearing to be the major injury. Jack had seen similar injuries in his training, usually on the victims of professional hits.

"Twenty-eight chest tube with a trocar." Jack took a plastic tube from the scrub nurse. With the metal spike in the middle, he punched the tube into Suzy's chest. Immediately, a flood of blood flowed through the tube as he hooked it up to a drainage system.

"Lateral decubitus position." Jack was already turning her on her side as the circulators assisted.

"You need a thoracotomy tray. We've probably got an aortic or subclavian injury!" He was painting her chest with antiseptic as the anesthesia team prepared for action.

With the release of blood from Suzy's chest, she could bleed more easily inside and the pressure released. They were calling for blood, fresh frozen plasma and platelets. They expected considerable blood loss and needed clotting factors to assist Suzy's clotting ability.

As Jack prepped her left side, her back was exposed as well. Carved into her back was a Chinese character that looked like a teepee with a line through it and a "J" below it. Quan saw it as Jack did. Though Korean, he knew Chinese as well. "It's Chinese for "Li." It looks like a brand. Chinese prostitutes are often branded by their pimps."

Jack was busy draping Suzy again. This time half of her body was exposed, her entire left side facing upward.

"Scalpel." Jack slit Suzy from under her breast to her back, this time leaving the renegade bleeders free to ooze.

"Turn the Bovie up, 75 and 75." The cautery sparked with extra power as it slid through the latissimus dorsi, the major muscle of the back, and the serratus anterior, it's partner in front.

"Get ready. We're gonna lose some blood," Jack warned the team above.

He zipped through the fifth and sixth rib, and blood poured out of Suzy as he spread her ribs with a retractor. Inside, Suzy's lungs were billowing into the cavity, obscuring Jack's view.

"Sponge stick." He placed a long clamp holding a sponge on the tip into Suzy's chest. He transferred the instrument to his assistant, exposing the arch of Suzy's aorta.

The largest artery in Suzy's body arched at the top of her chest, branching into vessels feeding her arms and brain then coursing downward through the chest and diaphragm and into the abdomen. At the top of her chest, he could see where the knife had slipped into her chest, the first wound before Suzy's carotid was stabbed.

The injury to her aorta had missed its mark by a millimeter. The aorta was squirting continuously into her chest, but it was a grazing blow with only a minimal injury. If the blade had been angled toward her back, Suzy never would have made it to the OR

"Pledgetted 3.0." Jack knew that his needle passes had to be perfect. If his repair wasn't perfect, her entire aorta would tear apart.

With a felt strip on each side of the knife wound, Jack gently tightened the suture, allowing the felt strips to kiss the tissue together, immediately stopping Suzy's blood loss.

"That did it," Quan bellowed from above. "The pressure looks good; heart rate is stable."

"I just hope her brain is okay," Jack responded.

Until now, Jack had been acting on reflex. His training and instincts had been sharpened through countless emergencies and he was able to suppress any fear, insecurity, or uncertainty. In an emergency, equanimity was the premier tool. During his training, he read, over and over, an address that Sir William Osler gave at the University of Pennsylvania in 1889. Sir William had stressed the importance of imperturbability, of maintaining presence of mind and clear judgment under all circumstances. Osler also stressed the importance of detachment. Osler maintained that a physician couldn't be a finished product unless he or she remained emotionally neutral. Jack understood all that completely, but now that Suzy's injuries were repaired what was left was a bright eyed, beautiful, intelligent girl who had suffered more than he could imagine. The blood loss and low blood pressure could leave her brain dead or the shock could lead to total organ collapse and death. He felt his equanimity, his emotional neutrality, slip away.

When he left her on the 7th floor, he left for duty, to help two people he didn't know who, as it turned out, were already dead. He could have stayed with her. If he had, none of this would have happened. Emotions now consumed him. He had similar feelings for her as his deceased wife, an attachment of spirit that transcends understanding. Now he not only regretted abandoning her on the floor but was enraged at whoever had hurt her. He was also fearful that she wouldn't recover and felt grief for what she must have endured.

Each pass of the needle through Suzy's muscle was painful to Jack. When his wife had suffered from leukemia, each shot and each needle stick gave him chills and he wished the pain could be his. It was the same now. He acted like he was fine, but Suzy did not represent an operation now, procedures to follow, problems to solve. Hers was a torn body, a brokenness that sutures couldn't restore.

CHAPTER 32

Dick, holed up in his lab, was making progress. Certain that the aluminum encasement of the lab would block any signal from the clip, he labored tirelessly and fearlessly.

Frank was asleep in the media room. It had been a long 24 hours. He was finally able to relax. The shower had washed away most of his blood and grime, and Grant had sewn his thumb together, delivering a long acting anesthetic to help dull his pain.

Luckily Sand's had an infirmary. Being isolated in the marshlands of Mobile County presented unique problems. Early after opening business it became clear that a fully stocked medical area was necessary. Copperheads, cotton mouths, and a variety of rattlesnakes had shared venom with employees. Similarly, black widows and brown recluse spiders were frequent visitors. One employee had been attacked by a black bear when she got too close to its cub. There had even been stories of seeing a panther in the marshes one day.

Grant and Harper had awakened early, partly out of habit but mostly from worry. The coffee tasted good and was a starter for them both. Sand's was a no-smoking facility, and so they went outside for Harper to light up. The marsh had its own character, especially before dawn, and they listened to the constant whistles and squeaks that were interrupted occasionally by the croak of bull frogs, the hoot of an owl, or the scream of a coyote.

"How long can this take?" Harper took a long drag, the red of his cigarette lingering.

"Who knows?" Grant was still apprehensive, looking and listening for any sign of trouble.

"Did Dick say he was getting anywhere when you went in to his lab."

Grant scanned the shadows fully before speaking. "I really don't understand communications that well, so what I say might not be fully accurate." A fish splashed in the water to their left.

"Dick explained that communications had simply exploded in the last few years. What was impossible a few years ago is now old technology. Wiretapping is still necessary, but methods are different." He watched the flight of a plane, even suspicious of it.

He continued. "Surveillance, counter-intelligence, and counter-counter-intelligence have had limitations in the past. Since all bugs are based on wavelengths, then bugging devices can use any wavelength between DC and light. Apparently, years ago there were 3,500 bugging frequencies used around the world. But now, according to Dick, an unlimited number of frequencies can be used for bugging."

Harper sucked on his cigarette. "I know a bit about this stuff. I'm a trooper and we don't bug people, but we have to be careful it doesn't happen to us."

"Okay, so nowadays acoustic, optical with visible or invisible light, and radiofrequency bugs anywhere from three kilohertz to three terahertz can be used. It used to be, when I studied physics, that electromagnetic radiation couldn't be measured in the sub-millimeter bands. Now the terahertz waves are able to work, even in highly magnetic fields."

The woods were waking, the creatures of the area preparing for the first rays of sunlight. Birds started to chirp, and rustling in the underbrush became louder.

Grant said, "The sub-millimeter bands were considered useful at high altitudes, like between satellites or aircraft to satellites, but not in the low atmosphere. Water vapor causes adsorption of the signals and it hasn't been practical.

"Things are different now, though. I remember back in 2012 when a team at the Tokyo Institute of Technology developed a resonant tunneling diode that produced waves in the terahertz range. That transmission allowed data transfer to be 20 times faster than the Wi-Fi of the time."

"You've lost me now." Harper crushed his spent butt. "What you're saying is that somebody can monitor us, like maybe through that clip you've been talking about, and nobody can detect that it is transmitting."

"That's basically it. Plus, there would be an unlimited number of wavelengths that could be monitored. Basically everyone in the world could have their own personal frequency, a bug of his own."

"So, what is he trying to figure out in there?"

"He's hoping to find the wavelength fingerprint of that microdot for one thing. He's also trying to process the material in the dot. He's trying to make some kind of connection between the clip, the dot, and whatever agency or company is using it."

"Shit. That could take forever. Even if he was Einstein, and I'm not sure he ain't, he'd still need the CIA and the Pentagon to figure all that shit out."

"Well, he told me he'd already figured out the band. He was working on the encryption."

"Encryption?" Harper blasted. "What the fuck are you talking about?"

"You know about encryption." Grant chuckled. "Everything you send through the Internet now is encrypted. It has been for a few years. It is simply an algorithmic scheme that codes messages or conversations and prevents others from listening in on your frequency or reading your messages."

"This is more fucked than I thought." Harper lit another cigarette. "We've got a fucking Big Bang scientist in a laboratory in the middle of the Alabama Amazon trying to solve the riddles of the universe. You and your buddy were almost killed by fuckers who are using Martian technology. We have no idea what fucking planet they came from and can't ask for help because the aliens who are after us might be us!" He took two long drags, coughed, spat, and continued. "I've got a fucking gun. You've got a car. Let's go get the other two and go to the state troopers office and let them know what we know. Our guys aren't fucking Martians and we'll be a hell of a lot safer around them than out here in the middle of nowhere."

The lights in Sand's suddenly turned off. "Must be the daylight trip switch to save electricity," Grant thought. At that moment another red dot appeared on Harper's forehead, just above the embers of his cigarette.

There was no sound, no flash, no Hollywood tracer. Harper's head simply exploded in front of Grant.

The laser was now tracking him. Grant hit the ground as he felt the vacuum and heard the whizz of a shot that blew by his right temple. He jumped to his feet and started to run, but he tripped and fell as another bullet zipped past his forehead. This time he caught the ground squarely and catapulted to the garage. He could tell that the shots had come from his left, possibly from the far end of the plant, maybe even from the other side of the river.

When he reached the garage, another shot ripped the concrete off the wall to his left. He turned toward the right, ready to fly back through the door, but it was too dark to identify the entry. Then a flashlight inside illuminated the doorway. He didn't have far to go but the shots were coming from a different angle now.

He squatted beside his car, which was parked 10 yards from the entrance. Then he heard a Ducati engine.

The flashlight at the entrance grew brighter as the door opened.

"Someone's shooting out here. Be careful."

It was too late. Frank stood at the door. Swaying in a night robe with "Sand's" printed on it that he had found to replace his clothing, the flashlight crashed to the ground as Frank's chest opened up. He looked down, dropped to his knees, and fell forward, half in and half out of the door.

The Ducati roared around the corner as Grant raced in the door. He pulled Frank back inside and slammed the door. The bolt clicked shut as the motorcycle hit the door.

The Ducati was no match for the reinforced steel. The acceleration of the cycle was too powerful and the stop too abrupt. The bike accordioned and sent a rod through the rider's chest.

"Dick! Are you alright?" Grant yelled, groping for Frank's face. The flashlight had fallen out of his hand outside, leaving Grant in the pitch black inside.

"Where are you?" Dick's voice was far away.

"At the entrance. The guys on motorcycles are here. They shot Harper, and I'm pretty sure Frank's gone, too." He found Frank's head in the dark and traced it to his neck. There was no pulse. He felt lower. Frank's chest was gurgling. Grant had heard and felt this before. The bullet had ripped through Frank's lungs and heart, leaving them useless, blood dripping into a pulverized cavity.

"Follow my voice, Grant." Dick was loud but not frantic.

"Coming..." He heard other cycles outside as he followed Dick's voice.

"I'm not far away. Just keep following my voice."

"I thought this plant was run on a generator. How did the power go off if everything is self-contained here?"

"The generator is in a separate building behind us. Someone must have cut the line." Dick stayed where he was, waiting for Grant to reach him.

The morning's first light was finding the corridors inside, and Grant could see Dick's outline now. He ran to his side. "Harper and Frank are dead. Harper had a gun but he's outside on the pavement. Are there weapons in here?"

"No. Strictly forbidden. The new federal laws restrict businesses from having any firearms inside."

"I don't give a shit if it's the FBI, CIA, or the pentagon. I'm calling 911 to notify the local police. Where's a phone?" Grant searched the dimly lit halls for a phone.

"Come on in here." Dick opened a door to his left, the one he had been standing by.

"There should be a flashlight on the wall to your right."

Grant entered the room and groped the hardwood inch by inch. Then he expanded his search, making broad sweeps with his arms and hands. "Here it is." He pulled a heavy-duty light from the wall and switched it on.

There were a number of telephones in the room. He picked up the closest one. No signal. One by one he picked receivers and realized they were all dead.

"I figured they'd be out. I can't even get cell phone reception." Dick was still standing at the doorway, looking outside for any motion. "Whoever is out there has pretty high-tech gear. They must be blocking signals somehow."

"Do you have the clip?"

"Well, in a manner of speaking!" Dick returned.

"C'mon, Dick. This isn't the time to be fuckin' with me."

"Well the dot on the clip is definitely a transmitter of some kind. I've never seen anything like it. It looks like it has the ability to reflect or bounce sound to a receiver. There must be a highly sophisticated and powerful satellite up there that can pull out the sound, encrypt it, and send it back to whoever is listening in."

"So we still don't know who's behind this," Grant barked.

Ting, ting, ting. They looked down the hall to their right. The morning sun reflected off the Xuanlong improved Type 93 assault rifle. One of the motorcyclists was firing into the window, aiming directly at them. The 5.56 millimeter rounds cracked into the glass, splintering but not penetrating the multilayered polycarbonate glass.

Grant ducked back into the office, leaving Dick in the hall. "He can shoot all day and he won't get through that glass," Dick said, unmoved. "That glass can take more than Kevlar. It's the newest line against hurricanes, tornados, and bastards with guns."

The Xuanlong emptied 36 rounds into the glass, leaving a pattern of webs. The biker stood in disbelief, looking through the buckled glass at Dick, who walked toward the window. He grinned as he walked, returning a glare of superiority.

"All we have to do is wait them out. Tomorrow there will be a fleet of workers here. Unless...!" He stopped, turning back to Grant.

"Unless what?" Grant urged.

"Unless the troopers who were supposed to be following us see what's going on and unless your wife or my parents get concerned and let someone know."

"Don't count on my wife. I called her before I left and told her not to expect me for a day or so. As far as she knows, I'm in the OR."

Grant crept out of the side room and joined Dick. The biker was reloading his weapon. The morning sun was stronger now, filling the halls with light. The air conditioner was off, leaving the air stuffy, humid and warm. Sweat was already beading on them.

"What I did discover on that clip is that the dot and the stapler were manufactured in the same location. Welding had been performed. There wasn't a glue to bond the dot to the clip. They were actually coalesced through some process that joined them. They work together, maybe allowing the clip itself to act as an antenna. But the clip was made in China! If I had to guess, those are Chinese under the face masks." Dick was looking straight ahead, staring down the shooter who was advancing more toward the window.

Grant stayed back. "What are you doing?"

"I want to get a good look at that guy." Dick marched forward, confident that his father's construction was reliable.

Another burst of bullets pounded the glass but fell away, impotent. Dick was at the window now. He fired a universal finger at the shooter.

"Are you crazy!" Grant yelled from the hall.

The shooter stood still in full body gear, a bandanna and helmet, his rifle aiming directly at Dick. Then he slung the weapon over his shoulder, the sling fitting snugly. With a slow stroke, he straightened his hand and slid his hand over his throat, making a slicing gesture. Next he pointed at himself, then Dick. He walked to the left, out of sight.

It was already a sauna inside. The day had barely begun, but without air movement the retained heat of the building did quick work.

Dick and Grant took different posts. Dick stayed at his window while Grant moved to the front of the building.

"Do you see any of them?" Dick yelled.

"Two."

"Didn't you say there were three in the woods when they attacked you?" Dick hurried to Grant's side of the building.

"I don't know what happened to the one who tried to blow through the door." He wiped his brow. "He could have died in the crash. He was going pretty damn fast."

"Do you think it's safe to open the garage and see if the other one is out there?" Grant asked.

"Unfortunately, there's no way to get a view of that area without opening the door. Dad didn't want the parking area disturbing the view from inside. But if someone's out there waiting for us, it would be bad."

....

The heat was really building inside, and Dick and Grant were dripping. It had been some time since they'd seen the bikers. Two had disappeared into the generator annex, which was the last time they were seen.

Suddenly, the labored churn of a generator thumped in the background, bringing the first movement of air in hours. Instead of air-conditioned coolness, however, the flow was suffocating, musty at first and then thick with dust and humidity.

"The generator is working again, so why don't the lights come on?" Grant searched for a view of the bikers. He was glad he'd worn blue jeans, a T-shirt and tennis shoes to the hospital last night when he returned. They had served him well through the night. But now they were pasty from sweat and dirt from his romp in the woods last night.

"They can control the electricity and a lot more from the generator room." Dick sniffed the air. "These guys aren't your average hit men."

"What now?" Grant sniffed, also. The smoke trickled in at first, bringing the familiar ashen dryness, but it also carried a pool-water pungency. "Smells like chlorine."

"That's what I thought. Our generator runs off of hydrolysis. Hydrogen is the energy source but the brine water around us acts as a perfect substrate for the hydrogen. Salt in the brine is made of sodium and chloride. When the reaction takes place between water and salt, hydrogen and chlorine gas are formed." Dick paused. "We usually use the chlorine to produce polycarbonates, polyurethanes, silicones. and thermoplastic polymers, but..."

"Yeah, I get it." Grant knew his chemistry and history. "Chlorine gas. They're recirculating the chlorine gas like in the concentration camps. The chlorine turns into hydrochloric acid in our lungs, melting us from the inside out."

"You've got it. We're gonna have to get out of here," Dick snapped.

"Is there any way to turn the vents off in certain areas of the building?" Grant asked, hopefully.

"All of that is centrally controlled so that there is uniform distribution throughout the plant. The mechanism is in the building with the generator."

"Check your cell phone again. See if you get any signal!"

"Dead."

The vents were active now, blowing hot air in waves. The dust swirled around them, carrying the sour gas.

"This is bad." Grant wiped his eyes, the biting acid drawing streams of tears, and his nose ran furiously.

"Come here." Dick ducked into a bathroom and pulled cloth towels from the racks. "Soak this in water."

Grant turned on the faucet. No water. "They must have turned off the water supply."

"Piss on it, then, and start breathing through the towel." He saw Grant's surprise. "It's how they avoided poisoning in the war. The urea binds the chlorine. It will buy us a little time. We've got to get out of here quickly, though. The chlorine is heavier than air and will fill the lower floors first."

Grant's eyes blistered with the caustic haze that was growing denser and denser. His lungs wheezed, trying to pull air through the cloth. They had urinated on the cloth, but it just made breathing thicker. Dick's eyes were closed, the cloth pressed tightly to his face, his breaths slow and deliberate.

"Are you thinking, praying, or giving up?" Grant was looking down both sides of the hall, wondering where the bikers were.

"Thinking and praying. I never give up." He grabbed Grant's scrub shirt, pulling him close. "No matter what happens, I want to thank you for saving my father. Now, you've got to trust me. We have only one chance to get out of here!"

All Grant could think of now was Carol, Ree, and Beth. He had left home, like so many nights before, ready to face challenges but never once thinking his life might be at stake. He had operated on countless AIDS patients, been soaked in the blood of patients with hepatitis, and his hands bore scars from needles and scalpels carrying viruses or bacteria. He had been sprayed with pus, feces, and blood in his eyes, even in the mouth. He had wrestled guns and knives from thugs in the emergency room. But he had never considered that any of these threats could really end his life. Even with his appendectomy, malignant hyperthermia, and assault...

Now, the acid was melting him and the heat suffocating him. The bikers were waiting to shoot him or slit his throat if he tried to escape the toxic building, but his only thought was the time he had wasted, times he'd returned to the hospital instead of to his daughter's rooms. Through the acid, he tasted Carol's lips and smelled her hair, her neck. In only a few minutes, if he lived, he knew his eyes would be burned beyond repair, the corneas blistered and clouded and his eyelids permanently open from structural damage. Even if he survived, he would never see his family again. His breathing came harder and harder, as much from the reality of his situation as the toxic vapors.

CHAPTER 33

When Yao sent the Tiger on a mission, he never worried about the outcome. The Tiger had no trouble making it through the terminal at the Hartsfield-Jackson Atlanta International Airport. He had made the trip several times before and his razor-sharp Beidao polymer knives had never been seen during airport screenings. Even if they had been seized, however, his diplomatic immunity would protect him. He carried the knives as much as an act of defiance of the law and contempt for those who tried to uphold them as a need to have them. Every part of his body was a weapon. He only used the blades for enjoyment.

Bao Chan, who was working on a neuroscience project at Emory when he received the call, had met him at the airport. His postdoctoral work could wait when it came to Yao. Buying a Suzuki Hayabusa was a new experience for the 25 year-old nationalist who lived in an apartment with three other students and ate rice with vegetables every day. Paying cash made him feel important and plugged into the mission. He proudly took the Tiger's suitcase to his apartment for safe keeping. He knew that the Tiger had business that required he travel light, and so he didn't ask questions. The answers could be dangerous. He knew that the Tiger always showed up with a suitcase and carried the suitcase back to China untouched.

The wind whistled over the Tiger's head as he watched cars behind him disappear like insects. Zero to sixty in under three seconds made policemen and state troopers a joke. Even if they saw him, and even if they could catch up to him, he would escape off road if necessary.

"*Gǎibiàn jìhuà.*" Yao's voice was clear, even at 120 miles per hour. Nevertheless the Tiger slowed enough to hear the signal clearly. He was on the way to Mobile, but Yao calling with a change of plans was common.

"*Shénme shì xīn dìngdān!*" The Tiger asked for new orders.

"Everything is under control in Mobile. You need to go to Tuscaloosa. You are almost in Montgomery on 85. You need to take 65 north and then 82 north to Tuscaloosa. I'll let you know when you need to make turns. There are no policemen that I see." Yao's screen showed the Tiger zipping past cars, leaping forward on straightaways.

The Tiger's jaw tightened, not against the wind that clawed to pull him from the speeding bike but because he imagined his knuckles finding their target, a single blow below the sternum, the heart bouncing from his fingers to the backbone and back again. Perhaps he would have the time and privacy to use one of his blades that he had taken from his case, to watch blood spray from the neck to the wall, to watch a face turn from pink to pale, to see the final twitches of another *Móushā*.

CHAPTER 34

Church was a priority, and starting his rounds at 4:00 A.M. usually gave Jack time to make it to Sunday School and the 11:00 service. But he still had to rush through his rounds on Sunday, and today was no different. He had to see 20 patients, including five discharges and two new consults and place one central line for a patient in intensive care who needed an intravenous catheter under her collarbone.

However, instead of jumping into his car at 9:30 for a quick ride, he hurried to Intensive Care room 303 for his final patient. He would make up for church next week. Today he had other business. He had already spent an hour or so last night talking to policemen about the murders in Lizzie's room and the attempted murder or suicide of Suzy. He had more questions than answers at this point.

"She's doing fine, Dr. Wade," Blanche welcomed him as he approached. "Her breathing tube came out a couple of hours ago. The police were here asking questions, but she wouldn't tell them who did this. They left a little while ago. She told them she had no intention of filing charges."

Jack pulled the chart to check labs, x-ray reports, vital signs, and fluid shifts. "Looks like she's been very stable...anything else?"

Blanche winced, her typically stoic appearance twisted into confusion and revulsion. "Dr. Wade, have you seen her? I mean..." She gathered herself. "Have you really seen her?"

"I know she has a bunch of scars, yes."

"Dr. Wade, she doesn't just have scars. She's been mutilated, and recently." Blanche could hardly speak. "I've been nursing for 30 years, and I've worked on psych wards, but I've never seen anything like this."

"That's why I'm here, among other reasons."

"She couldn't have done all that to herself, to her privates." Again, her body shivered with her words.

"What are you talking about?" Jack asked cautiously.

"Dr. Wade, her clitoris was cut off, and recently." Blanche pushed her words out. "She has a brand on her labia that looks like some Chinese or Japanese writing."

Jack's face twisted into a grimace of anguish mixed with rage. Slowly he opened the door to Suzy's room. The light, drifting through the window, bounced from the floor to her face. Her skin was whiter than usual in the glare and from her blood loss. A tube exited her left chest and coiled into a plastic container that collected bloody drainage.

"Dr. Wade!" Her eyes brightened as he entered, then she sank back into a shell of shame.

"Hey, Suzy." He approached gently. "You're a tough girl." He shared a soft smile.

She tried to return a grin but simply stared back in disgrace. "Dr. Wade, thank you for saving my life. The nurse told me what happened." She felt the wound on her neck and reached for the incision on her chest. "I wish you hadn't wasted your time, however. I should have died."

Suzy began to weep, trying to conceal her tears with her hands, which shook as she held them over her reddened eyes.

"Suzy, you've got to trust me." He was beside her now, reaching for her hand.

Instinctively, she brushed his hand away, but then grabbed it and pulled it close to her chest. Her other hand joined the embrace, holding his with all of her strength.

She let go with her right hand and reached toward Jack's pocket, then pulled a pen from his Oxford cloth shirt and pointed to a piece of paper on the bedside table. Jack handed her the paper with a clipboard.

"I can't talk. They are listening!" Her hand trembled as she wrote.

Jack moved back slightly. Suzy's face was chalky, her pupils widening with every tremor. His rotation in psychiatry included managing paranoid schizophrenics and so he knew the classic signs: delusions, hearing things, feelings of persecution, suicidal thoughts. He had misjudged people before and now had to admit that perhaps Suzy had done these terrible things to herself and could be totally crazy. He held her hand tightly.

"Who is listening?" He wrote back.

Suzy tried to relax but her hands betrayed her. They tightened in spasms as he went to get more paper.

"I have a transmitter in my finger." She continued on paper, looking at the tension and tremors in front of her.

He had seen this exact sign of paranoid schizophrenia in some of his patients who thought that Martians had planted transmitters in them. Some thought that the government had put electrodes in their brains, controlling their thoughts. Some thought Big Brother had a telescope, watching every move they made.

She rolled her little finger toward him, palm up. A healed incision was barely visible at the base of her finger. Pointing to her fourth finger, a matching scar appeared.

"The more transmitters, the better the signal. I have four," she wrote before showing him her other hand. Two more incisions, and again her fourth and fifth fingers.

Jack shook his head in disbelief. He looked from the paper to Suzy, then back. "Who?????" he wrote.

"I don't really know! I just know they know everything I do and say!" Suzy's face now had enough blood to blush. She searched Jack's face for a sign of belief, anything to show that Jack was with her and didn't think she was crazy, or worse. She knew it was a risk, but at this point, she didn't care about herself. She finally wanted to be honest.

Jack's eyes betrayed him. Not that he didn't believe her. But, suddenly he understood more than he had dreamed.

"Who are you???" He returned.

"My name is Suzy Yuan, and I really am studying here in America. I really love America, but I have to perform certain duties for my boss as payment for being here." She looked up, expecting contempt.

Jack wiped her forehead, motioning for her to continue.

"I don't know everything. I just do what I am told." She paused again, looking up. Jack was dazed, silent. "I am supposed to go through the hospital, to every floor every day, and I have a sensor that goes off when it detects a frequency. My sensor registers the frequency and I am supposed to record the name of the patient with that frequency."

Jack's mind was racing. HIPPA violations. Hospital violations. Patient privacy violations. Suzy might be a victim in all this, but she would likely go to jail too.

"I don't know what is being done with the information. Every day I log it into my computer. I send it to www.yidatrack.com. All I know is that Li Zhang makes sure I do my work." She looked up again as Jack recognized the name. "He is a representative for the company, for Yida.

"He knows everything I say, everything I do, and everywhere I go. He is the one who tried to kill me." The pencil fell from her hand as she shook uncontrollably. Shivers took over her muscles. Her eyes widened and she looked toward the door and then the window and then scanned the room. She was filled with panic and relief mixed into one. She'd finally done it, finally told the truth, but now she was certain she would die.

Jack remained vacant, trying to absorb everything.

Suzy continued. "Do you know Li? He calls himself Lee." She spelled the name for Jack as her boss used it with Americans. "He works for a surgical staple company."

Jack nodded. Visions of Lee running from the waiting room on the 7th floor would never leave his memory.

"Do you believe me?" After Suzy wrote, she looked directly at Jack, waiting for signs.

Jack sighed. It was all too much, more than he wanted to hear and not enough at the same time. Her actions and her story were too bizarre not to doubt her, but he nodded in affirmation and scribbled on his own paper. "We have to let the police know!"

Suzy's eyes flashed and she shook her head violently. "Anyone I talk to will be killed." She scribbled furiously. "I shouldn't have told you. They will come after you if you say anything or if they suspect that you know!"

Jack remembered that Lee had looked him in the eye before he found Suzy, and his throat tightened as the power he had felt so often in the past surged through him. It was the combination of determination and courage that prepared him for every hit he delivered as a linebacker in college.

"So we just act like nothing happened?" Jack's brow rose at the prospect. That wasn't his style. He was ready for a fight.

"Please, yes!" Tears were streaming down her face as she wrote this. She had such relief that she had shared something of her torment with someone, with Jack, who was the only person she had ever felt comfortable with, the only one she wanted to believe in her.

Jack had always felt comfortable holding and touching patients. Hospital requirements now forced him to wear gowns and rubber gloves with any contact, which seemed to spoil the relationship between patient and physician. He understood the importance of infection control but detested the encroachment of rules on relationships. He pulled close to Suzy, her body covered only with an over-laundered thin gown. The chest tube in her left side tented the fabric, showing her breast. He pushed the tube closer to her side, shading her exposed skin, and slipped his arm under her back. Suzy curled toward him, ignoring the pain from her position. She felt his warmth, smelled his strength. She wondered what it would feel like to be kissed, to taste him, to hold him.

Jack was content to hold her, just to feel her. He had felt that way with Kate, but no one since. He was torn. Suzy made him feel peaceful, content simply next to her. He was content to remain silent, sharing silence, sharing himself—but there was also an inner storm.

Jack knew he wouldn't be able to obey Suzy's request. He would find a way to get at Lee, or at least to protect her, but for her safety at present and without more evidence, he would have to restrain himself. Thirty minutes by her side was enough to give them both the trust and energy to remain silent for now.

After a parting nod, he left Suzy with the first smile she had shared in years without fear or shame. Jack closed the door behind him, aware that Blanche had been careful to leave them alone for a while.

"Is she going to be okay?" Blanche asked when she joined him.

"I'm sure she will!" he reassured her with a thumbs up.

"Is there more here than surgeon and patient?" She had been around a while and knew Jack as well as she knew any of the surgeons. She had never seen him react to another patient like that.

"You're pretty clever, Blanche." He tried to deflect her gaze but it wasn't worth it. "She's really special to me. Take care of her."

Jack knew Blanche would watch her like a mother, and as long as she was in the Intensive Care, Suzy would be safe. But the energy inside him needed to be released. Sunday at Jim's Gym was the perfect place to blow off steam, to pump iron alone, to exercise to exhaustion and bring some focus to his scattered thoughts and emotions. His mind whirled as he left the unit, but he was aware enough of the motion to his left.

"Hey, Dr. Wade." Lee brushed against him, acting like he was avoiding a collision.

Jack recognized the voice, but when he met Lee's face, his feet turned to clay. It was too late. He never expected to see Lee again, and Lee saw his response. Not only his surprise and hesitation but fear. It was all he was looking for. Jack stood motionless but then realized that he had been hooked. He tried to recover but knew that this battle was over.

"Lee!" Jack tried his best to seem neutral and cordial, but he failed and he knew it. Lee acted totally innocent while Jack's face turned blood red.

"Is she okay?" Lee asked with a concerned brow.

"Who?" Jack asked instinctively. Then he realized how ridiculous his faux naiveté must sound.

"That girl." Lee's tone was caring and concerned. "I was running to find some help but saw you carrying her to the operating room."

Jack was used to this kind of banter. The last two years of medical school and residency were all about mind games. There is no way for a human being to perform as many tasks and remember as many facts as necessary, and so the key is honesty within the confines of the game. It is fine to *act* like you've done everything possible and studied everything as long as you don't *say* it. "Intern Poker" is a game to be won for losing means that the A's in high school, the all-nighters in college, and the fight get to the top in medical school could all be extinguished in one exchange. It only takes a moment during morning rounds to make or break a reputation, and Jack had sparred with the best.

"Oh, yeah." He regrouped. "I saw you last night before finding her." His voice returned from startled uncertainty to conversational. His feet found their traction again, allowing him to continue in a leisurely pace. "She's a lucky girl. If I hadn't found her when I did, she wouldn't be alive right now."

"It sounded awful. Someone tried to kill her?" Concern dripped from Lee's lips.

"I guess the word is out." Jack was able to look Lee in the eye now as he resumed his walk up the hall. "I wasn't sure, with HIPPA rules and regulations, what I could say. But if you know already, I guess I can talk. She must have tried to kill herself. She wouldn't talk to the policemen, and that usually means it's a gang thing or self-inflicted injury."

"My God." Lee recoiled. "That's awful."

"She's doing okay, but it looks like her mind is in worse shape than her body."

Lee's tone grew discernibly lighter. "She suffered brain damage?" He realized immediately that he sounded hopeful instead of caring.

"No. She is awake and alert, her cognitive function totally intact. But she looks like one of those self-mutilators." He struck his head, acting like he said something he shouldn't have. "Sorry, HIPPA rules again. I can't go there!"

"Well, everyone in the hospital thinks you're a hero, the DCH Superman," Lee said cheerfully. "I have to go back to the OR to check inventory. My work is never done."

Lee broke off, certain of what he must do.

CHAPTER 35

"Our only chance is this." Dick grabbed the scrambler from the R&D room.

Both he and Grant choked as they ran. The stench of urine on their faces and the sting in their eyes was almost unbearable, and waves of acid propelled by blistering heat surged through the vents, making their path just a blur, their corneas clouded with nipping tears.

"We're going up?" Grant coughed. He followed Dick obediently, racing up the stairs, the pungency less oppressive with each step.

"Don't talk. Just follow." Dick raced upward then threw open the roof latch, breaking into the freshness of pure air and the morning light but shaded from the sun, which hadn't cleared the trees.

They both gasped for air, their lungs pulling for life.

"Come on." Dick pulled Grant along the concrete surface to a bricked-in cubicle. The room was big enough for a dozen people, the air inside coated with detergent.

"Take off your clothes." Pulling a metal ring, Dick stood under a shower of water. He reached for another ring and pulled it. Grant was suddenly blasted with a similar spray.

The water burned at first, allowing the acid to moisturize and sink into their pores, but quickly the relief began.

"I thought they shut off the water supply," Grant said as the water bathed his eyes and flushed his entire body.

"They did. The water here is pumped and filtered like a well from the outside streams. We wanted to one-up OSHA and made our decontamination unit almost foolproof. The pump is powered by those solar panels." He pointed to the ceiling, which was transparent, the same bulletproof glass as the siding. Photovoltaic cells topped the glass like dominoes. "Even if the pump fails, water is stored in that cylinder for reserve."

Pulling another cord, Dick allowed the pipes above him to squirt blasts of liquid soap. The suds covered him quickly. He pulled a similar cord over Grant. They both washed and rinsed and repeated the cycle several times.

"Now wash your clothes. Quickly!" Dick's body still bristled from the sunburn of the acid, but his vision had returned and his lungs had recovered.

"Put this on." He pulled some tubes from a nearby closet. "It's Aloe, Bupivacaine, and a special epidermal growth enhancer we developed."

They rubbed the cream over their bodies, feeling the Bupivacaine work its magic as a topical anesthetic and soon they were free of the burning sensation.

"This, too." Dick squirted his eyes with drops from the cabinet as well. Grant followed his lead.

"Now put your clothes back on. We're gonna need 'em."

They pulled on the dripping clothes and soggy shoes and went back out on the roof. Dick carried the scrambler, a camouflaged 10 x 3 x 3 contraption that was part flashlight and part rifle scope. He carried it like a Star Trek phaser, aware of its potential.

"We've been working with Homeland Security on a new crystal for this baby," he said as he and Grant peered over the building's edge searching for the bikers.

The edge of the building erupted as 5.56-millimeter rounds tore into the concrete, powdering the edge, and the sound of two Xuanlongs blasted the morning air. The rounds started low and worked up, giving Grant time to duck under the wall. Dick wasn't so lucky. A single round clipped off the lower third of his left ear, but he was able to avoid the spray of other bullets as he joined Grant below the barrier.

"Shit! They know everything we're doing. Everywhere we are." Dick huddled down next to Grant.

Above, the Yaogan Weixing satellite hovered. The synthetic-aperture radar sensors with electro-optical digital imaging sent joy back to Yao. He hadn't expected the two Americans to make it this far, but he smiled as he watched them crouch. It wouldn't be long now. This was better than he had hope for. Assuming that they were dead inside the building, melted from acid, wasn't as fun, or as certain, as watching them suffer and die.

"They must be watching us, even listening to us." Dick shot a bird into the sky. "Fuck you!"

Yao's smile vanished and he shifted his head as if to avoid Dick's aim.

"One of us must be carrying a similar clip or..."

"Shit. Of course," Grant screamed. "I had surgery a few weeks ago. I'll bet I've got a fucking clip in me."

Dick flipped an "Of Course!" with his index finger and thumb united. "Let's stay quiet unless necessary!"

Yao's face tightened. The automatic translation hit him hard. "*Ràng nàxiē bùyào liǎn de.*" He spat into his microphone.

"Yes, sir," the one Dick had labeled Big Guy back in the woods responded. He knew when Yao yelled that there was a problem. Big Guy was already furious. He had wrapped his best friend, Monkey, in a body bag and dragged it into the woods. The Americans would pay for this. Monkey's neck was broken, and a pipe must have crushed through his chest the instant his neck broke. Even with his helmet, brains were dripping out of his ears when Big Guy found him in the garage. Now it was just he and Ghost.

"Climb up that tree," Big Guy grunted to Ghost as he pointed at a nearby tupelo. There were enough lower branches to make the climb possible. Perhaps at the right elevation, Ghost would have a shot at them.

Ghost nodded and ran to the tree. He climbed limb by limb like an acrobat, his Xuonlong strapped to his back. He could almost see the top of the building when a branch snapped. He didn't fall, but Dick heard and backed away from the ledge of the building in time to see Ghost, who had taken off his helmet but still wore the full motorcycle gear. He slithered up the tree, moving quicker and quicker with the more frequent branches.

Dick brought the scrambler to his eye, sighting in the Ghost. An earlier version had already found its place in skirmishes on the border and Iran. The spectrum of light emitting diodes on the head of the device only had to be directed at the Ghost's eyes to work. A laser spotter for daytime use allowed Dick to find his target. The laser itself could cause permanent blindness, so it automatically shut off when it found Ghost's retina, a requirement by international law. Dick pulled the trigger and the rainbow of light sunk into his eyes. No one knew how it worked, just that it worked, and every time. The synapses in Ghost's brain immediately scrambled, and the connections that maintained his coordination turned him into a nauseated jumble of vertigo.

He reached for a branch but the branch wasn't there. Everything was a mirage. His hand searched through the air but only found emptiness. His body followed, toppling from his perch. He held back a wave of nausea, but he was already lurching to the left, away from the body of the tree. Then his footing collapsed and he tumbled through the branches. He bounced from limb to limb until his head wedged between two branches and he came to an abrupt stop. His body convulsed for a moment or two, then was limp.

"What the Hell?" Grant watched his pale face turn blue, a hangman's death.

Yao couldn't see Ghost. The tree cover was too dense. "Where is he? He should have shot by now!" he hollered at Big Guy.

Big Guy had heard the crashing and saw Ghost fall to his death. He ran to the base of the tree and looked up at his only remaining friend, stiff and suspended out of reach, looking like a piece of meat on a fork.

"He's dead," Big Guy groaned as much to himself as to Yao.

Yao sat dumbfounded. Anger turned to alarm. He looked back at the rooftop, but it was too late. He had seen the scrambler work before but hadn't noticed these two had one until now.

Grant stood and wave on the edge of the building, ready to duck if necessary. "Hey!" he yelled as loud as he could.

Big Guy looked up as the laser turned off. Dick pulled the trigger and Big Guy staggered, then went down. He fell behind the tree, out of sight. Hallucinogenic colors marbled through his brain, leaving him drifting in a vapor of fantasy.

Yao realized what had happened now. He jumped out of his seat in disbelief. Big Guy was out of sight to him also. "*Nǐ hái hǎo ma?*" Yao hoped for "Yes, I'm okay!" But he just heard grunting.

"Okay, we don't have long. The effects of the scrambler vary. He could be down for several minutes or just a brief period. We've got to move," Dick yelled. He pulled Grant and they raced to the opposite side of the building. He pushed a lever and there was a squeaking brush of metal crashing below. The fire escape ladder pounded to a halt as the last segment reached the ground.

"You go." Dick pointed.

Grant jumped on the ladder and scrambled down, Dick following, keeping an eye around each side of the building. He thought, "The road is the only direct exit, but the closest stop is Lula's Café, too far to outrun a Ducati. Surely the bikers have their keys and didn't leave them in the cycles. Otherwise, we could make a break for one of them and we be off before Big Guy comes around. No. Too risky. Besides, he could catch us with his own motorcycle and machine gun. Our best option is to split up and take our chances in the wild."

They hit the ground quickly. Dick didn't know if the satellite could see them, but he assumed they could be heard and so he shared hand signals with Grant, then both took off on a sprint into the swamp. Dick ran upstream and Grant downstream. The river was low, typical for this time of year, and so swimming was an option, but running was the best choice for now.

....

Grant was a strong runner, his strides usually lengthy because of his height, but the downed trees and patches of marsh and his fear of snakes limited his velocity. He remembered Combat Survival Training at the Air Force Academy years ago, all fun and games and a chance to show off. They had been told that a day might come when survival techniques would be for life or death, but as a 19 year-old cadet, everything was a game. He knew that the government would watch out for him that night. After all, they were paying him for his education and already had a significant investment in him as a potential officer. They were nearly as interested in his safety as he was.

He and 20 of his classmates were placed in a tent together, prisoners of a mock Middle Eastern regime.

Their mission was to organize an escape. They knew where "Friendlies" could be found. So, if escape for one was possible, the others had a chance. Grant was selected the go-man. They'd been playing prisoner of war for days, living in a tent and pissing and dumping in cans that sat inside with them, breathing dust and stench, sweating through filthy fatigues and wondering when it would all end,—and how. A chance to escape the stench and filth was worth the risk.

During a night in Saylor Park a few miles northwest of the Academy in Pike National Forest, Colorado. The camp, which was large with 20 tents containing other cadets on similar missions, was surrounded by concertina wire, barbed wire coiled on the ground in stacks. He was the go-man because of his flexibility. As a wrestler, he could maneuver under the razor wire better than any of the others. The only problem was the searchlight that could easily spot him, and he could not time his movements because the searchlight was erratic. He had heard that the torture chamber wasn't a pleasant place, and the guards were more than happy to send him there.

His first step was simple, squeezing under the tent through the dusty base. His buddies were there to help him through. He would be alone from then on. He sucked in a breath of mountain air as his last foot slipped from the tent, from the stench of urine and days' old perspiration to the freshness of nighttime in the Colorado Rockies. The air was so thin that stars seemed only a touch away and coated the ground with their icy stare.

He remembered crawling to the wire with the board his buddies had hidden beside the tent. Then, lifting the wire with his board, he squirmed under the wire. His only other concern was the guards patrolling the outer perimeter, but his wrestling skills came in handy again. Staying low and moving fast was as easy for him at 6'2 as for the short guys. Hand after hand, foot after foot, he kept moving.

That part was all too easy, too much a game, and then reality, including the limitations of government, the frailness of flesh, and the danger of nature, bit him—literally in that last case. He still remembered the sound of the rattler before his shoulder took the hit. He had heard that rattlesnakes couldn't live above a mile high, and he was certainly higher than that. After a week in the hospital, he found that western rattlers could live up to 9,500 feet. He also learned that the reason he almost lost his shoulder was that the venom of a rattlesnake digests the surrounding muscle and that his headache, abdominal pain, and nausea were common side effects.

What he knew at the time was that two four-inch fangs could hurt even more than the destructive venom when they both hit underlying bone. He remembered the immediate shock of pain, the terror of realizing what had happened, and the next two bites as he fell onto the reptile in pain.

That was when he realized that life isn't a game, that everyone back in that tent was preparing for circumstances far more dangerous than a rattlesnake bite. He also developed a true phobia, the mere thought of a serpent making him shiver.

....

Grant knew right now that a bullet represented more immediate danger than a snakebite, and he ran as quickly as he could in these conditions, stopping only briefly at times to listen behind him and to decide on paths to take. He knew that the clip inside him was sending signals far above and tracking his steps. His only chance was to move in a straight line and not to get confused about direction. If he doubled back or zigzagged too much, the one Dick called Big Guy could easily catch him.

He tried to ignore the movements in the water to his left and the ripples in the swampy area ahead. As long as he followed the river's path, he would eventually reach civilization. The river was to his left, tangled with logs and debris. It wasn't contained, though, opening at times into areas of marsh, and so staying on course wasn't easy. The trees were too dense to see very far ahead, but he kept telling himself, "Onward. Keep moving, just like in Combat Survival Training." Only now, it wasn't training, and he was well aware of his own frailty out here alone.

Big Guy wasn't far behind. His two friends were dead and he was furious. It wasn't just a mission now. He wanted to deliver some punishment. He knew Yao would enjoy watching that, too. Yao had told him about the scrambler. Big Guy didn't need to worry about that, though. He had taken care of Dick. Grant was alone and his clip was working perfectly.

Big Guy didn't need his weapon. He was thinking of different ways to kill Grant, different ways to apply his skills. He brought a rope just for that purpose. Hanging upside down, hanging by two thumbs, rope bondage, these were all fun, but he hoped to find a snake. Most Americans hate snakes.

CHAPTER 36

Wang's bodyguard wasn't used to being without his master, and he enjoyed the separation. Though he was big and looked like a mindless ape, he was capable at most tasks. He didn't care if his job meant looking like an intimidating monster. He enjoyed being frightening. Besides, finding employment in Beijing wasn't easy with his appearance. Business owners didn't want to feel threatened by his size.

And working for Wang had its rewards. Wang was always fair when it came to that. He could pick whichever girl from the orphanage he wanted, as long as she wasn't Wang's. That perk alone was worth any risk, but this time Wang told him to leave his passport and return plane ticket behind. His mission at the hospital was delicate. If he was caught, Wang didn't want any evidence that he was behind the plan.

The mammoth looked even bigger in his white laboratory coat, but it was sufficient disguise to allow him to get to the basement unhindered. He studied the halls and entrances before passing, careful to mask his face from the cameras. He knew all the tricks of video surveillance: behind mirrors, in corners, in clocks. But the cameras were always above. A lowered head, a hand, or his newspaper could hide him easily. The locked door to the basement was not a problem. Digital locks were no problem for a guy who worked security before being hired by Wang. He knew the basement would give him access to the tubing system. The hospital had installed a completely new pneumatic labyrinth of tubes to allow the rapid transport of medicines, blood products, intravenous solutions, and medical supplies. Central Pharmacy sent its mixtures and medicines directly to the floors, and the Blood Bank had its own delivery station. Central Supply did too, from the basement. The entire system was completely new.

The fluorescent-lit expanse was a city all its own. Skyscrapers of metal cages reaching for the ceiling 18 feet above were filled with supplies, all stacked and labeled for rapid delivery. And everything was robotic. The hospital had saved money on personnel, and errors were virtually nonexistent. In addition, supplies now were charged electronically, giving proof of use for those who wished to dispute their bills. The new federal government agency, Health Administration, which had replaced the Health Care Finance Administration, had given the hospital a bonus for its innovation and cost containment.

The robotic arms were active: lifting syringes out of packages, sending three-inch silk tape to 6 North, suture removal sets to 2 Center, a hemostat to the Neuro ICU.

The giant found a manual override button with the listing of patients and room numbers. It was a cinch to send an order for a new bag of IV fluid. He punched in the name and room number and an order for a liter of normal saline and watched the metal arm take off to the intravenous fluid shelf. Simple and quick.

As the robot shifted into gear, the squeak of a door broke the silence from behind. The monster knew there might not be much time. It could be a guard or worker. He watched the arm bring the bag of fluid back toward the tubes. Before the exchange between the arm and the tube, a scanner posted the fluid delivery in the system and labeled it as the giant injected it with his own syringe.

"Bù fāsòng!" a deep voice growled from behind him. The Tiger wasn't in time to keep the giant from sending the fluid. He had been slowed by a guard. Killing the security guard felt good, but the task had delayed him just long enough for the giant to complete his task. The giant had already twisted the surveillance cameras to the wall.

The fluid travelled through the tubing system like lightening, arriving at the Cardiac Surgery Intensive Care Unit in a moment. The giant knew that the fluid would do its trick. Cyanide was a timeless poison. It causes asphyxiation by inhibiting an enzyme that allows oxygen to be utilized. He had placed so much cyanide in the fluid that death would be certain after only a few minutes.

Death was certain in the basement, too. The Tiger was half the size of the giant, but each knew that the other was lethal. The Tiger sprang from the darkness when he realized that the fluid was on its way. His fingers were clawed in the infamous tiger fist, the last two joints of all of his fingers bent at 90 degrees, except his thumb which only had the last bent. His claws fanned into position.

"Nǐ shì shuí?" the giant asked as he slid into a crouch, ready for an assault at any moment.

"Don't worry about who I am. Worry about your life and your foolish boss." The Tiger approached with the grace of a ballerina but the power of a stalking cat. When he was within striking distance, he stood with relaxed focus, his arms extended to shoulder height. His palms slowly turned upward, baring his claws that shook in anticipation of a quick slice.

"If I don't know who you are, I won't know what to place on your headstone."

The Tiger was the first to lunge. Starting from a crouch, his right foot slightly behind the left, he sprang forward, releasing his right leg. The first kick missed as the giant batted it away with his left forearm. But his left foot followed in the same motion, clipping the elbow of giant's right arm. The Tiger felt the joint falter but it did not break. Before his leap was finished, his right heel returned from its initial shot and landed a sting in the giant's rib, just above his kidney.

The giant swung to his right, using his left arm to catch the Tiger's descent. His arm caught the Tiger squarely below the shoulder blade, launching him into a concrete pillar. The Tiger's left hip took the blow. He had felt the nausea of bone injury before, but he knew how to mask any sign of injury. He bounced back to his feet, watching for the next moment to spring again.

The giant tested his right arm, pulling it into a tuck. He hoped to make the move look like a gesture of readiness, but the Tiger saw the hesitation. Another lunge and the Tiger pounced toward the giant's neck. The snap of his right heel grazed its target as the giant bent lower and to his left. The second and third kicks bounced off the giant's left then right ear, sending lightning through his skull.

As the Tiger flew past the giant, his left hand shot toward his throat but was met by a blocking sweep that popped his wrist. His right claw slashed forward with a sweep that met the giant's left eye. His fingernail sliced through the moisture, scalding the giant's face.

But, once again, the giant countered with a broom kick, sweeping the Tiger into a spin. He caught the Tiger's claw with his right hand and held with all his might. The Tiger's knuckles were hinged like metal but buckled under the beastly power.

The monster, temporarily blinded, pulled the hand to his left, reaching for a hold on the Tiger's throat. The smaller body zipped back under the power of a grinding grip.

The Tiger yo-yoed back, but his left claw did more work. It caught the monster with an upper cut, driving his nose inward and upward. The power of the blow continued backward, crushing the bones inside. The sequence was predictable. The giant's nasal bone sunk into the sphenoid bone that macerated his hypothalamus and optic chiasm. It didn't matter that blindness was immediate; the hypothalamus is the brain of the brain.

The giant's grip released and his legs began to buckle, but three more heel kicks from the Tiger sent him backward. His head shook the concrete pillar, bursting like a watermelon.

The Tiger scurried to the door as quickly as he could. Yao had told him the layout of the hospital. Intricate details of plumbing, electrical wiring, and even future architectural schemes were easy enough to obtain through his sources.

The guard wasn't big. His uniform made dragging him through the basement easy. All the Tiger had to do was take off his uniform and lift him into the chute at the back of the basement. It would only take a moment for the guard to fall into the grinder, then pass to the incinerator going from corpse to carbon dioxide and water in moments. He would simply follow the path of amputated limbs, extracted kidneys, and infected tonsils that fell from the pathology lab above to the air and earth outside.

The giant was a bigger struggle, but hearing him bounce off the metal chute on his tumble brought a sense of closure to the Tiger, whose hands relaxed in a moment of victory.

The Tiger then ran to the computer, hoping to erase the last sends. But they were already logged in. One liter of normal saline intravenous solution was already on its way to Governor Richard Sands.

CHAPTER 37

The acid in Grant's lungs had done some damage. He couldn't control the secretions that shortened each breath or the wheezing that was constant now. But he could control his pace, which had slowed considerably over the last hour or so. Surely there would be a sign of civilization at some point, a hunting lodge or a house or a person.

An avid wrestler, he had sparred with the best until his appendectomy and the malignant hyperthermia. The poisoned dart and recent acid had not helped his conditioning any either. Now, as he ran as best he could through the tangle, he tried to focus on his morning runs when he was at the Air Force Academy. The runs began each morning at 5,280 feet altitude, a mile high, sometimes in T-shirts and tennis shoes and other times in full fatigues and combat boots and carrying M-14 rifles. The mornings with full equipment were always the worst and yet the best. They taught him endurance and brought him confidence as his unit ran in formation, chanting side by side, knowing they couldn't drop out. Dropping out meant that an upper classman would be all over you, screaming demeaning things and threatening the recruit's very existence. Grant found that he could chant louder than the rest, run longer and faster, and do it with less effort than the others. The chanting required effort and took away precious gulps of air, but it could be done in rhythm, the timed breaths distracting him from thoughts of fatigue. By concentrating on each breath, his arms didn't falter under the weight of the rifle and his feet and legs simply churned ahead, tempo and pace more important than the finish line.

But now, in the thicket and on a spongy surface, rhythm and pace were impossible. Each movement forward was more of a leap than a glide. He concentrated more on the ground and its potential hazards than his breaths. His lungs were simply a pipeline now, sending streams of sputum upward, either to strangle him for moments at a time or to be quickly spat into the air. His lungs, once the engine of his endurance, now wheezed and choked for relief.

Overhead, a turkey vulture, named for its bald red head and feeding habits, followed Grant's path, circling with lazy patterns. Known locally as simply a buzzard, it waited patiently above, identifying the struggle with nature below. Meanwhile, Yao tracked both Grant and Big Guy from the satellite, satisfied that the chase would end soon.

Earlier, he talked Big Guy back to his senses after the scrambler had left him nauseated and disoriented for a few minutes. He recovered fast enough to see Dick slip into the woods.

Dick never saw it coming. He thought he had enough separation to escape safely. Careful to keep the canopy of trees over him to avoid detection from the satellite, he paralleled the river, running in the opposite direction Grant ran. But Big Guy's rapid recovery, speed, vision, and aim allowed him to fire one shot with his Xuanlong. The bullet tore into his left shoulder, splintering bone and throwing him into the river.

By the time Big Guy reached the strike zone, Dick was nowhere to be found. He searched for a while but was satisfied that the shot was mortal. Blood on the ground had sprayed on a neighboring tree, leaving no doubt that the bullet had hit its target.

Now, as another vulture spotted Grant, Big Guy readied himself for another shot. Grant had paused, pulling for air, just before an open area he wanted to avoid. He assumed that the satellite knew where he was anyway, but he had no idea if Big Guy would know where he was. On the other side of the opening was a building that looked like an abandoned hunting lodge, but at this time of year, all lodges were vacant. Grant thought there might be a telephone or even a weapon inside.

Big Guy's Xuanlong was fitted with a Taijing advanced combat sight. The scope, fitted with reticle illumination, automatically removed glare and shadows from his view. In addition to giving a perfect view of Grant's head, the bullet drop compensator allowed for distance. Either the American would die or the bullet would do what he hoped.

A single 5.56 millimeter round rifled through the air, striking Grant before the sound arrived.

Both Big Guy and Yao smiled as Grant hit the ground.

CHAPTER 38

Katie's first rotation as a nurse in training was on the unit she had requested, the Cardiac Intensive Care Unit. Nursing School at the Capstone was her goal from the time she graduated from Hillcrest High School. Historically, the University of Alabama had been referred to as the "Capstone" of learning in Alabama so the nursing school was now referred to as the Capstone College of Nursing. It was established in 1975 in response to the need for nurses in Tuscaloosa, but now the institution was one of the top 10 programs in America. Now, working in the Open Heart Unit, she was filled with pride and couldn't wait to tell her parents when she returned home at the end of the day.

Her first job was to hook up Governor Sand's intravenous fluid, a simple task, but her first time to do it, and on the governor! She would call her grandmother, also. Governor Sands was Maw-Maw Jean's hero. He had helped her brother out with a job in Mobile when the economy had tanked years ago.

"Okay, Katie. We're gonna act like you've done this a thousand times," Tamala instructed her as the new fluid bag zipped through the tubing and into the unit. It only took five seconds to make it from the basement. She pulled the bag from its outer plastic wrapping and handed it to Katie. "Just push the tubing connector into the bag and then slip the tubing through the computerized pump. Set the rate at 100 cc's per hour and then hook the other end of the tubing up to the governor's intravenous needle."

Katie had seen the sequence several times before and walked into Richard Sand's room with confidence. Tamala followed, acting as she always did in these training situations. As a veteran nurse, she could take care of any problems, even if it meant explaining to the governor that everyone needs to start somewhere.

"Sir, I need to change your IV line." She smiled as she entered the room. "My name is Katie and I'll be helping take care of you today."

"Okay, Katie," Governor Sands responded. "I haven't seen you before. Are you new on the unit?"

Katie looked at Tamala, hoping for support, but part of training was letting the young students stand on their own two feet.

"Yes, sir. Governor, I'm a nursing student. I'll be working up here for the next month and so I guess I'll get to see a lot of you." She hung the fluid bag from a long metal pole and winked at the governor with confidence.

"Well, I'll enjoy seeing you. If you're as good as all the other nurses up here, I'll have to send a note of appreciation to your nursing school and the hospital administrator here."

Katie glowed with pride as she slipped the tubing through the mechanical pump and set the rate. As she hooked the last connection up to the governor's wrist a shrill screech blasted over the intercom system. "Code White. Code White. All personnel, this is not a drill. Code White."

Katie had no idea what that code might mean. If a patient was arresting on the floor, it was a Code Blue and the announcer said the room number that emergency responders needed to get to. She looked at Tamala again.

Before Tamala could make eye contact with Katie, the doors to the governor's room blew open, the Plexiglas doors slamming against the wall as four state troopers stormed into the room.

One officer swung his pistol around the room, clearing it mentally as he checked all angles. He ended his sweep with Katie, his pistol pointed directly at her chest.

Katie, screaming hysterically, backed into the IV pole that crashed onto the ground. The bag of fluid exploded as it hit the floor. Katie, retreating from the troopers, slid backward. Catching herself before she fell to the floor, she threw her arms forward and skied across the floor, hitting his bed with her pelvis and landing on the governor's groin with her face.

The governor, aware that danger was possible, held onto Katie for her protection. He grabbed her shoulders so she wouldn't fall back on the floor, which this made her tumble into bed with him.

The troopers surrounded the governor, their radios blasting.

"We have a breach of security in the basement, sir," one of the officers shouted. "We have reason to believe that this could endanger you!"

Katie curled into a ball, housing herself under the governor's arm. He held her gently, realizing she was scared out of her wits.

"It's okay, sweetheart," the Governor comforted her. He held back a groan as she lifted herself off of him, pushing on his chest wound.

One of the troopers helped her the rest of the way off of his bed, making sure she had her footing before letting her stand on her own. Tamala had pulled towels from a bin in the room and was mopping the floor as Katie tried to regain composure. She stood motionless, white faced and hands trembling, and then collapsed on the floor. Halfway to the ground, the trooper who had been with her caught her head, preventing any serious injury.

"Take her out and make sure she is alright," Governor Sands directed the trooper. "Can you help my officer, Tamala?"

"Absolutely, Governor." Tamala helped carry the tiny student out of the room, leaving the governor and three troopers.

"Sir, we're sorry to barge in like this," the gray-haired officer said. "There was an event in the basement, apparently a fight. Hospital security had a warning that the secure area where supplies are distributed in the basement was broken into, and they found blood on the floor and supplies thrown all over the place. The robotic system was broken, but according to the records, the last item it delivered was the IV fluid to you." He looked at the floor. "That must be the fluid."

All officers and the governor looked at the moisture that still shimmered on the floor.

"Was anything caught on surveillance cameras," the Governor asked.

"We're not sure at this point, sir. As far as we can tell, this was professional. Whoever broke into the basement did it with high tech equipment or they knew the code to the lock. They turned all cameras away from their work. Hospital security is working on it, but we have no answers at this point."

"Alright. Stay on top of this with building security." He pulled himself up in bed, looking at the gray-haired trooper. "Any word from the officers who were trailing Dr. Miller or from Dick?"

"Yes, sir. We just found the troopers' car wrecked on the highway." He lowered his voice, wanting to hide his next comment. "They were both dead. Not from the wreck but from gunshots!"

Richard tightened his jaw, considering the painful possibilities. "Where is Molly?"

"She was in the waiting room. When we were alerted of the basement incident, we pulled her into a secluded room for security. She's okay." He read Richard's thoughts. "She doesn't know about the troopers. We just learned that, also."

"Has anyone checked our plant?" Richard sat up in bed.

"Sir, we have a couple of cars going there now."

"Alright. I'm on the verge of getting the FBI involved, but for now, keep me informed of everything: the hospital investigation, the downed troopers, Frank, Harper, Dr. Miller, and Dick." He wiped his brow as he looked at the older trooper. "Let's not tell Molly about this for now."

CHAPTER 39

When Grant woke, his head pounded from the blast of Big Guy's weapon. The bullet from his assault weapon only grazed Grant's left temple, but at 2800 feet per second, the impact and shock wave left him down long enough.

Big Guy had received permission from Yao to have his way with Grant, and it didn't take long to find his tool of choice. A five-foot cottonmouth now waited in the river, a noose tightened around its neck.

The last time he had used a snake was in China. Yao needed to know about a counterespionage gang hacking into the Internet. Instead of sharing findings with Yao, the gang's boss had used it for personal gain. Big Guy found a mountain viper and taped the snake to a broomstick, its long body fully stretched and taped from the base to the end. Then he held the snake like a frog gig, the snake's bites precisely aimed at eyeballs, nose, ears, genitals. He was able to find out everything he needed.

Today would be even more fun.

"Ahhh!" Big Guy grinned as Grant's eyes focused on him. "You are a sleepy head!"

Grant was woozy, but he realized quickly what had happened. Dried blood crackled on his cheek. His hands and feet were tied, leaving him pretzeled on the ground. He looked around but remained quiet. Big Guy stood over him, watching him awaken with hungry eyes.

"Your friends are dead." He kicked Grant in the rib cage, hard enough to take his breath away but not enough to break bones. "The one you called Frank died too easily. He didn't have the opportunity to suffer. A gunshot is no fun if it doesn't bring pain. That's why I didn't kill you like I did him and the one you call Dick."

Grant's breath stopped when he mentioned Dick. That was his last hope. He had envisioned Dick following him and showing up to save the day. Reality set in: there would be no Dick, no gallant savior. Big Guy saw Grant deflate and was thrilled that this *gwailo* was so easy to read, so easy to control.

"This is going to go badly for you." Big Guy kicked him in the other side with the same intent. "I don't really like sex with men, but I like relationships."

Grant imagined the possibilities and wished the bullet had finished the deal.

"You can talk to me for a while, or I'll just have to have other relations with you!" Big Guy rubbed his groin. He had an Asian accent but spoke with clear and precise diction.

"Okay." Grant's voice sounded like it had echoed out of a dungeon. "Who are you and why are you going to kill me?"

Big Guy grinned. "I'm going to kill you because I have orders to do it. I'm going to do it my way because you killed my two friends. My name is Ping."

"Who gave you orders to kill me, Ping?"

"No, let's play it like this. I ask a question and then you ask a question." Ping licked his lips as though he was about to begin dessert. "First, I want you to know that it was me and my friends who put you down close to your house. I could have let you die then, but that wouldn't have been fun, like this..." He kicked him again in the left side. "Where is the clip and what do you know about it?"

Grant knew better than to lie. He assumed that the clip inside of him had allowed their conversations to be monitored the entire time. They knew what he knew. "As far as I know, the clip is being melted by acid in the plant. Dick examined it. I guess he dissected or dismantled it and decided that it was a surveillance bug. I don't understand high-tech surveillance but assume it is a tracking device and also has the ability to send audio through a satellite."

Ping nodded his approval of this answer. There was a pause as he listened to Yao through his cochlear implant. The Chinese had perfected the design in the last five years, having stolen the plans from Audionomics in Sacramento. Instead of the older implant, which required a microphone to pick up sound, a signal processor and a radio transmitter cord that sent impulses directly to the inner ear cochlea, Ping's microphone was a single chip, like the one inside Grant, implanted in a bone behind ear. The small chip allowed Yao to communicate directly, bypassing his eardrum and going directly through his auditory nerve to his brain. Yao sometimes found it ironic that this technology, stolen from the Americans, was now being used to steal further secrets from them.

Yao could see and hear everything. He was licking his lips, too.

"Okay!" Big Guy grunted. "Your turn!"

Grant's head was still pounding and his back had tightened, pulled by the ropes binding his hands and feet and the kicks to his ribs. He squirmed for some relief, but Big Guy popped him with blow to his left kidney. The deep pain made him feel like he would throw up.

"What does the governor have to do with any of this, and who is the satellite sending signals to?" Grant knew that the end was coming. He was completely helpless, tied down and alone in the wilderness.

In front of him, three feet away, Big Guy had placed a squirrel with a knife through its breast. The squirrel hung head down, its tiny eyes staring helplessly at Grant. Grant didn't know what was behind him, but he knew from his view before the bullet hit him that there was a stretch of swamp and the building. Above him was an opening into the late afternoon sky, the satellite watching, the buzzard circling.

Ping waited for Yao to give him permission to answer Grant's question. "Go ahead and tell him about the clip! Let him die knowing that more is lost for him than just his life."

"The clip is manufactured by the Yida Company in China, and you are right. It has the ability to send GPS coordinates and audio through a satellite. Our country knows better than yours how to coordinate knowledge." Big Guy delivered another blow to Grant's rib. "We got the design for a new capacitor from one of your electronic companies. The capacitor allows the clip to send off powerful signals through a tiny processor that another American company developed. Still another company was working on signal magnification. You see, the more clips that are in you, the stronger and clearer the signal. Soon, the clips will even be able to process the heartbeat, chemistry levels, and internal physiology of the people it is in." Ping grinned with superiority.

"Your governor has many clips..." Big Guy stopped speaking abruptly. Yao was yelling through his microphone, bouncing nerve signals to his brain.

"Stop!" Yao screamed. "Don't tell him specifically who has the clip inside, just that we stole the ability to individualize the signals so every person with a clip has their own personal signal. Tell him how we have gotten everything from America and now we have access to all the information in America and in every country."

Big Guy did as he was told, but he found this kind of foreplay boring. He looked up, eyeing the buzzard above. "That big bird above us can smell dead meat three miles away." He looked at the dead squirrel. "In China, the vultures have beaks strong enough to tear through skin and break bones. Your birds are weaker, like your country. Meat has to rot and decay before the birds can eat. That is what China has let America do, rot. You are now decayed enough for us to eat you."

"Does anyone else know about the clip? Does anyone else suspect that the clip has transmission capabilities?" Big Guy continued, already knowing the answer.

"No. No one." Grant responded, expecting another kick. It came rapidly and more powerfully, crushing into his lower back.

Grant assumed that the conversations in the hospital were all wired. He expected that Ping was aware that governor and his wife were aware of the clip's existence. But Grant was certain that his time had come and he wasn't going to implicate anyone else at this point.

"Bad answer, Dr. Miller. You forgot about Dick's parents, Governor and Mrs. Sands." Another blow struck him below his right shoulder blade. "I'm afraid I can't trust you anymore."

Ping twirled Grant like a top, spinning him so his head faced the river. The bank wasn't steep, giving him a clear view of the lazy flow of water and the angled tree with a rope hanging down at the edge of the stream.

"Do you like rivers?" Big Guy smirked.

Grant remained quiet, wondering if his death would be by drowning, hanging, or something slower and more painful.

"It doesn't really matter, of course." His voice grew deeper as he approached the river's edge. "You see, I have a friend right here who loves the river, which is his home. He gets very angry when someone trespasses on his territory."

Grant knew about water moccasins, that they are very territorial and very mean. He felt his body shiver as he searched desperately for an escape, knowing deep inside that it was pointless. "What a way to go!" He thought to himself.

Ping tugged on the rope, lifting the serpent into the air. The rope lassoed his thick head. The snake wrapped his tail around the rope, lifting himself upward, toward Big Guy, until being lowered back into the water. The big Chinaman saw the horror in Grant's eyes.

"So you don't like snakes." He returned to Grant, wiping perspiration from his forehead. "Well, before my spineless friend gets to taste you, there's something else you should know." He waited for a moment, then huffed with laughter. "Your wife must not mind that you are at the hospital all the time." He wiped his crotch, pumping three or four times. "It seems she likes it when you're away."

Grant tumbled from fear to disbelief and then into utter emptiness.

"After me and my buddies searched you for the clip, we wanted to make sure you hadn't hidden it anywhere. Luckily, you didn't mention it to your wife or I would have to kill her." He watched the color fade from Grant's face, knowing he had injured him more than any bullet or snake could.

"But we did put a bug in your house." Big Guy went on, enjoying the moment. "It seems your wife has a...friend. He comes to your house while your daughters are at school and leaves before everyone comes home."

Grant was totally blank. He'd never dreamed, never suspected. His life was going to end and he realized he had lived a shadow life, a life in darkness. He was about to die and his killer knew more about his wife than he did.

Visions and voices swirled through his head. He had heard Carol's muffled voice on the telephone, arranging meetings. He had never questioned her. He'd never had a reason. But now, he remembered how she would find another room to talk or a reason to call back. He knew that the Chinese monster was going to make his death painful and he could easily be lying. But, he also recognized that he hadn't paid full attention to her needs. The reality of his words seemed painfully possible.

"Ha!" Big Guy gloated at Grant's distress. "I guess you didn't know. In the homeland we used to put adulterers in pig cages and throw them into a river, but I guess she wins and you go into the river." His laughter grew louder by the second.

Walking slowly back to the river, Big Guy planned his strategy. He would cut a hole in the snake's tail and tie the rope through it. Then he would tie the other end of the rope to Grant's neck. The rest would be like a movie. He was thrilled with his plan.

He stood at the tree and lifted the rope. Initially, there was a tug. But then the pull was effortless. Big Guy raised the head of the cottonmouth out of the water but the body was gone.

Looking at the snake head, and then at Grant, who was watching everything in stunned surrender, he took one more look at the river. Big Guy was two feet from the water's edge and holding the line as it dangled in front of him. The snake head opened and closed its mouth, snapping at the air as though a target was there.

Then the water exploded with furious splashing and the thunder of crushing bone. The same gator that had feasted on the moccasin moments ago had a firm grip on Big Guy's leg. The roots and moss that had steadied his perch were simply slippery ice now, and Ping lost his footing with his good leg and slipped forward.

The 10 foot, 800 pound beast, a firm grip on Big Guy's calf, made three spins and twirled him into the river as easily as Ping had spun Grant on the ground. Big Guy grabbed for the roots he had stood on, but they were too slippery and large to grasp. The dark water was all over him as he spun and thrashed. Downward, the gator pulled, tugging his prey with merciless force. Big Guy tried to fight, reaching for the gator's head, but a series of spins pushed him back. Water filled his lungs as he gasped for air. Then he went limp and Ping's body and the gator disappeared beneath the surface of the water, submerging together to the crocodillian's den.

Grant didn't have the strength to hope that Big Guy was dead or to believe that he had just been saved by an alligator. He rolled to his back and looked upward. A green anole lizard was perched on an overhanging limb of a long leaf pine slowly chewing on a baby field cricket. Flickers of sunlight bounced on and off the chartreuse lizard as a lazy breeze played through the leaves above. The hardwood leaves danced playfully in the late afternoon. The light green of the five inch reptile gradually muted, mimicking the brown branch where it feasted. Two last gulps and the cricket was no longer a thought. Instead, the two beady eyes searched for another snack or danger.

Grant simply gazed upward. He watched the simplicity of life and death, the indifference of nature, the ability to be green at one moment and brown the next.

Even higher up was the buzzard, still patiently soaring. Its five foot wing span caught currents of heat, lifting it in drafts that required no effort. Living required death for the bird of prey. Its simple circles weren't out of idleness, but necessity. Perhaps it had lost a bigger feast than it had hoped, but the squirrel at his side was enough for a day's work.

Still higher, Grant assumed, the satellite was still there too.

"Oh, my God!" He simply couldn't move, frozen by knowledge he couldn't process and overcome by the shades of reality he was afraid to see.

"What have I done?" Guilt was the deepest claw that sank into his thoughts. "What am I even doing here?" He was a husband first and a father second, a surgeon third. "What in the Hell am I doing in this place? I'm not a Marine. I'm not a federal agent. My life wasn't even in jeopardy until I launched off on some movie drama vigilante expedition."

He squirmed to the knife that was bayoneting the squirrel to the tree. Part of him wanted to be cut free and part of him wanted to lie back down and wait to become the buzzard's meal. Cutting himself free of the ropes around his hands and feet was simple, but his next challenges were not so simply achieved.

There was so much to do now: find a phone and call home, retrieve Dick, notify authorities. One step forward.

Yao had seen it all. He couldn't believe this *gwailo's* luck, but he had seen it. Now he watched Grant through the satellite, tracking him by GPS.

CHAPTER 40

Lee knew it was only a matter of time until Yao would find him. He also knew the end would be ugly. At this point, he had nothing to lose and was determined to make others pay. He was going down, but Suzy, Dr. Wade, and others were going to pay first.

Everything was going just fine until Dr. Miller screwed up the clip in the operating room. It should have been a simple thing to lose it, to find it and destroy it and then kill anyone who knew about it. None of those things had worked. The clip was his ticket to wealth, power and fame, his Trojan Horse, but now it was going to be his ticket to a hangman's noose.

He had worked his way up the ladder at Yida Tech, sucking up to anyone who could launch him on his mission in America. He knew that he could be his own man in America, build his own kingdom of servants and women. And in fact he had Suzys in every city he worked. He'd had access to the three hit men, who were now dead, and could make a telephone call and have a free ride, free meal, free sex... Anything he wanted or needed.

The only thing he had to worry about was the clip being discovered. Mr. Hu, the owner of Yida, had given him full authority to market the Yida Clip. Lee not only marketed it but received 20% of all sales. It wasn't that Lee was so good but that he was clever. Lee knew Mr. Hu hated Yao, who had imprisoned his father and kept Mr. Hu on a leash. Mr. Hu had developed the Yida Clip with Yao's help, and they used the resources of Chinese

Intelligence and Yida's technology to do so. The clip was just the first in surveillance options. Soon, new orthopedic prosthetics, vascular stents, cardiac devices, pacemakers, and even internal glues would have the capability of transmitting GPS, audio, chemistry, and even visual data to Yao and Chinese Intelligence.

Lee saw the opportunity to gain the upper hand and made sure that Yao knew Mr. Hu was not his friend, that Mr. Hu was looking for a way to destroy Yao. Lee placed bugs throughout Mr. Hu's house, throughout the Yida plant, and even in Mr. Hu's car. With Lee's help, Yao made sure Mr. Hu was under constant surveillance. It didn't take long for Yao to learn that Lee was valuable and that Yida was too.

As payment, Yao demanded that Mr. Hu give Lee the income he wanted, the power to market the clip in America, and Lee took full advantage of it.

Lee also knew that the penalty for failing Yao, for the clip being discovered and risking the entire program, was worse than being charged with international espionage. The last contact with Yao was hopefully the last he would ever have.

Yao had told him about the death of his three hit men and that Dr. Miller was still alive and knew about the clip. Yao also said that he knew that the governor and his wife were suspicious of the clip but had no proof of its capabilities or even suspected that the Chinese were involved. He knew that Dick, the governor's son, knew about the clip but Yao felt that he was dead.

Perhaps Lee could salvage victory if he could kill Dr. Miller before he told anyone about the clip, or if he could discredit Dr. Miller. He knew that the clip was destroyed, that Dick had dissected it in Sand's lab, and acid would have completed the job. It would be a challenge for Dr. Miller to convince the FBI that a clip that was now destroyed could do everything it really could do.

Yes, victory would be very hard and was perhaps impossible now, but he also knew that he, Lee, was too big a risk for Yao to let live. Lee had never been trained in resisting interrogation techniques, and if he was captured by federal agents, it would just be a matter of time until he would break and tell all he knew. He knew it and Yao knew it.

Lee's only chance of survival at this point was to go into hiding. He couldn't do it with the surveillance devices that Yao had implanted in his hands, but it wasn't hard to deactivate them. A quick walk by the MRI machine in the hospital and the strong magnet would destroy their capacity to function.

The only problem would be that he was totally in the dark. No one could track him but he had no idea what was going on with Yao or his men either.

....

Lee believed he knew Americans. They were odd creatures, more confident of their survival instincts than wary of death, more curious than cautious. He had worked with doctors enough to know they were off the bell curve in terms of self-confidence and taking risks.

As a representative for Yida products, Lee had access to all of the surgeon's cells, including Jack's. He zipped off a text, then waited for a response. "Dr. Wade. Please meet me at the spillway, Lake Tuscaloosa. This is Li Jiang (Lee). I just spoke to you at the hospital. I have important information to share with you about Suzy. I have to speak to you in private. It is a matter of life and death for her."

Lake Tuscaloosa officially became a lake in 1970. At a cost of over 7 million dollars, a dam was constructed blocking the flow of North River in order to contain 5,885 acres of surface water and 40 billion gallons. New Watermelon Road, crossing over the edifice, allowed two different views. To the west of the road, a gentle breeze teased the lake creating lazy ripples on the otherwise glassy surface. Fingers of the lake stretched between rolling hills, filling the valleys with water pure enough for human consumption. The glistening surface reflected spectacular homes sitting like castles over the expanse.

To the east, a constant spray jetted into the air, shot through a cannon-like tunnel that travelled through the boulders forming the dam. The spray, steamed through the power of thousands of pounds of pressure and the late summer sun, misted the valley below. The Appalachian Highlands make their final surrender to the Cumberland Plateau in this transition zone of erosion-carved cliffs, evergreen coated hills, and the white water descent of North River as it continues its path to the Warrior River.

North of the dam, a spillway allowed overflow of the lake, pouring tons of water a second into a reservoir that then sends the furious water swirling downward and onward into the final vestiges of North River. Recent storms had already lifted the water level to record levels. Warnings lined the entrance to the spillway and a gate prevented the unwary from falling 20 feet into the reservoir below.

Lee had been at the spillway for some time, checking out different angles and deciding where to position himself and how to coerce Jack. Part of him wanted to torture Jack. A simple gunshot didn't seem enough for the rage he felt. Everything had fallen apart, and although Jack wasn't the reason for all of his problems, he was guilty enough to pay. He probably knew about Suzy, that Lee had attacked her. Jack probably would learn more from Suzy if he remained alive, if Suzy remained alive. But worse, Jack was trying to move in on his property.

Suzy was Lee's, and if he couldn't have her, Jack couldn't have her.

"When do you want to meet?" Lee received his text response from Dr. Wade.

"Now, if possible," He responded.

"Okay." Jack texted back. He wasn't a fool. He had already called his buddy Miles, the Chief of Police, and given him enough time to position a SWAT team in the hills above the spillway and on the shore opposite.

Jack drove slowly toward the lake, waiting for Miles to call him and confirm that his team was in position. Even when the affirmation came, he was in no hurry. As his Chevy truck rumbled down the hill toward the lake, he spotted movement at the spillway across the lake.

The overlook, sometimes frequented by sightseers, was empty with the exception of a single person. When he was halfway across the dam, Jack could tell it was Lee. He looked on the hill above the spillway and glanced to his left, hoping to see evidence of his support, but saw nothing.

Jack slowed as he approached the left turn into the spillway parking area. Lee was standing by the gate watching him as he parked next to his sedan.

"Thanks for coming," Lee called, remaining positioned at the gate. Behind him water poured over the concrete, crashing into the basin below.

Jack approached cautiously, watching Lee for any sign of threat. "What's up?" he questioned, keeping his distance.

"I wanted to talk about Suzy!" Lee waved for Jack to join him, knowing that Jack would come.

"What about Suzy?" Jack approached, anger and curiosity propelling him forward.

"She works for me, you know!" Jack was sizing up Lee as he approached. He measured Lee at 5'10, hardly a match for Jack at 6'5. And Lee had the physique of a successful salesman. Wining and dining had made their mark under his chin and at his waistline.

"No, I didn't!" Jack was hesitant.

"Yes. She has worked with Yida for years. She is a student at the University of Alabama with expensive tuition." Lee seemed surprisingly relaxed and unguarded. "I hired her so she could pay her expenses and not be sent back to China."

"What does she do for you?" Jack decided to play along, now seeing movement in the hill over the spillway.

"She helps log patients who have Yida products that are implanted in them." Lee laughed slightly. "I don't really need her, but I want to do what I can for her." His laughter stopped, changing to ice instantly. "She's crazy, you know. She hurts herself, does crazy things to her body!"

Jack held back his anger. His first instinct was to hit Lee, but he wanted to hear where Lee was going with this. "No, I didn't realize that!" His tone was all disbelief.

"Sure, she's studying neuropsychology at the University, hoping to figure out where her wires got crossed. She's psycho, a paranoid schizophrenic who thinks other people are trying to get her."

The water was pouring over the spillway behind him with a deafening thunder as it crashed in the reservoir. He intentionally softened his voice, making Jack come close enough to hear him speak. His words never stopped, and neither did his eyes, occasionally focused on Jack but mostly scanning the lake, the road, and the opposite shore. Finally, Lee saw movement he was expecting...across the lake at the boat landing. The reflection of metal and a lens was unmistakable.

Lee continued, his voice even softer. "She was a prostitute in China and got in deep with the mayor of Beijing. He didn't want his family to find out about his relation with her, and so he paid for her to come to America."

Jack's mind swirled from disbelief to uncertainty. He wanted more information, something to convince him one way or the other that Suzy was who he felt she was. After years of exams and patient evaluations, he thought he knew people, but doubt had surfaced. He pulled closer to hear Lee out.

Jack was within whisper range now.

"I've tried to let her work for me, but money doesn't mean anything anymore and she can't stop whoring." Lee's voice dredged for a deeper cut, trying to slice Jack with every word. "She's really just a sperm bank now. I've had her in the ass more times than in the mouth!"

By the time Jack realized that Lee was lying, Lee had already drawn his pistol from his front pocket, hiding it from the hill behind him but flashing it visibly to the other shore. He grabbed Jack by his collar and pulled him backward, swinging the pistol to his skull.

The thunder of water was joined by more thunder as Lee pulled the trigger.

CHAPTER 41

Grant tried to make it to the building across the clearing but could not get through the swamp, which he was not going to cross after seeing what happened to Big Guy. Even if Grant had the assault rifle, which was now at the bottom of the river, falling into the water with Big Guy because it was slung across his back, he wouldn't risk the water and weeds. Grant's only weapon was the knife, but at least he was only being tracked from above. But whoever had been watching and tracking him from the satellite was certainly still invested in killing him. After all, if Dick was dead, he was the only one who knew about the clip, about the surveillance, about the Chinese. He had no idea how close more henchmen might be, but his choices were limited.

He hurried as fast as his lungs, legs, and emotions would take him. Wary of snakes and wilderness hazards each step of the way leaving the Sands facility meant that retracing his path back was no trouble.

Not a natural worrier and generally not suspicious, but basically trusting and dutiful, his imagination was nevertheless having its way with him. Who was in his home with Carol when he was at work? The question wouldn't leave. He tried his best to erase the question and imaginings from his mind, but his dark thoughts continued to assault him.

Maybe Big Guy was just trying to torment him before killing him. Maybe there was nothing to it. Surely there was nothing to it.

He had given everything he could to her: a house, two wonderful daughters, money to use as she wished...

He had abandoned her, leaving to work every day. Every day, always work, and he had left her out of his day every day...

He had been faithful, never cheated. Thought about it, maybe, but never followed through. He would never...

Would she ever be unfaithful. Could she have feelings for anyone else? How would he know if she did? He was never there...

How were they going to work things out? Could he forgive her? Could she forgive him?

What about the girls? Would they side with him or her? Did they know? Could they keep it a secret from them? How would it affect them?

Who was it? Was he handsome or just available? Did he show her affection more than he did? Had he not given her the warmth she needed...

What was she doing now?

The questions, the visions, rocketed in, exploding with answers he couldn't control. Jealousy, anger, bitterness, regret, forgiveness... The emotions and thoughts wouldn't leave.

Minutes turned to hours, the torture of uncertainty and the power of suspicion making the journey seem endless. But, at last, the view of Sands appeared through the early evening shadows. Grant crashed through the thicket, racing toward the building, which stood eerily dark, still without power.

"Grant!" A voice came from his right, under the tree where Ghost hung.

Dick sat at the base of the tree, paler than the corpse hanging above him. He had yelled with all the power left in him. Blood no longer dripped from his shoulder, but plastered his back to the tree, dried into glue.

Grant raced to his side, horrified even as a surgeon at the cavity the bullet had left. A bloody trail showed the path he had taken to crawl up the tree and retrieve the assault rifle from Ghost. Dick held the rifle with his good arm, but at this point he was too exhausted to raise it let alone fire it.

"You're a welcome sight, buddy!" Dick's voice painted his joy with weariness.

"You too." Grant quickly examined the blast wound, careful not to stir up more bleeding or to cause pain.

"I thought you were dead!" Grant admitted.

"I thought the same about you!" Dick mustered enough energy for a smile.

"What about the biker who shot me? Do you know where he is?" Dick pulled the rifle closer to his side.

"Eaten by a gator." Grant nodded. "Long story. I'll tell you later. Let's get out of here and get to a phone."

"Oh shit." Grant pulled his hand to his mouth. "I forgot about the clip." He looked at Dick, then up in the air. "I guess the bastards know we're both alive now!"

Grant took a visual sweep of the plant and surroundings. "I'll be back. I'm gonna see if any of the motorcycles have keys or if my car can be started."

"Sounds good. I'm not planning on going too far." Dick shared a muted grin.

Just as Grant stood up to leave, the sound of an automobile purred in the distance. Grant heard it first but Dick was the first to acknowledge it. "Do you hear that?"

"Yes."

They both felt a shiver of concern. "You think it's good guys or bad guys?" Dick's finger tightened on the rifle.

"I don't know, but we better be prepared for the worst." Grant pulled the weapon from Dick's grasp. "I know how to use a rifle." He looked at Dick's shoulder. "I don't think you'll be able to fire too many shots in your shape."

They huddled behind the tree, waiting and watching. It was dusk and the breeze of coming darkness cooled the air, carrying the organic odor of the wilderness. The heat of the day had worked on the undergrowth and nearby water, allowing decay to lift sulfuric vapors into the air. Invisible crickets chirped. Grant listened to the one closest, counting 35 chirps in 13 seconds. Having tested this folk fact as a child, he added 40. "It must be 75 degrees," he calculated. Then focusing intently on the approaching engine, he isolated two pitches. There were at least two vehicles. The drone grew louder and louder, joining the symphony of chirps, croaks, and squeals that marked the end of the day.

Then the beam of headlights turned onto the straightaway, closing rapidly on Sands. Grant froze with paranoia. How would he know if they were good guys or not? His thoughts were jumbled at this point. What if the police or Feds are involved? The police car that was supposed to be trailing, to be support, hadn't been anywhere to be seen when they were in trouble. He shouldered the rifle, ready for whatever came.

Dick was awake but detached from his blood loss. Grant had seen it many times before, morbidly sick patients on the precipice of death, tumbling over the edge without fear, without hurting, without regret. He left Dick undisturbed, hoping that, if things ended badly, he would drift away painlessly.

There were two cars, one was clearly marked as a state trooper vehicle and wearing rooftop lights like a crown. The lead sedan was unmarked. They stopped in tandem, 100 yards from the plant. Obviously, they sensed danger. Grant and Dick were opposite the garage, which is what the vehicles must have seen. Likely, the destruction in the garage had warned them to stop.

Grant peered through the scope on the Xuanlong. In spite of the shadows of dusk, the infrared illuminator and image intensifier made it easy for Grant to identify what was going on. Inside the first car a trooper took off his hat and was pulling on a protective vest. His partner was on the radio with the car behind him, looking through the rear window and exchanging hand signals. There appeared to be confusion, maybe with the radio. Those in the rear car were active as well. Two men, both in uniform, were checking their shotguns, preparing for a fight.

The first car pulled forward, leaving the other in place. The two men in the marked car both pulled binoculars to their eyes, surveying the property. Both Dick and Grant were well out of sight, but Ghost, hanging above, would be clearly visible if they scanned that high.

Grant's paranoia gradually eased as he watched the troopers work. They were coordinated, the two on the ground working together to check the perimeter and then the building. The first to see the spray of bullet marks on the plated glass rapidly called the finding in to his buddies in the other vehicle.

Grant looked back at Dick, realizing that he needed urgent care. He felt confident enough that the troopers were legitimate.

"Hey, over here," Grant yelled, staying low behind the tree.

Both troopers crouched, their pistols pointing in Grant's direction. "Who's there?" the closest yelled back.

"I'm Grant Miller. I have Dick Sands with me," Grant returned, staying low.

"I need you to come out slowly with your hands up," the lead Trooper continued.

"Okay. I'll come out, but Dick has a rifle pointed at you just in case you're not who you seem to be." Grant lowered the weapon and placed it on the ground beside Dick.

Grant then reluctantly raised his hands above his head and walked toward the troopers.

"Why wouldn't we be who we seem to be?" The officer kept his pistol aimed at Grant.

Grant continued forward, looking at the other trooper. He seemed frustrated trying to use his radio. He, also, kept his firearm readied. "It's a long story." Grant tried to smile, hoping it would ease tension and they would bring down their weapons.

"On your knees, hands behind your back." As quickly as his hands fell, the handcuffs clicked around his wrists. He had felt the panic of captivity earlier as he faced certain death, but the shame and vulnerability of total surrender tore at his essence.

"Can I see some identification?" Grant looked up, making sure he met the officer's eyes. He knew eyes—honest, deceitful, professional, worried, angry—knew them all. These were distracted eyes.

"Sure. But where is the Dick you were talking about." The officer kept his pistol on Grant, making quick study for weapons with his other hand. The other officer had ducked behind the building.

Darkness was coming on quickly now. The cars' headlights produced their own shadows, leaving witchy images in the distance. The churn of the engine in the background suddenly took on new character as Grant remained motionless. Instead of idling, the rumble seemed to deepen as if preparing to charge.

CHAPTER 42

Lee's pistol fired a moment after the Remington M40A7 bolt action sniper rifle delivered its magnum at 3,500 feet per second to Lee's chest. A foot-pound of kinetic energy has the ability to lift one pound a foot into the air. At 3,000 foot-pounds of energy, the newly designed hollow point bullet expanded on impact to three times its diameter, spreading the energy and blasting Lee backward and through the gate behind him.

Lee was holding Jack's collar as the round made its impact, his grip firm enough that they both crashed through the fence and downward. Jack, stunned and deaf from the .38 special bullet that missed his temple by a millimeter, tumbled through the air, hitting the angry slurry of water in the spillway.

The exit was immediate. Under the power of tons of water, Jack shot out of the spillway and into the fury below the spillway. Tumbling over boulders and bedrock, he was 50 yards downstream before the surge pushed him up for a breath. The rumble in his brain after the gun blast was only a whisper compared to the water's rage. Darkness pushed him forward. But the stream, only 20 feet wide in areas, plunged him through narrow chutes, lifting and lowering him, tumbling him onward.

Back at the spillway, the SWAT team rushed to the gate. Felix, the captain of the team and the sharpshooter who tagged Lee, looked into the swirling water below and then back at the gate. "Shit. The fucking gate was cut. I hit the bastard in the chest, but my round wouldn't have had the power to throw both of them through the gate." His hand studied the freshly snipped strands of wire.

"Call the Dive Team and Air Patrol," Felix yelled as he ran to the east side of Watermelon Road, searching the rapids for any sign of life.

One member of the team called headquarters as two others bounced down the hill, jumping from boulder to boulder toward the water. Felix called Miles directly. "Sir, we have a problem."

The Chief of Police was already on Watermelon Road. When Jack called, he left a crime scene across town to join the SWAT team because he was indebted to Jack. Two years earlier, his wife had been diagnosed with pancreatic cancer, and Jack performed a Whipple operation on her, removing a portion of her stomach, duodenum, pancreas, bile duct, and gallbladder. The cancer was advanced at the time of surgery, but Jack performed an advanced technique. He removed all lymph nodes in the abdomen and implanted a chemotherapy pump in the abdominal cavity, using a Geiger counter-type of nuclear scanner to remove areas in the abdomen at risk for recurrent cancer. The operation took 15 hours and she never had a single problem postoperatively. Jack checked on her every few months, calling and visiting her at home.

"Sir, we have the helicopter on its way and we've mobilized the Dive Team." Felix was talking the moment Miles' door opened. "We don't know the status of either man. We've got their meeting and the shot that put them in the water on tape."

Miles walked across the road to see if the officers along the river were having any luck. They were about 500 yards away, paralleling the stream. One of them started waving his hands and yelling, but the roar of the water was too loud to understand them.

"We have Dr. Jack Wade." The radio signal was loud enough for them both to hear as Felix received his call from below.

"He's okay."

Felix and Miles looked through their binoculars as the SWAT members pulled Jack up the bank.

"What happened?" Jack panted. One of the officers helped him sit on a nearby boulder.

"The man you were with tried to shoot you," the other SWAT member answered. He was tucking in his shirttail like he'd just finished dinner. "He must have missed by a frog's hair. Felix, our team leader, put 160 grains in his chest. Y'all went through that gate into the drink like shit through a goose." Smiling like Boss Hog, he looked at Jack like a prize.

Jack looked up the hill at the water spouting furiously from the spillway. "How the hell did I survive all that?" His head still pounded from the blast beside his right ear, but he hardly cared. Lee was dead and he was alive.

"Can't wait to find that bastard. I'll bet he realized he was gonna die when he saw his heart flying toward Walker County."

Overhead, the percussion of chopper blades batted the air. "We have one here alive. You're looking for the body of the perpetrator now," the man relayed the message to the chopper. "This is a recover mission now, not a rescue." He clicked off the radio. "The divers better hurry up. We pulled one ol' boy outa the drink here 'bout a month ago. One too many beers and he fell outa his boat at night, and by the time the divers found him, the catfish had all but finished him off." He fanned his nose. "I was off that day but decided to watch the search. When they pulled him out he looked like a mummy without clothes, and he smelled it too."

Jack was on his feet. "Well, let me know when you've found him, but as far as I'm concerned, the catfish and buzzards can fight over him."

The trek back up the hill was easier than he thought it would be. As steep as the incline was and in spite of having churned through the rapids, he marched up the bank like on a Sunday hike. Miles was waiting at the top.

"I thought y'all were going to protect me, not make me a human torpedo." Jack smiled as he took the last step onto Watermelon Road.

Miles grabbed his right hand for a formal shake, then fully embraced him. "We didn't know you could swim. Otherwise, we'd of let the bastard blow your brains out." He released Jack and they shared a laugh.

"Come look at this." Miles took Jack to the fencing over the spillway. "It looks like the bastard wasn't gonna take any chances. He must have cut the gate before you got there. Once he shot you, I guess he was ready to push you through the gate. You'd never have been seen again except by the fish downstream. That's why you went into the spillway. The bullet he was hit with took you both through the gate, but only because it was already cut."

Jack brushed his hair to the side, which had dried, leaving it plastered over his brow. With a sweep of his hand, it returned to perfect position. "Do I have to fill out any paper work or answer questions."

"Actually, yes," Miles responded. "I guess you've watched enough TV to realize we have to write up the incident. You can either come with us now or come by the station tomorrow."

"Maybe tomorrow, if that's okay. I'm pretty whipped right now." Although Jack was tired, he was not too tired to talk. He wanted to take care of something before talking to the police.

CHAPTER 43

Dick had dozed off, his mind hidden in dreams and emptiness. His shoulder didn't really hurt but provided background impulses of pressure, until he slipped from his perch on the tree. A slight slip to the right and the pins and needles in his shoulder became a hot poker, startling him as they burrowed deeply into his neck and arm.

"AHHHHH!" His vocal cords couldn't handle the burst of air that exploded from him and his scream slid into a moan, bringing him back to consciousness.

Grant, still bending at the feet of a trooper, realized that his paranoia might cost Dick his life. "He's behind that tree." He pointed with his eyes. "The one with a dead man hanging in the branches."

"What?" The officer bent to one knee, minimizing himself as a target and keeping Grant between himself and the tree.

Grant abbreviated the story as much as possible. "That's Dick Sands behind the tree, the son of the governor, who owns this place. We came here to investigate something, possibly espionage, and three people attacked us. They killed two of us and shot Dick in the shoulder. He's badly injured and needs to get to a hospital quickly." He turned, looking at the officer. "I wasn't sure if you guys might be trying to kill us."

"Here." The officer pulled out his badge and identification. "I'm Officer Kelly and my partner is Officer Jones. We're here to help you, not to kill you."

The officer spoke into his radio. "Check out the tree at one o'clock." No reply.

"Hey, John." He yelled this time.

"Yeah." Officer Jones wasn't far way. He edged forward from the building.

"Our communications are shot. I've got this guy. He says there's someone down under the tree." He shouted again.

Within moments the other officer was at Dick's side. "Got him," he yelled. "You're right. He's got a bad shoulder wound."

"Is there a body hanging in the tree."

"Shit!" The car lights lit Ghost's face, now a jack-o-lantern of swollen darkness. "Yeah, there's a body hanging in the branches."

"Any ID on the wounded guy?" Kelly asked.

"Looks like a Richard Sands, Jr." Jones had found his wallet.

"I can make this simple for everyone." Grant squirmed. "I can make a quick call and have the governor on the line to let him know about his son and he can confirm who I am." He shifted his weight on his knees. "And can I get out of this position?"

"Sir, you can stand up."

The handcuffs made it difficult, but rising to his feet ended the numbness that had set in. "Just a single call and we can get things going. We need to get him to a hospital as quickly as possible, anyway. If you call the governor, I'm sure we can get air ambulance services right away, and he can let you know what hospital to send him to."

"We have a problem," Officer Kelley admitted. "We lost radio and cell phone communications about a quarter of a mile from here."

"Well, drive down the road to where we have communications. You don't want the governor's son dying, do you?"

"I'll be right back, John," Kelly called to his partner. "I'm going to call in back-up and an Air EVAC. I'm taking this guy down the road where we lost communications."

"Ten-four."

Grant and the officer ran back to the car, handcuffs still in place. Grant wondered if the satellite was able to block communications, who was listening to him now, and what he could tell the governor if he got through.

Kelly informed the other two officers, "We're going to make a call back where we lost communications. You guys help John with the governor's son. We'll be right back."

When they were a few miles up the road, he told Grant, "This ought to do it."

"Okay. Call 205-751-7663 and tell them you have Dr. Miller and he needs to talk with Governor Sands," Grant directed.

"Shit, you never told me you were a doc." He unlocked the handcuffs. "Here. You can make the call yourself."

Grant took the phone and quickly dialed the number. He left the phone on "speaker" mode so that the officer could hear. When the governor answered, taking the phone from the nurse on duty, Grant noted he sounded strong, a relief.

"Governor, this is Grant Miller and I'm with Officer Kelley. We're on a speaker phone."

"tell me what's going on, Grant!" The Governor knew better than to waste time asking questions.

"Governor, Dick has been shot. I'm pretty sure he will be okay if we get him to the hospital quickly. We were attacked by three men." Grant paused, but the governor did not ask questions, allowing Grant to proceed.

"It's a crazy story that I really need to tell you when I see you, but right now I need you to pull whatever strings necessary to get a Air EVAC down here as quickly as possible. We are at the Sands facility but all radio and communications are out at the building and around it." Grant paused again.

Molly, who was in the room with Richard, knew when the call came that it was about her son. She knew by Richard's eyes that there was a problem.

"We need to get an air ambulance to our plant. Dick's been shot in the shoulder. He's okay."

Molly was already on her feet. Her mouth held back a quiver. "What do I need to do?"

"Go tell Daniel what's happened. He'll take care of things."

Next to Frank, Daniel Cooper was the Governor's closest companion. A state trooper for 10 years, he had been Richard's shadow since he took office. Before becoming a trooper, he had been a Security Guard at Sands. Always loyal and honest, Richard handpicked him as his personal attendant. He and Frank were a perfect team. they protected Richard, anticipating problems and helping him avoid awkward or dangerous situations. Richard and Molly considered them family. Holidays and special occasions were celebrated together. The governor's family even held birthday parties for them.

After Molly left the room, Richard straightened himself in bed and said, "Tell me more."

"Governor, I'm sorry. Frank and Harper are both dead, killed by the three men who tried to kill me and Dick." Grant looked at the officer next to him, wondering if he could talk freely.

Officer Kelley realized Grant was no threat and that he had things to share in private. "I'll step out of the car for a moment if you need to talk alone to the governor." He turned off the engine and took the keys with him, though.

"The helicopter should already be in flight if I know my people," the governor said.

"They also need to know that they might lose radio communication when they get near the plant. The bikers must have used some scrambling device. No communications in the plant worked, and the troopers who just showed up lost their signals about a quarter mile from the plant..."

"Are you okay, Grant?" Richard interrupted.

The question took Grant by surprise. He instinctively answered but knew what he said wasn't fully accurate. "I'm fine. How are you?" Grant asked.

"I'm doing really well, physically."

"Governor, where do want to take Dick? The closest place would be Mobile, but we have excellent orthopedic surgeons in Tuscaloosa and he would be close to you."

"I want him in Tuscaloosa."

"One favor. Can you arrange for me to ride on the helicopter back to Tuscaloosa."

"No problem. I'll even send another one down for back up."

....

The combination of moonlight and infrared imaging gave Yao a clear view of Grant's car and Sands facility. Four people were huddled around the tree where Ghost hung. He could hear them, through Ghost's transmitter, tending to Dick's wounds.

"Too many mistakes," he thought. With all of his technology, all of his potential to gather and integrate information, and all of his intuition for where to concentrate his surveillance he had still failed to use his resources fully.

Quickly, he flipped another switch, commanding the EMIT to broaden its communications blockade. He didn't want Dr. Miller to have any more communication with the governor.

As he watched the four men under the tree, he realized that if he had used thermal tracking earlier in the day that it wouldn't have come to this. Instead, the clear optics that daylight allows had distracted him. Watching the action at the Sands facility had been too easy and too disturbing. The chase had distracted him as well. He chose to follow Grant through the delta, to direct his agent to him and watch him suffer. As a result, he didn't think about using his daytime infrared tracking or he might have seen Dick come out of the river where he had fallen from the rifle shot. He could have sent the Tiger to Mobile to finish what his other three agents had failed to do.

Computers whirred in the background as Yao pivoted in his chair. His skin had almost adopted the greenish blue haze that filled the globe of monitors around him. Instead of streaming from screen to screen, eavesdropping with the click of a button, recording conversations and events with precision, he simply twirled aimlessly on his chair. The countless monitors surrounding him seemed hungry, seemed to be watching him as they sprayed their monochrome images of red, green, and blue with delight, feasting with him and enjoying their power of distance and anonymity.

....

Skipper Jenkins was in the air. His father had started SkySave as a small scale air ambulance service in Atlanta, but it was now the main flight service for transporting patients from hospital to hospital and providing trauma services in the Southeast.

None of the flight crew wanted him as their pilot, not only because he was an asshole but because he was a cowboy in the sky. The crewmembers took their jobs seriously, their entire mission centered on the patient, but for Skipper, everything was about Skipper. They also knew that Skipper would fly the missions he wanted to fly and fly them how he wanted.

When Skipper heard that the governor of Alabama's son was down and needed immediate pickup, he was in his Cumulus 585 before the full message zipped through his cell. At 250 miles per hour, he would be at the Sands facility before any other regional service could arrive. This was a chance for glory. Skipper didn't care about the money—he had plenty—but he always brought his PR man with him, hoping for the perfect rescue, his heroism recorded for the world to see. His last trip had been a bust. He took an Atlanta Braves pitcher to Boston and didn't have a single picture to put on his wall or send to the Associated Press because athletes don't allow pictures of themselves when they are going for medical work. This would be different: pictures, video, primetime.

"Yahoo!" Skipper waved his arms as the Cumulus did its work. He could play like Slim Pickens riding a nuclear bomb if he wanted to. It was his helicopter and his dad's business, and everyone inside the chopper knew it. Luckily, the helicopter didn't really even need Skipper. The inertial guidance system was taking the helicopter to its destination as digital processors automatically corrected the roll, pitch, yaw, altitude, latitude and longitude in the aircraft. The Rolls Royce twin turbine system combined with new quadrotor propulsion allowed the engineering marvel to slip into the tiniest alcoves for quick pick up and delivery.

Once again Skipper waved and yelped, watching the infrared camera paint the projected landing area ahead. "Yeah, baby. We're coming in." He flipped his favorite switch, turning on the music. Wagner's "Ride of the Valkyries" rumbled into action. Skipper was no Robert

Duvall, but the panorama of woofers and tweeters bellowed out enough energy and sound that even the flight crew became energized.

The helicopter's sensors had identified the exact spot for landing, the potential dangers of surrounding trees and the flight speed that would be necessary to maneuver the landing. Moonlight sprayed off the chopper blades as the Cumulus whirled over the Mobile Delta. Outside, the mighty rotors roared, tearing through the thickened air that carried a taste of salt and the vapors of swamp. Inside, the drum of Wagner's masterpiece blasted as the helicopter began its descent, Skipper posing for a video shot.

"Governor, this is Skipper Jenkins." The music automatically muted as he spoke.

Skipper had been in touch with Richard throughout the flight, assuring him that he would have his son in Tuscaloosa before the second showing of O'Reilly.

"We are about there. If your information is right, we may lose radio contact for a while. But don't worry, this sky carriage will be clickin' home before a night owl can hoot." He winked at the video recorder and tipped his captain's hat.

Below, Grant watched the lights approach, feeling a sense of rescue and relief as the monotony of crickets and buzz of mosquitoes quickly surrendered to the dominant rotors above. "Here it comes." Grant knelt beside Dick, who was now awake.

"I'm ready to get out of here." Dick's head rested on some uniforms that Kelley provided from his trunk. "That's a pretty sight."

The helicopter passed over the road where Grant had made his call, still traveling 150 miles an hour. That's when the communication from the three axis autopilot system suddenly lost its inertial guidance. That's also when Grant lost communications again with the governor.

·········

For years, NASA and the Chinese National Space Administration (CNSA) had been battling to develop defenses against radiofrequency interference (RFI). Satellites occasionally had difficulty receiving and transmitting data due to transmitters from earth broadcasting on the same frequency they used. It was known that RFI directed at satellites could have various effects on communication systems and microwave sensors. Military and commercial programs had existed for some time, developing strategies and techniques to use RFI to degrade data in satellites and block communications.

However, Yao, in concert with the CNSA, had been the first to successfully disengage satellites through directed RFI. They used their technology on their own satellites initially but had toyed with those of other nations as well. Not only did Yao have the ability to apply this communication's weapon to satellites, he could use the same weapon technology wherever he wished.

Big Guy's Ducati was armed with an EMIT, Electromagnetic Interference Technology. Simply by triggering it through his satellite, Yao was able to cut off communications in the Sands building and for a few miles around it. That's why Grant and Dick had lost all cell phone and landline communications and why the troopers had lost their radio capabilities. That's how he was able to end Grant's conversation with the governor and bring down a helicopter.

·········

The aircraft bounced like it was hit by a nuclear shock wave, then tumbled through the air. The four sets of propellers chopped at the air, each battling the others, totally unsynchronized, and the helicopter lost all control. Skipper was frozen in his seat. The cyclic control between his legs shook aimlessly, waiting for him to take manual ownership of the mechanics. His feet on the anti-torque pedals were simply bricks, hardened with terror. Instead of the rotors continuing to slow in the approach phase of landing, the autopilot sensed a stall and sped up.

All blades sliced furiously at the air, but there was no hope. The helicopter crashed on the road leading to the Sands compound, metal flying in all directions and flames following the wreckage. The cabin bounced three times then disintegrated into splinters of wiring, aluminum, acrylic glass, and bone.

Yao watched the infrared display of the helicopter crashing, his eyes wide with excitement.

"*Lā shǐ!*" (SHIT!) Yao slammed his fist on his knee. Suddenly he realized that he had made another mistake, maybe his worst. He could have used the EMIT to bring the helicopter down with Dick Sands and Dr. Miller on board.

Yao stopped spinning, furious with himself for negligence. He wouldn't make that mistake again.

CHAPTER 44

Jack put the wadded note, now soaked and faded thanks to his swim, Suzy had given him into the pocket of his dry jeans pocket. Her request: "Please go to my apartment and get my computer. Don't let anyone see it."

He knew he had better find the computer before he spoke to the police. Surely Suzy and her story would be part of the interrogation, and he wanted to be honest and thorough with the authorities. But there was something about Suzy that had captured him. He hadn't figured it out yet. Maybe it was compassion or concern, maybe sorrow or duty, maybe desire or affection... He couldn't sort everything out, but he knew that Suzy was a piece of the puzzle in his life.

After a quick shower and donning fresh clothes, he typed the address into his car's map and was off. West on 15th Street and past Martin Luther Boulevard, he traveled toward Highway 11. Stillman College was on his left. Over a hundred acres in size, it had been eclipsed by the 1,000 acre University of Alabama long ago.

Jack continued past the college on Highway 11, the lights of the city quickly fading. He followed instructions from Sophia, his mapping guide, turning right then left and then going forward 50 feet until he arrived at Suzy's apartment. A single yellow light on the porch of the desolate shack was all that stood as a reminder of civilization at the end of the road. Moonlight hardly found the structure in its nesting of hardwoods and pines.

He knew Suzy lived on the fringes of the economy, but he had never considered that a student at the University of Alabama might live in a hovel. He hadn't forgotten what it was like when he was growing up on a farm, waking up hours before school to take the chickens scraps of vegetable peelings and bones that had been discarded the night before and milking Mammy, their aged cow, to have fresh milk for a breakfast of eggs from the chickens before heading off to school. Still, in the era of student loans and government support, he expected Suzy to have more.

After checking the address and GPS once, twice, and yet again, he stepped out of his car and onto the broken asphalt leading to her home. The yellow bulb on her porch glowed with faltering consistency, fading in and out but never failing. He stepped onto the porch, a square of crate-like weathered pine, testing it with his weight before committing himself. It gave slightly with creaking weariness but was more sturdy than it looked.

Jack knocked on the door, certain that there would be no response but careful not to be shot breaking into someone's home. He waited 10 seconds. No response. Suzy had told him the key was under a mat next to the door. He looked down at the coir mat, faded and saturated with dirt, that must have grown up with the building. He could barely read the "welcome": GO AWAY! The key was under it, dusted with filth from above.

The smell of sardines, rice vinegar, and fried rice met him before he could find the light switch. When the lights came on, the odor was all that was there. The kitchen cubicle housed a Chambers gas stove, the white paint now yellow from layers of smoke and 60 years of faithful service. There was one shelf with a bag of rice and one can of sardines. No refrigerator. The sink, rusted and cracked, couldn't have held water in years. Inside the trashcan was an empty cardboard box, the last remnants of sweet and sour pork licked from the edges of a China Yum take out.

The vacancy of food was surpassed only by the tidiness of the room. The floor was neatly swept and there were no crumbs on the stove and no clutter. Through the kitchen shone a tiny blue light, the power signal of the computer he hoped to find.

Jack flipped another light switch and found the computer on a wooden table, a single plastic chair tucked underneath. Papers were carefully stacked beside the machine. In the left far corner of the room was a single folding metal bed, the mattress stained with dry blood. Smudges around the blotches showed signs of efforts to wash away the marks. Two pairs of jeans, two T-shirts, and undergarments were carefully folded beside the bed.

The left closest corner was a half bath, a toilet and standing shower the only inhabitants. Five bars of soap were stacked on the back of the toilet, probably still too little detergent to wash away what Suzy needed washed away, he thought.

Jack stepped hesitantly to the table, feeling like he was intruding on revered space. The papers were organized in stacks, each labeled with a cover sheet: Intellectual Functioning, Academic Achievement, Visuospatial Processing, Visual Learning and Memory. Jack flipped open the laptop. He expected the screen to be blank or for a password to prevent his intrusion, but her screen was open to anyone.

The icons were simple universal prompts, but Chinese characters made her computer incomprehensible. He did recognize one of the icons. Having presented a paper recently at the Southern Surgical Society in which he had to include Spanish translations, he knew the value of Language-Shift. Tapping the icon, he easily maneuvered from Chinese to English.

In a flash, the screen was totally in English. He zipped through her research: Neural Pathways of Meriones Unguiculatus, a species of Mongolian Gerbil; Functional Preservation of Rubrospinal Tract in Spinal Preparation in Rattus Norvegicus; Spinal Recovery after Traumatic Transection, DCH Regional.

Jack's fingers danced with excitement as he entered the DCH file. Patient after patient was listed, their physical findings, emotional progress, and objective improvement. The data was thorough and perfectly organized, and Suzy's follow-up was impeccable.

Then his heart paused. "Lizzie White!" Jack read the name, then stared blankly at the screen.

He remembered the name clearly from the death certificate he had to sign. He remembered the little girl's body, the horror. Then he remembered Suzy hysterical in the waiting room.

"Who is Suzy? The innocent victim or devious monster? What does she have to do with Lizzie? Did she have anything to do with her death?"

Jack's mind spun with more questions than answers as he opened the file.

Lizzie White was a 10 year-old child with a spinal cord injury high in the neck resulting in paralysis of her arms and legs and diaphragm. That was the reason the little girl was on the respirator, her diaphragm wouldn't work as a piston to allow her to breathe on her own. Suzy had performed daily exams, all confirming complete paralysis.

Reading on, Jack's heart melted as he found communications between Dr. Weng Fang, Professor and Chief of Neurosurgery at Nanfong Memorial and known internationally as a pioneer in spinal cord injuries. Suzy had been in contact with him from the day Lizzie came into the hospital, sharing what she was able to find out from records and her own interactions with the girl. Government regulations prevented her from access to early information that she might have used to improve Lizzie's chances of recovery.

However, when Lizzie left the intensive care area and arrived on the seventh floor, Suzy was able to learn more and to do more.

"Dr. Fang, I have implanted the biosensor in Lizzie. You should be able to receive the data on Lizzie White (patient LW583) immediately." Jack read Suzy's communication to Nanfong, China. "Biosensor," he thought. Maybe that was the same implanted device she had in her, the receiver that prevented her from talking to him.

The next day, she continued her correspondence. "Dr. Fang, I have given Lizzie the Lithium and Methylprednisolone that you suggested."

Dr. Fang had responded, "Excellent. I can already tell that the circulating serum Leptin and S100B levels are improving. Keep up the good work, Suzy. Do you need money for supplies?"

"No, sir. I have plenty of money!"

After Suzy's response was a notation: "$223 U.S. for supplies, my week's pay from China Yum!" She had posted a Smiley Face beside her notation.

Suzy must have been working at China Yum late at night, Jack's favorite takeout place in Tuscaloosa and he would have noticed her there during regular hours. Perhaps she cleaned up after hours or prepared food for the next day, All he knew for certain was that she had spent her entire week's pay on a little girl. Jack knew Lizzie wasn't just a research project for Suzy.

Above the tiny shack, tall pines swayed under the clouded sky, brushing away any light from above. The darkness around the tiny structure found crevices to sift into, bringing a draft of coolness through the room. Jack read on, feeling the tugs of the night to accompany his need to know more.

"Lizzie White (LW583) now shows neural pathway activity in Vestibulospinal Tract. Give 1 ampule of stem cell growth factor. This is great news, Suzy. It looks like Lizzie will walk one day."

Dr. Fang's communication must have come the night before Lizzie's death. There were no more entries from him, just another notation from her.

The wind outside had picked up. A breeze whistled through a break in the kitchen window. Jack felt a chill, probably not unlike those that Suzy experienced in her isolation.

"Li Ziang must have seen this. He probably knows that I have used one of his transmitters to send data to Dr. Fang. I hope he has taken out his anger only on me. I am afraid he might hurt Lizzie. I am going to Lizzie's room. When I know she is safe, I am going to tell the police everything."

Jack read what was probably the last entry in the computer for Lizzie, almost Suzy's last communication ever. He knew Li Ziang was Lee. He knew why Suzy was so broken when he found her in the waiting room the day of Lizzie's death. He knew some of the things that Lee must have done to her. What was she going to tell the police?

Jack looked at the screen of her computer and saw that it was 1:30 AM. That's when he heard a strong wind raging through the surrounding trees and snapping limbs like twigs. The distant howl of a siren was almost inaudible but slipped through a momentary break in a wind gust.

He remembered stories of the April 27, 2011 EF4 tornado that ravaged the city. It killed 52 people and destroyed 2,000 buildings. Nearly a tenth of the population were immediately out of work. The mile-wide tornado stood as an ever-present reminder to those who had experienced it that weather sirens needed to be heeded. For Jack it was another reason to head home.

Just as Jack folded the laptop closed, the lights in the house went off and he heard what sounded like footsteps on the porch.

CHAPTER 45

Grant and the troopers had no hope for the helicopter passengers. The cabin had crashed close enough to them that any further search was unnecessary. It was destroyed, the devastation complete. Now the distant sound of a second helicopter was thumping toward them. There was no way to warn them, no radio contact.

The second helicopter's lights had found their landing zone, turning the road in front of Grant into daylight. Reflections of hundreds of eyes in the night flickered in the woods and wetlands around them.

The landing was smooth and the medical team quickly examined Dick, placing needed intravenous lines and delivering fluids and antibiotics. His shoulder was a dried carpet of blood, tendons, muscle, bone, and river wash. They simply covered it with a dressing, careful not to reactivate bleeding. Then, as quickly as they landed, they were back in the air.

Yao waited until their airspeed hit 100 knots. He had reprogrammed the EMIT. Now its range was two miles. His brow furrowed above a chilling stare as he flipped the switch, watching the flight of the helicopter on infrared magnification. The helicopter was going fast enough by now to provide a similar crash to the previous chopper's.

The helicopter, a Bell 206 Long Ranger based in Mobile and the oldest air ambulance in the Southeast, flipped to its left and then to its right, throwing intravenous tubing and packets to the floor of the chopper. Grant was seat-belted in directly across from the paramedics.

The lurch whipped his head forward then snapped it back against the seat. Tubing from Dick's intravenous line whipped his cheek as it rebounded.

"Son of a bitch. We've lost our compass and autopilot," Finney, a veteran of Afghanistan, growled, more to himself than anyone onboard. Finney had flown more missions from the Forward Operating Base Pasab, Kandahar than he could remember, returning broken warriors to Kandahar Hospital Role 3 and Hero. He knew how to fly a Black Hawk without instruments in dust storms or at night and could land a whirly with his eyes closed, sensing the ground like radar.

Finney turned off the autopilot and took manual control of the chopper, relieving the confused computers under the sticks of their command.

....

Yao's stare burned into the screen, watching, waiting, and then disbelieving. He switched EMIT off and on again, retriggered it, expanding its territory. On. Off. On... Rage fired through his hands.

....

The panel in front of Finney was schizophrenic, point-on accurate and then crazy with disorientation. It flipped on then off, the gyroscope whirling mindlessly and then recapturing its focus. Finney stayed cool, letting the professionals behind him do their thing while he did his.

"Sir, you asked me to call," Finney barked. "We lost radio connection there for a while, and actually lost our autopilot and instruments for a while."

"Is everything okay now?" The governor asked, watching Molly's prayerful stare.

"Yes, sir. Everything's back now," Finney grunted, looking at the instruments with disgust. "We should be there shortly."

"Great. Be careful. Let me know if you have any problems. We'll be waiting for you."

·········

Yao was plugged in to the governor and Grant, listening as he watched the helicopter zip toward Tuscaloosa on infrared. He also watched the signal from Grant's clip, making sure he was aboard.

"Anything else on Dick?" The governor's voice was choppy as Yao listened.

"Still having chills and fever. Paramedics say he's still talking out of his mind." The nurses taking care of the governor had explained the paramedics' assessment as well as they could. Dick's blood loss and injury, the contamination of his wound from the river, and hours in the elements of the Mobile wetlands had likely made his son delusional. His blood pressure was probably low as a result of blood loss but may well be a result of infection setting in on his shoulder wound.

"The paramedics say the quicker he gets to the operating room to clean up his shoulder, the better. I'd just make sure the doctors and hospital are ready for that. They say he's really strong and hanging in there but could get into trouble soon without rapid care." Richard kept his cell phone on speaker mode so Molly could hear the conversation.

Yao could hear the telephone exchange clearly as well. He quickly called the Tiger.

244

CHAPTER 46

"Governor, we should be down in 10 minutes." All systems had been working normally since south Alabama. Finney had stayed in constant contact with Richard, busier on the radio than with the chopper.

Grant watched the lights of Tuscaloosa grow brighter as the helicopter chopped through the air, drawing them closer and closer. He had played chess in high school, but never had to consider so many moves—so many options and the consequences of them all—as were before him now.

He couldn't talk to the governor about the clip. Whoever was trying to kill him and Dick would be after the governor as well if he knew what they knew. And he had to assume that anything he said was floating over the airwaves. The governor himself might have a clip in him, however, and so he needed to be aware that his communications were also being monitored. Grant had a responsibility to let him know, but timing was everything. If he didn't have a clip that was being monitored, then telling the governor prematurely was potentially dangerous to him... Grant skipped from scenario to scenario, considering the impact of telling the governor or not telling him. And in case neither he nor Dick survived, his pen had furiously recorded the last 24 hours as well as he could remember. Although he was muzzled, at least his story would survive. Besides, he really had two missions, and one was more important to him than the other.

The midnight lights of Tuscaloosa were mainly white—headlights and street lights—but the various shades of green, blue, and red of late-night businesses added color below as the helicopter made its final approach to the landing pad. DCH Hospital's helipad had been active the last few hours, bringing in trauma patients and sending others for specialty care in Birmingham. The blue lights marked the target as the blades changed their pitch and velocity for landing.

The paramedics gathered their equipment for rapid transfer to the Emergency Room or Operating Room, wherever they were told to go. Finney, wary of the autopilot, was locked into his destination, using his hands and feet to steer the chopper manually. The descent was smooth, perfect. Only a slight bounce welcomed them back.

Finney cut the power to the blades and allowed them to idle. Grant unbuckled his seatbelt and stuffed his recent notes in his pants pocket. He was careful to let the paramedics do their work, but he took Dick by the wrist. His pulse was thready and rapid. Sweat met his fingers. A clammy film of moisture was already chilled despite the feverish flesh underneath. Grant recognized the signs of sepsis, signs of a body being conquered by bacteria. There wasn't much he could do at this point. He knew the trauma service at DCH was tops and would do all that could be done, but he closed his eyes momentarily.

The helicopter doors opened. Emergency room personnel were present to assist the paramedics and Dick floated from the helicopter to the ground and then the Emergency Room. Almost riding a wave, he came to a stop in Trauma Bay 5.

"Tetanus. Clindamycin, 900 milligrams. Vancomycin, 1.5 milligrams. Meropenem, one gram IV, now." Bud Rivers was the emergency room physician taking care of Dick. He had finished a residency in general surgery only to find better hours and pay as an ER physician. But his experience had many returns. He was able to identify situations that others might miss. "And type and cross for four units of blood. We've already got necrotizing fasciitis."

He had peeled away the dressings over Dick's shoulder to find the classic signs: a brash-water drainage seeped from the underlying mangled bone and muscle, remnants of twigs and leaves buried inside, gifts from the river. The putrid smell and brackish blisters surrounding the wound were the dead giveaway.

"This is bad, really bad." He didn't recognize the nurse who had joined him but continued to deliver orders. "He needs to go to the Operating Room ASAP. Call Dr. Taylor. He's been waiting on the call."

A thin nurse took orders, the epicanthic fold of her eyes, high cheek bones, strong jawline, and round face not at all familiar to him. But nurses came and went from the Emergency Room, and so he didn't worry. He knew his staff was consistently good.

Bud had managed necrotizing fasciitis before but with mixed results. He knew this was usually due to a mixture of different bacteria, all with the potential to rapidly spread though injured tissue. The bacteria give off poisons as they divide and spread, destroying more muscle and fat in the process, the destruction spreading like a wildfire. The only treatment is multiple high powered antibiotics that he had ordered and immediate surgery to remove all dead tissue.

"Dr. Taylor, this is Meirong. I am Dr. Rivers' nurse. He asked me to call about this patient, Richard Sands, Jr. He says he needs to go to the OR immediately." Meirong nodded to Dr. Rivers, signaling that the message was delivered.

Bud knew what was ahead for this patient and was glad that he would soon transfer care to someone else.

Bud didn't want to be the doctor who couldn't save the governor's son, or his arm should he survive. He had been waiting for the last hour and a half for the patient to arrive. Fifteen calls regarding this particular patient had come in while he was trying to see other sick patients, the first call from the Cardiac Surgical floor, warning him of who was in the helicopter. The CEO of the hospital called, the chaplain, the OR, and finally his own wife to ask him what was going on because she had heard the governor's son was flying in from Cuba with a bullet in his heart. So much for HIPPA rules. So much for accuracy in the grapevine.

"Dr. Taylor said to send him on up. He's already in the OR, waiting on him." Meirong placed two more intravenous lines in Dick as she spoke loudly. The scars on her hands were hardly visible.

Another nurse administered a tetanus shot while two others hooked up the antibiotics. Dick was semiconscious, drifting in and out of the twilight zone. His lips twisted as he tried to speak, but the mumbles didn't have enough energy to form words. Even he could speak a full sentence, his mind was cobwebs, jumbled and disconnected.

"I'll stay with him and make sure he gets there," Meirong offered.

"Thanks, but I'll make this transfer personally." Bud wasn't leaving Dick's side until he was sure his responsibilities were over.

As four nurses and Dr. Rivers pushed the gurney through the halls, he shouted to clear a path to the elevator. Then they went up to the second floor and into the Operating Room. The OR staff had probably had the same number of telephone calls Dr. Rivers received because two nurse anesthetists, an anesthesiologist, three circulators, two attendants, and Dr. Taylor were waiting at the door.

Dr. Zac Taylor's five o'clock shadow was now a two-day shadow. He had switched call with his partner, not anticipating 60 hours without sleep. The pointed toes of his Stetson cowboy boots had already broken through the worn blue footies that were supposed to protect them from blood and other stains, but everyone knew, when he took the protectors off, his boots looked like camo with patterns of blood, bile, and fecal stains.

"Mother fucker, Bud. He looks like hammered shit." Zac Taylor wasn't one to hold his words. "Get the fucker into the room right now."

The anesthesiologist was looking at the bottles of antibiotics and medicines running into Dick's IV's, counting the number of intravenous lines and checking Dick's pulse.

"I said get the fucker into the OR room now!" Zac snapped, pushing the stretcher himself.

Meirong watched the activity as every staff member in the OR rushed to catch up with Dr. Taylor. "Is it okay if I stay and watch this?" she asked Dr. Rivers. "I've never seen anything like this before?"

"It's fine with me if it's okay with staffing downstairs." Bud was already heading back to the E.D., relieved that his duties were over.

Meirong was already in scrubs, and so fitting in as an observer was easy enough with all the commotion. She placed her mask and bouffant hair cover on and stood in a corner, watching and listening. Dick was asleep, his breathing tube in place.

One of the circulating nurses, vigilant in sterile technique, was carefully preparing a scrub setup. It was the way she was trained, the only way she knew how to clean an area before surgery.

"Give me that fucking paint." Zac had scrubbed his hands and was wearing his surgical gown. "It's a fucking sewage tank in there, honey." He took brown iodine based antiseptic and sloshed it freely over Dick's shoulder, pouring and wiping the liquid from his ear to his navel, lifting and coating his entire left arm and chest. "This is the kind of case that you scrub your hands AFTER you scrub the patient." He splashed the fluid, thoroughly wiping inside the wound and pulling out chips of bone, lumps of dirt, remnants of leaves and twigs.

"It doesn't matter if you scrub this wound with toilet water," Zac muttered to himself. "You can't turn a shit hole into candy by flushing the toilet."

Zac sloshed antiseptic paint over the wound, letting it pool in the cavity. Then, after squaring off the field in drapes, he began snipping away with scissors, cutting out dead and dying tissue. The he went deeper, trying to find bleeding muscle. His excavation went down to Dick's ribs on his chest. Muscle was no longer muscle but gelatinous lumps of stench dissolving in front of him. His fingers swept under Dick's skin, separating planes of muscle from the fat above. The tissue was melted butter seeping out of the wound, vapors of composting flesh filling the room.

Finally, after seeing red instead of dead in all areas, his scissors took a break.

"Irrigation," Zac snapped, expecting the machine to already be there for him.

A two liter bag of saline hung above the table attached to a battery powered wand. The circulating nurse clicked the final connection and Dr. Taylor was spraying clear fluid through the wound. The pressure washer did its work, removing any remaining debris and leaving only healthy tissue behind.

"This is going to be bad." He surveyed the well of blood, ribs, and exposed blood vessels and nerves in his shoulder. The open wound extended from his nipple to the middle of his chest, from his neck to his upper arm. "It's gonna be hard to explain this bomb blast to his parents." Zac paused. "Gov'na's gonna put me in shackles under the outhouse."

Zac kept spraying. Finally, there was nothing but blood, no dirt, pus, or odor. "Call hyperbarics. We need to get him in the tank as soon as possible."

The infection that Dick had was obviously caused by bacteria that live without oxygen, and Dr. Taylor knew that recent studies had confirmed the use of hyperbaric oxygen in gas gangrene and anaerobic infections. The bacteria in his wound grow in dead tissue and oxygen is poisonous to them, just like the lack of oxygen kills human tissue. The hyperbaric tanks in the hospital were available for wound healing but were rarely used emergently. Arranging for their emergency use would be problematic.

Meirong had never seen hyperbaric therapy before. She was determined to follow the governor's son as long as she could.

CHAPTER 47

Grant was the last to leave the helicopter, giving Finney a set of notes and a message before he stepped out. When his feet hit the ground, his legs launched him toward home. His lungs were still stiff, the lingering effects of the acid, but his legs knew their job and he wasn't going to let anything delay his reunion with Carol. He made a turn onto University Boulevard and crossed the bridge over McFarland. His strides stronger than he had expected, he picked up his pace. Things were darker than usual and he noted that the traffic light ahead was out. The lights from the hospital were strong enough to fill the road behind him, but ahead everything was shadowed.

Oak branches and leaves were scattered over the road as he entered the Highlands, signs of a recent storm. Overhead, low level clouds resisted the moon's efforts to lead Grant home. Obviously, the hospital's generator was keeping the place lit and all the equipment running for there were no lights in any of the houses around him.

Behind him, a branch cracked maybe 50 yards back. Grant's legs continued to churn, but his ears were on alert. His lungs were making too much noise to identify what was behind him, but he knew better than to look back.

The tapping of footfalls faster than his was unmistakable and quickly approaching. He searched the darkness, spotting his home at the end of the road. He would never make it. Whoever was behind him was a sprinter. It was time to face whoever was behind him.

The Tiger was enjoying the chase, the game of cat and mouse. He could run faster, but there was no need. He let his steps fall as heavily as possible to announce his presence. Silence wasn't necessary with men. He had killed too many to change his ways. No matter where his attack took place, he'd never had a man call for help or scream out of fear. It was an honorable approach to death.

Darkness was the Tiger's co-conspirator. His eyes preferred the grays and silhouettes of ambush, and takedowns were even better in the deepest shadows. Fear and panic made his work more entertaining, darkness adding flavor to his work.

Grant hit the brakes and did a one-eighty. He crouched, both arms up, ready for battle.

The Tiger swerved to his right, swishing past his prey. Five steps later, he whipped back, anxious to meet his target. His fingers tightened into claws, his knees ready to spring.

"My boss wants me to give you a choice." The Tiger crept toward Grant, examining his posture and deciding on a point of attack.

Grant's crouch was defensive, protective, but his lungs truly gave him away. His rapid breathing made it clear that he wouldn't last long in a skirmish. His legs would be the first to go. A front sweep with the Tiger's left foot followed by a slash across his throat would end it quickly.

"Who are you?" Grant heaved for oxygen.

"That is not your concern." The Tiger's accent was easy to identify, and expected.

"Then what are my choices?" The darkness was intense and the Tiger was a blur rather than invisible.

"You can die right here..." The Tiger let that choice linger. "Or you can take an oath of silence." The Tiger hoped Grant would turn the second choice down but knew that Yao was listening as well as watching. He would give the *nuò ruò de rén* (coward) a single chance, and then his fists would fly.

"I don't really want to die," Grant responded, his tone partly sarcastic and partly terrified. He kept his position, knowing his only chance was to engage his opponent, gain a hold, and hope for the best. Even in this light it was apparent that his adversary had skills. He had seen kung fu fighting in his training as a wrestler, and the Tiger's crouch was unmistakable.

"Then listen very carefully," the Tiger said, disappointed but obedient.

"You will forget everything that happened in the last 48 hours. Everything!" The Tiger was close enough to attack and yearning for the feel of flesh, the snap of ligaments.

"I can do that!" Grant returned. The Tiger knew he was lying.

"Very good. I thought you would say that, but just in case your memory returns, we have surveillance inside your house." Seeing Grant make a slight movement backward, he paused. "If your memory returns, we will know and your wife and children will be mine." He paused again. "And that would please me more than ending your life now."

Grant's crouch weakened and then gained energy. "You don't want to..."

"Yes, I do." The Tiger's eyes widened, hoping Grant would give him a reason to strike.

"Go on," Grant said, holding onto his emotions as well as he could.

"Return home now. Tell your wife that you've been busy, that you can't talk about it if she asks. Then return to the hospital, to your patients and your work. When the governor asks what happened, refuse to say anything." The Tiger saw Grant's legs stiffen, weakening, now aware that he was indeed a coward and not willing to die with honor.

"Why don't you just kill me? What's in it for you?" Grant was willing to consider his offer, the options before him not attractive.

"You might be called on to do some things for us, things that will keep your family safe, that will keep you alive."

Grant saw where this was going and realized that things were about to end right here on the street in front of his home. His life had never been a secret and it never would be. Death would be better than the life of a traitor, living in fear, living a lie.

The Tiger watched Grant's knees bend again. A sign that maybe this one wasn't the coward he had expected. It would be over quickly, but he would enjoy it while it lasted. His fingers had never lost their intensity, but now the muscles in his arms returned to triggers, ready for the right moment.

"You should know that your friend, the governor's son, will be dead soon. We will take care of that if he doesn't die on his own."

Grant said a silent prayer while maintaining his guard. "Father, if it's my time, take me, but I ask you to protect my family, especially Carol, and those in danger."

Then he said to the Tiger, "So, if I'm about to die, can't I at least know who you work for?" Grant knew that his attempt at distraction probably wouldn't work, but he hoped for an opening, a chance for a first strike.

"Sure. If you are brave enough to die, you deserve to know that I work for your government, your CIA." The Tiger laughed to himself. Yao had told him to blame everything on the CIA, FBI, or Homeland Security. It

255

seemed like a good idea. Besides, death to him was spiritual and so he wanted to kill his victims' spirits before he killed their bodies.

"The CIA?" Grant responded instinctively. Grant was stunned momentarily by his response. The Tiger saw his opening and now decided on a different tactic. Instead of a quick kill, he would have fun. After all, like many Chinese, he believed that the flavor of meat was enhanced by the degree of suffering and had extrapolated that belief one step further: the degree of suffering made death more rewarding. He would reward Dr. Miller greatly.

The Tiger sprang forward, his left leg pointing toward Grant's left shoulder, his right tucked, ready to launch an attack on Grant's chest. Both arms were at 90 degrees, defensive only. He would let his feet break bones and his hands would gouge and pluck later.

Grant felt the crunch on his left shoulder well after he hit the ground. The Tiger's right leg had followed his left, catching him in the middle of his sternum after his left leg had done its work. The wounds from Big Man's kicks to his ribs earlier in the day were reawakened.

The pain was extraordinary, but sucking for a breath that wouldn't come was first priority. His chest had forgotten how to breathe, but he pulled back to a crouch, wheezing. His entire chest felt like burning kerosene.

The Tiger's face suddenly transformed from shadow to vivid detail. A car had turned onto the street, its halogen headlights hitting him directly. His face matched his accent, Chinese. A squeak of air entered Grant's airways as he prepared for another strike. He knew this might be the last.

As the Tiger leaped forward, the white light was joined by blue and red and a siren. He was still able to dart both hands toward Grant's throat. A broken larynx would end it all. But the high intensity light took his vision temporarily and made the Tiger's aim guesswork. Grant skirted to the left, feeling the iron of Tiger's fingers on his right forearm. His right missed its target completely.

Grant rolled out of the way, using intuition instead of technique. He wasn't far enough away for another attack, though. He still had no breath and knew he wouldn't stand long.

The Tiger, ready for another assault, winced with pain, the cochlear implant thundering in his head. Yao was yelling. The Tiger bolted toward a house, leaped a gate as though it wasn't there, and was gone.

Grant's breath was slowly returning as the police car stopped in front of him. He was bruised but able to stand. His chest hammered with pain.

"Go down to your knees, sir," the officer commanded. Both policemen were out of their vehicle but waiting behind their opened doors for Grant to obey.

It wasn't hard this time. He had rehearsed the drill earlier. Grant was on his knees, both hands behind his back, before any other orders could be voiced. The patrolmen had simply been checking on neighborhoods that had lost electricity after the storm, the timing of their arrival fortunate to say the least.

It didn't take long this time to identify Grant and escort him to his front door. One of the policemen knocked on the front door while the other stood several feet back, making sure a domestic situation hadn't taken place. He stood between Grant and the front door.

Carol woke up when she heard the siren and saw blues and reds spinning around her windows, but she couldn't tell what was happening when she peered out the window into the darkness. There were flashlights and voices but nothing distinct.

She opened the door cautiously at first, then swung it wide, horrified. "What happened to you?" Carol's voice trembled, echoing off the flickers of candlelight that filled the foyer and joined the beams of flashlights outside.

Grant knew he was a mess but took a moment to review himself. His shoes were hidden with dried mud and bird nested with twigs and pine needles. His pants were shredded, left mostly behind on fallen trees and broken limbs. Blood was hard to separate from perspiration and swamp liquid, which had congealed on his shirt, hiding the lumps of black, blue, and purple that circled his chest. His whiskers were frosted with dried saliva and the left side of his face painted with blood that still trickled from the bullet wound on his temple.

"I haven't been at the hospital." He pulled dry humor out of exhaustion, confusion, and unfiltered alarm. "Quickly, go get the girls. We're going to the hospital."

"What?" Carol was still. Confusion left her motionless.

"I don't have time to explain right now, but get them. We're all going to the hospital." Grant really didn't have a plan. He didn't know what his next moves or conversations would be. All he knew was that the hospital was the safest place for him and his family right now. He could figure some things out there, but his family wasn't staying the rest of the night alone in their house.

CHAPTER 48

The policemen waited for Grant to take a quick candle-lit shower and change into clean scrubs. Meanwhile, Carol gathered the girls, toiletries, and clothes. Then they all rushed to the hospital and to the governor's room in Intensive Care. It was a breach of privacy, of Intensive Care policy and procedure, of HIPPA rules and regulations, but no one was going to tell Dr. Miller that he couldn't bring his family and two policemen back to the governor's room.

As Grant made the turn, escorting the procession toward Governor Sands' room, a guard posted in the hall stood up rapidly from his chair. Daniel was giving a report to the governor and Molly when he heard the commotion and saw the guard stand. Daniel drew his 9 mm Glock and was in the hallway before the guard had a chance to talk.

"Dr. Miller!" Daniel's pistol hand relaxed.

The policemen escorting Dr. Miller had crouched defensively when they saw weapons drawn. They relaxed, also.

"I'm sorry to barge in like this." Grant looked at Carol and his girls. They were terrified but following obediently, clueless as to why there was so much potential gunplay in their midst.

"Grant!" The governor's eyes brightened when he saw his surgeon. "Thank God you're alright!"

"I'm fine, Richard." He waved Carol and the girls into the room and introduced them. "And these are the policemen who saved me when I tried to go home."

"What?" Richard puzzled.

"Governor, I have no idea what's going on, who tried to kill me or why." He caught a glimpse of his children, who morphed from confused to terrified. He had tried to hide his face from them to this point, but now the lights and his words allowed them to clearly see his bruises, scratches, and bullet wound on his face. "But I'm afraid Dick is still in danger."

"Yes, we just got the report from the surgeon. Dick has a terrible wound that is badly infected. They cleaned him out and they're sending him to hyperbarics for high intensity oxygen therapy." Richard looked at Molly, who stood next to him, holding his hand hopefully. "By the way." He looked at Carol. "This is my wife, Molly."

"Nice to meet you, Molly." Carol smiled politely but continued looking at Grant incredulously. "Now, can you tell me what's going on?" Her voice was rarely sharp, but she was ready for the suspense to end. The last time she saw her husband before two policemen brought him home, he was going into the hospital for an extended period.

"I will... I mean..." He paused. "I will try my best to fill in the blanks." He looked at Carol, then back at the governor. He knew his family had been threatened if he did not remain silent, but Dick was in greater danger than anyone now. Grant scratched out a note but remained careful with his words, suspicious of everyone. Once again he was even afraid that the CIA was involved.

The clip that we investigated is a transmitter. Someone is listening to you right now. You have clips in you. I have them in me. In fact, anyone who has had an operation may have a transmitter in them. We are being monitored, and I thought it was the Chinese but it might be the CIA.

Whoever it is, they are going to try to kill Dick. I think they are in the hospital. If they know I am telling you this, my family, and they have no idea that I went to Mobile at this point, is in danger.

The governor started to say something but then caught his words. He saw the certainty in Grant's face, which was confirmed by his wounds. He showed Molly the note. Molly's face turned white, then flushed with anger. She looked at Carol and the girls, careful to disguise her concerns for them. Then she winked at Grant, acknowledging his note and its implications.

As Carol watched these exchanges, she grew more and more frustrated and angry. Grant recognized her irritation and quickly brought his finger to his lips, signaling for her to remain quiet a bit longer.

"I'm going to check on Dick." Molly mouthed silently. She pointed at Daniel to follow her. Richard twirled his finger in Daniel's direction and mouthed to get more troopers around him, his wife, Dick, and the Millers.

Grant scribbled another note and gave it to Carol.

I've been in Mobile this weekend with the governor's son. At this point, I can't talk about it except to say, when I had my appendectomy, a device was implanted in me and my words and location are constantly being monitored. If I talk about this weekend, you and the girls could be in danger. But I need to talk to you privately.

Carol's face glossed with confusion, but she followed Grant's lead. He indicated to Beth and Ree that they should remain in the governor's room and then led his wife to an adjoining unoccupied intensive care room.

"I can't talk about this weekend," he said as he closed the door behind them. "There's a bug inside of me and someone is listening to everything I say and they know everywhere I go."

"What are you talking about?" Carol's emotions finally exploded. Her voice roared through the walls.

FORD SIMPSON, M.D.

Beth and Ree, huddled next to the governor, trembled. They couldn't pick out the words but heard their mother's exasperated tone coming from the adjoining room. They had never heard their parents scream or fight. Richard pulled them close. "It's going to be alright."

"When I had my appendectomy, apparently a surgical clip was placed inside of me. I'm being monitored now. Everything we say can be heard," Grant continued.

He didn't have a clue how to ask what he needed to ask. "On my way home, someone attacked me and told me that, if I talked about the last 48 hours, they would come after you and the girls." Grant was careful with his words. The clip had been placed before the weekend, so he felt he could share that with Carol.

"Are you kidding me?" Carol responded incredulously. "You're telling me that we can't talk because our conversations are going out on a party line?"

Grant said apologetically, "I haven't figured out the extent of it all yet. All I know is that, for now, I can't talk about this weekend."

"Alright." Carol's tone still held disgust. "Then what can we talk about, and what about the girls?"

"I'm going to make sure the girls are safe. I give you my word." He realized that this was all too much for her. He saw it in her face. He even doubted his own sincere tone.

"Your word?" Carol's voice pierced through the walls again. "You leave town when I think you're working hard in the hospital, your life is threatened, our lives are threatened, you could have been killed... I could be a widow and your children without a father, and you want ME TO TRUST YOUR WORD!" Her eyes blazed through tears.

"Carol!" Grant reached for her arm but she recoiled.

"I understand there is a trust issue here." Grant tried to shift the conversation. Ever since his experience with

262

Big Guy, all he could think about was trust. Visions of unfaithfulness, thoughts of possible years of deceit had consumed him.

"Trust issue?" Carol echoed. "I'd say there's a trust issue." Her words stung.

"Carol, I have to know." Grant couldn't hold back any more. "Has a man been coming to our house while I've been at work?"

Grant stood straight, ready for any answer. He just needed to know. He couldn't think of anything else until he had an answer.

Carol looked dazed. She shook her head, not in answer but bewilderment. It took longer than Grant expected, but then she understood the question. Fury took the place of resentment. Grant watched her carefully, looking for guilt and hoping for honesty.

"Yes. There has been someone." She glared at him defiantly.

Grant had promised himself that he would work things out no matter her answer, that he would be forgiving. He loved Carol too much to let her go because of infidelity. The entire helicopter flight back to Tuscaloosa was a conversation of "what ifs" with himself. "What if she had been having an affair?"

Carol let her answer percolate. She wanted it to burn for a while. He would have to ask more specific questions before getting answers.

Grant didn't move. Carol's answer hit him harder than he expected. He stood, empty and hoping for remorse, but Carol faced him boldly. She waited for another question, unwilling to provide a narrative on her own.

"How long?" Grant's voice was filled with disappointment. He again searched her face for any sign of remorse, but there was none. "How long have you been seeing someone?"

"A few years," she returned with a snap. "But more frequently over the last year." It was as though she enjoyed the pain she saw in his eyes.

Forty-eight hours of skirmishing with death, of beatings, physical and mental, of fear for the lives of his family and feelings of responsibility toward the governor and his son was now capped off with unfaithfulness. The daggers were too many. Grant sat in a chair, feeling his life drain through every pore.

Carol recognized his anguish. She had intentionally misdirected her answers up to this point. Having been blasted with surprises, threats and accusations, her initial response was to parry with evasiveness and thrust with equal intensity. But she had never seen her husband so defeated, so helpless.

"Sweetheart." She knelt at his feet. "What are you thinking?" She took his hand. "Do you think I've been having an affair?" She let the question drift, hoping he felt ridiculous.

Grant took his eyes off of his knees, raising them to her eyes. "Isn't that what you were telling me?"

"Not at all." Tenderness had taken over. "I've been seeing different people for the last few years, some men and some women." She waited for a response. He tried his best to stay calm. "I've finally found a counselor who has really helped me."

Grant remained motionless.

"When we lost Matthew, I thought I was strong enough to put it behind me, to go on, to face each day like you do." She took both of his hands. "You go to work every day. You have operations to do, patients who need you and responsibilities that make you focus on the present and the future." Moisture streamed down her cheeks. "But I don't have those things. I wake up every day and think of Matthew."

Matthew was their first-born. They had just arrived in Tuscaloosa, cute couple with a precious and healthy little boy of eight months old with blue eyes and a Gerber smile. He had been crawling for two weeks, his eyes now accommodating like an adult, and little Matthew smiled all the time. His hands were precocious and he used them with precision. They were sure he would follow in his father's footsteps as a surgeon.

Carol had grown up in a broken family. Her parents had divorced when she was a baby. Her mother worked long hours and her father was MIA. She was determined to give her boy a better life, to be there when he needed her and never let him down. Although she also was determined that Matthew would have a father who gave him baths, changed his diapers, fed him, helped him with homework, and coached his Little League teams, Carol had accepted Grant's work hours as part of being married to a cardiac surgeon.

One day, Carol was giving Matthew a bath, which was always a fun time for her. The aromas of baby shampoo, the warmth and softness of Matthew's skin, the playful smiles of enjoyment in the water were memories she still carried. It only took a drop of shampoo, one meant for his hair. The yellowish orange pearl fell with laser precision into Matthew's nose. At first, the mistake seemed negligible, causing a sneeze and coughing.

But Carol would never forget how quickly the pink skin turned blue, how Matthew's smiles and giggles turned into gasps and sputters. The horror on his face would be painted in Carol's thoughts forever, as if he was asking, "Mommy, why did you do that?" Maybe if Grant had been home, things would have been different, but as usual, he was late, tied up in the operating room. Maybe she didn't call 911 fast enough. Maybe it was meant to be! Questions outnumbered the answers.

After an investigation and the autopsy, it was clear that the shampoo caused asphyxiation. Everyone supported Carol and grieved with her. Grant did everything he could to struggle through his own grief and to comfort her, but the guilt and emptiness would never leave completely.

"Matthew?" Grant winced.

"Yes, Matthew." She sobbed. "I see him constantly. I hear him in my dreams and when I'm alone. Counselors have helped, but the nightmares won't leave and the tears won't stop." She held his hands with determination. "You didn't see him. You didn't hear him. You can escape in the hospital, but when the girls leave for school, I'm trapped in my nightmare."

It had been years since Grant had thought of his first-born. The loss was inconceivable at the time and the grief seemed unbearable. But he had to return to work, and the hospital had, indeed, been his house of recovery. Not only did the distraction of operations allow him to refocus, but the loss and grief in others' lives seemed to erase his own.

The week he returned to work, a father had an argument with his wife. Drunk, he backed out of his garage in a fury to escape the emotions of the moment and ran over his son who was playing in the parking court. Grant couldn't save the child, who had mortal chest wounds, but he could cry with the family and share the sorrow and guilt.

For Grant, each day was filled with decisions that could mean the difference between life and death. Each operation carried the burden of an individual and a family. The joy of success with any one patient was always shadowed by the certainty of failure and sorrow in another. Matthew was always there in Grant's heart and memories, but he was hidden behind panels of duty, barriers of emotions, and stacks of failures.

"My God." Grant dropped from his chair to join Carol on the floor, kneeling beside her. "Why didn't you tell me?"

"I couldn't." Her voice shook through gasps of guilt. "You are so happy with your work, such a wonderful man and surgeon." Tears eddied above her lips. "I didn't want you to worry about me. I didn't want you to think about Matthew." She paused. "You never talked about him after we lost him. I assumed you either didn't want to or that you were simply able to move on, to put him behind you." Wiping her face, she looked at the ceiling, searching for words. "God, help me. I wanted to do that. I wanted to have a job that I could go to, somewhere I could escape to forget just for a moment. I wasn't going to take that away from you."

She was right. He knew it. He had forgotten Matthew in terms of daily thoughts. His work had given him a burial ground, a place to put Matthew in a casket and buried only to be visited on special occasions of his own choosing.

"I've been so selfish." He realized, for the first time, one reason why he had become so absorbed in his work. "I have ignored you, I never even considered what you were going through."

The days and weeks and months after Matthew's death were blurred. But he remembered one thing for sure. "You're right. I never talked about Matthew." He knew now that he had done it for himself. It was his escape. He had buried Matthew as quickly as he could in order to bury his grief. He had never considered Carol's battle.

"I've been so selfish!" he repeated.

"No, you haven't," she reassured him. "You really love what you do. I didn't give you any reason to worry about me. I know you would have been there for me if you knew I needed you, but I wanted to be strong. I didn't want to be a disappointment to you, and so I never said anything."

The counselors had helped her sort out her emotions, helped her identify her demons and call them by their names. They had encouraged her to confront them and to destroy them. They had suggested that she could do this by doing what was happening right now, sharing them with her husband. She thought it would be more painful, but it actually felt good. Layers of onion were being peeled away. The vapors stung her eyes, but there was freedom in the escape. She knew there was one last demon to confront.

"There's another reason I didn't want to bring up Matthew." Her heart raced with the anticipation of shedding the last layer of guilt. "I didn't want you to think about Matthew because I didn't want you to blame me and resent me." Weeping turned to wailing as she emptied her secrets.

"Oh my God." Grant pulled her into him, feeling her chest heave with sobs. "How could I have been so blind?"

"Do you blame me?" The question was in her heart from the day Matthew died but never made it to her lips.

"Please don't blame me," she begged before Grant could respond.

"Sweetheart, I've never blamed you." And he never had, but he realized that he should have voiced it long ago. "I had to go into my shell, my cave. That's where I go when I fail, when I'm wounded. It's a lonely place, but it's only me in there and so it's a safe place. But it's a selfish place, too. When Matthew died, I had to go back to work, and work was my cave. But I left you outside with the lions and tigers." He took a long sigh.

"No, I never blamed you. I blamed myself, if anyone. I blamed myself for not being home when it happened, for going back to work and leaving you alone at home."

He wiped tears from her eyes, then kissed her cheek. "Can you ever forgive me?"

"I don't know how you found out about my visitor at home, and I don't know what you've been up to this weekend. I don't know what secrets you're still hiding either." She found the energy to send him a cutting glance. "But I know who you are and what you stand for. I'm glad you found out about my visitor so we could have this conversation. I know you would never intentionally hurt me or our family, and I know whatever you do is because you think it's the right thing to do." Her tears had stopped. "There's nothing I need to forgive you for. Nothing in the past and nothing now. My counselor says that forgiveness is giving up the right to hurt someone who has hurt you. So there's nothing to forgive."

"I love you so much." Grant pulled her tighter, feeling her warmth and realizing how much he really did.

CHAPTER 49

It must have been debris from the wind that sounded like footsteps. Jack didn't like darkness, especially in the middle of nowhere. The loss of electricity and the storm, in combination with the assault by Lee, had him spooked.

He hurried out of Suzy's house after checking all angles outside. The darkness wasn't complete. Moonlight crept through pores in the overhead clouds, but only enough to distinguish shades of black. He held the computer like a fullback, protecting it from flying debris and ready to shield it if he tripped.

Luckily, the headlights provided a visible pathway to his car when he tapped his remote to unlock it. He hurried into the sedan, carefully placing the computer next to him on the passenger seat. He wasn't sure how long Suzy would be in the hospital or what she might need, and so he had packed the remnants of her clothes in a bag that was sitting beside her desk. He placed it in the back seat on top of his lab coat so he wouldn't forget it in the morning.

After a quick trip home and a few hours of sleep, he would be able to make rounds, check on Suzy, and answer questions at the police station. As he tapped the ignition button and the engine fired, the driver's window exploded, spraying diamonds of glass everywhere. Jack's first thought was that the wind had blown something into the window, but then he felt the metal against his head just like earlier in the day.

Lee had planned well. The police would be searching the Warrior River for the next week, only to give up hope of finding his body. Li Jiang was dead as far as the world was concerned. The authorities would assume that the catfish got his remains. The bullet at the spillway would have torn his chest apart if he hadn't planned for the shot.

Shrapnul, the newest and strongest bulletproof vest, was hardly visible, and its Mouton cushioning to minimize impact trauma had delivered him safely into the spillway and even protected him from injury as he crashed down the river. He knew that the police would go for a body shot instead of a head shot when he pulled the pistol on Dr. Wade. He also knew that the shot would come from the south side of the lake instead of the northern end because he had hidden the gun he pulled on Dr. Wade from every sight angle but that one. If the police had not been there, Dr. Wade's head would be vapor and his body could have been pushed though the cut fencing. Since the police were there, he knew he would be hit in the chest and take Dr. Wade, dead or alive, into the drink. He had cut enough of the gate to allow them to fly together into the spillway.

He knew his bullet had missed its target when he saw Dr. Wade emerge from the water upstream. It was no problem for him to swim into an alcove and escape. He had parked in the shopping center above the lake and easily made it back to his car so he could trail Dr. Wade.

Now Dr. Wade was his.

"Get out of the car, Dr. Wade!" Jack knew the voice, and he remembered the advice he had heard about carjackings: never get out of the car and try to get away in the first seconds. But he didn't expect Lee to miss a second time.

The lights in his car came on automatically as he opened the door. Lee must have trailed him from the lake for his hair was matted with grime and his clothes torn and dirty.

"Let's take a walk." Lee's voice was scratchy but piped with victory. "The river's not far from here. You should recognize the water."

Jack looked at Lee, then the darkness. A quick bolt into the night might do it. He took a deep breath, ready to launch into the shadows, then felt the metal on his neck again.

"Here, place these on your fingers." Lee handed him two sets of finger traps. "My company makes not only clips but these devices. You won't get to use them in the hospital, but they work very well."

Jack had seen the Chinese finger traps used in orthopedics. Patient's five fingers were placed in the traps and suspended in the air for shoulder operations. They opened easily, allowing his fingers to slide into the plastic slips, but tightened with wiry stiffness as he tried to release his fingers. The traps were attached to nylon cords that Lee tied behind his back.

"Now, Jack... You don't mind if I call you Jack, do you?" Lee tightened the cord, pulling the traps tighter.

"I think you can call me whatever you like." Jack still looked into the darkness, his legs ready to bolt. He knew that it was now or never. The clouds had given him the cover he needed. When Lee closed his door everything went pitch. Jack launched forward, feeling the thrust of his thighs. As a linebacker in college, he knew he could get a quick start.

He took three steps, then felt the strain on his fingers and the fire in his shoulders as he toppled to the ground. The leash Lee held that were tied to his finger traps almost popped his shoulders out of joint.

"Oh, Jack. Don't do that again." Lee's voice dripped with insincerity. "You might hurt yourself." He laughed with delight as Jack rolled and then legged his way back to his feet.

"I almost forgot." Lee snapped the cord, throwing Jack back to the ground. "I almost forgot Suzy's computer." He pulled Jack on the ground back to the car and retrieved the laptop.

"This is my treasure, Jack. I can't leave this behind." He pulled the 18-inch out of the front seat and tucked it under his arm.

"Now be a good boy, Jack. Let's go back to Suzy's house and put this inside so it doesn't get hurt."

Jack was back on his feet again, his shoulders still ripped with the pain of near dislocation. Lee trailed him to Suzy's hut, then jerked on the leash as they reached her door.

"You know I have a key to this place." Lee's voice turned from sarcastic to sensual. "Suzy is very good. She does whatever I want, and I want a lot." He unlocked the door and placed the computer in the kitchen.

Jack was on fire with pain, anger, and fear. He remained quiet, trying not to listen to Lee, hoping for an idea or opening for escape.

"She likes it when I take my time. She likes to scream!" He closed the door behind him. "But now she won't like it at all. She lost her toy." Lee laughed uncontrollably.

"Now keep walking," he said when he regained his composure. "I know this place like the back of my hand. The river is just through that opening."

Jack could see a break in the tree line ahead. There was no road, but the ground was firm. His eyes had adjusted as much to the night as possible, but things were still murky.

"So why did you have to kill those people in the hospital?" Jack decided to try to distract Lee. If he became angry, he might lose his focus.

"Ahh. You want to talk!" His sarcasm returned. "You see, Suzy did a very bad thing. She was supposed to be working for me, doing only what I told her!" His voice tightened with resentment. "She was using our equipment for personal use and that just wouldn't do!"

"What personal use? What equipment?"

"Okay. If it will make you feel better before you die, I will give you some pleasure." Lee knew he had several hours of darkness left to torture Jack. "I work for the Yida but also with Chinese Intelligence. The clips that you use every day are going into patients like Trojan Horses. They sit inside patients and hold blood vessels and intestines together, but they also transmit information through a satellite back to Beijing."

Jack's steps shortened, partly out of interest but also to lengthen his trip.

"Suzy doesn't even know what's going on. She just does what she is told. She thinks she is helping the Chinese government with medical research. She goes through the hospital with a receiver that logs patients with clips implanted and records their frequency. Each patient has his or her own frequency. Chinese Intelligence can know where each person is, what they are saying, and what's going on inside of them." He grunted.

"Instead of doing what she was told, Suzy decided to use the clip for her own purposes. She used the clip to help that girl with paralysis." He hissed. "She knew better than that. I'm not through with her either."

Jack was still looking for an escape, but his thoughts returned to Suzy. He not only wanted to escape, he wanted to pound Lee into the riverbank. He also wondered how many people he had placed clips in, how many people were walking bugs.

"You see," Lee continued smugly, "after I kill you and Suzy, then I will have her computer. I will be able to return to China and can name my position in Intelligence." His voice deepened with resentment. "I won't have to act like a servant, a salesman. I won't have to call people 'doctor' or 'sir' and will be respected and honored for who I am and what I have done."

"Why did you risk your life by being shot?" Jack's arms throbbed, the joint capsules in his shoulders stretched to their limit. Each step ricocheted lightning into his bones. He wasn't sure if he would be able to escape even if an opportunity came.

"I knew that my boss in Intelligence in China was aware that Suzy had used the clips without permission. He also knew I had killed the family. He would have wanted me dead, and so I obliged him. I killed myself." He laughed again. "He doesn't realize that I might soon have his job." Again his laughter was violent.

"The idiot thinks he's smart. I'll show him smart." Lee jerked on the leash. "Stop here," he commanded. "You're a surgeon. Do you have good hands, strong fingers?"

Jack knew something bad was going to happen. He remained silent.

"Down on your knees." Lee placed the pistol on his ear, letting it follow him to his kneeling position.

The darkness was powerful and wind still swished through the pines, but Jack was able to hear another rope traveling over a tree limb above him.

Lee pulled on his side of the rope. Jack's shoulders ripped with pain as the rope tightened and pulled him into the air. The finger traps were nooses pulling mercilessly on his hands, but his arms stretched backward nearly breaking out of their sockets.

As Jack hung in the air, his head swung in front of Lee. "Stick out your tongue, Jack," Lee commanded. The weight of Jack in the air must have been something he didn't expect. His voice was muted as he struggled to hold the rope.

"I said stick out your tongue," Lee yelled a second time. "I won't ask you again."

Jack knew what was coming. As soon as his tongue passed through his teeth, Lee kneed his jaw. His teeth almost severed his tongue, but Lee still had plans and wanted him to be able to talk. He was enjoying the conversation too much. The taste of iron filled Jack's mouth as his tongue went from numb to an open nerve.

Lee released the rope, letting Jack fall to the ground. His face hit first, smearing blood from his mouth over his eyes. All vision was gone now. His breath had been taken away by the fall as well. He lay on the ground sucking for a breath, pounding with agony from his shoulders up. He heard more activity but couldn't see what Lee was up to and didn't care.

Behind him, Lee had taken a blow to his back, just between his shoulders. He collapsed, his spinal cord sheared from the blow. His arms swung wildly as he tried to recover, but two more blows came. His elbows snapped, leaving his forearms dangling uselessly like a puppet's. The Tiger wanted him alive.

Lee thought that the clips in him had been disabled by the magnet in the MRI suite, and they had been for a time. But Yao was able to pick up his location by GPS. He couldn't hear what Lee said, but he knew where he was.

With Lee alive, the Tiger would be able to find out what he said and what his plans were, where the computer was, and then some.

The Tiger threw Lee over his shoulder, carrying him like bagged game. Lee hung helplessly, watching Jack, lying motionless on the ground, recede into the darkness.

CHAPTER 50

Monday morning was a long time coming. The storm had passed and the clouds had thinned, leaving only remnants behind. Brilliant oranges and yellows streamed over the horizon and DCH Regional Hospital gleamed under the canopy of sunrise.

Electricity had been restored in the city, but there was still work to be done on the streets. Branches and leaves were scattered, but drivers hardly cared as the day had begun.

"The FBI has been busy," Governor Sands reported. He had just hung up the phone.

The slumber party hadn't ended. Grant, Carol, Beth, Ree, the governor, Molly, and Daniel were all together. Dick had completed his hyperbarics without incident and was tucked in a bed next to them in Intensive Care. His wife had arrived from Mobile and was at his bedside.

"A team is already at our plant trying to piece together who the dead men are and their connections. They're also trying to figure out how the electronics went haywire down there." Richard looked strong. He was still pale from the anemia of his operation, but was in command again.

"I called the FBI in before you arrived in Tusca-loosa." He looked at Grant, careful to establish that he had involved the FBI before Grant arrived in Tuscaloosa. He didn't want anyone to suspect Grant of leaking infor-mation. "They are looking here in the hospital, also.

There's some concern that a security breach in the basement may have been related."

Grant remained quiet. He still didn't know who was listening and who might be a threat.

"So far there are a lot of theories, but we don't know anything for certain," Richard continued. "Another crazy thing happened last night also." He paused, thinking. "A surgeon from this hospital by the name of Jack Wade was almost killed yesterday at Lake Tuscaloosa. The person who tried to kill him was a sales representative at the hospital here."

"Jack?" Grant shouted.

"Yes. I guess you know him."

"Sure, I know him. He's the surgeon who operated on me recently and a close friend."

"Well, he must be a cat with nine lives," Richard responded. "He was almost shot in the head. The bullet missed and he went over the spillway with the person who tried to shoot him. They thought the shooter was dead, but apparently he came back after Jack last night."

Grant's eyes were wide. "Is he alright?"

"Sounds like it. He's been in the police station for the last hour or so answering questions. But the FBI thinks everything might be tied together. Everything points to the Chinese at this point. The dead men at the Sands facility are Chinese, and so is the person who tried to kill Jack. Apparently the same person who tried to kill Jack may have tried to kill another Chinese student at the University of Alabama. She's in Intensive Care."

The governor had considered his words carefully. He wanted to make it clear to whoever might be monitoring them that the game was over.

Beth and Ree were still standing by the governor. They had remained quiet, almost motionless since they had arrived in the intensive care room. They had been pulled from their beds and rushed to the hospital, heard their parents screaming through the walls, and listened to stories of attempted murder. And seeing bruises and blood on their father's face had pushed them from nightmare into near hysteria.

Grant saw their alarm and knelt beside them. "Girls, everything's going to be alright." He wrapped his arms around them, pulling them in tightly.

"Do you remember when we were in Florida in the rip tide?"

Neither girl said a word but both nodded.

"Do you remember how we were all hanging onto the same raft and we couldn't paddle fast enough to get back to the shore?"

They nodded again.

"What did we have to do?"

They looked at each other but remained quiet. Neither wanted to offer an answer. Neither wanted to test their voice.

"We kept going farther and farther out in the ocean, didn't we?" His voice lowered, drifting like the raft.

"Do you remember what I said as the water got darker and darker, cooler and cooler?" His voice almost shivered. "I said that we would all be alright, but we had to stay together."

"I remember!" Ree offered, her voice strained. "You promised we would be alright." Her voice now strengthened. "You told us to start paddling to the side and not fight the current."

"That's exactly right." Grant pulled them even tighter. "I said that, no matter where the current pushed us, we could beat it if we worked together." His voice brightened.

Then Grant released them so they could look into his eyes. "Sometimes things happen that we can't control. Sometimes the current sweeps us away and we can't fight it." He rested for a moment, letting them catch up to him.

"But even though things might seem scary, even if we don't understand where the current is taking us or why, there are two things you can count on."

Beth joined in. "I remember what you said now!" Her expression had come back to life. "You said we can trust you, that you will never let us down, and you said that we have to stay together and each do our part."

"That's right, sweetie." Grant smiled.

"So what's going on, Dad?" Beth snapped. "You've been in the hospital for the last 16 years and now you show up and rush us out of the house like we're in a suspense thriller."

Grant's face betrayed his surprise. He'd never heard either girl confront him. Beth's 16-year-old's courage had emerged, though.

Silence filled the room. Even the governor remained motionless, as anxious as the girls for his response.

"Really, Dad." Ree's tone was less challenging but just as powerful. "What's going on?"

The room was silent only for a second. Grant started to answer just as the tremor hit. The window behind Grant shook first, and then the floor.

There are two fault zones in Alabama, but most earthquakes in Tuscaloosa's southern Appalachian seismic zone are detectable only with instruments. The rocking and foundational unsteadiness came first, but instead of a momentary rumble and then calm, an explosion rattled through the hall followed by a sonic boom. It wasn't an earthquake.

The lights flickered, and then alarms blasted through the halls. Two state troopers ran to the governor's room and took up posts on each side of his bed.

"Code Red, Hyperbarics. Code Red, Hyperbarics." The announcement came over the loud speaker.

Molly looked at Richard, then rushed out of the room to make sure Dick was next door.

....

The Tuscaloosa Fire and Rescue Service had grown from one horse-drawn fire wagon in 1878 to 11 stations, more than 300 firefighters, and a proud history of community service and successful containment of fires.

Roscoe Tucker was new on the Rice Valley fire team. He had just finished the fire college and had been talking to his wife before the call came. It had been a slow morning: raising the flag, washing the engine, checking equipment. He had been with the team for a month, and so far his most dangerous task was to respond to a dog attack in a nearby neighborhood.

His wife was excited for him but uneasy when he told her that the call had come for a fire in Riverchase. It was Roscoe's chance to use his skills and to prove to the veterans that he was worthy. After all, Riverchase was one of those neighborhoods where everyone knew each other and everyone knew the families there.

The house on Saratoga Lane was about 40 years old, one of the oldest on the street, but it was next to Verner School. That made it a perfect house for the Peppers. Their two children could walk to the elementary school by simply crossing the field between the school and their house.

Sally was about to enter the front door of the school when she looked back at her house and saw smoke billowing out of the chimney. She knew her mother was home because that's where she had been since she was diagnosed with multiple sclerosis. She also remembered that she had left the toaster on. She'd been told time after time to turn it off because it could cause a fire.

Sally screamed, pointing to her house, alerting a teacher who called 911. But Sally was already on her way, streaking across the field. By the time she reached her house, smoke was seeping through the kitchen door, everything inside a black cloud. The door was locked. She raced to the front door only to find it locked also. The fire engine arrived moments later, and Sally explained what might have happened and that her mother was still inside, maybe trapped because of her MS.

Roscoe was the first in the house, searching in darkness for any sign of life. He didn't realize that Sally's mother had made it out of the house and had crossed the street in her wheelchair to notify the fire department. When Sally and her mother saw each other, they were too busy hugging each other to notify the firemen that they were both safe. It could have brought Roscoe out more quickly.

But he wasn't going to leave the house until someone told him that everyone was out and accounted for. He knew the warning signs of carbon monoxide poisoning but ignored the lightheadedness and headache. He knew that the poison gas was caused by fire and lack of oxygen and that the colorless, odorless gas was all around him. But he didn't realize that his oxygen tank was depleted. The gauge had frozen. Nausea was the first symptom that alerted him he was in trouble, but it was too late. He went to his knees, then to the ground as the darkness and smoke swallowed him.

Luckily, his buddies were able to find him and pull him from the house, but his carbon monoxide poisoning was more than dangerous. His blood level was lethal. He would be dead in two hours without rapid treatment.

Dick Sands was scheduled for a second hyperbaric treatment within an hour of Roscoe's arrival at DCH. One of the hyperbaric tanks was down, being repaired, which meant that Roscoe would have to take his spot.

Hyperbaric oxygen at three times the normal atmospheric pressure would pull the poison out of his blood four times faster than oxygen by face mask. It might have been his only chance of survival if Meirong hadn't gotten to the tank first.

Meirong knew that Dick Sands would have to come back for the second of three hyperbaric treatments in a short time, and so she placed the Velcro inside. She was aware of American tragedies, especially high profile ones emphasized in classes as a child. She remembered Apollo 1, which was supposed to be the first manned flight to the moon; but in 1967 the American spaceship exploded, killing all three crewmen. She was taught that the American's lined the cockpit with Velcro. The plastic was good for holding things, but friction causes sparks and sparks in concentrated oxygen cause explosions. It happened once and it could happen again.

Roscoe didn't have a chance. He was going to die of carbon monoxide poisoning without hyperbarics, but the Velcro that Meirong placed in the tank sealed his fate. As soon as the tank hit three atmospheres, Roscoe squirmed on the pad, scratching the plastic against itself. The spark wasn't enough to see but the heat was enough for ignition.

The tank would have vaporized if the energy had exploded in all directions. But the blast shot the tank forward, throwing it through the walls of the hospital. It torpedoed 30 yards though the building, crashing through steel and bricks before falling into an elevator shaft.

Meirong was back in the Emergency Room. The explosion rocked the entire hospital. When she heard the Code Red, Hyperbarics, she knew her plan had worked. She tried to hide a smile of success, but the thrill of accomplishment bubbled inside of her.

CHAPTER 51

Jack Wade could hardly talk. His tongue pounded with every heartbeat, the near amputation leaving his mouth swollen and raw. But he was still able to communicate in writing as well as with nods of his head.

His walk to Sanders Ferry Road, his hands still lassoed behind him and the tendons and ligaments of his shoulders stretched to the point of detachment, was the hardest part of getting to the police department. Luckily, a policeman saw him on the road and picked him up. Now he was telling Miles everything about Lizzie, Suzy, Li Jiang, the shack, and his release after being tortured

The puzzle came at the end. Jack was expecting a lethal blow after being tortured, but Lee simply let him drop to the ground and left. Jack never saw him again. Apparently he made off with Suzy's computer, which was all he really needed for it contained information on all the patients Suzy had catalogued. It probably had considerable more information that Jack had not seen, but it was gone.

He made it clear that Suzy was still in danger. She had a clip in her that allowed someone somewhere to hear her and monitor her. She was certain that she would be killed if she talked. If she told her story, THEY would hear and finish the job Lee started.

The policemen drove him back to collect his car and they escorted him back to his home. They even stayed in his home while he showered and dressed. No one knew where Lee went or when he might show back up.

....

When Jack arrived at Suzy's room, her smile filled her face.

"Dr. Wade!" Her voice floated with joy.

"Hey, Suzy." His tongue stuck to the roof of his mouth, too swollen to let the syllables do their work. He was able to smile, however, hiding the pain inside.

"What's the matter?" She winced, aware that he was hiding his mouth.

"Suzy, I was almost killed by Lee, the man who tried to kill you." The words came out with drool and slurs.

Her face swept from pale to white and her eyes widened but then became blank. "What?"

"Don't worry, Suzy. I'm okay and so are you." He knew she was worried that he was saying things out loud, things that could be monitored.

"I know everything, or almost everything," he continued. "Before I was attacked, I saw your computer." He saw her eyes light up with hope. "I saw that you were trying to help Lizzie. I know that you were recording data for Lee too, but he explained that you didn't even really know what you were doing."

Suzy was still anxious. He was saying too much. She mouthed to him, "Don't talk!"

"Suzy, I've told the police everything. They know about the clips in you and they know about your computer. They know what happened to you and will protect you." He reached for her hand.

She received his palm, pulling it toward her heart with both hands. "I'm so scared, Dr. Wade."

"I know, but the police are going to be with both of us. We will be safe." He continued.

"No. I don't mean that I'm afraid for my safety." She searched his face, hopeful, uncertain.

Her voice broke. She tried to hold back tears, but they couldn't be restrained. "I've never wanted anything for myself before." She fought with emotions she had never felt. "I don't deserve anything." Tears were free flowing now and her voice trembled. "I am a terrible person. I've done terrible things."

Jack wanted to say something to comfort her, but he was empty.

"But now..." She took a gulp of air. "Now I want you." She pulled his other hand to her heart. "I'm afraid that the only thing I've ever wanted, which I don't deserve and never even dreamed of before, is an impossible dream!"

"Why do you think your dreams are impossible?" He squeezed her hand.

"Because they are too strong and I am too weak. We don't have a chance." A grimace of reality stretched over her face.

Jack asked, "Who are THEY?"

"I don't know exactly, but the Party, the Chinese..." The words came out in puffs. She didn't think she had the energy or courage to say them. She looked at her hands, at the location of the clips. She wiped her hands as though she was washing them clean of their control over her.

"Don't worry. The police are already on it." Jack's tone was all confidence. "Apparently the FBI is already on it. You don't have to worry about the Chinese or the Party."

Suzy tried to trust his words but seemed to know better. "No, it's probably too late." She pulled the sheet to her eyes, wiping them clean. "It's my fault again. I could have said something, done something..." Her voice drifted again. "Everything I've ever done has been wrong. I've never done anything right." She tore at herself with disgust. "I've always been too scared to do the right thing, too scared to say no to the wrong things and yes to the right things."

"Suzy, don't worry." He wiped more tears from her eyes. "I know Lee has raped you. I know he has done terrible things to you!"

Her face relaxed again, then stiffened. She reached for every bit of courage inside of her. "Do you have my computer?" Her voice trembled with hope. "There are things in my computer that I need to share with the police, with the FBI." Her entire face brightened with newfound conviction. "It's time for me to do what I need to do."

Jack hesitated, then continued. "Lee took the computer. He has it."

"No!" She gasped. "There were things in it that I need to share, things that I can't remember."

"But I read a lot of what was there, and I have told the police that you were an innocent victim of anything that was going on."

"No. I'm not innocent. I knew that the Party was collecting information on America. I knew that the Chinese are using the information to hurt America. I don't know exactly who is doing it or what they are using the information for, but I know they are bad people. The Party is as evil as it is powerful."

"Don't worry, Suzy. The FBI and Homeland Security are on board now, and they will figure things out. You're gonna be okay. I'll make sure of it."

Suzy glanced at Jack. "You have no idea what you are promising."

"I give you my word." Jack brushed her hair from her brow. "You're going to be alright, and WE are going to be alright."

"You have no idea!" Suzy thought.

"I have another meeting with the police." I'll be back when I'm through. "I think the FBI will be there as well."

"Good." Her voice was as far away as her thoughts.

"There will be a policeman outside your room for your safety." Jack knew she wasn't really listening any more. "By the way, I picked up some clothes for you. They're in the bag." He left her belongings on her bed. "I'll be back."

Suzy watched him close the door behind him. All that was left was silence. The beep of her heart monitor was the only sign of life in her room. Her thoughts were scattered, her recent courage exhausted. She fumbled through the bag Jack had brought, exploring aimlessly.

Then she felt something familiar with her hand. Her body stalled, then ignited. Another touch and she was sure. It was her Socrates, a computer backup module that had everything in it that her computer did. Her eyes closed with thanks. There was hope.

Her eyes were still closed when the door to her room opened again.

"Hello. My name is Meirong. I will be your nurse today."

CHAPTER 52

"Governor, we need to talk." Malcolm Winters looked more FBI than an actor portraying one on a TV show. He could have been Agent Smith in *The Matrix* but without sunglasses. "My name is agent Winters. I am with the FBI. There's a lot going on that involves you." He showed his identification card, his hand steady and his demeanor commanding.

"Yes, it's time," Richard returned.

Grant, Carol, Molly, and Richard had been exchanging notes and mouthing conversations to avoid verbal exchanges that could be overheard. But it was time to face things head on. Beth and Ree were in a conference room only five rooms away. Two troopers were with them.

Malcolm scanned the room. His navy tie had a perfect double Windsor. It seemed more pasted to the white Oxford shirt underneath than hanging freely. Neither the tie nor the shirt had a wrinkle, both institutionally pressed. Even his blazer and grey pants were picture perfect.

"Governor, you and I need to talk." He looked at Grant, Carol, and Molly in turn, spotlighting each with a glare of dismissiveness.

"Agent Winters, do you have a first name?" Richard asked. He'd dealt with enough people who felt they only had last names and titles.

"Malcolm." His response was immediate and emotionless.

"Well, Malcolm. This is my wife Molly." Molly smiled passively. "And this is my surgeon Grant Miller and his wife Carol."

Nods and manufactured smiles followed.

"Very well. Now can we get on with things?" Malcolm looked only at the governor, hoping the others would take the hint and leave.

"Certainly. Feel free to talk. We are all anxious to hear what you have to say. My staff told me you were coming to share some information and to ask questions." Richard knew that Malcolm wanted to be alone with him, but he wanted the others present.

"Governor, these are issues of national importance and include information that is classified. I'm sure you understand." Malcolm never changed expression or tone but simply maintained eye contact with the governor.

"We'll be next door. Let us know if we can be of help." Grant had already gotten the message. He lazily escorted Carol and Molly out of the room.

Malcolm pulled a black box out of his briefcase and sat it on the bedside table. He hooked a cord to it and waved a wand in front of the governor. It crackled with static, then was silent. "I need to check you for a bug, sir." Malcolm lifted the wand, waiting for the governor's approval.

Richard waved him on. Malcolm proceeded to scan him at precise geometric angles. The governor's left leg had a vein removed for the heart procedure. Although the vein had been retrieved with scopes and there was only one incision at his knee, the agent's device beeped repeatedly, registering a number on the black box. Malcolm continued making passes at angles, recording the same numbers when the wand passed over Richard's chest. He nodded with emotionless interest and dialed the same frequencies on the controller on the box that he had just recorded.

"Now we can talk" Malcolm continued. "You have been bugged but I interrupted the transmission frequencies, two of them."

"I thought so. I've been careful with my conversations after Dr. Miller told me that I had been bugged."

Malcolm tilted his head with surprise. "How did Dr. Miller know you had been bugged?"

"He figured it out with my son in Mobile, at our plant."

"Is that why the assassins tried to kill them?" Malcolm's question flew without a pause.

"Assassins?" Richard returned as quickly as Malcolm.

"Yes. The two dead men at your plant were Chinese assassins. Their finger prints match some recent American deaths, all by hit men." Malcolm paused momentarily to decide whether to offer more information. "We are still looking for a third, but we know who he was also. They work for the Chinese government, specifically for the Ministry of State Security. All of their activity has been associated with cyber spying. The Chinese are evolving much faster than the United States in this. They are using HUMINT much less."

"What is HUMINT?"

"Just an abbreviation for human intelligence. You remember the early part of the century when the Chinese were stealing our military and technological secrets? That was done using agents who bought, recorded, photographed or in some other way stole American intelligence."

"Yes, I specifically remember a DuPont employee, Tze Chao, who pleaded guilty to giving trade secrets on titanium dioxide. As I recall, he gave the information to the Pangang Group, which worked for the Chinese government."

"Everyone remembers Larry Wu-tai Chin, Katrina Leung, Gwo-Bao Min, Chi Mak, and Peter Lee. But Americans didn't realize until too late was how extensive the espionage was. Chinese citizens were compelled to do the dirty work of the Chinese government. Regular citizens would come to the United States for scientific meetings, technology fairs, family reunions, and vacations and return with trade secrets, nuclear technology, military secrets... Hell they almost flew a Lockheed Martin F-35 Lightning back to Beijing a few years ago."

"I remember that." Richard chuckled.

"Yes, but Chinese intelligence has been evolving into cyber attacks. They attacked Google in 2009, and they haven't stopped. We haven't been identifying quite as many human intel sources over the last few years, but the Chinese always seem to be a step ahead of us as if they know what we're thinking, what we're planning."

Malcolm became stiff faced. "The People's Republic of China has become expert in identifying security flaws in software. They add attachments to e-mails, allowing cyber agents access to companies and their resources. Once they are in a company's computer, they have full knowledge of their financials, business plans, and weaknesses. The same thing goes for our defenses."

Richard knew most of this and wanted to move on. He knew about malware and knew that e-mails were unprotected since the revelations of 2013. "So what you're saying is that the Chinese aren't using manpower now in the same way. Instead of using agents to steal information, they do it through cyber-warfare, and the human element is used for support, like hit men."

"Well, yes. I guess you could say that. But now, I think we've got a few answers." Malcolm finally allowed himself a slight grin. "A Chinese student at the University of Alabama here in Tuscaloosa might be the key to recent mysteries. A surgeon here at DCH Regional Hospital has given us clear evidence that the Chinese have infiltrated our medical system. They have developed surgical clips that go into patients during operations and serve as transmitters, sending GPS locations of the patients as well as voice transmissions and even biochemical data."

"I'm pretty sure that's why you scanned me. I had a recent operation, and that's what was placed in me."

"Exactly."

"Well, actually, the gentleman you sent out of here had already figured out most of that with the help of my son."

"We assumed so and that this is the reason they were targeted."

"Well, I think they are still being targeted. My son was next up for the hyperbaric tank that blew up, and Dr. Miller was almost killed by another assassin when he was going home. That's why he and his family are here, for protection."

Malcolm's brow furrowed. "Yes. I am aware of your son and the hyperbarics. Who is guarding Dr. Miller's family?"

"My state troopers. The person who tried to kill him on his way home said he was with the CIA, and that's why he was scared to share anything with authorities...plus, his family was threatened if he talked." Richard pointed at the agent. "That man saved my son. I'm going to make sure he and his family are safe. You see, he has a clip in himself and knows he's being monitored."

"That's perfect," Malcolm returned, speaking as quickly as he thought.

"What do you mean?"

"I mean we can use him."

"What in the hell are you talking about?"

"If they think they are monitoring him, that he is their Trojan, we can draw their people in and identify who is working this from HUMINT on their side."

"He's a surgeon, for God's sake, not a spy."

"Well maybe you need to start thinking about things from the standpoint of a governor, a representative of the people." Malcolm's face was stone, his voice harder. "Or, if you want to look at things from the standpoint of an individual, that of a husband or father, then I've got some good reasons for you to look at my side."

"Okay, fire away Malcolm. Give me some reasons why I should encourage my surgeon, the man who saved my son's life and a family man, to be a decoy or spy for you."

Malcolm spoke like a robot, using his fingers to indicate numbers as he went. "One: this is a national defense issue. As governor it is your duty to coordinate state level intelligence and fuse it with that at the federal level. You have a legal responsibility to respond to a potential defense threat. As in all matters of national defense, the protection of the nation outweighs the protection of the individual.

Two: as a husband and father you have a responsibility to protect your son, to provide for your wife, and to protect yourself. Your son has been threatened by the same people who tried to kill Dr. Miller. He is still at risk. The sooner we identify the threat, the safer he will be."

Malcolm tilted his head mechanically, deciding whether to share more. "We suspect that the explosion in hyperbarics was targeted at your son. All the more reason for us to believe there is a clear and present danger and that we need to act quickly."

Malcolm continued. "Three: your life is in danger, governor." He paused, not as an act of compassion or sensitivity but to make sure the governor was following him. "The incident in the basement here in the hospital was likely an attack on you."

Richard's lips tightened. "What?"

"We haven't analyzed everything yet, but we know that the computer in the basement froze after sending an intravenous packet to your room. It is too much of a coincidence not to be meaningful. Someone likely was trying to poison you."

Richard remembered the intravenous fluid that hit the ground. He looked at the floor with gratitude. "That very well could be," he thought out loud. "Just as the alarm sounded in the hospital, the nursing staff dropped a bag of fluids on the ground."

Malcolm looked down. "We will run an analysis of the floor. Has it been washed with detergent since the incident?"

"No." Richard shivered slightly. The close calls were too frequent and too personal. The likelihood that he had been targeted made him furious, but the thought of his family in the crosshairs turned concern into alarm. "What happened in hyperbarics?"

"We aren't completely sure. The nurse who was supervising the treatment session was killed in the explosion. However, there has never been an incident like this in DCH. The protocols are followed explicitly. Whatever happened had to have been planned. Since your son was supposed to be in the tank, we feel certain that he was the target."

"Who died?" Richard's voice softened.

"A firefighter. He had a wife and one child. He was here because of carbon monoxide poisoning from a house fire."

Richard looked through Malcolm. Beyond Malcolm's insensitivity, beyond his mathematical approach to life and death, there was logic in his thoughts.

"What do you suggest we do?" Richard asked quietly.

"Well, if we are going to use Dr. Miller as a 'walk in' agent, then we need to talk to him. We had better talk to his wife, also."

Richard shrugged, then wiped his face. Obviously torn, he conceded with a nod. "Okay. Why don't you bring him and his wife in here?"

CHAPTER 53

"Is there anything I can get for you?" Meirong asked. She had just received her report on Suzy and was taking over as her nurse.

Suzy was deep in thought. The bag of clothes that Jack had brought her also had her Socrates, her backup drive, which had everything in it that her computer contained. She would be able to share all of her information with authorities. She knew what this meant.

Suzy's was a life of obedience. She was obedient to her parents before their death, always doing as she was asked. This was the foundation of Chinese culture, an influence from Confucianism, which established how people should act in society and within families. Suzy accepted that the subordinate owed obedience to the superior, and everyone was superior to her. Unfortunately, she was too late in realizing how those who were her superiors were also evil and had taken advantage of her. She knew from the day she was taken to Beijing that they were taking advantage of her, but she never had the opportunity, or the courage, to resist those who controlled her life.

Now, she had both the opportunity and the courage to make a stand. She could turn over the Socrates and reveal all of her secrets and contacts. She could explain to the Americans what she had been doing. She also knew that this meant she would go to prison for espionage. Now that Jack had given her a reason to live, she wanted more than ever to experience life. Every time anyone had touched her since her parents died, it was like sandpaper scraping away every layer of dignity that she had. But any contact with Jack, verbal or touch, was color and warmth, springtime breaking through the winter of her life.

Meirong slipped a thermometer in Suzy's mouth and recorded her blood pressure. "You seem to be recovering nicely from your injury." Without Suzy noticing, she peeked in the bag Suzy held, unable to identify what Suzy held.

Suzy suddenly broke out of her thoughts. She recognized the accent. Her hand stiffened in the bag.

"Yes. I'm doing better than anyone thought I would." She looked up to find what she expected. Meirong's fleshy monolid and rounded eyelids identified her ancestry.

"I'm so glad. It sounds like you had a terrible experience." Meirong's compassion was present in her words, but her tone betrayed her.

"What part of China are you from?" Suzy tiptoed into danger.

"Oh, I'm not from China. I am a native American." Her answer was rapid, almost rehearsed. "My grandparents were from the mainland. I'm not even sure if my parents could speak Chinese."

Suzy carefully folded the clothes in her bag over the Socrates, stuffing it deeply into the bag. "Oh. Where were you born?"

"Florida," Meirong returned. "My parents were school teachers. They taught math."

"How did you get interested in nursing?"

"Oh, I've always wanted to help people. I was good in science in school, and nursing seemed like a good fit for me."

Suzy noticed more in her voice than simply accent.

Meirong's cell phone rang. "Hello!" She answered it rapidly.

Suzy acted uninterested as Meirong listened. Other than saying okay a few times, Meirong remained silent. The conversation was short.

"Nice cell phone. Is that the newest version?" Suzy asked, noticing the sleek design she had seen advertised recently.

"Yes. I love it." Meirong relaxed.

"Was it made in China?" Suzy faked a giggle. "You know Shanzhai. " Suzy spoke in perfect Shanghainese.

Meirong burst out in laughter, then vacuumed it back with horrified silence. The dance was over. Meirong realized she had been tagged.

Suzy recognized the Wú accent. Even in English, Meirong couldn't disguise the characteristics of the language spoken by 14 million in Shanghai. The joke also gave her away. Shanzhai means "fake" or "copied" in Shanghainese. Suzy knew that Meirong had grown up in Shanghai, or at least the Wú-speaking region of China, and not in Miami.

"Pretty smart girl." Meirong sneered, speaking in native Shanghainese. "But not smart enough."

Meirong noticed the pallor on Suzy's face and then the furrowing of her brow, an initial sign of a headache. Suzy loosened her hold on the bag and its contents.

"What did you do?" Suzy wheezed as her breath became labored.

"Oh, I forgot to tell you. Your temperature is 98." She looked at her thermometer, taking off a plastic sleeve coated in cyanide and placing it in her pocket.

Suzy's diaphragm was active, taking in 30 to 40 breaths per minute, but her arms and legs felt like lead.

Meirong turned off the monitors hooked to Suzy and slipped her bag out of her hand. "I'm sorry but I have to leave you. That was an important telephone call."

Meirong grinned, taking one last look at Suzy before she walked out of the room. Suzy was barely panting, foam dripping from her mouth.

CHAPTER 54

"Are you kidding me?" Carol was incredulous. "First my husband tells me that we can't talk, that we're being monitored by someone in the sky who is listening to everything we say. Now you tell me that you want Grant to say things precisely because he will be heard so that you can catch the people who have terrorized us?" Her eyes were wild. "Do you think this is a James Bond movie?"

Malcolm had already disarmed Grant's clip. Once again, they were all together. Molly held her husband's hand, understanding the weight on Carol and Grant.

"Tell me one more time what you just said, about the governor, about the basement," Grant said as he turned to Malcolm.

"Someone broke into Central Supply. We are still looking over the surveillance videos, but it looks like there was a fight. It also seems likely that someone was trying to poison the governor," Malcolm recounted.

"Sir, we have some information that might be helpful!" A tap on the door preceded the intrusion.

"Yes, Jeffers."

"Three things." Agent Jeffers' starched white shirt matched Malcolm's, pressed without a wrinkle. However, without a coat, he appeared less plastic.

Malcolm noticed Jeffers' reticence. "You may speak freely. Everyone in here has my clearance for secrecy." Malcolm looked at everyone, making sure they understood the importance of his words.

"First, the Homeland Security detail is onboard. They are already aware of everything. They have given us the go-ahead to proceed with our investigation but they want updates on everything we know and any plans we might have."

"What's that?" Grant interrupted.

"You may not be aware." Malcolm rapidly responded. "The Department of Homeland Security and its subordinate agency, the Transportation Security Agency, has had agents in most towns across America since 2014. It was an Executive Order issued on October 26, 2012."

"Two." Jeffers continued, brushing off the interruption. "We've done a brief analysis of the spillage you requested."

Malcolm saw the excitement in Jeffers' eyes. "And..."

"Cyanide," Jeffers barked. "The chemical analysis isn't complete, but there was definitely cyanide on the floor."

Richard turned Molly's hand loose. "Cyanide?"

"Yes."

"You mean the intravenous fluid that almost went into my veins, that pretty little Katie spilled on the floor, had cyanide in it?"

"That's right." Jeffers was becoming impatient. He wasn't used to repeating himself. "We had already notified Homeland Security, but with the possibility of an assassination attempt, we notified Washington directly."

"Assassination attempt?" Molly screamed.

"That's what it would have been if the poison had worked." Jeffers words bulleted out. "Assassination: the murder of a prominent person or political figure by a sudden attack." He was quoting from the FBI manual. "May I continue?" Jeffers pulled out a pad and clicked the video key.

Everyone could see the screen clearly. Jeffers launched the series of video surveillance shots that he had received.

"Stop there," Richard yelled only a moment into the action.

Jeffers hit pause. The picture was somewhat grainy but the image was unmistakable.

"That's the gorilla who was with Mr. Wang during our negotiations for the automobile industry." Richard sparked.

"You recognize him?" Malcolm's tone remained flat but direct.

"Yes. Definitely." The Governor sat straight up in bed. "He is Mr. Wang's bodyguard." He scratched his face, pulling out a memory. "I'm almost certain he was standing behind me at the celebration downtown when I had the heart attack."

Now Grant was deep in thought. "Wait a minute." He paused. He tried to remember the heart catheterization findings. There was something odd about them, something that only now made sense.

CHAPTER 55

Jack had forgotten to ask Suzy a few questions before his meeting with the police and FBI. He arrived just as the policeman came back from an errand.

"Aren't you supposed to be guarding this room?" Jack snapped.

"Yeah, but I got a message to help with a fight on the first floor." There was no concern in his voice. "Got there, looked for a fight, and nothing was going on. So I came back."

Jack had already opened the glass door to Suzy's room. The curtain was drawn. He whipped the curtain back, praying to find a smile and Labrador eyes.

"Get the crash cart!" Jack yelled.

The policeman looked past Jack into the room. Then he lost his footing and collapsed. He had seen one dead person, but they were more grey than blue; but Suzy, although her body laid there lifeless, was deep blue. She wasn't making any effort to breathe and her head was slumped to the left. A puddle of drool had collected over her collar bone, one bubble still floating in the pool.

Two nurses joined Jack as another kicked the policeman to the side, wheeling in the cart.

"What happened?" one of the nurses screamed as she collapsed the bed flat. "She doesn't have any monitors on!"

Jack was already pushing on her chest as another nurse slid a plastic sled under Suzy for support. The heel of his hand was a piston, pounding the frail breastbone underneath. He worked the drill, two inch compressions for 30 strokes, to the beat of "Stayin' Alive."

"Where's the face mask?" Jack roared. "Isn't the cart supposed to have equipment for ventilating?"

"It looks like the mask and intubation equipment has been removed," one of the nurses screamed, searching the cart for gear to deliver oxygen to Suzy.

"Shit!" Jack bellowed. "Get another fucking cart and call for anesthesia. Get every fucking nurse on the unit in here right now."

Jack tilted Suzy's head back, lifted her chin, and pinched her nose closed. As he bent down to deliver a breath, he smelled the almonds just as he tasted the bitter salty saliva on Suzy's mouth.

"Shit!" He spat and ran to the sink to wash out his mouth.

He knew Suzy was too blue for a natural death. He also knew the signs of cyanide poisoning. As a resident in surgery, he had almost killed a patient, giving him sodium nitroprusside for extremely high blood pressure. The dosage was too high and he had continued the medication too long. He wasn't aware at the time that the routine medicine for hypertensive crises had five cyanide groups per molecule. The cyanide binds to an enzyme preventing the use of oxygen. Suffocation is rapid. It was used in gas chambers in Germany during the Holocaust and has been used for the death penalty in the United States. After almost being fired for negligence during his training, he learned everything he could about the poison. For one thing, he knew that it is rapidly absorbed through mucous membranes, and he didn't want to share her poison.

Another crash cart bounced through the door as the entire Intensive Care Unit focused on Suzy. Jack tore the plastic lock off of the drawers and grabbed a breathing tube. He suctioned a puddle of saliva from her throat and slid the transparent tube into her airway.

"Oxygen, 100%. Bag her!" He returned to chest compressions, knowing the respiratory therapist in the room knew what to do.

The therapist squeezed her Ambu bag every five seconds. The football shaped soft plastic delivered full breaths with each compression, expanding Suzy's chest as Jack pounded it.

"Call the pharmacist. Get sodium thiosulfate 25%, 90 cc's, and hydroxycobalamin, 5 grams." He was pounding furiously, Suzy's body still lifeless.

"On second thought, tell the pharmacist to bring it with him when he comes here—and I want him here in a minute or less!"

Jack watched the team do their jobs. It was routine for everyone except him. For Jack, it was everything, his life as much as Suzy's he was trying to save. One nurse had already turned the monitors back on. The heart rhythm was irregular, her pattern widened and slow.

"One amp of epinephrine and one amp of bicarb." He continued the compressions, sweat dripping from his chin.

Another nurse was popping vials and squeezing medicines into Suzy's intravenous line as another recorded all deliveries of medicines and their times.

"Oh, my God!" One of the nurses had tripped over the intravenous tubing, pulling the line out of Suzy's vein. Bright red blood squirted out of her arm. "The line must have been in her artery, not in her vein. Look at the blood. It's scarlet."

"That's venous, not arterial blood." Jack scolded. "She's been poisoned, probably with cyanide, and the body organs can't metabolize the oxygen so the oxyhemoglobin level is high."

In spite of the oxygen traveling through Suzy's breathing tube, in spite of Jack's chest compressions sending oxygenated blood through Suzy's body, the oxygen simply was passing through Suzy's tissue. All of her cells needed the oxygen to stay alive but none of her cells could use the oxygen. The biochemical reactions in every cell had stopped. Suzy's brain cells would all be dead soon.

"Two more amps of epi and another bicarb and one atropine." Jack was pounding harder than before, watching the EKG pattern on the monitor. Suzy's heart rate was in the thirties, hardly doing anything on its own.

"Where's the fucking pharmacist?" he yelled, wildly pumping.

"Here!" Patrice ran through the door carrying a bag of supplies. She popped an ampule of amyl nitrate and sprayed it into Suzy's breathing tube. "The nurses said you had a cyanide poisoning. The amyl nitrate will start things."

She handed vials of medicine to the nurses for them to deliver. "You can give all of those intravenously. Give both of them over about five minutes."

"Who was watching her?" Jack demanded. "Who is her nurse?"

"Julie had her earlier, but she got called away," one of the nurses offered. "I've never seen the girl who took her place, and I'm not sure where she is now."

The policeman was still outside the room. He had been watching all of the activity. His face was white with the realization that he was partially responsible. "It was the nurse who told me I needed to help with the fight downstairs."

"What?" Jack was incredulous.

"She told me there was a huge fight downstairs involving guns and knives. She said that the hospital guards can't have firearms and that I needed to go help." He took a hard swallow. "She said she would make sure everything was okay until I returned."

Suzy was still lifeless. At first, her breastbone had popped back ready for each returning beat, but Jack had broken several ribs as he pounded on her chest. Now, her chest was simply a massive bruise, still absorbing blows but exhausted, and her tiny breastbone sank with each compression.

"How long have we been going?" Jack looked at the clock. He knew Suzy had run out of time.

"Thirty minutes, sir." The nurse recording the code responded.

"Shit!" Jack screamed. "Shit, shit, shit."

Jack kept pushing on Suzy's chest, but his eyes were now searching her bed. His eyes went from the bed to the floor and then around the room.

"Does anyone see a bag, a blue bag with clothes in it?" The room was cluttered with carts, sheets, discarded vials and paperwork, but no bag.

Everyone in the room was looking about but no one responded. Jack's eyes were bloodshot. He couldn't even see Suzy through the moisture. He didn't want to. He simply kept pushing.

CHAPTER 56

Grant and the governor made it to Cath Lab 5. Carol, Molly, Ree, and Beth remained in the Open Heart Unit. Troopers and policemen swarmed both areas.

"Look at these pictures." Grant pulled the cine angiograms on a video screen.

Richard was in a wheelchair but pulled close enough for a good view.

"You've got to tell me what you're looking at." Richard squinted, trying to make meaning of the black on blue images.

"This is dye being injected into your coronary arteries," Grant explained. "Can you see these narrowings in your heart vessels?" He pointed to the screen. Instead of wide open vessels, the images showed bird-beaked tapering of the arteries.

"Yes, I do see them." Richard conceded. "That's why you operated on me. It's why I had a heart attack."

"Well, I'm not so sure." Grant shook his head. "Do you see how there are several areas of blockage?"

Grant pointed to the blood vessels that appeared as moth eaten lines of spaghetti. "Yes, but why did you have to bring me here?"

"Because I'm going to repeat your heart catheterization to see if my hunch is right!" Grant waved an olive-skinned middle-aged man into the room.

"Hello, Governor. My name is Dr. Bahar. I will be performing your heart catheterization." Dr. Bahar was six feet tall but his Pavarotti beard and Turkish jaws made him seem taller.

"Well this is a bit of a surprise," Richard said cautiously. "Shouldn't I have Molly down here? Isn't this a procedure with potential risk?" Richard's surprise was obvious, but he also appeared willing to do what the doctors suggested.

"Absolutely!" Dr. Bahar responded. "I wouldn't want to proceed without her here. This is an invasive procedure." His deep voice rolled over his beard. "Why don't you call for her to come down?"

Grant was already on his cell phone. He dialed Carol's number, knowing she would pick up rapidly. Her phone was always close by.

"Hey, honey. Will you bring Molly to the Cath Lab. We're going to repeat his heart catheterization."

"Right now?" Carol knew Grant was taking Richard to the lab but wasn't sure exactly why.

"Yes." Grant continued, "I'm concerned about something."

"Well, do all of these security people need to come with us?" Carol looked in the hall. Everyone was represented: FBI, troopers, Tuscaloosa police, DCH security...

"No. We should be safe in the Cath Lab. We already have enough security down here, and it won't take long."

"Grant." Carol whispered. "Is the governor there with you?"

"Yes."

"Well, I guess you don't have to tell him now. Maybe it would be better not to." Carol was still with Molly, Beth, and Ree. They had just been updated by Dick's surgeon.

"What's going on, Carol?" Grant asked.

"Dick has taken a turn for the worse. The infection is in his blood system." Carol repeated what the doctor had just said. "The entire hyperbaric area is shut down because of the explosion, and so Dick won't be able to have any more treatments."

Carol's voice was low at first but now came clearly through Grant's cell phone. Richard was close enough to hear.

"I heard that. Dick's in bad shape." He wiped a grimace of surrender from his lips. "All the more reason to get to the bottom of this."

"You and Molly come on down here," Grant continued. "Leave the girls upstairs."

"Grant," Carol whispered again. "Go where the governor can't hear you."

Grant edged away from the governor, obviously shielding him from the message. "Okay. He can't hear me now."

"The surgeon said Dick wouldn't make it through the day." Carol looked at Molly as she spoke. "Does this have to be done today? Now?"

"It doesn't have to be done now, no." Grant understood that this wasn't urgent, but the procedure would give them some answers immediately.

"Grant," the Governor called. "Let's get on with this. If Dick is getting worse, I want to get back upstairs as soon as possible, but if this has anything to do with the people who hurt my son, I want to know about it now."

"Did you hear that?" Grant asked. He knew Richard had yelled loudly enough to be heard over the phone.

"Yes," Carol replied. "We'll be right down."

CHAPTER 57

Yao was wired. His knees wouldn't stop bouncing. All screens were zoomed in to Tuscaloosa. DCH Regional looked like a tomahawk from above, but zooming in allowed him to pinpoint Grant and the governor's positions.

He had lost radio contact with both of them for a while, but he had ways to restore communications. Now he was on them. Maybe the problems of the last few days could be wiped out with a final assault. They were both together. His blueprints of DCH placed them exactly where their conversation was. Cath Lab 5 was the spot.

The Tiger was on it. He had contacted his team. All they needed was the green light and everything would be over quickly. The Tiger had already put Suzy's computer in the mail to Beijing so there was no more evidence, no link to Yao or his agency.

Meirong had done her job and Suzy was dead. She had also already destroyed the Socrates and was in contact with the Tiger.

Dick would be dead soon. No one else would be able to uncover the trails of the Yida clips.

Yao had all but given up on the clip. It had served its purpose to a point, but all forms of spying eventually become obsolete, especially in today's world. Yes, he was willing to forfeit the clip, but he wasn't willing to risk the Chinese automobile industry in America.

What was Wang thinking? Hadn't he learned that he couldn't do anything without Yao knowing. How stupid!

Luckily he had sent the Tiger to fix things. Luckily the Tiger had killed Wang's bodyguard in the basement of the hospital. If Wang had poisoned the governor, as Yao suspected, everything would be exposed. An autopsy would reveal that he had been poisoned and then the clues would pile up.

There was enough surveillance at the governor's speech to show that Wang's gorilla, his hit man, stuck the governor with a dart. There was no heart attack, at least not the kind that brings people in with calcium and cholesterol buildup. No, the governor had an intense spasm of his coronary arteries to stop his heart and then suffered the same fate as others with normal blockages. It would only be a matter of time before Wang was identified as the villain after an autopsy and the inevitable investigation when it was discovered the governor did not have blocked arteries. The Chinese automotive business would be in hibernation for decades, not only in America but worldwide.

That's why everything must end now. It was time for everyone to go who was a threat. Grant and the governor, their wives if convenient, would be the first. Dick, if not of natural causes, would be next.

If only the Tiger had killed Jack while he was snooping around Suzy's. At least he didn't have proof of anything without the information on the computer, without Suzy. But he would have to go too.

Clean slate. Checkmate, except for the link to the Chinese. But that was easy enough to fix. He would frame the Hammer!

Yao's mouth watered with eagerness. The moment was almost upon him.

CHAPTER 58

The Tiger knew that the hospital only checked for firearms and knives in the Emergency Room, and there were lots of other ways in: the main entrance, the Cancer Treatment Center, directly through the Cath Lab, Supply Receiving... He preferred bringing death with his hands and feet, but he found the smell of gunpowder and the power of assault weapons exhilarating as well. Two AK-47s fit nicely in the Red Cross boxes used to transport blood and blood products. The AK-47s had all been taken off the streets and catalogued in Detroit and had rested, dormant, in the police station until stolen several months ago. Yao had no idea how the weapons would be used when he arranged for them to be heisted, but he had the foresight to plant one in the Hammer's garage.

The Tiger had already contacted several local Party loyalists. There were plenty to choose from, all with different skills. Since 2011, the number of Chinese Students at American universities had increased every year by more than 200,000. Recently, those picked to travel overseas were picked for special purposes and their academic ability was not primary.

Huang, a 24 year-old expert in electrical engineering and commercial wiring, was already in the hospital. He had been in America for two years, studying, waiting. He already had wiring blueprints for most commercial buildings in Tuscaloosa, including DCH Hospital. Xun, whose specialty was surveillance systems, stood with him outside of the power station. Xun also had his black belt in kung fu, dragon style.

Baozhai was barely five feet tall. Quantum Physics was second nature to her. Her head was the size of a small cantaloupe but contained more knowledge of angular momentum and the uncertainty principle than a mega-computer. She also knew more about assault rifles and how to use them than the Tiger. Her timid nature was a disguise. She, Jinjing, Chunhua, and Lanying had all arrived together in the second floor waiting room. They huddled in the southwest corner, quietly waiting for orders.

The Tiger had pulled up to the entrance outside the Cath Lab. The DCH security guard who had questioned him about parking in a restricted zone lay in the back of his cargo van, his nasal bone shoved into his brain with a single blow. The Michigan license plates on the van came from a junk yard and so served as an arrow pointing at the Hammer.

"Where have you been?" the Tiger snapped.

"Hui was in class." Jian bowed quickly. "We had to get him out."

Hui was six feet tall. His broad shoulders and chis-eled chin were clear enough evidence that he was fit, but his mind was even sharper. Receiving a PhD in Applied Calculus was no problem, but teaching it was difficult with his cultural biases. He had grown up learning that Americans were inferior and unable to understand concepts or to reason with analytical precision. Teaching classes seemed such a waste of time. He would enjoy releasing some of his frustration and had been looking forward to this call.

Hui, Jian, and Kang helped the Tiger carry the Red Cross crates to the Cath Lab door. They waited outside for the Tiger to give the signal. They all wore white uniforms, baseball caps, and gloves and kept their heads down.

Yao heard what he had been waiting for.

"Okay, Governor, you'll feel a needle stick. We're about to get started." Dr. Bahar's voice was clear.

"Richard, we're just going to use local anesthesia. We won't be sedating you." Grant's voice was unmistakable as well.

Both transmissions were crystal clear, and the GPS coordinates for both showed them in Cath Lab 5.

"*Xiànzài!*" Yao gave the order.

Xun opened the door to the power room, ready to be swift and silent. Anyone inside would never know what hit them. A quick look to the left and then the right revealed the room to be empty. Xun waved Huang in. Within moments Huang was flipping switches as Xun relaxed.

The door to the Cath Lab opened upon Huang's signal, the security lock disarmed. Immediately, the Tiger and his crew carried in their Red Cross crates and took a right turn into an empty waiting room. Huang disconnected power to all security cameras in the hospital and then to all alarms. The Tiger waited for his final signal, which came after all power in the first two floors was shut down.

Inside the crates with the AK-47s were Hyena digital night vision goggles. As quickly as the crates were opened, Baozhai and her helpers arrived, taking their weapons and placing ski masks over their faces. Each went to their positions, blocking anyone from entering the cath lab. Meirong joined them on the run.

The Tiger and his men were already on the move.

Green phosphor intensifiers in their goggles turned darkness into green images with distinct lines and borders. Finding room 5 was easy enough. The team crashed through the door, their weapons raised.

CHAPTER 59

The Tiger trailed the others, ready to protect them as they moved in on Cath Lab 5. It was 10:00 Monday morning. If the governor was having a procedure, where was his security detail? He looked past his comrades, down the hall and then behind him, his ears straining to hear voices or activity. Where were the other patients who needed studies? Where were the hospital employees?

The ceiling tiles above him were easy to slip through as he spring boarded, catching the cross tees that supported them. A tucked pirouette swung him up and onto the supports. He placed the ceiling tile back behind him as the yelling began.

"Put your weapons down!" a deep voice commanded.

The Tiger tiptoed toward the voices, ready to assist his team from above and to make sure his mission was complete.

"Put your weapons down."

Sprays of light zipped through cracks in the ceiling tiles as flashlights and lasers lit the lab below. One beam hit the Tiger's night vision goggle, immediately blinding him and automatically turning off the image intensifier. The distinct crackle of AK-47s stormed below as lightning bursts thundered underneath him.

Yao wasn't expecting the commands in English as he listened to the barrage of gunfire through the Tiger's sensors. He waited for the Tiger to respond, paralyzed with anticipation.

The Tiger tiptoed above the battle as bullets sprayed through the ceiling and tore into glass and cement below. He crept over and through tangles of wires and ducts until the barrage ended.

Flipping the goggles up, he saw all he needed to with the flashlights below. There were enough holes in the ceiling and splattered tiles for him to see that his team was down and blood covered the floor and was splashed on the walls around them.

"What is happening?" Yao whispered even though his words could only be heard by the Tiger. There was no answer, no motion from any of the transmitters of his team, and no voice signal.

The Tiger searched through the streams of flashlights for the governor, for doctors. All he saw were men in SWAT uniforms moving like ants below.

Then all the lights were turned on, filling the room below and the Tiger's loft with fluorescence. There were only dead Chinese below him.

The Tiger had seen enough. He snaked through the ceiling ductwork and was gone.

CHAPTER 60

Wang's compound was locked down and had been for a week or so. He hadn't heard anything from his gorilla in days. His new bodyguards, who were expensive but worth it, circled the grounds, ready to use their QBZ-97s or martial arts as necessary. He had been reading local and state newspaper reports over the Internet from Alabama, learning that someone else had tried to kill the governor.

So far, it appeared that Chinese students at the University of Alabama had been hired by a Detroit labor union boss to kill him. But Wang knew what that meant. Yao, who was the only one who knew about his deal with the American labor union boss, had failed.

"Great!" Wang thought. He was in the clear. At this point, it didn't matter why Yao would have organized the attack.

What mattered was that Wang held the trump card. He knew that Yao was behind the attack and knew that Yao had failed. He knew that Yao was behind the investigation of his Detroit connection. The governor was alive and would do everything to keep the union out of Alabama now. Wang didn't need the labor union. It would have been easier for him to use them, but he could still get his automobile built in Tuscaloosa without them.

The bottle of scotch, Glendronach 1968, was half empty, and a Cohiba cigar still smoldered in the ashtray beside his bed. The lines of cocaine were hidden in the bathroom. Remnants of sushi lingered on the dresser.

Both of his *baopo* were happy that Wang had finally relaxed. The guards were no longer posted in the bedroom, watching them perform. The monster dogs had even grown bored with their constant activity. Prostitution was illegal in China, but "packaged wives," *baopo*, could be bought easily for the right price. Ai and Bo enjoyed each other more than Wang, especially with fresh powder tickling their nose. They were good at their work, finding enjoyment even through the stench of cigar breath and crusty linens.

Ai's red garter had been in constant motion for the last 12 hours. It clung tightly to her soft thigh, five inches below her freshly waxed pelvis. Bo liked the look. The frills and color gave contrast to Ai's delicate simplicity. Bo chose the perfume that drifted from the garter. Shanghai Satin and Ai's moisture made a perfect mist. Wang could care less. He just knew that Ai was the one with the most enthusiasm, the most ideas. For the moment, her red elastic band wasn't being touched or shaken but gliding with precision from the bottom of the bed. Ai's small breasts were bruised from teeth, and so the silky sheet felt wonderful as she slid toward the other two.

Bo was on top of Wang. She had straddled him for the last 30 minutes, disgusted by his teeth and constant grunting but imagining that the grinding and series of warm spasms were from her lover. The blinds were pulled, but glimmers of sunlight painted her breasts as they bounced freely, her eyes closed, her mind dreaming.

Ai looked to the left. The block-headed Boerboels were asleep, the biggest with its head on the other's belly. In front of her, Bo's buttocks danced up and down, her knees churning, slowly for a while and then rapidly, swaying to the left and then the right, circular and then back and forth.

Ai slid between Wang's legs, licking them as she inched forward. Her fingers massaged and explored as each millimeter brought her closer to the action above. She took her time, rubbing Yangmei Strawberry Gel on his thighs as she ascended. The gel was a new product, developed from the fruit of its name and the toxin of a pufferfish, causing numbness at first but quickly leading to a sensual sting. Ai had started on his toes, letting him get used to the excitement as she moved up. The aroma of the gel excited her, making her massage more focused. Her thumbs inched higher and higher, working with her fingers to mix pain with relaxation, allowing the gel to anesthetize and then stimulate. She felt Bo bouncing above as Wang grunted and shoved.

Her left hand drifted toward her garter, pulling the capsule from its pouch. She continued to spread the gel with her right hand, pressing firmly now with both of her hands. She felt the pop in her left hand as a tiny needle emerged from the white capsule.

Even without the gel, Wang probably wouldn't have noticed the prick. But the razor sharp needle entered his thigh unnoticed; triggering the capsule to empty its content beneath his skin.

Ai looked to the left again, this time above the Boerbels. They were still asleep, and above them was a picture of Wang. There was enough light in the room to see him at a younger age. At one time, he didn't have a double chin or yellow teeth. Twenty years earlier his hair was so dark that it was impossible to see the microchip glued to the picture.

Ai couldn't see the chip, but she knew where it was. She winked at it as she heard Yao congratulate her on a job well done. The cochlear implant was working perfectly.

Wang's lips felt slightly numb. He was willing to experience more excitement. Ai had brought more toys and ideas to his bedroom than he had ever known. Maybe his whole body would sting like his legs. He felt his heart racing and was ready for his body to respond. Bo's eyes were open now, peering deeply into his. He knew this would be thrilling. He felt it.

Then a prickling sensation electrified his body and his heart was wild, his breathing short. He had felt this before, as a gasper with other *baopo*. Maybe Ai was saving the best for last. Neither Ai nor Bo had tried to squeeze his carotid arteries. That's how he had experienced it before. It was one of the most erotic experiences he had known. He had even used it on himself. But he knew it could be dangerous, also. He knew to be careful, but in the hands of professionals, he simply waited for the climax.

The carbon dioxide was building quickly inside of him, bringing on a familiar giddiness and lightheadedness. But this was different than before. His lower body wasn't responding. Instead of his erection growing stronger, his entire body was weakening. He couldn't move.

Bo and Ai were on each side of him now, watching him. Sunlight stood dormant on his chest. His eyes were open but everything was blurry. His chest wasn't moving at all.

Ai had learned a lot about the poison of blowfish and pufferfish. The sushi they had eaten was sashimi fugu and would still be in Wang's stomach if he had an autopsy. The gel would also be an innocent accomplice. The poison of the pufferfish is 100 times more toxic than cyanide, but Wang's death would be easily explained.

Ai and Bo waited and watched. They knew what they would report to the authorities. Such a tragedy! Wang had ordered the sashimi himself. Several tubes of the gel were in his bathroom, all with his fingerprints. His death was an accident, his own fault.

CHAPTER 61

"Was that good for you?" Yao asked.

"I like to play," the Tiger grunted. "I would rather be in the game than in the audience." He had joined Yao a minute or two before Wang's death, and together they had watched everything.

"Ha!" Yao sneered. "You like watching people die as much as I do." Yao had enjoyed the whole show, the sex and the death.

"Who was that?" The Tiger continued.

"Wang Chien." Yao snickered. "A fool!" He zoomed the camera in and out, enjoying the scene.

"Ah! He was the one who sent the monster to kill Governor Sands." The Tiger smirked, remembering the fight in the basement. "Why did he want the governor dead?"

"He was trying to get his automobile, the Astor, built in America, in Tuscaloosa." Yao was careful not to tell too much. "The governor didn't want any labor unions involved in production. WE DID."

"So he tried to kill him because of that?" The Tiger knew there was more to it.

"Wang's bodyguard poisoned the governor at an announcement ceremony. Once it was certain the Astor was going to be built in Tuscaloosa, Wang wanted the governor out of the way." Yao continued playing with the camera, adding color and brightness to Wang's corpse. It now looked like a copper paperweight. "He didn't expect the governor to survive, and I didn't expect the good fortune of the governor living."

"What do you mean?" the Tiger asked.

"Wang didn't know that the clips existed and Lee didn't know that the automobile was coming to town." Yao grinned. "I knew everything!"

The Tiger knew how to get more. "You are too smart, I guess! I don't have a clue what you are talking about."

Yao spun his chair around. Greens and blues from the surrounding screens drizzled shadows over his face. Pride spewed from every pore. "Of course I am too smart," he bellowed. "Li Zhang, Lee, was a salesman for Yida Technologies. I had developed a special clip with them that is used in surgery. The clips are put in patients, but they are Trojan horses." Yao thought the Tiger was smart and was disappointed that he couldn't understand his plot. He wanted the Tiger to at least acknowledge his brilliance.

"The clips are similar to what you have in your body. They allow me to hear conversations and know your position at all times." Yao's words flew like bullets. "When the governor didn't die and received a clip in his surgery, I knew he would be more valuable alive than dead. I could hear him in meetings and have inside knowledge of his state and the country."

"Ahhh." The Tiger, scratching his head, acted like he still didn't understand.

"Wang still wanted the governor dead, and so he sent his bodyguard to finish the job. That's why I sent you to stop him. I wanted the governor alive."

"Then why did you give the order to kill him and his surgeon?" The Tiger was still scratching his head.

"There was still a chance to keep the Yida clip secret, still an opportunity to have a microphone in every room in America." Yao turned back around, zooming in and out on Wang's body. "Still a chance!" His voice faded. "Still a chance."

"So I killed Li Zhang because he knew about the clips?" The Tiger knew better but wanted to hear Yao explain.

"No!" Yao roared. "No! I killed him because he thought he was smarter than me!" Yao whirled back around and glared at the Tiger, suspicious now. "He thought he could steal my show!"

Yao's eyes narrowed. "I could forgive Li for the Americans finding out about the clip. It was purely luck. It wasn't his fault that the men I trained failed, that they let the Americans outwit them and kill them in Mobile." His voice grew sharper. "It wasn't his fault that the girl tried to use my clips for her personal work."

The Tiger remained motionless and emotionless, his face a rock. He watched Yao rise to his feet. The stench of Yao's breath proved that he hadn't left the control room in days.

"I wouldn't kill someone simply for failure." Yao let his words linger. "But I would kill anyone who tries to deceive me or to cross me."

"How did Li deceive you?" the Tiger asked, no fear in his voice.

"He played like he was dead, like the Americans killed him, and tried to disengage the transmitter in him." Yao growled. "He thought I wouldn't know, thought he was smarter than me."

Silence filled the room as Yao studied the Tiger, who stood motionless. "I don't know what Li was going to do with Suzy's computer, if he was going to give it to the Americans for money and amnesty or if he was going to use it for his own purposes." Another moment of silence followed. "We'll never know, but he won't cross me ever again."

The Tiger turned, meeting Yao's gaze directly. "So whose fault was it that the men were killed in Mobile and the Americans know about the clip. Whose fault is it that the governor, his son, and Dr. Miller are alive while 11 Chinese died in an American hospital and now their Homeland Security is looking into our involvement?" The Tiger's eyes were green, his blood icy.

This time the silence lasted longer than either expected. Yao had seen it in the Tiger's eyes, heard it in his voice. The Tiger was here for more than congratulations and more orders.

Yao was the first to move. When he stood up, he had carefully drawn his knife from its sheath on his ankle. He was holding it at his side, ready for action. His first motion was with his left arm, expecting the Tiger to defend a blow from that side, but the Tiger had already seen Yao draw his knife. Yao's left hand swung toward the Tiger's face as the knife lifted toward his chest. The Tiger never lost eye contact with Yao but snapped the knife out of his hand with a chop from his right hand and followed with an eagle claw punch to Yao's throat.

Yao felt the cartilage of his trachea shatter as the Tiger landed his blow. The punch was so quick that he never moved. His diaphragm sucked for a breath, but there was no airway left. Yao tried to hold a grimace back, but his muscles betrayed him. A series of contortions seized his lips and then his cheeks. His chest wouldn't obey him either. It strained involuntarily for oxygen. Yao fell backward, dizzy with hypoxia.

Behind the Tiger, hidden in shadows of greens and blues, sat another figure. He had heard everything.

Yao looked at the Tiger, then recognized who was behind him. Yao closed his eyes.

CHAPTER 62

"So are we going to be on TV like I saw last night?" Ree asked, eagerness bursting in her breath.

"What?" Beth answered. "That was the Prime Minister of England eating Thanksgiving dinner with the President." She tried to hide her mockery.

"Honey, this is Montgomery and we're eating Thanksgiving dinner with the governor." Grant snickered. "We're not going to Washington, and we're not going to be on TV."

They walked up the last steps between the four stately columns, the flags of Alabama and the United States floating proudly above them. Grant reached to open the front door just as the attendant opened it.

"Wow!" Ree's eyes widened, dazzled by the crimson runner draped like a robe down the ivory white staircase in front of her. "It looks like a throne." A bouquet of flowers was perched as a crown at the top of the steps with a chandelier and two sconces showering the scene with prisms of royal light.

"Dr. and Mrs. Grant." The gentleman was well tailored and spoke with perfect diction, Alabama style. "Ladies." He bowed respectfully, looking at the girls. "You must be Beth and you Ree."

Ree was still looking at the entry hall. "Are you the curator?" Her eyes were wandering as she spoke.

"Ha." He turned, ushering them forward. "No, but I agree with you." He laughed. "This place truly is a museum."

They continued to the rear of the mansion, the inlaid parquet flooring silent under their feet, muffled by a toasty breeze.

"Ahhhh. Greetings." Richard and Carol were there to greet the family as the doors to the dining room opened.

The mansion had been closed to the public early in the century, and the kitchen had only recently been reactivated. The aroma of turkey, ham, sweet potatoes, and chocolate crept into the modest room, coating the crown molding and circling the mahogany table.

"It's great to see you again, Governor." Grant matched Richard's strength as they shook hands with sincerity.

"Please call me Richard. After everything we've been through, I consider you one of my closest and dearest friends."

Carol and Molly had already hugged. Molly bent to kiss both of the girls on their cheeks. "And we consider all of you family." A twinkle of moisture shimmered on her eye, brightened from the overhead crystal chandelier.

"Don't leave me out." Dick hurried in from the back entrance. "We're still part of the family, too. Don't forget." He waved Crista and his two girls in.

"You look great." Grant was careful not to squeeze Dick's hand too vigorously. But Dick seemed to have recovered fully and made a point of employing his grip vice-like when he shook Grant's hand.

"Thanks to you and your hospital, I'm alive." He pulled Grant toward him and bear hugged him.

"You're more than a brother to me," Dick whispered in Grant's ear.

"Likewise," Grant returned.

"We all have soooo much to be thankful for this day," Molly chirped loudly. "Happy Thanksgiving to everyone."

The entry door opened again from the foyer. "Hey guys." Jack's arms were spread. "Happy Thanksgiving to everyone." His corduroy jacket was tannish gray and thin, unable to conceal his broad shoulders. His blue jeans were tailored and dark like his hair.

"Welcome, Jack." Richard hurried to greet him. "Your girlfriend couldn't come?" Richard's disappointment was audible.

"Oh, she's in the foyer looking at the pictures and portraits." He smiled, looking back.

The governor stepped out of the dining room. Suzy was standing below a portrait, her posture stiff. He calmly approached her, stopping four feet from her to give her space she seemed to need.

"Hello, Suzy."

"Oh, Governor." Suzy stumbled over her words. "I shouldn't be here. I don't deserve to be here." She looked around the room, from the brilliant poinsettias lining the walls to the chandeliers to the governor and back to the portrait.

"Do you know who that is?" Richard's voice was soft.

"No." Suzy lowered her head, ashamed.

"That was a governor of Alabama, George Wallace. He was one of the most famous governors. He even ran for President of the United States." He paused. "Do you know why I put his portrait up and none of the other great governors?"

"No."

"Because he learned something about life that most governors and most people never learn!"

Suzy waited but Richard remained silent. "What was that?" she finally asked.

"Governor Wallace achieved power by stepping on the people who were the weakest and siding with the people who were the most powerful. He made a political stand against blacks, drawing a line in the sand by trying to keep them out of schools and universities, trying to keep an entire race of people shackled in history simply because of the color of their skin."

"I think I heard about him." She nodded. "I have been to the door at the University of Alabama where he stood in an attempt to keep the first two black students from registering in 1963, at the entrance to Foster Auditorium."

"That's right. Well he decided to run for President in the 70s."

"I think I remember." Suzy smiled. "He was shot and paralyzed, wasn't he?'

"Yes. He had to drop out of the campaign but returned to Alabama as governor and then was elected for a fourth term. But after being paralyzed and after a period of rehab with a bullet lodged in his spinal column, he decided he was wrong about segregation and racial discrimination. He appointed blacks to cabinet positions and apologized to black civil rights leaders for what he had done and said in the past." Richard nodded. "He became a born-again Christian. He said he didn't want to meet his maker with unforgiven sin."

"Was that just because he was paralyzed?"

"There are events in everyone's lives that change us." The Governor paused, thinking of his own life. "When Wallace was paralyzed, I think he had time to think about life in a different way, to see through different eyes."

"What do you mean?"

"Well, Governor Wallace became the member of a minority." Once again Richard paused. "Governor Wallace learned what it was like to look up to everyone from his wheelchair, to depend on others to drive him places, to feel weak."

"So, it all happened because he was paralyzed." Suzy was a scientist. One plus one had to equal two, and so paralysis had to equal conversion. It seemed to be an awkward conclusion.

"Not exactly, Suzy." The Governor backed up, returning to his original thoughts. "I think that Governor Wallace changed his mind because evil touched his life. A man who simply wanted the power of national recognition visited Wallace that day, and that moment the bullet entered his spine changed everything for him."

The governor wiped his eyes as he looked at the portrait. "Governor Wallace was given the opportunity, through his pain and anger and weakness, to respond. He responded out of forgiveness and repentance. He asked for forgiveness from the black leadership and he forgave the man who shot him and delivered 20 years of pain to him. He realized that his life had more importance than simply human power."

Richard's eyes lowered, locking with Suzy's. "Evil has touched all of us, hasn't it?"

"Yes." Suzy wanted to look away. Guilt and shame tugged at her, trying to pull her head down, but she resisted, holding her connection with the governor. "Evil is very strong."

"Sometimes evil comes to us directly or visits others in our lives. It comes with its own agenda but it can be defeated. The governor defeated it. The man who was attacked more ferociously than anyone before or after defeated it."

Their eyes shared the past. The governor didn't need to say anything further for there had been enough evil recently to speak for itself. But his stare drifted even farther back, back to events he'd never shared. Suzy knew evil. She had felt it, tasted it, seen it...

She thought of Lizzie. She remembered Lizzie's mother and her grandmother. Evil had visited them, and maybe for one purpose. Suzy took in a deep breath, filling her lungs with strength. Evil came to take them away in order to finish its work on Suzy. But it didn't work. Lizzie was no longer paralyzed, and it wasn't drugs or operations that did it. Lizzie was just fine now and so were her mother and her grandmother. So was Suzy. The silence was now filled with voices from the past, visions of Lizzie and others, sadness and pain and regrets all turned to joy.

"I think I understand." Suzy finally whispered.

"Well come on in and enjoy the meal." Richard wanted to stay longer, but he knew it was time.

"I want to thank you for everything you've done to keep me out of prison." She stayed where she was at the foot of the portrait.

"Suzy, all I've done is tell the truth to the right people. Besides, you're more valuable to America and our safety out of prison."

Then Suzy walked with the governor and they joined the others. She realized that she was out of prison on a far larger scale than just having avoided iron bars and locked doors.

CHAPTER 63

"Thank you both for joining us." Richard ushered Grant and Jack back into the foyer. Dick joined them.

"I'm the one who's grateful," Jack said. "The meal was delicious. Thanks. But thank you even more for asking the President to pardon Suzy."

"No problem. I'm just glad you've been able to fill in the blanks and act as her character witness. It made all the difference that you let the police copy her Socrates before you gave it to her. Without it, I don't think we could have gotten a pardon. With it, our Homeland Security will be busy for some time."

"Well, you've given her a new life, and you've given me a chance for happiness again, a chance I've waited many years to have."

"I hope and pray that everything works out for both of you!" Richard winked.

The silence didn't last long. "The truth is, I am more thankful to all of you." He looked at Dick. "Yes, you too."

Dick had heard his father's praise before, but he knew something was different this time.

"The fact is that Homeland Security has come to me." Richard sounded almost apologetic. "They wanted me to ask you all..."

CPSIA information can be obtained at www.ICGtesting.com
Printed in the USA
BVOW03s0928151213

339164BV00006B/54/P